# THE GIRL YOU FORGOT

GISELLE GREEN

Boldwood

First published in Great Britain in 2020 by Boldwood Books Ltd.

A CIP catalogue record for this book is available from the British Library.

Paperback ISBN 978-1-80048-202-9

Large Print ISBN 978-1-80048-198-5

Ebook ISBN 978-1-80048-196-1

Kindle ISBN 978-1-80048-197-8

Audio CD ISBN 978-1-80048-203-6

MP3 CD ISBN 978-1-80048-200-5

Digital audio download ISBN 978-1-80048-195-4

Boldwood Books Ltd
23 Bowerdean Street
London SW6 3TN
www.boldwoodbooks.com

*To Andrew*
*May you always be a light to others in dark places, when all other*
*lights go out.*
*(Paraphrased from J.R.R Tolkein: The Two Towers)*

# PROLOGUE

*'Why are you doing this?'* Will was sitting on our bed in the dark, plucking the strings of his guitar, I remember that. I remember striding in and flinging the curtains open wide and how, outside, the snow was falling, gently and steadily, covering over all the joyful pansies I'd planted out, freezing over all the bright and colourful things...

And also... how he never looked up, just carried on ignoring me while all I could do was stand there, my heart going nineteen to the dozen, feeling so scared. How he scared me with his single-minded purposefulness, his ability to block everyone and everything else out, me included. And then, above even that, I was just so sad because by then I already knew I had lost Will.

I knew there was nothing I could say and nothing I could do to make him budge and change his mind because he was always so damn...

'Why are you being so stubborn?' I went right up to him and put my hands across the neck of his precious guitar so he couldn't play any more and he couldn't ignore me or how he was breaking my heart.

'How could you tell me you'd prefer to die rather than... than face your own pain?'

He looked up at me then, eyes sunken in sorrow and something in his despair stopped me in my tracks.

'Please,' I choked. '*Please, please*... think again.'

He sucked in his lips. 'There is no point, my love.'

I sat down on the bed beside him, clinging onto his hand.

'How can you...?' I gulped. 'How can you call me *my love* when you won't do this one thing for me? This... one, simple thing.'

Did I see a small, sad smile cross his lips at that?

'Sometimes, *living*,' he said, 'is the most difficult choice any of us ever have to make.'

'Yes!' I shook at his hand, desperate for him to hear me. 'Yes, it is, Will. For me too, don't forget. Upon us all, a little rain. – sometimes a whole sky full of rain – must fall! And you... yes, you've had your share, I don't deny it...'

'You think?'

'That doesn't mean you get away with killing yourself over it! That doesn't mean it's right and fair. What about me, what about your...?'

If only I could've said *your child*.

'I'm not killing myself.'

I looked at him, my heart breaking. 'What else do you call refusing a life-saving operation, Will? What else do you call it when you have the chance, *you have the choice and you won't*...?'

He shook his head, but I couldn't let it go.

'This is about...' I took in a deep, shuddering breath. 'This is all about the baby, isn't it?'

Head bowed, he went back to strumming his guitar. Anything, rather than listen to me. And I wanted to take that guitar and chop it up into little pieces and set fire to it with a match.

'You're...' I was almost choking; let him have it. 'You're seriously willing to let yourself just... die... simply because the baby you thought was yours isn't? That's insane, William!'

I tried another tack. 'Do you really hate this child I'm carrying so much?'

That one hit its mark. I saw it instantly. He looked up at me, shocked.

'I don't hate the *child,* Ava. How could you say that? I hate...' He did something then, and there was this loud, reverberating *twang* as one of his guitar strings went flying off with some great force. His hand stretched out, and when he put it up to his face, I saw that he was crying, brushing tears away. My heart swelled with hope, because maybe it meant that he wasn't freezing me and my words out any more?

'I *hate...* that I won't...' He stopped then, lost for words. Closed his eyes for a brief moment. By the white daylight coming in through the snow-veiled window, all the little lines of pain on his face spoke louder than anything else so far. I saw his pain. That maybe this child I was carrying would always be a reminder of another man's fertility?

'I'm sorry, but we can't turn the clock back, even if we wish...' I gulped, not quite able to say the words, because how could I feel any regret for the outcome of my mistake?

'I know.' He touched my knee softly then. 'And I, too, am sorry.'

'Will...' I paused for a second. 'You can't forgive me... is that it?'

'I can't *forget*, Ava.'

'And that's it?' I moved back then. 'That's what makes life *not worth living*? I messed up one time and now you don't trust me any more?'

'Jeez,' he came back in a pained voice. 'It isn't *just one thing*, is it? This is all happening... much too fast, can't you see?' I saw him gulp then, and for a moment I caught a glimpse of the deep scare he'd been masking. 'I haven't even had time to get over what's gone on between you and me and now my back's immediately up against the wall with this op! There's been no chance to process any of it.'

He paused. 'Even if they save my life – from what we've been told, I'll remember nothing at all about the past few years. Have you ever considered – I might not be the same man at all, when I wake up? What about... my music? What if I don't like the man I am, when I wake up?' He looked at me pointedly. 'What if *you* don't?'

I shook my head then, denying that could ever happen, but he hadn't finished.

'I'm sorry for what I'm doing to my family and everyone else who knows and cares about me, but most of all to you, because I do love you, Ava. You need to know that. I wanted this baby so bad, and I only wish...' he said, voice breaking. 'I wish I'd never known.'

He gave a sad laugh. 'If only we could wipe everything out, right? Just like...' He indicated through the window, where a thin blanket of snow lay over the ground outside, the world a clean, white slate, waiting to be walked on.

'*God*, Will.' I leaned in then, without even thinking what I was saying. 'You won't remember *anything* after the op, if you have it, will you?'

His hands went back to lock behind his head. He stared up at the ceiling for such a long time, I didn't know where he'd gone.

At last, his eyes had crinkled in pain. 'That's true, I wouldn't. *You* would, though? You'd remember.'

I nodded. 'But... if you have this operation, if you'll only agree to give life another chance, I swear, Will, I'm the one person who'll *ever* know it.'

When he turned to look back at me, I thought I saw something shift deep in those blue-green eyes of his.

'You'd do that?'

'I'd do anything, Will! Whatever it takes to keep you alive, only don't... don't throw your whole life away on a whim, just because of a mood that will surely pass in time.'

'And time,' he said softly, 'is the one thing I'm about to run out of.'

'Will, we are *already* out of it!' He knew it as well as I did. He'd been resisting the steadily mounting pressure to have this operation for the past week.

My voice got caught in my throat as I realised the truth of that. We didn't know how long he'd have, but without this operation – it really would all be over. Will put his guitar down and pulled me to him, holding me close for a few, long minutes while I sobbed in his arms.

After the longest time, he spoke again. 'This is all happening too quickly. It feels as if my whole world's being ripped out from under me without warning but... maybe you are right.'

When I looked up, shocked, he finally said the words I'd been longing to hear.

'I'll have the operation. Because afterwards, I won't remember anything about the baby not being mine, or about how I can't...' He swallowed. 'And, if you don't ever tell me...'

'I wouldn't, Will. I'd never breathe a word.'

His hand tightened in mine. 'You *swear*?'

'I swear! Do you really imagine I'd ever risk putting you back in the terrible state I'm seeing you in, right now? Not in a million years. Not for anything.'

He gave the tiniest nod and I sent up a prayer of thanks, then. We had a solution. All I had to do was promise him he'd never know the truth about this child...

I thought in that moment that disaster was averted, that everything was going to be okay. He'd live, and my child would be blessed with the best, most loving daddy in the world, and we would all go on and be just fine.

That's what I thought.

I didn't see it, then.

How our carefully constructed plans could be wiped away in an instant. But maybe I should have. When I went to the window in a joyous daze, afterwards, there'd been a fine rain pattering down on the patio outside, melting the top layer of snow, wiping it all away, but underneath, my pansies – my bright and beautiful pansies, planted out with all my dreams of the glorious summer to come – they all lay battered and broken.

# 1

## WILL

'Don't try and move yet, please.'

Someone's injecting something into my arm; I can feel it going in. *Move?* I feel as if I've plummeted out of a deep dream, the pit of my stomach not where it should be. He's withdrawn the needle. Now he's shining a light in my eyes.

'Hello? Can you tell me your name, please?'

I squint, trying to get away from the glare.

'That's better.' The light clicks off. When I refocus my eyes I'm not where I expected to be, even though I can't remember where that is, either. There's an unpleasant wooziness in my head. A sense that I'm circling somewhere up high in the sky, waiting to find somewhere to land. I make to sit up a little, but the man is staying my arm.

'Can you tell me your name?' His eyes peer intently into mine.

'Will. Tyler.' My mouth is dry. My lips feel swollen, tasting faintly of blood.

'Perfect,' he says, pumping up one of those blood-pressure bands around my arm. 'You were away for a good few minutes there, Will.'

Away – *where?* I wait for the feeling of fear to subside in my chest and he adds, 'You're in hospital, Will. D'you know why you're here?'

I have no idea but I've got the sense that I should.

'Did I...? I took a tumble off my motorbike?' My eyes close again as I try to remember.

Bits and pieces, like coloured confetti thrown up into the air on a windy day, shoot through my mind. I'm on my bike. Travelling fast, yes, but not too fast, enjoying the ride. And I'm feeling good. Impatient to meet someone who I've been longing to see. The sky is blue and clear and there's practically no traffic about. I don't remember coming off my bike, and I have no idea how much damage I might have done, but I feel a shaky relief at recalling at least that much.

'Try and stay awake for me, please.' His hand is pressing gently but firmly on my arm. 'Are you in any discomfort?'

Am I? I lift up my hands in front of me and look at them.

My mouth feels a little swollen but I am not in any real pain. Is this a good thing or a bad thing? Then a thought occurs to me and I feel a shot of pure fear in my stomach. I can't move my head.

I croak, 'Is my neck broken?'

'Your neck is fine.'

I can't turn my head, I realise, because it's bandaged and there seems to be some clear plastic tubing coming out of it, too.

'Christ, what the...?' I'm learning I can't move my legs, either. Maybe I've done some real damage – *I don't even want to look* – but I'm praying it's only the bedsheet wrapped round me too tightly. Suddenly I'm feeling cramped, locked in and I can't breathe and there's a strange smell. I feel something placed over my face and now I'm breathing in deeply through an oxygen mask.

'Take some slow breaths for me, that's right. Try and stay calm.' He's letting the armband down. There's a *whoosh* and the pressure on my arm eases off. 'You've come out of an operation and you're in Intensive Care. My name's Andy and I'll be taking yours obs every fifteen minutes for the next few hours. Right now, I need you to stay awake and talk to me. Can you do that for me?'

An operation? Why don't I remember that?

Reluctantly, I blink my eyes open for him. I need to *breathe* and stay awake. I know this is important. After a few minutes, he takes off the mask.

'Can you tell me your age, Will?'

That one's easy.

'Twenty-seven.'

He sucks in a breath through his teeth at that and so I reassure him by elaborating. 'I'm twenty-seven. I celebrated my birthday last month, in Berlin.'

He's frowning.

'Have I been in an accident?' I ask shakily. 'I came off my bike?' Perhaps they brought me here by ambulance? I don't remember that but they must have done.

'No, Will.' He's still looking into my eyes intently. 'You didn't come off your bike. You won't remember this, but you walked in here under your own steam yesterday morning and checked yourself in for elective surgery.'

I blink.

'I... *yesterday*?' I didn't. He's wrong. *What's happened to me?* 'What surgery?'

'You had a malignant tumour on your brain that we've been monitoring for a while,' he says. 'We needed to remove it.'

A wave of pure dread runs through me on hearing that, because I might be confused right now but I know for a fact *that's* not true.

'No, I was on my bike,' I insist. 'I was on my way to...' My mind stretches out into the void of a reluctant memory. Like a dream that stubbornly refuses to come. I blink at him, unable to shake my head, feeling lost.

'I appreciate it must be hard for you to take this in. You'll be able to talk to your people, soon, check it all out for yourself, I promise you. But you knew going in that it would be like this, that you wouldn't remember.' The look of sympathy on his face is genuine enough. 'Believe me, we've spoken about this, many times.' *Many times?* 'Right now, you're going to need to trust me on this one.'

We have never spoken about this.

'I have never seen you before in my life,' I tell him. He seems like a nice enough bloke, but...

'Will, I am so sorry, but you have. You last saw me yesterday when you booked in.' He lays his hand gently on my arm. 'Besides, you told me you think you're twenty-seven years old.' He glances over automatically as the instrumentation on the side of the bed starts to beep, checks the oxygen monitor attached to my finger, then looks back at me.

'You'll need more thorough and extensive assessments done but at first glance – it looks as if you might have lost seven years...'

What is he... *what*?

'Are you saying I've been in a coma?' *Seven* fricking...

'No. You've just forgotten. The brain is a complex organ, Will. Even small adjustments to its network can result in significant changes and your tumour was close to the area responsible for storing your most recent memories.'

'I cannot,' I tell him, 'have lost seven years.' But he's looking at his watch, writing something down in my notes. 'Listen, I... I...'

'I know. I'm sorry.' He stops what he's writing and looks over at me, apologetically. 'At least, Will, you're still alive.'

My voice comes out like a croak.

'I was alive when I woke up this morning.' I don't remember this morning, but it was probably like every other morning, I imagine. I must have woken up and done my normal things and made some plans. I was on my motorbike, *going* somewhere that made every part of me light up with happiness, I know that much.

'You'd be surprised.' He finishes putting away some of the bits and pieces of equipment he's used, and pauses to look at me properly. 'They tell me you died for ten minutes on the operating table.'

I was *dead*?

He's nodding at me, completely serious. 'Sometimes it just takes a knock-back like this to remind people.'

'That they're alive?' I say faintly.

He glances at me significantly.

'To *remind* them, Will Tyler, what that's worth.'

## 2

## AVA

'It's all gone as well as we could've hoped.' Dr Gillian Mason's looking quietly pleased. 'It took us eight hours to get here, but in the end... really well.'

'Thank you so much.' I can hardly speak for the lump in my throat. It is the early hours of the morning, and they'd hoped to be done by midnight. Still.

'It's over. Thank God.'

'In many ways, this is just the beginning. He's not going to recognise you, I'm afraid.'

I nod rapidly.

'They warned us about that.'

'I'm sure they did.' She's taking me in thoughtfully. 'This might be your one-hundredth meeting, but, to Will, it'll feel like the first time he's ever laid eyes on you. It doesn't matter what we tell him. As far as *he's* concerned, he's never met you before.'

'I know.' They'll have taken out the part that was killing Will and, along with it, every part of him that ever loved me. I push away the sadness that threatens to rush in and swamp me.

'It's okay.' I force myself to smile. 'I'm not expecting Will to be the same, but where there's life, there's hope, right?' That's what this op was all about: keeping him alive.

'Ava...' She touches my arm lightly. 'This'll be harrowing enough for him, but there's nothing that can really prepare *you* for it, either. When someone you know and love can't recognise you...'

I know she means well but, right now, all I need is for them to let me in to see him. I glance towards the white doors of the ICU, wondering when she's going to let me inside.

'I figure as long as he's physically okay, we'll be able to start again.'

'Hopefully.' Dr Mason holds open the door of the little private side room where they're looking after Will. 'I'll leave you both to it, then, but... remember to give it some time.'

'Sure.'

'Above all...' her voice sounds a little sad '... remember not to take it personally.'

*Personally?*

I shake my head at her, bemused. This isn't about me, is it? All I want is to see for myself that Will's come out of this intact. That he's okay. I step inside, both eager to be alone with him and dreading it at the same time. The young male nurse who's in there with Will looks up, immediately cheerful.

'Ah, here's your girlfriend I was telling you about, Will. Her name's Ava.' To me, he says, 'He's all yours, but for fifteen minutes only, today. I'll be just outside.' I watch as he leaves.

Then there's only Will and me and he's looking over at me.

'Will?' My knees want to buckle with relief. Because Will's still – he really is still here and alive.

*'Will?'* I take a few steps nearer to his bed, drinking in the fact that he's looking at me curiously. His eyes aren't vacant and staring; he's still him.

'Hey,' he says. He sounds just the same.

'Hey.' I come over and lean in. He can still hear and understand. And he can still see. Jubilant, I send up a silent prayer of thanks. *We made it, babe.* Will shoots me a small smile, and my heart dares to hope for a fraction of a second.

Does he *know* me?

'God, Will, I'm so glad it's over.' Leaning in automatically to kiss him, I feel him pull away slightly at my approach. Of course... I move back a little, giving him his space.

'I realise that you don't know me any more. Not yet. But I want you to rest assured that I'm here for you, Will. I'm going to be here for you, come what may.'

He doesn't look very reassured. I swallow.

'They're all very pleased with how your operation went.'

'So I'm told.' He indicates the small drooping bunch of blue and white flowers I've been clutching in my warm hands. 'What're those for?'

'Forget-me-nots.' I let out a laugh. Every time we've come here, we've been passing by these, growing in the stone planter outside St Bart's main entrance. These were going to be our little sign. I hold up the flowers I just went downstairs and picked.

'Before the op, we said that we'd...'But I can see I've rushed in too fast with assumptions because there is no recognition in his eyes; none whatsoever. 'I promised I'd bring you these,' I finish lamely.

He shakes his head. 'I don't remember that,' he says.

'No.' My throat's suddenly gone scratchy and dry. 'I know. We knew, going in, that you wouldn't remember them. It was just...' I don't know what it was, really, this thing with the flowers. Our way of trying to defy reality, maybe?

'I'm sorry, I didn't quite catch your name,' he says politely. 'Did he say Aila?'

I blink. 'My name's... *Ava.*'

'Ava,' Will says. He puts out his hand, the one with the IV drip attached, and we shake hands like polite strangers being introduced in the workplace. I close my second hand over his. To me, at least, his hand still feels warm and familiar and I'm longing to reach out and kiss him. Despite what we've been told, despite everything, something in me imagines that if only we kissed, then surely *something* would click? He'd know me then; he'd recognise my kiss?

But I don't do it. Instead, I sit down on the chair beside Will's bed, still holding onto the flowers, my knees weak.

'Have we... known each other long?' he asks.

'Three years.'

'Three.' His eyebrows go up, wondering at that. 'They tell me I've lost seven.'

'Yes, you've lost all the best years.'

The puzzlement on his face is bordering on devastation. I explain myself.

'Sorry. That was my little joke. I meant the ones with *me* in them.'

'I see.'

Even in this brief interaction it's clear that I'm a complete stranger to him, but the worst thing of all is he's feeling like a stranger to me, too. I hadn't anticipated that, and I can't quite get my head around it.

'The three years with you, and then four more, before I ever even met you,' he muses.

'That's true, yes.' Looked at from that perspective, I realise immediately, *our* three years together might not feel that important. Not if you didn't know any better. But *I* do. Those were among the most important years of both our lives.

He nods, glancing around the room.

'I'm kinda bummed DelRoy's not here, to be honest, seeing as I've apparently had this major operation.'

'DelRoy?'

'Yeah, I really thought he'd have...'

'Your mum's coming down later.' We both speak and then stop, at the same time. He motions, *you go on*, so I clear my throat and tell him.

'Sylvie's coming later. She was on the train down from Leeds but they diverted it somewhere else and there's been a massive delay, otherwise they planned to have sent her in first.' I pause, then add, 'A face you'd definitely have recognised.' The idea that he might prefer to have his mum here at his bedside, rather than me, still feels weird. I know all about Will's complicated relationship with his family up north. His mum, Sylvie, pined for a long while after he left home young, didn't stay up there to be near her, but now she never comes to visit much, either.

'Sure.' Will's mind is still elsewhere, though. 'I went to see my mum shortly before my birthday,' he tells me. 'She was pretty tied up with her family at the time.' He glances ruefully at me. 'That's how it generally is, with her. I don't imagine she'll be able to stay down here for long.'

'No,' I say. Will's looking towards the door curiously – perhaps wondering why no one he *actually knows* has come to greet him on awakening.

'I take it there are other people – my friends, who know about this... operation I've had?'

'They know. But they're not being allowed in here to disturb you. My sister, Robyn, waited up with me for part of the night but she left. She wouldn't have been allowed in, anyway.'

He pulls a pained face. 'So... you're the one who stayed up all night, waiting for me to come out of this op?'

'I did.'

'Thank you,' he says stiffly. I can see the thought makes him slightly uncomfortable. 'And am I...' another thought occurs to him '... still ousted from DelRoy's band?'

*He's asking about the band, now?* Wow. We really have travelled back in time! I'd hoped he might have been a bit more curious about us on waking up. It's disappointing, in all honesty, but understandable and Dr Mason did warn me.

'You left the band, voluntarily,' I say. *Eight years ago, and five years before you even met me.*

'Only because they stopped playing the kind of music I liked.'

'They never went back to playing it,' I give him. There was a time after he left the band where he'd been drifting for a bit... Is that where his memory has stopped, at that period in his life?

Will takes that in, unhappily. 'Where do I work, then?' He's pale and exhausted from his op, and yet the thought still makes him anxious, I see. In that regard, at least, he has not changed. 'I do work, don't I?'

'Sure, you do.' I lean in. 'You're going to like this. You're a songwriter now.'

'No shit.' I see his mouth drop open slightly. 'One that actually earns money?'

'Definitely,' I enthuse. 'You've written a number of songs for some well known bands that've gone straight up the charts.'

'Bloody *hell*.' Will looks puzzled and astonished, as if he can't for the life of him imagine how he got to *there* from where, in his mind, he still is.

'I can see I'm going to need to ask you a lot of questions, Ava. I hope you won't mind?'

'No,' I reassure him quickly. 'I won't mind at all. We expected this, Will. We planned for it.'

'I planned for it?' He pulls a pained smile.

'*We* did,' I correct. He's like Will's doppelgänger. He looks and feels like the man I love in every single way and yet... how much is he really still the old Will?

'I know that, in your mind, there isn't any such thing as "we",' I tell him softly. 'But I promise you... out here, in the real world, there is.'

'Is there – can there still be – any "we"... if I don't know you?'

I stare at Will for a moment, then look away. He has a point. But then again, this state of affairs is only temporary, because I'm going to help him rebuild his memories. It's what we agreed, and what I promised him, even if he doesn't know it any more.

So I need to have patience. I take in a breath. 'You don't know me now, but you will. Look, they'll probably be discharging you before too long.' I deliberately put on a bright voice. 'After we get back home, you'll be able to—'

'Home?' He's looking at me uncomfortably. 'You and I live together, Ava?'

I blink.

'Well, you've still technically got a lot of your gear at DelRoy's place, but I naturally assumed that you'd...'

'I see.'

There's an uncomfortable few moments' pause while we both take this in. I'd imagined him moving back in with me, at least, would be a given.

'You'll be wanting help with everything after you get home,' I put to him. 'You're going to need time to adjust and I thought...'

He looks up as the door opens and the nurse moves unobtrusively back in.

'I'm sorry, Ava,' Will says. 'I don't think I'm ready for this.'

Ready for what?

I look at him in consternation, not quite sure what I'm hearing. This was part of the plan. The plan he's forgotten.

'You wrote down your wishes...' I scrabble about in my handbag, looking for the notes he made before the op. The things he wrote so he could tell himself what it was he'd want, who he could trust, and so on... I'll show him the notepad so he can see it's all in his own hand-writing.

'I understand,' he's saying gruffly. 'But I can't. You and me living together. That feels too... weird.'

'Okay.' I stop searching through my bag as the stark realisation hits me. Those handwritten notes – what we'd both thought of as an insurance policy against him not knowing or believing his own wishes, going in – they're not going to mean a thing more to him at the moment, now, than *I* do.

They're not going to mean anything at all.

I let that sink in, watching Will's amazement as he turns his attention to his mobile phone that's suddenly *so* much more advanced than the one he left behind seven years ago. He actually seems more interested in that than he is in me. I get it, his brain's been wiped and he doesn't know me so no one could blame him for not wanting us to move in together, but right now... that does feel pretty damn personal.

The nurse, Andy, is giving me a quiet *time's up* signal. But this hasn't been nearly long enough! After all the hours last night when I was sitting outside, getting progressively more worried and stiffer and colder, counting the creeping minutes till the sun finally came peeking through the waiting room windows, I really, really want to ignore the nurse, and carry on talking to Will. I want to carry on our conversation till I see some small, tiny little glimmer of *something* still there between us. But instead I get to my feet.

'Take care,' Will calls out, the way he does to everyone. 'See you soon, Ava.'

Seeing my forlorn face, Andy presses my arm gently as I head out.

'This is all normal, all what we expected, remember,' he reminds me. 'People take differing amounts of time to adjust to this situation.'

'I know. I only...' Everything in front of my eyes has gone blurry.

'Did he remember anything?' the girl at the desk asks, on my way out. She's been my shoulder-to-lean-on for the last few hours since she came on duty. I shake my head, feeling all the weariness and the despair I haven't felt up to now.

'Maybe some of it will come back eventually?' she consoles, even though I've explained to her that it's all gone. Him and me. What we've been to each other. I imagined I might somehow still be... *in there*. If not in Will's mind, then still in his psyche, somewhere. Like soulmates. That's what I always thought we were.

'Give it time.' She kindly hands me a tissue.

Time. I get the feeling I'm going to be hearing that a lot in the coming days. Along with what I already know about *how lucky we are*. He's made it through the op. He's alive. We can start again.

But what if it turns out that giving it time isn't enough? What if no amount of time ever will be?

# 3

## AVA

I should go home, I know, but when I make an autopilot right turn into Pilgrim Street, heading in the direction of work, that's where I end up going instead. Sitting quietly in the deserted Butterfly Gardens car park for half an hour, I realise it's too early for any of the other staff to have arrived yet so I let the events of the long night wash over me. Reminding myself that Will is *alive and intact* and that, going in, that's all I ever hoped for.

I knew there'd be changes in him. I knew he wouldn't know me. But I hold onto my stomach, stemming the wave of nausea – it's one thing *thinking* you know what to expect, and another thing altogether experiencing it. Maybe I still had a place deep inside where I was expecting too much?

I glance at the time on my phone but it's too early to ring my folks. I already sent them the same text I sent Robyn but as they're in Spain currently, helping out an old mate with his restaurant, they don't usually rise till late. Besides, I'm not up for putting on a brave face and reassuring them yet.

My folks won't understand it and I couldn't explain it to them but there's something missing that's *more* than Will not recognising me.

Somehow I had convinced myself that the spark of magic that's always been there between Will and me would still *be* there. Even if he needed an operation and came out not knowing me.

Only... I see now, I couldn't locate it earlier, that spark. It's that which has upset me more than anything. Not his innocent questions about *what was your name again?* Or *how many years?* None of that, no. Those are only the facts that go to make up a life, facts that he can learn again. I could get over that. We both could. What's bugging me is how that magical spark seems to have vanished the moment he couldn't light up his end of it...

I shove my mobile into my bag. Apart from the earlier feeling of nausea, I now also urgently need to pee.

Exiting the car, I spy a small window open on the upper floor – will the cleaner still be in there? Please, still be there, Bess. If she doesn't show in *five seconds flat*, there'll be nothing for it, I'll have to go behind the large purple buddleia that management have recently planted out front. Bess doesn't open up.

'Ouch!' Before I can even get into position a branch has twanged me in the face and I hear an elderly gentleman calling out.

'You all right, there, miss?'

'Uh...'Sheer determination not to humiliate myself in public gives me the super-human power to hold on. One. More. Minute.

'I need the toilet.' Face reddening, I extricate myself from the buddleia. 'They haven't opened the doors yet!'

'Haven't they?' Old Harry Briers can tell you more than you'd ever want to know about insect breeding programmes – he's been involved with them for the Butterfly Gardens since the seventies – but when it comes to mundane matters his mind's like a sieve.

I squirm.

'It's a Wednesday. They won't open up here till ten o' clock.'

'You don't *look* like one of our volunteers?'

'Harry, I work here a couple of times a week,' I remind him. 'I've done so for a few years. Look, I really need to pee!'

'Righty-oh, then. You should've said.' Mercifully, he unlocks and when I finally come out, full of relief at a disaster averted, he's still waiting for me in the courtyard; at least, he's standing there with his eyes half closed, breathing peacefully.

'Better?' he says.

'Much better.' I join him by the lipstick pink, feathery cosmos as half a dozen small mauve butterflies flutter in and out.

He asks casually, 'Been up carousing all the night?'

'No,' I breathe. 'I gave up on my carousing days when I left my job working in the fashion industry.' We've spoken about all of this before, but Harry doesn't remember. Apart from all the things he learned years back, all the things he does automatically, Harry doesn't remember anything for more than a couple of hours. Not any more. So, I fill him in, again.

'I was waiting at the hospital for my boyfriend to come out of a long and very dangerous operation.'

'Oh. That work out all right, then?' Harry's attentive, but he's still got his eyes closed, face turned towards the sun. Like one of his giant daisies, I think, drinking in the light through his closed lids.

'He survived the operation and it was a success, yes.' I pause. 'He doesn't know me any more, though, Harry. He's forgotten.'

'He's forgotten a handsome young woman like you?' Old Harry mutters softly. 'Wants his head examining, that one.'

Despite myself, I give a soft laugh.

'I hoped we could start again.'

'You love him?'

I nod. More than the world.

'I love him, and I hoped he could get to know me again, that we could go back to how we were but...' I rub the heel of my palm against my chest where the dull ache I recognise as sadness won't go away. 'Right now, I'm not sure if he even *wants* to get back with me, Harry. Not only does Will not remember me, I get the impression he's no longer interested.'

He's quiet for a bit, then he asks, 'Did he love you, too?'

'Once,' I breathe. Will loved me and being loved by him made me feel a way I can't even begin to explain.

'I see.'

'But he won't remember any of that. That's gone.' *Is it really gone?*

'He won't,' Harry agrees. 'The mind's a bugger that way, sometimes. I feel it, myself.'

I feel my shoulders droop as he says it, but I'm fond of Harry and he's trying his best to be kind. I remember my manners, suddenly.

'Thank you for opening up the doors for me. I'd have peed in the bushes if I'd had to, it was that urgent.'

'They'd have survived. Besides, my wife was always the same,' he says without missing a beat. 'Throughout all her pregnancies, she lived beside the bathroom, she did. Bit of a bother for her, really.'

I stare at him, and he asks, 'This is the cause of it, I take it? Bladder unable to take its usual strain?'

I nod, feeling caught out.

'Hearty congratulations, then.' Harry's eyes remain resolutely closed even as he says all this. 'When's the bairn due?'

'November.' I'm not too sure how I feel about saying this. Nobody here knows it, yet. I guess, even if Old Harry knows it, that's not too much of a problem because he won't recall it by the time he sees the next person.

'And if he's forgotten you, no doubt he's also forgotten...?'

'That I'm having a baby and how overjoyed we both were about it? He'll have lost it all, Harry.'

'You'll have to tell him soon, I expect?'

I bite my lip. I'll have to tell Will that we're expecting, yes. Even though the child's not his. I'm not looking forward to that moment. I'll have to work myself up to it and then...? Just... say it, and then force myself to forget, as he has, that it isn't the truth.

Because from now on, it will be.

It will be the new truth.

'We only had fifteen minutes together this morning and I didn't want to overwhelm him,' I tell Harry. 'There wasn't a good moment to bring it up and Will was shocked enough, coming to terms with waking up to discover he'd lost seven years and finding *me* there...'

'Perhaps it won't all be as bad as you think?' Harry's opened his eyes and is looking directly at me.

'No?'

'No.' He's smiling sweetly. 'Because he loved you. Rest assured, the heart always remembers, even when the mind's forgotten.'

I smile at him sadly.

'You reckon the heart remembers?'

'Oh, yes,' Harry says.

If that's true, it could be a double-edged sword. I look down, doing up the buttons of my jacket, feeling the morning chill on my skin for the first time. If Will only recalled all the good feelings he once had towards me that'd be peachy, but what if, deep within him, Will still has some remnants left of everything else he was feeling before the operation? The sadness, the despair and the depression? I'm praying not.

Standing there with Harry for a while longer, I watch the sun as it rises over faraway buildings, casting light across the old stone courtyard out front. Looking on as it makes all the tiny white mayflowers along the wall turn a warm orange colour and then a glowing, May morning pink, I tell myself that it's all going to be okay. I tell myself that I am resilient and patient and strong and I don't need to worry because I can weather all this.

And I ignore the small, quiet voice inside that's already begun whispering to me, traitorously: *Ava, I don't know if you can.*

# 4

## WILL

'Hey.' The young nurse, Andy, is back, shaking my arm gently. I haven't seen him since they sent me down from ICU onto the general ward, yesterday. 'I promised I'd pop by; see how you were doing.'

'Was I sleeping again?' I'm mumbling, embarrassed to admit to it. The last few days have been a bit of a haze.

He leans in to help me get up. 'Brain ops tend to do that to you,' he says cheerily. 'Still. Have we had you moving around yet, today?'

I shake my head. They wheeled me down for a barrage of physical and cognitive assessments earlier. That was tiring enough.

'We need to do that. Keep the circulation going. Prevent muscle stiffness, blood clots and so on...' He glances at his watch.

'We've got thirty minutes. Fancy a stroll around The Park, Will?'

'What?'

He motions upwards with his head. 'Top floor. The most beautiful garden of any hospital building you'll ever see, overlooking part of Holcombe Bay and tended entirely by a group of enthusiastic volunteers.'

'Sure.' I force some enthusiasm into my voice. Garden space, fresh air, that'll all be good for recovery, right?

In the lift up to the eighth floor, he asks casually, 'Expecting any visitors today?'

'Uh?' I was concentrating on standing upright all by myself, focussing on the little light jumping up the floor numbers, 3, 4, 5... We stopped at five and the doors opened for what felt like *a very long time* as a porter wheeling a vacant chair got out. I kept thinking how much I'd like to sit down in that chair. How much energy it was taking me simply to keep standing up.

'Anyone coming in to see you, later?'

'Mum, I suppose.' I was happy to see her when she finally made it in. My stepdad, Joe, came with her too, but between the travel mess-up and her constant fretting over leaving Auntie Doris alone, it's not been that much comfort having them around.

'Apparently I told *everyone else* I know to stay away?'

He nods. 'After this kind of op, we generally only encourage visits from the people who'll be most important for your recovery and support.'

I nod and he winks at me.

'Like your girl, Ava?'

My girl. That still feels odd, so I don't answer him. At floor eight he holds the doors open as I tortoise my way out onto the open terrace, blinking in the welcome, bright daylight, suddenly and unexpectedly surrounded by huge fronds of *green*. I breathe in, deeply. A clear, crisp breeze hits my lungs and the stifling, rarefied air I've been breathing for the last few days melts away. For one glorious moment, I feel human again, *alive*.

'This feels like paradise.'

He grins broadly.

'That's what they're hoping you'll feel.' He takes my arm and guides me slowly around to the other side of the building. I'm enjoying taking some deep breaths as we walk around The Park in silence for a bit. I have to concentrate, but it's gratifying to find I can actually walk by myself, with no aide. *Sayonara bed pans,* I think. Thank God. The distinct smell of the lunches being prepared wafts up from the kitchens below.

'Apple crumble and cinnamon with a hint of...' I take in another deep breath. 'Pear?' I never usually notice stuff like this. It's as if everything hitting my nostrils has been dialled up a few notches. Kinda cool.

He smiles. 'A heightened sense of smell is sometimes a thing, after this kind of op.'

'Is it?' I laugh, more than usually aware of the fragrant scents of the plants surrounding us.

'Reminds people there's a great, big, beautiful world still waiting for them once they get outside this place.'

'I guess there is. I'm looking forward to that.' To getting out of here anyway. Even if – I stiffen slightly at the recollection –I have so little idea what kind of life, beyond these four walls, currently awaits me.

'Everyone does.' He pauses now, smiling. 'D'you have any idea about what you used to do for work?'

'Last I recall, I'd left my band and spent a year making ends meet.' I open up my hands. 'Apparently, I'm still a musician for a living... a songwriter.'

'Impressive!' he says.

'Too impressive,' I admit. 'Ava's been playing me some of the songs I'm supposed to have written. They're damn good, and I have *no clue*, man.' I look away from him, aware of that lost feeling again. How I felt when I first woke up after the op and my last memory was of me riding out on my motorbike.

I'm still not entirely convinced that it *wasn't* the last thing I did.

And that's only a tiny part of the whole scary business of Will Tyler's life that I'm going to have to figure out how to slot back into. How am I supposed to come to terms with it, this sense that the rest of my life just blinked out at that point, leaving me cheated out of a whole chunk of time? How does anyone? I swallow, putting out a hand to steady myself against the wall.

'Does it get any better?'

'Sure, it does. All in good time.' We wait there for a few moments before we start walking again.

'You've lost a portion of your past, but people *can* still form new memories of old events.'

My ears prick up – new memories of old events?

'It's like… when we see pictures of ourselves as infants,' he goes on. 'Barely anyone recalls too much before their third birthday. Half the time we only think we do, because we've been told by our parents how it was.'

'Ah, I see.'

Somehow that doesn't leave me feeling reassured. Andy bows his head. We're both silent for a bit, taking in the morning air. The scents and fragrances dancing in on every little breeze are like musical notes in my head. They're like a beautiful symphony, threading through the strong feelings of disappointment that've just hit me. I close my eyes.

I thought for a bit there, he might be talking about something else, some sort of remedy. There is none, though.

I know Andy brought me up here partly to help get me grounded, but now that he's mentioned it, my mind can't help bouncing back to the *seven missing years* again. The great, big, blank space inside that everyone else is going to want to fill in for me, *all the events of my own life* that I'll now feel I was never even present for.

He admits softly, 'It's okay, man. It's quite common to experience something that feels a bit like grief.'

'Is that what this is?' He'll know, I tell myself. He'll have seen it all before. I take in a deep breath, pulling myself up straight, taking heart from his matter-of-factness. If he says it'll get better, then it surely will.

'Most likely.' We've stopped walking again. Andy points out, 'Look what else is out there, waiting for you…' We've come to the end of the wall, and there, over to the east, is a faint but undeniable view of Holcombe Bay, shimmering in the distance, just as he promised. It's never looked quite so beautiful to me as it does this morning.

Andy's looking at me thoughtfully. 'Look familiar?'

'Very familiar.' I've got a lump in my throat. 'My grandad was an old sea salt. This is a bit like the view from his place.'

'I know.' He smiles. 'You asked me to bring you up here, after your op, for that very reason.'

*I asked him to bring me up here?*

'I'm afraid I don't...'

'No,' he says softly. 'You wouldn't.'

He must see the look on my face because he adds gently, 'Hey, I brought you up here to show you that you haven't lost *everything*. You recall your Gramps' place. There are things you can, and will, build on, in the coming weeks and months.'

'Yes,' I say. Because – what else is there? He's right. I've had a big setback, clearly, but I've got to focus on what I *do* know. Build on that.

Our time must be almost up – he's indicating we need to be heading back towards the lifts.

'First things first, though,' Andy says. 'Sister wanted me to ask, have you settled on your going home arrangements?'

'My...?' I look at him, blankly.

'We got the sense there was a bit of confusion over your advance wishes, regarding going home arrangements, yes?'

'I don't know. Is there?' I want to keep breathing in the fresh, scented air, forget about the day-job I no longer have any confidence I can do, and everything else that's coming, but he's already mentioned *going home* twice.

'They're planning to discharge me, sometime soon?'

They told me it'd take between two to seven days depending on many different factors and, so far, the doctors have been making encouraging noises about my progress. I pull a small frown. Everything's been a bit of a blur and, though I'm keen to leave, I haven't given any real thought to what getting out of here will look like. Now that I'm up here, feeling for the first time as if I'm slowly thawing out, I see I'll have to address it, soon. Then I realise what he's said.

'Advance *wishes*?'

'You stated in your wishes beforehand that you'd be going home with Ava.'

'I did?' I shake my head, slowly. 'I don't think I've seen those, yet.'

'Haven't you?'

Now I think about it, I probably have. A nurse did bring something like that in, along with a load of other paperwork and instructions soon after I arrived on the general ward. We were going to go over it all, when someone came along to take me away for a physiotherapy assessment, and it never happened.

'So... I've changed my mind,' I tell him slowly. 'I won't be going home with Ava, after all.'

'No?'

'No.' He's looking a little puzzled, so I add, 'I don't know her.'

'Many people need to be tended to by agency carers when they get home,' he points out reasonably. 'They won't know their carers either.'

I look at him uneasily. 'My point is, I don't know her, but she still feels she knows *me*.'

'Some people might say that was a good thing.' He glances casually at the watch-fob he's got hanging off his uniform. 'Ava's the one who's going to help you get back to yourself soonest, Will. She can, because she's the one who knows.'

I blink, recalling the pained look on her face when she came in after the op and I didn't recognise her. The *hope* she had in there, I can't even... I shake my head. The expectation that we could re-set everything back to *whatever it was* from before, easy as flicking a switch, but we can't. I can't.

He comes back after a while. 'In circumstances like this, advance wishes are put in place as a safety net. You knew that you'd remember nothing, and you agreed to what you believed would be in your best interests while you were still in a position to judge that.'

I shift my whole body so I'm facing the view, away from him. I don't feel comfortable hearing all this. Sure, it all makes good, common sense, but common sense isn't sitting too well with me, right now.

He persists gently. 'She seems like a nice girl though. Attractive, caring, and...' He grins suddenly, man-to-man. 'She's clearly into *you*. You should be happy about that, dude!'

I let out a breath.

'Yeah, sure. I know. I should be happy.'

Maybe I should. Maybe someone should tell that to my wary, shocked, and over-burdened heart – how *happy* I should be that I've got this successful life and wonderful, ready-made relationship I'm supposed to jump right back into. I suspect this nurse Andy's not going to be the only one having trouble seeing it. I sigh heavily, and he pats my arm.

'It's okay, Will. As long as you've got *someone* to support you. You're going to need that in the coming weeks, believe me. Your mum, maybe?'

'Perhaps,' I tell him faintly. With the best will in the world, my mum's got enough of her own concerns. She's got hospital appointments coming up and my Auntie Doris to worry about. My stepdad, Joe, offered to stay on, but he knows that'll never happen and even if Mum manages to stay down here for a few days more... he just said *weeks*. Is that how long it's going to take me to recover from this operation? And that's only the physical side of it. What about all the other things it's becoming increasingly clear I have lost for good?

I feel as if I've been left, stranded on the shore of my own future, with no ship that's ever coming to take me back.

'Time's up, I think,' Andy says regretfully. As we make our slow way back down onto the ward, I've got more worries going around in my head than I had when I went up. Tearing up those advance wishes is going to have consequences, no doubt about it. No doctor's going to sign my discharge papers if I've not got the proper home-care arrangements in place. I know this.

I have to figure something out. I just don't know what, yet.

## 5

## WILL

'Let me get this straight – you want me to *lie* for you?' Ava's taking this surprisingly well. She's sitting calmly by my bedside looking elegant and fresh with her auburn hair tied up high in a ponytail and – given what I've requested of her – she's not looking in the slightest bit put out.

'Um... not exactly lie,' I put it to her. 'I need you to be a little... economical with the truth.' I swear, she should be mad at me, but instead there are two little dimples appearing on the outskirts of her cheeks that suggest she's actually finding this amusing. I have no idea why.

It's Friday afternoon and, as Andy predicted, the discharge team are currently doing their rounds on the ward. Having drawn a blank on every other option I tried to dream up, I've asked Ava to imply that, yes, of course, she'll be there to support me once I go back home.

'I want you to tell them you're coming back with me, to mine. Only to *tell* them that, you don't have to actually come.' Mum and Joe have gone back to Leeds already. Auntie Doris had a fall while they were down here and there was nothing for it, but it's left me in a difficult position.

'They'll be happy with that,' I tell Ava. 'And then, once my mum's sorted out someone else to look after Doris, she can come down and be the "named person" instead.'

My mum won't be back down here, I know that much. But does Ava? Do I sound as if I'm pleading with her? I am! It's amazing what a bit of intensive bed rest and professional care can do. I feel so much stronger, so much more coherent but she has no idea how badly I have to get out of here.

'I see.' She looks down at her hands, neatly folded in her lap, but I get the definite impression it's more to hide her smile than anything else.

'I wouldn't have asked you,' I say, 'if there'd been anyone else.'

'I know.'

'You know?' Does she know I was trawling through the contacts on my phone earlier to see if I could find someone – anyone else – I could ask, but, whaddya know, apart from DelRoy who's never around, I could hardly find a single person to ring who I actually *knew*. It seems I have left behind pretty much everyone in the last seven years. And, yeah, I know we're doing this 'no one come and visit Will' thing, but none of the new people have even sent me a 'Get Well' card, so what does that say about them? Did I really want to phone up Jerome or Fenella, only to find out they're no mates of mine but my plumber and my dental hygienist?

Or... something else? I've actually got this guy called Red Sphynx up there. Red Sphynx! God knows who *he* is.

Which only left Ava.

Ava who really has been with me for the years she claims she has, because there are photos of us on my phone to prove it. Photos where we're lounging together comfortably and laughing in the way only real couples would do. Photos I must have snapped in off-guard moments, taken of her, sitting at breakfast, or looking out of a window, looking wistful. And some which she must have taken of a *me* I barely recognise. I've been staring at them, long and hard, those pictures, trying to figure out who he is, this new version of me. But I don't know him. He only feels like some older brother who I'm a little envious of – maybe even a little in awe of, right now.

I really wish I knew Ava as well as I'm supposed to know her, and I could trust her to say the right thing, because now Dr Mason and a group of other staff are heading towards us. There's a *zip* as the nurse closes off the curtains, leaving me in my own private cubicle with *my girlfriend* and the medics, and my heart's pounding so damn loud I'm sure they're going to need to pull over the heart reviving equipment any moment. Ava didn't give me an answer yet, did she?

'You've already met your surgeon, I believe.' The tall, grey haired man at Dr Mason's side leans in to offer me a firm handshake. 'Mr Tripoli's the consultant who performed your procedure.'

'Yes,' I say. 'I remember.'

His eyes narrow.

'You recall our *pre-op* consultations?'

'No,' I admit. 'I remember your name being mentioned on the ward, and seeing your picture in an online hospital brochure I've looked at, since.'

'Ah. Excellent.' He seems pleased at that; taps the folder he's holding in his hands. 'Well, Mr Tyler, you'll be very happy to hear that the MRI scans we took post-op showed we got it all. You're clear. There's no residual swelling in the brain and absolutely nothing to currently indicate to us that you won't make a full and complete recovery from this.'

'Amazing,' I say. 'Thank you.'

'Swelling on the face going down nicely, too, I see. Not experiencing problems with pain or any headaches, at all, Mr Tyler?'

'Not actual headaches.'

'Oh?' His eyebrows go up; he's immediately on the alert.

'The bit on my *scalp* where they tell me they stapled the bone of my skull back in place hurts like hell.'

'I see.' He glances over to the nurse. 'Usual painkillers for that one, I think?' Then to me. 'But, no actual deep brain aches?'

'None.'

'Good to know. It's very important that you report them to us if they do occur. Headaches could mean brain tissue swelling, which we'd then have to treat with a course of steroids.' To Dr Mason, he says, 'OT assessment come up with any transient deficits that we know of?'

'Speech, cognitive awareness and memory *since* the procedure are all stated as excellent. No reported motor function loss, either.'

He beams.

'We did a great job, it seems.' Mr Tripoli turns back to me. 'Only the last few years of your life we couldn't manage to retain for you, eh? So,' He smiles at his colleague. 'Any plans for discharge in place?'

Dr Mason glances at her notes.

'Will's due to go home with his girlfriend, Ava Morley, who'll be taking some time off to support him.'

'Um...' I clear my throat and they all look over at me, now.

'Is there a problem?'

'Not exactly a... er... I'm, you know, feeling *so well*, I wondered if it was really necessary for...'

Dr Mason and Mr Tripoli exchange a glance. I get the sense they've already had some wind of my being about to renege on my advance wishes.

'It's absolutely necessary. The most challenging period of recovery following this type of surgery often happens in the weeks after,' Dr Mason impresses upon me. 'You'll want someone to be on hand, I assure you. Shopping, cooking, even showering...'

'Showering?' I say.

'Even going to the bathroom may be a problem for some,' she continues. 'I'm sorry, Will, but this is the reality of the situation. There is no way we are going to discharge you, until—'

Ava clears her throat quietly. 'It's not a problem at all,' she tells them. 'We knew what would be required from the start. The only change to the plan is I'm moving into Will's apartment instead of him coming over to mine. To keep things as consistent for him as possible.'

'Oh!' The medics smile at each other, relieved. 'That's all right, then,' Dr Mason comes back. 'In that case we'll certainly be able to let you go home today, Will. Just a little bit of paperwork to do, and then we can get you organised.'

They hang about for a few minutes more, making observations on how well things have gone, and telling me that I'm doing brilliantly and how lucky I am. *I know,* I think, my heart's not stopped pounding yet. *Damn lucky.*

Once they've gone, I breathe out, *'Thank you,'* I tell Ava sincerely. 'Thank you so much.'

'You're welcome.'

'I wouldn't have asked you.' I apologise once again. 'I'm sorry to have to dump that on you.'

'I know you wouldn't have asked me, but that's perfectly all right. I'm more than willing to do whatever I can to help you with your recovery.' Her warm green eyes are gazing into mine, intently. When I look right into the depths of hers, searching for an echo of something I can recognise, I don't find it, but... I feel a small zing of warmth in my belly, instead. A little bit of happiness that's found its way into my day.

And even better it sounds as if, later on today, I'm going home.

## 6

## AVA

'Let *me* carry that.' Exiting the car, Will grabs the holdall containing his belongings before I can... his face immediately twisting in a wince, which I pretend to ignore. 'It's not that much of a weight,' he says.

It's not. It's only going to feel like it, to him. They warned us, and I can see it on his face. Normal, everyday things are going to be a real strain for a while and he doesn't need to play macho man. The steep stairs up to DelRoy's flat aren't going to be too much fun, either. I catch Will's face the moment we enter the stark high-rise with its concrete façade.

'This where I live, then?'

'Sure.' I look away, awkwardly. He doesn't, and I already told him so but I'm not opening up *that* whole can of worms. We pause at the bottom and he peers up the dark stairwell.

'Not the cheeriest place.'

'It's... a bachelor pad, isn't it?' He looks at me blankly and I offer, 'I don't suppose you ever expected to be around here for much more than kipping and heating up the occasional microwave meal.'

'I see.' Going up the stairs, Will seems to be holding his breath. If it's the super-charged sense of smell kicking in again, I can see why he might want to do that. Good. The less he likes it here, the better.

Inside the flat, which DelRoy was subletting to him for a while, Will drops his bag on the narrow hall floor, immediately pouncing on a guitar he's spotted lying on the sofa.

'I recognise this one. It's mine!' The discovery of the guitar seems to soothe him, a familiar thing in a familiar place. He looks overjoyed, cradling the guitar on his lap, allowing his fingers to run softly up and down the neck. Then, he gets up in an instant and has a nose around in his old bedroom, running his fingers along the top of all the clothes he finds hanging in the wardrobe, pulling out an old leather jacket, lingering to inhale the familiar scent of it, before putting it back.

'I recognise some of these, but not many.' Will turns, glancing out of the window. The block next door obscures most of the skyline, the wall facing him a discoloured, smoky grey. He gives a deep sigh, gazing up at the small patch of visible sky.

'Is this really what I open my eyes to, every morning?'

'It isn't, not normally,' I say.

If things had worked out the way we'd intended, he'd have been coming back with me. I had Beach Cottage all ready and waiting for him but there are so many facts I still need to apprise Will of. So many, *complicated* things...

Will is peering into the kitchen. 'The place where I microwave my meals? Nice!' He's wrinkling his nose. 'I feel as if I haven't been here in a while, but I do recognise it.'

He would. Will's been friends with DelRoy ever since he came down from Leeds to live permanently with his grandad in Holcombe Bay in his early teens. Coming out to stand in the middle of the lounge, looking around again, he's taking it all in.

'It's all coming back to me, Ava. I used to stay here at DelRoy's on and off whenever the band weren't touring. I can actually remember...'

He goes over and picks up a tacky wooden spoon with the picture of a tulip painted on the back, *a gift from Amsterdam.*

'I remember visiting Amsterdam one summer with the band not long after we started. We were doing a low-key tour of the continent. I remember long, hot, summer nights when we'd go to bed in Krakow and wake up in Warsaw.'

'Yes.'

'You were there?'

I shake my head, reminding him, 'We've only been together three years.' All the way down here, he's been full of questions about the past but he's not asked me the first thing about us, yet. It's understandable, but I'm starting to feel a bit like a spare part. Is he genuinely so uncurious about our time together?

He looks up at me, swallowing suddenly.

'It took a while but I think the band were starting to go places, y'know. I always thought I'd get back with them, I thought we'd get over our musical differences but... it never happened?'

The band again? I go to fill up a glass of water from the tap. *Anything*, for him not to see my face right now. I'm glad for him if he's finding some solace, reminiscing about all the bits and pieces in here that he remembers, but why couldn't some of the nostalgia he's holding onto from those days have been wiped as well? I lean up against the fridge, sipping my water.

I can't let this go on for too long, can I?

'Will, you should know. DelRoy's band broke up a few years back. He still tours, but as a session musician with other bands. That's why his flat is so often empty.'

'Oh, right.' He sighs, sitting down heavily on the small sofa. The news seems to deflate him somewhat.

'So, I'm on my own, these days?'

I sit down gently, beside him.

'No. You have *me*, Will. Me and everybody else.' He's still looking a little lost – does he imagine I'm going to disappear any minute, now that I've delivered him to the flat? It might be all that he asked of me, but I've no intention of doing that.

'I've stocked the fridge and I got in everything else I could think of that you'll need and... I'm here for you.'

He looks at me appreciatively. 'Wow. You've gone to a lot of trouble. Thank you.'

I bow my head, silently.

He adds, pained, 'It does still feel... odd, accepting all this help from a stranger.'

I lean in, pulling a small smile. 'Only, I'm *not*, am I?'

He takes in a deep breath. To my surprise, when he comes back, it's a little shyly. 'Is it too soon to ask how you and I met?'

'That one's a *little* bit embarrassing,' I admit.

'For you or for me?'

I give a short laugh. 'For me, I'm afraid.'

He puts his head to one side, smiling, and waits. 'Are you going to tell me?'

'We were both attending an R-Time concert. It was a hot day and I'd had a couple of drinks before going in. When it got to the interval, the queue for the Ladies, as usual, backed into the following Tuesday while the queue for the Men's...'

'*Whoa.*' Will's got a disbelieving grin on his face. 'You're not telling me we met in the...?'

I nod.

'In the Gents?' He throws up his hands. 'Please tell me there wasn't anyone else in there? Apart from me, I mean?'

'If you're imagining that I walked in and came across a whole line of guys standing there with their dicks out...'

He takes in a breath, glancing up at the ceiling.

'There wasn't. You had the field completely clear. All to yourself,' I give him. '*Pas de competition.*'

'That was... lucky.'

'For you or for me?' I hide a smile. It's not all as bad as he thinks. 'Look, I'd borrowed a "No Entry, Works in Progress" sign and stuck it up outside the door. All the other blokes were obligingly using the loo on the next floor up.'

'Not me, though?'

'No. For some reason *you* didn't seem to feel it necessary to follow the rules...'

He gives a hearty laugh. 'I see you're the kind of woman I should be making a beeline for. Resourceful! Good in a crisis.'

'True. I am all those things, and more...' I laugh. '*Now*, you're staring at me!'

He's looking at me just the way he used to when we first started going out. Back then, his gaze would often lock onto mine, as if he was looking for something deep in my eyes. I never could figure out what. I'd be the first one to look away, every time. Back then, there were no secrets I was keeping from him, though; I was open in the way you only ever can be with your first true love, nothing yet to hide.

'I was trying to see if I found any of your features familiar at all.'

I toss my hair back, batting my eyelids at him.

'And... do you recognise anything about me?'

He just gives an apologetic shake of his head. 'I'm sorry, but no.'

His reply hits home. For a moment I had dared to think we'd recaptured something, but maybe it was like one of those elusive butterflies we only catch rare glimpses of at the tea rooms; we know they're *there*, somewhere, but we have to take it on faith...

I smile sadly. 'It's how they said it would be, Will.'

'Hey. Isn't that...?' He's not even looking at me any more. His gaze is locked on the picture hanging on the opposite wall, of a pretty, dark haired girl, pouting and posing provocatively up against a gate. 'That girl has legs up to her neck,' he says, a little too fondly. 'And huge eyes.'

*Eyes as big as a chihuahua*, the guys used to say, hence her nickname. I let out a small, quiet breath, clenching my hands briefly. He recognises her well enough. Why couldn't it have been *her* who was erased from his memory and not me?

Her and DelRoy's bloody band.

'That's ChiChi,' he says out loud. He sounds pleased with himself. 'I'd know her anywhere.'

'Sure, well, I imagine you would.' I swallow. 'Being that you two were an item *over seven years* ago. Which is,' I add, feeling annoyed, 'rather a long time ago, you'll agree.'

He considers that for a moment. Then, 'And I've still got her picture up there because...?'

'Because...' I check my first response, riled at his automatic assumption that he's the one who put it there. *He knows* he and I have been together for a while. 'That's because DelRoy's going out with her now.' I add quietly, 'And this is his flat.'

That takes a moment to sink in. I see it, his look of surprise and disbelief.

'DelRoy's dating ChiChi?'

'Yep.' The news has taken him aback, no question.

'Well, son of a gun.'

'And you're going out with me,' I remind him.

Will looks straight at me.

'Were,' I correct, noting his bemusement. 'You *were* going out with me.' Hell, we were getting on so well. I was planning on getting in our baby news, today! He tilts his head to one side now.

'I guess I must have upped my game somewhere along the way, then?'

I make a surprised noise, which comes out like a snort. 'You definitely upped your game.' I add, tentatively, 'D'you remember why you broke up with her?' My heart is actually aching. ChiChi was always the wrong girl for him. If he remembers the real reason why...

'Sure, I do.' He comes straight back. 'She had a bit of a roving eye and we had our ups and downs, but, if there was one thing that was ever going to be a deal breaker for me, it was the day she told me she never wanted kids.' He clasps his hands together, head bowed.

I breathe. 'Do you still want them, Will?'

He frowns.

'Hell, yeah, if I ever get the chance. I've wanted them ever since I was in my twenties. Now I'm thirty-four, it's become...' He does a regretful motion with his face. '*It's become more important than ever.*' He says, very quietly, 'Especially now that I've had a taste of how fragile our lives can be. I don't know if this was something you and I ever spoke about, Ava?'

I nod, aware of a feeling of sadness growing inside me. 'We spoke often about starting our family.'

He shoots me a soft smile. 'Did we, really?'

'We did!' I take in a deep breath. 'Will. There's something really important I've been wanting to let you know about since you woke up, but I've been waiting for the right moment.'

He looks over curiously but I have ground to a halt. Will's obvious enthusiasm over his ex has left me feeling a little lost. I lean down to pull my mobile out of my bag. Perhaps he'll take the news better if he hears it in his own words?

# 7

# AVA

When I scroll through my mobile it doesn't take me long to find the twenty seconds of video I took of Will, sitting in the garden on the sunny morning before his op.

'This is you.' I hand my phone over so he can see. 'Right before the op.'

*'I know what this is gonna mean,'* Will is saying in the video. 'I'm going to forget everything and everyone I've known in recent years. I'm going to forget Ava and all the medical discussions that led up to this and I'm even going to forget I made this video.' He smiles into the camera then, a wonky, self-deprecating, typical Will smile.

'Which is why I'm taking this video. So, I'll know, coming out of it, that I'm still sane. And also, to let my future self know...' there's a pause, while he looks to be marshalling his thoughts '... to let myself know that I *wanted to live*. That I had every reason to...' his voice catches here '... to want to live, and that waking up potentially like a zombie was a price I was prepared to pay.' He does a cut-throat motion into the camera, clearly feeling overcome. The video snippet comes to an abrupt end.

Will's looking a little startled, staring at the phone. I give him a moment for it all to sink in.

There's another little snippet, one I took before this one, where he talks about *how happy he was* for us to be expecting this baby. I was planning on showing him that one next. Only, he's already handing the mobile back to me.

'Actually, there was another little piece there that I—'

'I knew?' Will still sounds a bit stunned. His hand goes up to touch the bandage around his head, distractedly. 'I knew I might wake up like a zombie?'

I blink. 'Well, you *didn't* wake up like that, obviously. I guess you had to sign a disclaimer form saying you knew that it was a possibility.'

What's this about? Maybe I should have started off with the 'we're expecting' clip? I didn't imagine he'd react like that to the other video, but now, 'I need to visit the bathroom, Ava.' He gets up abruptly. 'Excuse me.'

I put the phone to one side while I wait for him to come back, folding my arms. I don't know what's up with his strange reaction. I'm still telling him about this baby today, though. I've waited long enough. I'll do it as soon as he comes back.

As the minutes tick by, Dr Mason's warning that some people may need help visiting the bathroom for a while after returning home enters my head briefly, but I don't think Will's in any place for me to make that offer. Instead, I get up and go to stand in the hallway. Near enough to hear if he falls while in there, near enough to come if he calls. But instead, it goes quiet for a long time. At last, I give up, knocking tentatively on the door.

'You okay in there?'

'It's open,' he says faintly.

When I push the door, Will didn't appear to have needed the loo at all. He's standing by the tiny bathroom cabinet, staring into the mirror. For the first time, I catch a glimpse of him as he must see himself. Wan, with dark rings under his eyes, and that huge white bandage still covering the entry wound on his head. He's stroking the skin of his face as if he can't quite recognise what he sees, looking upset.

'Can you believe, I hadn't looked until now?' he says softly. 'I hadn't actually *looked*.'

It must have been the comment about the zombie that did it. I come up behind, joining him in gazing at his reflection in the mirror. His dismay at what he sees makes me sad. *I* see my boyfriend, that's all. A little battered and worn from his trials, maybe, but to me he's still the same handsome, amazing dude I fell in love with. And still the man I wish would fall in love with me, again.

He's muttering, 'I don't care how many disclaimers I signed; no bugger ever told me I might come out of this looking like Maracas Man!'

I stifle a gasp of surprised laughter. 'I'm sorry, what?'

Will frowns. 'Maracas Man. The worst zombie monster the Hamlin Horror studios ever created. I could've ended up looking like him, *being* like him, you tell me. That's what I risked to have this...'

Oh, Will. I know he's upset, but, really? A spurt of unwanted laughter escapes my lips. I know I need to be the caring, solicitous girl-friend that he wants me to be, but the truth is, Will, *there was so much more troubling you before you had your op than this.*

He looks at me unhappily. 'You find this funny?'

I bite my bottom lip. 'The thing is...' A silly, off-topic thing has occurred now and I can't for the life of me get it out of my head. 'One night – about six months back – we'd had a tiff and you were sleeping on the sofa downstairs. I couldn't sleep without you and I came down at about three in the morning and there you were, watching this *Maracas Man* film...'

'And?'

'I made fun of you,' I admit. 'I made some comment about *who even watches terrible, Hamlin Horror, black and white movies like this, made back in the year dot,* and you said you were channel hopping and that'd been the first thing to come up.'

He's still waiting.

'You swore that it was the first time you'd ever seen a Hamlin Horror film.'

'*And?*' He's still annoyed, and upset.

'And that can't be true, if you remember it, can it?'

He's quiet for a moment. 'Okay.' He tells me straight to my face. 'I must have lied, then.'

'Oh, you did?'

'I must have. Because I do remember *Maracas Man*. I watched all the Hamlin Horror flicks back when I was a kid and they scared me half to death at the time. Especially him.' He pauses. 'Did I really tell you I'd never watched those movies before?'

I nod.

'You caught me out then.' He sounds contrite.

'Hey, it's nothing!' I assure him. 'You told a white lie because you were embarrassed, I imagine.'

Never mind *Maracas Man*, there's still the second piece of footage I've got to show him. Or maybe I should simply *tell* him? Will's in such a funny mood, though, holding his head in his hands.

When we go back to the sofa, it's still on his mind.

'No, really, I shouldn't have lied, and I'm sorry. That clip. What I said. I'm finding this really... difficult to...' Will is silent for a few moments. Eventually, he says thickly, 'It's dawning on me that if I'm going to recover from this, I'm going to need you. More than I first thought.'

'I'm here for you, Will.'

'Not only for help with physical things,' he continues. 'Every day I'm discovering how little I really know. I'm going to need you to be the map of... my life.'

'Sure, I will.'

He looks stricken. 'Ava, it would reassure me a lot if you and I could agree to always be 100 per cent transparent with each other.'

I baulk slightly at that. 'Hey, I'm perfectly fine with fibbing if it's about silly things, non-consequential things. Like your horror films. We all tell the odd white lie at times, Will.'

He presses. 'Promise me, at least, that I'll always be able to trust you.'

I close my eyes for a second, panicking slightly. Promises are like the glue that stick the core of you together. Once you begin breaking them there's a danger that the person you are inside will start peeling off and falling apart, until one day the moment comes when you wake up and you don't even know who you are any more.

How can I promise Will this, when the *first* promise I made him – to never tell him the truth about the baby – is still sticking in my throat? When I open my eyes, Will's looking at me expectantly. He doesn't look away till I give him the answer he wants.

'Okay,' I say at last. 'I promise.' Even though that makes me feel so cheap and miserable inside. He doesn't know it, but he's just asked me for the moon on a plate. I've given it to him, with a side serving of all the stars.

But in doing so, I am lying to him anyway.

# 8

## AVA

After he's extracted his promise, Will goes to have a quick sort through his old belongings. I leave him in the privacy of his bedroom while I find a deep saucepan to heat up some soup, searching out some bowls to serve it in, but my thoughts are a million miles from here.

Laying the table, I'm aware of his ex's photo, pouting down at me from the wall. He'd been happy to see her, a familiar and well-loved face, I saw that much. Whereas I'm just a kind stranger to him, a person who's turned up out of the blue to show him some tenderness and love when he needs it most, but... will I ever be any more to him than this?

I lay out the spoons on the bare table, carefully pondering it all.

I could be. Will still wants this, what I can give him – the baby would help us draw a line under the past we've left behind. It's our start-afresh moment. He's going to be overjoyed when he hears about this pregnancy, I know it. He'll see me in a whole different light.

He'll take me back in a flash, only... There's something about that that doesn't feel right.

It's as if I'd be trapping him. I push back my hair, blindly going around the table, putting down salt and bowls and butter and crisps.

How did I not see this before? How did I never factor in how it would make me feel?

Abandoning the table, I go to take in some fresh air at the window for a moment. Will's asked for complete honesty between us, but – could he ever really want me again if he *did* have that? I think I know the answer to that one. The thought saddens me deeply, though I try to push it aside.

And when I think about it, I don't want him getting back with me only because of the baby, or because I'm the one sticking by him in his moment of need. When, *if*, we get back together, I want it to be because Will's truly, deeply, fallen in love with me again.

Then – only then – can things go back to how they were, before.

# 9

# WILL

*Saturday, 12th May:*

*I've been at home just over a week. It doesn't feel that long and most of that time I've spent sleeping. Today's the first day I've woken up feeling I have any real energy.*

I pause. Is this really what the Occupational Therapist was after, when she asked me to keep a journal? 'It's really important that you write things down, Will,' she advised me. 'There may come a point where it's the only means you have, to judge how far you've come.'

Have I made *any* progress so far? I turn the pages back to reread the few, brief entries I've managed in non-sleeping moments over the past week.

*Tuesday, 8th May:*

*Tried to get into my online bank account, today. Cue fun and games and multiple requests sent for a new password. I hope they realise none of this is a joke, and send me one, soon.*

I flip the page over.

*Wednesday, 9th May:*

*Woke up gripped with the strongest sense that I've been trapped in a nightmare for the past week. Feeling very unhappy that there's so much stuff about myself that I still simply don't know. Spent some time with Ava trawling through some of our social media accounts and, by every measure, I appear to have a wonderful life! I am a success. A song I wrote that was a freak runaway hit worldwide still brings me in a modest but viable income. I'm free to follow my passions. Ava assures me I have adequate funds and many friends.*

I should be cock-a-hoop.

But, none of it felt relatable. It all made me feel even more hollow, like a doughnut with a great big hole in the middle. Who the hell am I?

That feeling hasn't gone away. I'm still feeling it. This deep desire to reconnect somehow with... *myself*. With the life I abandoned when I elected to have that operation. *Elected? From what they tell me, I didn't have much choice.* Still, this sense that what I've lost is something more than memories... that remains. When I'm not racked with utter exhaustion, trying to do the simplest practical things, it's the one, constant thing that I'm feeling.

I sit back and chew at the end of my ballpoint pen for a minute. Then I write,

*I've had several visitors during the week, but they mostly cut it short because of the falling-asleep thing. My stepdad, Joe, came back down for a day or so but as soon as he saw I was in good hands, he was happy to leave. I didn't know most of the others who came, including Ava's people. Her parents are away helping a friend abroad, but when some of her friends came they definitely seemed to know me. Her younger sister, Robyn, kept asking me questions as if she could jog my non-existent memory. Did she think I was being rude? I hope not. I'm aware of that all the time, how I must be coming across to other people. Other visitors who came didn't seem too sure what to say, either. They know what's happened to me, but how are they supposed to deal with it? Luckily, Ava explained I couldn't talk much because of the sore throat from having the anaesthesia tube down my throat. I got away with mostly thanking people for coming and putting them off till later.*

You see, you still have a life, I tell my aching heart. It might not be the one you remember, but it's still a damn good one. You have to make up your mind to accept it and re-enter it, William Tyler. Stop resisting.

I write,

*My new friends who I don't know yet seem like good people. I'm taking their word for it that I'll enjoy eating the chocolate covered fruit and the red Spanish sausages they brought me.*

*In other news, I've spoken to Mum over Skype a few times and things with Auntie Doris seem tricky. She seemed quite distraught. In all honesty, I'm glad I've got someone else here looking after me.*

I search the small patch of sky visible through the flat window, looking for further inspiration.

*Ava's been with me for pretty much the whole week as far as I can tell. She's been sleeping on the couch.*

I'm not writing that to please the medical people, either. She actually has been staying over. I wanted to hire a helper – turns out they were correct about just how much I'd need someone here with me – but in the end, Ava stayed and did everything I needed her to. I meant to protest but I've been too tired and she's been so accommodating.

I've been managing the bathroom and washing myself, I record, as that was one of the things the OT wanted to know. But Ava's been getting me my food, doing laundry, helping me change my pyjamas.

I pause. That should have felt awkward, but she was so matter-of-fact about it and I felt so weak I didn't care, I was grateful someone was here for me. I don't write that down, but continue,

*Yesterday she helped me with washing my hair for the first time.
Pretty gross stuff. My hair was still matted with blood and the jelly
stuff they put on my scalp. I'd got some scabs forming and the area
still feels bruised. She was really good about taking extra care to
avoid those bits.*

Physically, I currently do look like Maracas Man. I don't even want
to think about it. I keep going,

*Ava and I have taken small trips outside during the week – really
small. The first time we tried, we rode the lift down to the front
entrance. The smell was overpowering. Granted, I now have super-
powers in that regard, but seriously – how did I never notice that
before? I had to come straight back up and lie down for a bit. Second
time, we took the stairs. I did better with that, but the actual physical
demands of walking wore me out. I needed to head back after only
fifteen minutes. It was disappointing and frustrating. The third time
was for a hospital visit. Apparently, I fell asleep in the car on the way
and it's all a bit of a blur.*

Man, my handwriting is horrible. It feels painful and awkward to
even hold the pen. Still, I have written a huge amount today. Almost a
whole page. That's good. It shows I really do have more energy. Things
are not how I want them to be, but they *are* improving. Slowly.

'How're we doing?'

'Hey.' I cheer up a little as Ava walks into my bedroom. She looks
different from how she's been all week, dressed in an elegant white silk
blouse and cream skirt. Has she done something special to her hair? I
do a surreptitious double take. Is she wearing *make-up* this morning?
Her cheeks are looking brighter, that's for certain.

'I'm great,' I tell her. I am. Relatively speaking. I put the journal
down on the bedside table, done with it for the moment. Our eyes
meet.

'You're looking very lovely today, Ava.'

She's pleased, does a shimmying motion, indicating her new look.

'You like?'

'Oh, very much.' I add, 'I hadn't realised, actually, just how...'

Her eyebrows go up.

'... how pretty you are,' I finish lamely.

'Thank you.' She shoots me a smile under her lashes and for the first time I notice how, when she smiles, it's as if some burden lifts. *Is it me*? I get a shot of guilt – *am I that burden?*

'Um. Were you planning on going out anywhere special?' So far, she's nipped out to the shops a couple of times, but she hasn't actually *gone* anywhere, as such. I hadn't wanted her here to start with, but now a slight panic is gripping my heart at the thought that she might be leaving.

'Oh, Will. I thought I mentioned it earlier in the week?' She sits down gingerly on the edge of my bed. 'It's Saturday. I planned to nip back in to work for the afternoon.'

'It's okay.' I manage, with a monumental effort, to pull a smile. 'I can't expect you to stay a prisoner here with me forever.' I can't. I don't. I've just kind of got used to having this girl around.

'Will, please say, if you don't feel you're able to...'

'No, not at all.' This close to me, the powerfully sweet scent of her perfume is invading my nostrils. Iris and Bluebells, she tells me.

'I'll be fine.' I sit up manfully, feeling a touch of annoyance at myself as it strikes me that it's gone 11 o clock, and I'm still in my PJs. Something I've been happy enough to go along with all week, but not today. Today's different. I've woken up late, but feeling as if I'm back from somewhere.

'I'm a *bloke*,' I remind her. 'Of course, I'll be fine.'

I hear a throaty chuckle, at that.

'Seriously,' I say. I meant that. Did she think I didn't mean it? I can look after myself. 'Look, I'll admit it. I've been learning the hard way all week, how right those medics were about me needing someone here to look after me. They were right. You were right.' She looks at her hands demurely, that thing she does. If there's one sterling quality I can certainly give this girl, it's that she doesn't gloat.

'And you've done a really great job,' I allow graciously. 'I can't even tell you how grateful I am that you've been here.'

'My pleasure.'

Ava's taken time off from her private dressmaking that she's told me about, and also the Butterfly Gardens tea rooms where she works part-time, but maybe that time is up? If I didn't keep falling asleep all the darn time, I'd have a better idea of what day it is, and when things are happening.

As if reading that thought, she adds, 'And don't forget, I'm cooking you a meal at mine, tonight, William.'

I look at her stupidly. 'You've been cooking my meals all week, haven't you?'

She shoots me an enigmatic smile. Oh. Does she mean a *social date* kind of meal? We're moving things slowly onto the next level, is that it? But maybe not, because she says, 'I thought you might be ready for a change of scene, that's all.'

She's right.

Today, I want to put on some real clothes and get myself out of here. I want to go exploring, properly; I've got the energy for it, and the *desire* to reach out in some way and connect with everything in my world. That's stronger than ever. I look at Ava, feeling a pang of regret as she gets up, making ready to leave. Pity that my lovely helper's got to work today, really.

'Thank you again, for everything you're doing for me,' I tell Ava softly. 'I'm a lucky son of a gun, aren't I?'

She nods at me, smiling widely. 'More than you know.'

I say, without thinking, 'Well, I'm... looking forward to the chance to get to know how *lucky* I am.' Christ, am I flirting with her? Our eyes lock, for one, strangely intoxicating, moment.

'Will...'

'Yes?'

I hear her breathing out, slowly.

'You've got my mobile number if you need it,' she says in a strange voice. 'It's in your phone, don't forget.'

'Cool.'

'Work's only a short walk from here, so if you need me to...'

'Sure.' I do a nonchalant waving motion with my hands. 'I'm *good*.' I put on a big smile to assure her even though I've got this strange aching in my chest. 'You can go about your work today safe in the knowledge that I'll be grand.'

'Okay, then.' She doesn't want to go, and when she leans in a little to brush some crumbs off the bedclothes, the warm, sweet scent of her perfume floods over me again. I've been catching snatches of it all week and the strange thing is, it actually does feel familiar. It feels joyous and comforting and also sad at the same time. Like catching the scent of someone you have loved dearly and lost.

*Did I really love you once, Ava? As much as you're showing that you clearly still love me?* I hold my breath, and there's a moment when I wonder if Ava's going to kiss me goodbye before she leaves. Where I have to hold the powerful urge that comes over me, all of a sudden, to pull this girl towards me and kiss her, myself.

But she straightens up, before anything like that can happen.

'*Ciao*, then,' she says. And walks quickly out of the door without looking back.

Probably just as well.

# 10

## WILL

'Hey, hold up a minute!' I've just had to scramble like mad to catch up with Ava. I've caught her just as she was headed into work and the look of surprise on her face when she turns and sees me is a picture.

'*Will?*'

I stand beside her, panting for a minute. At least I'm not still in my pyjamas.

'You forgot *this*,' I say proudly. It's the ugly troll that's usually attached to her key ring. 'I found it on the kitchen floor,' I explain. 'I remember you mentioning it was some kind of lucky charm and you never left the house without it, so I thought maybe you'd...' I trail off, seeing the look on her face.

'You okay?' she says.

'Yep.' I bend over slightly, easing a stitch in my side. My head's feeling a tad light, too. Maybe I shouldn't have done that? I stand up tall as soon as it's possible. 'Came down here a bit too quickly, that's all.' I hand over her property. 'Your troll...?'

She pauses, looking a little bemused. 'Well, thank you. I'd have been searching high and low for that before too long...' The smile she's giving me is as if I've handed her a diamond bracelet. 'Though... I hope you didn't come out especially for *that*?'

I blink. I did, actually. Is she going to imagine it was an excuse to run after her?

'Not at all,' I say airily. 'I was looking up the place where you worked earlier, and I was already planning on coming into town.' *I was actually planning on going straight home, after this. I won't be able to, now, will I?*

'I'm so pleased you felt up to it!' She's genuinely happy. 'Plus, that was really sweet of you to make a detour, thank you so much.'

'*De nada*, I figure I'm already enough in your debt, Ava.'

'Not at all. You're good.' Ava adds, mischievously, 'I like your *hat*!'

I touch the bright red beanie hat – mine, presumably – that I found in the bottom of a closet. I wore it earlier this week when I went out to the hospital visit, to cover my bandage and she teased me then, too.

'Didn't want to frighten anyone,' I mutter. She leans in easily, taking a moment to adjust it slightly. It's an automatic, unselfconscious gesture; the type of thing you'd expect a girlfriend to do, but for my part I'm unnaturally aware of how close she's currently standing, of her small, deft fingers as she tucks in some loose strands of hair and the warmth of her breath on my cheek. *God damn*, Ava... I watch her out of the corner of my eye, standing very still, as she gets me straight.

'That's better.' She stands back after a bit, judging the angle, with her head to one side. 'A black beanie might look better, for this purpose. I'll see what I can find.'

'Thank you.' I smile, catching her eye. 'No point going out with a fashionista if you're not going to let them style you.'

She shoots me a grin. Says nothing, but, I swallow – *did I just say going out with?*

'So, um...' I glance about us at the old converted mill house she'd been about to walk into. 'This where you work part-time?'

She nods enthusiastically, indicating the place with a 'ta-da!' motion of her arms.

'This is it. Like the look of it?' Ava comes and stands right by me, disconcertingly close, to point out one of the windows. 'That's where I work, in there. If you ever want to come and stop by on a quiet afternoon?' She swings round to look at me again. 'Maybe I could give you the tour some time?'

I realise I've been distracted by how silky and shiny her hair looks in the sunshine.

'Sorry, what?'

'If you'd like to come in and check the place out?

'That's uh... very kind.' Ava's been feeding me titbits about pupae and caterpillars and the like, all week long. I'd welcome an excuse to stay and enjoy the sunshine with her on this blue-sky day. Not to mention that, to me, the sweet, rich scent currently coming off the swaying, purple spikes flanking what she's called *the lavender path* on either side of us is indescribable.

'Sure, I'll come in. If you don't need to rush off to work or anything?' I'm looking towards her, hopes rising.

'Oh, Will, not today. I'm so sorry.' She's leaned in, touching my chest briefly – *affectionately*? 'I'd love to stay and show you around myself, but I've got my sister, Robyn, coming in for a stint here this afternoon.'

Robyn? I snap out of my trance.

Ava's saying, 'She's been a bit upset about her uni grades. She needs some distracting so I've fixed her up with a few hours' work, here.'

'Kind of you,' I mutter. 'Uh... No worries, then. I'll take the guided tour another day, maybe? Besides, when it comes to butterflies, I'm okay with the colourful winged phase...'

'But crawling insects creep you out?'

'Yep. And...' I stop, suddenly shooting Ava a sideways look. 'You already knew that, didn't you?'

I hear her gurgle of laughter.

I'm regretting that she has to work. This part-time waitressing job is something she does to supplement her sewing commissions, but she seems to enjoy it.

'Crawly bugs aside, I can totally see why you'd love it here.'

'Can you?' she comes back earnestly. 'Most of my friends don't understand. They assume it's more a place for the old folks, but it isn't.'

'I think it's pretty cool.'

'It's very cool.' She tells me shyly, 'I've got this crazy little pipe dream that one day I'll have enough funds to take over this place, myself.'

'You'd do that?'

'If I had a lottery win, sure, I would!' The dimples have come out again. 'This place is so special. I've always thought it a shame that hardly anybody even knows we're here. I'd spread the word so more people could come and enjoy it.'

'Nice.' I point out, 'When you talk about it, your whole face lights up, did you know that?'

'What, really?' Her hands fly up to cover her cheeks. She laughs, suddenly a little self-conscious. 'So, there you go, now you know my little secret, Will Tyler.'

'I thought you had one,' I say, straight faced.

'Did you?'

'Oh, yes. I've been trying to work out what it was, ever since I met you.' I can't believe I'm still using that old chestnut.

'Have you, now?' She swallows, hard. My God, Ava really does have a secret?

'It's true! You've got the mysterious air of a woman who's keeping something close to her chest.'

Ava's face is going distinctly pink.

'I was hoping it wasn't some embarrassing secret about *me*,' I confess. I'm about to add, *'Only kidding!'* when she looks away from me so quickly, I don't get the chance.

'Anyway.' She's busying herself suddenly, putting her key ring away in her handbag. I shoot a puzzled smile at her abrupt change in manner – *what just happened there?* She says, a little more coolly, 'Were you planning on going far this afternoon, Will?'

This is definitely my cue to leave so I indicate the road out front.

'I thought I'd check out the high street,' I make up on the spot. 'And then, a bit later, I'll probably walk on down to the bay.'

Ava nods, still seeming strangely distracted, and I wish I knew what I'd done to make her look so uneasy.

'I'm not planning on overdoing it, don't worry,' I add, in case that's what she's worried about. 'I can always take the bus back.'

She looks at me, a little vacantly. 'Take the number ɪɪ from the pier, then. It stops right outside your place.'

'Will do.'

'See you tonight, Will,' Ava says. *Something's* definitely on her mind, isn't it? But, if I ever learnt how to read women in the last seven years, I've lost it again. I'm clueless. As she turns to walk away, a breeze wafts a huge scented wave of lavender over both of us. It's almost overwhelming.

But, walking away from me, Ava doesn't notice. It barely registers at all.

# 11

# AVA

Parting with Will, I'm left feeling flat even though he was just flirting with me and I should be overjoyed! I was so looking forward to coming into work today. I needed the change and yet now I find myself reluctant to go inside. Standing in the floral display section of the Butterfly Gardens for a few moments, I allow the tranquillity of the place to wash over me. Today, there are butterflies galore, fluttering all over the place. Everything's in new summer bloom, rose-blushed carnations, pale yellow and pink aquilegias and love-in-the-mist, all swaying gracefully in the light breeze, so I breathe it all in, slowly, relishing the sunshine.

Old Harry walks past me. 'Hello there, young lady! Always good to see a new volunteer.'

I spin around. 'Harry...' We have this exchange every time and he's never going to remember it, only today for some reason it *bugs* me that he doesn't recognise me. He's already gone, though. I gaze after him wistfully as he heads off with a ball of twine to rescue some drooping plants, leaving me standing there for a moment feeling like nothing more than a ghost. Before I get over that, my manager, Phyllis, is rushing out to greet me.

'Welcome back!' As she gives me a quick hug I see that, ever keen,

Phyllis has already got my 'Gardens' apron at the ready. 'It's really good to see you back, Ava.'

'Good to be here, Phyllis.' It feels more like a month than just over a week that I've been away and I'm struggling to recall what it was the staff here sent in with their card for Will. Mercifully, it comes to me.

'Uh... William really enjoyed that box of special biscuits you guys sent through...'

'You're very welcome! How have things been?' Phyllis holds my gaze, genuinely interested. 'We heard on the grapevine that his operation was a great success but naturally we've all been eager to hear it from you.'

I take my apron from her, tying it on loosely.

'He's doing really well, all things considered.' I hesitate. It's what people want to hear, I know, and he *has* been doing well after his op, but it's not just his physical recovery we're dealing with here, is it?

She's staring at me a little curiously, and I add, 'He's making a great recovery but it's just like they said, Phyllis. He's forgotten everything about the more recent years of his life. Will didn't know who I was when he woke up and... he still doesn't, really.'

'He doesn't recognise you?'

I shake my head.

'I'm sorry to hear it.'

I'm silent for a moment, recalling that her own mother has dementia now and how hard that's been for her. I bow my head.

'I know you were having a similar experience with your mum?'

'Unfortunately, yes. She has *no* idea who I am, any more.'

Sorry as I feel for Phyllis, I can't help thinking it's a relief to be able to talk to someone who actually understands.

'It's not an easy thing to experience at any age, but then...' my manager shoots me a sympathetic glance '... at least, most of us manage to make it most of the way through our lives before we ever have to encounter this.'

She's right about that much. *Her mum has already had her life and they've had all their good times together.* I gulp. Will and I haven't had ours yet! It all seems so unfair.

As we turn to walk back inside, she adds unexpectedly, 'The trouble is, when someone can't recognise you, terrible as it is for them, it can also make *you* feel a bit like a cuckoo in the nest, can't it?'

'Very true.' I rub the back of my neck uneasily. 'A couple of times over the past week, I've felt as if I'm an imposter, just posing as his girl-friend, crazy as that sounds.'

I pause and she says, 'Not crazy at all. Everything can start to feel a bit topsy-turvy, can't it?' She touches my arm, lightly. 'It will be the exact opposite scenario for you, thank goodness, but the woman my mother was is almost completely gone.'

We're both silent for a bit, then she says quietly, 'And I *miss* her. Can you believe, what I miss most is being able to share all our little bits and pieces of family gossip every week?' She gives an unhappy shake of her head. 'I never realised how much I valued that: having someone you can share all your everyday triumphs and your downfalls with.'

I look at her, sadly. 'You mean, like, bad news shared is halved, and good news shared... is doubled?'

'Absolutely! But to Mum, I could be anyone. My life's of no signifi-cance to her, any more.'

'I'm so sorry, Phyllis.' I look away, sad for her, pulling my hair up into a scrunchie, getting ready to go in and do some work.

'And even when she thinks she does recognise me, half the time, Mum seems to think that I'm *her* mother.'

'At least Will doesn't think I'm his mum!'

Somehow, we're both smiling now.

'That's something, I guess.' We're making light of it, but that would actually be unbearable, I reflect. At least, once we get over the preg-nancy hurdle – *which I've yet to do* – there's still the chance for Will and I to make things so much better.

'I just try not to take it too personally,' she says, pragmatic, now. That again.

'No, and to be fair to Will,' I reflect, 'in so many ways he's still the same person he always was.'

While she opens the kitchen door, I show her the key ring hanging off the handle of my bag.

'See this? He came running after me just now, all the way to work, to hand me Lucky Troll because he's figured out it's something important to me – that's pure, classic, old Will, thoughtful and caring.'

She smiles.

'Long may that continue!'

'And, it *has* only been a very short time,' I muse now. 'I can't expect to regain the three years of the relationship we'd forged, so soon. It'll just take a little longer.'

'Absolutely.'

Following Phyllis inside, I go and peek in our huge tea urn, checking that it's on and it's still got enough water in there. Going through all the familiar motions feels calming but our conversation has given me pause for thought. I can see now why I felt so leaden, walking in here.

It would've been so wonderful to be able to come in and shout about the baby from the rooftops, because, as I said to Phyllis, good news shared is doubled, but I can't. I can't say a word to them till I've told Will and now I won't do that until... I shrug my shoulders up to my ears. *Darn it.*

Blinking away the tears that've just come into my eyes, I tell myself it's like everyone says – I have to be patient. *Keep the faith.* There's absolutely no reason why we can't make new memories together – just as long as I never give Will any reason to suspect anything's wrong...

## 12

## WILL

Leaving Ava behind, it's no distance at all to the top end of town. When I lean over the edge of the old stone bridge, surveying the bubbling green brook flowing beneath, as I've done countless times before, it's a good feeling. My fingers brush against the weathered stone of the wall, searching for the indents where I painstakingly etched my initials on the top with a blunt penknife all those years ago. I got into some big, fat trouble for that at the time but hey – it's still here, isn't it? *W.T.* That's me.

A family of ducks stream past, making a neat 'v' parting in the water, and now the familiar sound of the early afternoon freight train honking its horn in the distance captures my attention and takes me back to the years I spent living at my grandad's place on Station Road. That horn sounded a lot louder and a lot nearer in the bedroom I occupied back then, but it'll always be a welcome sound to me.

A breeze carries over a gust of sweet fragrance from a mayflower bush that's growing on the muddy bank. I'm back with the duck family again. After satisfying myself that the straggler among them – there's always one – has made it up the riverbank to join the rest of his crew, I push off from the bridge, heading for the town centre, and in particular Gil's Music store. I'm looking forward to dropping in on him and I smile to myself as it dawns on me how the guys there are all going to appear seven years older than when I saw them last, even though – *in my head* – only a couple of weeks have passed.

I pull at the edges of my hat, squinting up at the sun. If it's going to be this hot all day long, I'll need to buy a bottle of water. My scalp's already feeling hot and itchy with this beanie on. I can feel where the skin around the sutures is beginning to pull. It's sore, but there's not a lot to be done about that. Maybe I'll nip into the chemist's, too, get some painkillers to take with that water?

When I get there, Mr Huang at the pharmacy has magically got white hair. He looks as if he's been out in the snow. Gratifyingly, he is so overjoyed to see that I've 'made it through okay' that he even comes out from behind the counter and gives me a hug! He knew me from a kid, was friends with my grandad, back in the day. I have to keep assuring him that I'm doing great. Like the snowstorm on his head, all the little lines on his face that were never there before come as a bit of a surprise. *But*, I keep telling myself, *seven years...*

'This must all feel very strange to you,' he says.

'What do you remember?' he wants to know, and now his wife comes out to look, too. 'What have you forgotten?'

The truth is, it feels the same as any other day. A few shops down the high street have changed. People who I see about town in the stores look a bit older to me, that's all. But, as Mr and Mrs Huang are standing there, smiling expectantly, I say, 'Well, this has got to be as close to experiencing time travel as it's humanly possible for anyone to get.'

The impressed look they exchange is worth the hyperbole.

'Speaking of which...' I look pointedly at my watch. 'It's time for me to leave.'

'It feels like time travel,' I hear Mr Huang telling his wife as I leave their shop. He'll be telling his customers this all week, I imagine. *William feels like he's been away travelling in a time machine, since his op.*

Which is kinda cool.

But, out on the warm pavement again, the super-comfy, super-expensive trainers I bought to wear on stage, just a few months ago, are so worn they're falling apart. They didn't time travel with me, it seems. They stayed behind and got old and used. Which is annoying. I never got to enjoy them new, did I? It doesn't feel like it.

Still, I'd anticipated this first outing might be a lot harder than it is. But all the nooks and crannies of my old home town look, feel, sound and smell the same as they ever did.

With everything in the town so familiar, it's hard to imagine that my break from the band happened years ago. Things had gone pear shaped, the music was changing and the band was broke, touring for peanuts, but still, making the decision to leave them felt like ripping a hole right out through the centre of me. I can still feel it now.

I'll ask Gil at the music store about all the other band members. What's happened to them? Gil will know. He'll fill me in on everything. Has he still got that crazy beard I wonder? Does he still smoke those cigars?

As I walk to the music shop I see there have been a few more changes at this end of the high street. The bank has been replaced by a hole in the wall, with offices behind it. The Cupcake Bakery has become a florist's, so I stop and pick out a bunch of flowers to give to Ava tonight. When I ask the girl at the counter to throw in some forget-me-nots, too, she smiles and comments, 'She's going to like these, whoever she is.'

It gives me a warm feeling in my belly, which lasts all the way to the butcher's shop where, much to my dismay, Watkins and Son is still there and still flourishing. If there's one person from my past I'd rather steer well clear of...

I frown, making to cross over the road, but, *'Oi!'*

Too late, *the son* – who we called Mule – the one guy in Holcombe whose mission it was to make my life a misery when I was younger, has spotted me. The brute's already at the door of his shop, yelling out, 'Tyler!'

I turn, wearily.

'Oi, *Tyler!'* To my horror, he's actually come out of his shop and walked right up to me.

'Heard about what happened to you,' he starts. 'I heard you had an op and you don't remember nuffink – that right?'

I feel a flash of shame at that. Has everyone in town heard about me? It seems they have. Mule's looking at me curiously.

'You remember *me*, Tyler?'

'Oh, yes.' That seems to please him. I wait for it. The taunts, the inevitable comments about *how he always knew I'd go soft in the head* or some such stupid quip, squashing the automatic feelings of panic in my chest at the thought of having to deal with this childhood bully. Of all the people I had to bump into in Holcombe on my first day out...

Mule's pointing a fat, unsteady finger at my beanie hat, eyes widening. He's staring so hard, I say, testily, 'You want me to take the hat off so you can see what's underneath?'

'*No*, man.' He swallows, backing off. For a butcher, he's surprisingly squeamish, which is strangely satisfying.

'It's not catching,' I say.

'No.' He glances back towards the safety of his shop. Then he says something I don't expect. 'I'm glad you made it okay, William.'

I frown, not sure what to do with that. He's wishing me well?

'So, we're *friends* now?' When did that happen? When did this dude ever wish me well, in his whole life?

'Oh, yes.' He's nodding soberly. 'We're friends. Ever since you jumped into the water off Holcombe Pier that winter's day to save my two year old son.'

I stare at him. So I'm some sort of local hero? Even more perturbingly – this man, who could never even get himself a girlfriend, *has a family*? I recognise the feeling deep inside me as envy.

'You have a son?' I say.

'Five last August.' He beams proudly. 'Missus has another on the way, too.'

'Congratulations.'

'All right, then. You take care, Tyler.'

'Sure, I will,' I tell him. He goes back to Watkins' where the customers are already beginning to queue up. Some have come outside and they're looking on curiously, seeing who he's talking to – *the dude who's had the brain op, the one who's lost all his memories* – and all my earlier feelings of happiness have drained away. Now I only feel strangely out of place.

I'm glad to hear I saved Mule's lad, but how did that even come about? Will Gil be able to fill me in? I hurry my steps onwards.

However, when I get to where Gil's Music store should be, I'm faced with the devastating discovery that Gil's has morphed into 'Hallit's Turkish Food Hall.'

I stand there, my heart going nineteen to the dozen and the feeling of betrayal is total. How could this have happened? Gil's Music store is the place where all the best bits of my youth and childhood occurred. It's where Grandad bought me my first, crappy little cheap guitar that I loved more than my life. I've still got it somewhere. At least, I think I have!

I stand there for a good few minutes, rubbing my arms, feeling all sorts of weird shit going on inside me, wondering, *how can this be?* How can I make sense of this? I've forgotten seven years. That music shop was a thriving hub of the local community here for at least twenty. Where's Gil buggered off to? Old stoners like him don't ever leave the scene, completely. They can't. It's in their blood. How could he do this to me?

'Cooeee...'

When I turn to see who's calling, the eighty-something year old woman with the knee high stockings and crimped grey hair seems pleased to see me. But this isn't someone I know. Who the heck...?

'You're out and about today, are you, William?'

'Yes.' I don't want to speak. I am gutted.

'You feeling a little lost?' She adds kindly, 'I'm your neighbour, Elsie.'

I stare at her. Clear my throat.

'I thought that young blond fella lived next door to DelRoy's? I saw him this morning on my way out. He said hello.'

'Oh, not your *flat* neighbour,' she says, smiling gently. 'I'm at the other place.'

'Right.' What *other* place?

Elsie is eyeing me curiously, just like Mule did. They'll be thinking, what's going on inside this bloke's head? Is he all okay up there? I'm okay. I just hadn't bargained with how much stake I was putting on Gil still being here. Him going was never on the cards.

'I'm...' I look at her helplessly. I'm lost for words and Elsie nods understandingly.

'I think I need to... get back home,' I croak. 'My head's starting to hurt.' My energy's gone.

'Let's walk back together.' She adds kindly, 'Don't want you passing out or anything.'

'I'm not going to pass out.' How bloody embarrassing would that be? 'Look,' I say, because it's bugging me. 'What *other place* are you my neighbour from?'

'Beach Cottage,' she says without missing a beat.

Ava's place?

'I live at DelRoy's, don't I?' I frown.

'I don't know where you live *now*, but you and Ava were living together at Beach Cottage for at least a couple of years.'

I gawp at her. 'And... I moved out? When?'

Elsie does a sucking sound through her teeth. 'That'd be around Christmas time, last year, I think. Yes, after the festivities, that's when you left.'

I pause for a moment, taking this in. '*Why*, though?'

'Oh, I think you'd both been having *words*,' she says delicately.

I stop walking. 'You're saying Ava and I were fighting?' If Ava and I had been at odds and I moved out of our shared place, she's neglected to mention it. Had we made up, then, or has she only come back because of the unusual circumstances or... what's going on? I look at Elsie.

'*Fighting over what,* exactly?'

Elsie looks coy, touching my arm gently.

'Not my place to say, is it?'

'No.' I swallow. 'Of course. I didn't mean to embarrass you, Elsie, but...' I look at her uneasily. 'My op. You *do* know what's happened to me, don't you?'

'Oh, yes. I know about your op.'

Everyone here does, it seems.

'My Don lost his memory too, after a fall. He forgot *everything*.' She smiles unevenly. 'But don't worry, dear. It turned out it was a blessing in disguise.'

I screw up my eyes and stare at her.

'A blessing?'

'Oh, yes. For instance – there were all sorts of things the family enjoyed that my husband refused to get involved with,' Elsie is saying. 'Like... liver and onions and holidays abroad in the Med. After he lost his memory, we told him the things we liked were also *his* favourite things and he went along with them from then onwards without a complaint.'

So they lied, basically. Because they could.

I'm struggling to hide the growing unease I'm feeling inside. 'Look, thanks, but I'll take it on my own from here,' I tell Elsie. Things aren't making sense any more and they definitely don't feel as simple as they did.

'Mind how you go,' she says.

Crossing the road, I quicken my pace, wanting to get back home. If this woman, Elsie, is correct in what she's told me, I don't... A flash of pain goes right across my brow and I wince.

I don't understand.

# 13

## AVA

Robyn's just popped her head around the kitchen door, looking a little nervous.

'Hey, *you came*. Thanks, sis!'

'Would I miss your first day?' I come over and give Robbie a hug. 'Besides, I thought this might be the best place to catch up with you, given the last week's been...'

'Pretty crazy, huh?'

I throw up my hands. 'You can't even imagine.'

She comes over and leans up against the fridge, tilting her head to one side.

'Everything okay? How're you and Will doing?'

We've had a couple of hurried phone conversations since Will came out of the hospital and she came around to see him one time, but I know people will still be wondering.

*'Good.'*

'You sure you're not overdoing it?' She picks up one of the bath buns I'd been about to arrange on a plate and takes a tiny bite, observing, 'You just look a little... *flat.*'

'Do I?' I manage what I hope passes for a smile, admitting, 'I do feel a bit flat.' Lowering my voice now. 'It's probably the anticlimax of coming here and not being able to share my pregnancy news with anyone.'

She stops picking the raisins out of her bun and looks up.

'You can't tell them about the baby, Ava – how come?'

'I *can't*, because I haven't told Will yet and he needs to be the first to know.'

'But... Will *does* know.' She stops. Says slowly, 'Ah, I see. He knew before but now he's forgotten...' my sister says, a little confused, 'Why wouldn't you have told him?'

Why, indeed?

'I was going to tell him, Robbie, until it dawned on me that Will would probably gladly pair up with *any* woman who was expecting his baby...'

'And?'

'And... it hardly seems fair to use that as an excuse to trap him into being with me.' I go and open up the top cupboards and Robyn mirrors my movements as we bring down all the delicate – if mismatching – ancient crockery, all the pretty teacups, saucers and plates, getting them ready on the counter. I glance at her.

'I want him to... want me too, don't you see?'

'I *guess*,' she says. 'Though, if it brings him back to you, it would get the job done, right?'

'I knew you wouldn't see it.'

'Hey, I *kind of* do.' She's busy matching up the gold-rimmed cups with their saucers. She's efficient, my sister, and quick. 'Either way, I guess you'll need to bring it up soon?'

She pauses. 'I mean, if you don't tell him, someone else is going to come out and mention it, like... his mum or somebody?'

'Don't remind me.'

I've spent the last few days trying to block just that possibility from my mind. Up to now, it's been only him and me at the flat but we won't remain in isolation forever. Sooner or later Will's going to want to reach outside the two of us and when he does... I swallow, the thought not filling me with a whole lot of joy.

'Y'know, I don't think I'd even *begun* to appreciate how difficult this situation is for you, sis.' Robyn adds, a little repentantly, 'And I'm sorry to have pulled you away from Will today. You've clearly got enough on your plate.'

'You're good. The last week at the flat's been pretty intense and... even if I couldn't share my news, I still wanted to come in.'

'I can totally see why.' She indicates around us now. 'It's *amazing* here!'

Despite myself, I manage a smile. She closes her end of the cupboard, turning to me.

'Is it really true what you told me about this place being about to go under?'

I'm nodding. 'The Butterfly Gardens runs at a loss, most days,' I admit. 'I think the main problem is not enough people know we even exist.'

'They don't? Then, maybe what you *need* is to bring someone on board who'll shout about this place from the rooftops?' She adds, confidently, 'I bet Carenza could do it for you.' She's got that look she gets on her face whenever she gets a good idea.

I pick up my tray, bemused. 'Your mate from uni, you mean – the one with the blog?'

'If she did a piece on it, you'd be astonished at the difference it could make.' She pauses. 'She has over a million followers, you know, Ava.'

'Impressive!' I smile.

'And you should see how many shares we got on the post we put up after my birthday party. That post was months ago, and it still has loads of traction.'

'Nice.' Then I twig what she's just said. 'She put up a blog post about *your birthday party*?' I put the laden tray down again. 'Why?'

'Yep. And it's already had over a quarter of a million views. You should take a look.' She smiles at me, pleased. 'Given that you're in quite a few of those photos yourself!'

'I'm sorry, what?' I give a small laugh, waiting patiently while she insists on opening up her phone to show me.

'This is one of our most popular blog posts so far,' she's saying proudly. 'Carenza's been showing me the ropes and we worked really hard to make it look this good.'

'Robbie…' I stiffen, feeling my face going pink. *What the heck is this?* All these photos of me, dancing with my ex – what are they doing up here? I cover my mouth with my hand, the implications of it pulsing through me like mini shock waves, gathering momentum. The party was ages ago. I'd pushed it to the furthest corners of my mind and imagined everyone else had, too, but all the time there's been this *blog* out there, waiting to be discovered by anyone who cares to take a look. I glance up at my sister in horror but she's looking pleased as punch.

'You're looking good, here, don't you think?'

'What?' I stare at her. Then look away. I sacrificed my peace of mind to tell Will the biggest lie of all. To make everything go away. Now I'm seeing that all it could take is something like these *innocent photos* to stir up questions that would force me to lie to him even more. This whole ugly mess isn't sorted, after all. It isn't over.

## 14

## AVA

I stifle a moan as Robyn reaches out smartly to catch the saucer that's just slipped out of my grasp, *panicking* just like on the day we first discovered the truth. There was nothing I could do about it then, either.

'You okay?' she's saying. I've turned away, feeling my insides go cold, wanting to stop what's happening, but it's too late, all the unwanted memories are already flooding back.

Memories of the bright morning in the spring when I'd come up with our coffee to find Will on the phone. Our mugs were hot and steaming and I laid them on the nightstand. I smiled, leaning in to kiss him, but when he looked into my eyes, something stopped me.

He looked away, continuing his call.

'There's got to be some mistake!' The small niggle in the pit of my stomach deepened. He was playing with a popper on our duvet cover, pulling it on and off with his hands, his mobile tucked under his chin. Will and I hadn't been back together very long so we were still in the honeymoon phase and yet here he was, clearly so upset and I didn't know why. What could possibly have come in to disturb the luxurious enjoyment of our lazy weekend?

I sat patiently on the edge of our bed, waiting while whoever it was on the other end gave him some lengthy explanation over the phone. When they'd finally stopped talking, 'No? You say not. There's *got* to be. Why? Because... she's pregnant, that's why!'

My hands flew to my mouth then... *who was he talking to?*

'*No* possibility of a mistake? I see. None whatsoever?'

I leaned in, and touched him on the shoulder, but he still wouldn't acknowledge me.

'Babe, what's...?' Heart thumping, I followed him after the call ended when he stood up and went to the window. When I sidled up to him, his shoulders had gone limp. He wouldn't return my embrace, and there was no trace of warmth coming from him at all. He only kept pulling the blinds down and then up again. When he stopped at last, staring out as if I wasn't even there, I grabbed at his elbow, the fear sticking in my throat.

'What is it, babe? What's wrong?'

He went quiet for such a long time, I couldn't bear it. I shook his arm, desperately, only knowing that something terrible must have happened.

When he sat down, holding onto his stomach, I whispered again, full of fear, '*What's wrong, Will?*'

He glanced over to a letter that had arrived that morning, which was discarded on the bed. Then he looked at me, eyes glazed, and he said, 'Everything is wrong, Ava. *Everything.*'

I blink away a tear, distraught at the recollection, and my little sister, *who has no clue*, is back again.

'Hey,' she says mildly. 'I didn't mean to upset you – they were only some pictures of you enjoying the dancing.' She nudges my arm. 'No harm in that, sis?'

I look away, unable to maintain eye contact with her.

*No harm in dancing, if only Max and I had left it at that.*

But back then, with me separated from my boyfriend and with my head so full of sadness, stupid jealousy and hurt, we'd taken it that much further, with no thought for the consequences. How could I have known I'd get pregnant with anyone else when Will and I had been trying for so many months? How could I have known, then, that Will was already making plans to get back with me? I clutch at my elbows, writhing inside at the memory.

Will has forgotten everything that was in that letter. It's meant to be *all over*, and yet... if I've been tagged online and Will does a search for my name, *sees the date*, clocks that I was at that party with someone else and I haven't even told him yet about our... *break*, that could open up all sorts of...

Choking, I grab at her arm. 'These photos have got to be taken down, Robbie.'

'What?' She takes a step back, shocked. 'Why?'

'Because... Will wasn't there with me, was he?'

She gives a puzzled laugh, still not seeing any problem. 'When you agreed to come to my birthday party you knew it was at uni and you knew what it would be like. You were happy enough to come along and enjoy the night *without Will* then, so why does it matter so much now?'

I stare at her, unable to come up with any good answer. My brain has frozen.

'Besides,' she's running on, 'this is one of our most popular blog posts so far. We worked really hard to make it look this good.'

'*We?*'

My sister gives a little uncomfortable laugh. 'I told you. I've been helping Carenza with it.'

'You can help her take them down, then?'

Robyn's shaking her head. 'She won't want to do that.'

'*She...*' My throat has clammed up. Carenza *has* to remove it. My sister will have to find some way to persuade her!

'Look – apart from the photos...' Robyn hesitates. 'Is anything else wrong, Ava?' Though she's got her hands on her hips, she's looking puzzled and sad. At the end of the day, she's still my little sister. Whatever else happens, I want to trust her. I *do* trust her, but...

'You're not going to tell me, are you?'

'Robbie, I...' I cannot share this with her. I made Will a promise I still need to keep and the outside world cannot show any different picture from the one I'm painting for Will. This blog... it needs to go away. I gulp, rubbing at my face. I am not going back there to face all that again. It is not going to happen.

Robbie hears my sharp intake of breath, I know she does.

'Fine, then.' She sounds hurt. 'I'll just have to explain to Carenza that, as you're still planning on getting back with your boyfriend, you'd rather remain, shall we say, *incognito*? There won't be any guarantees,' she warns, unhappily. 'And she'll most likely refuse!'

'Thank you,' I whisper, feeling my legs go weak with relief. If she'll at least ask her friend, that's a start. 'And... remember, not a word to anyone here about the baby, just yet.'

Robyn shoots back, 'You and your secrets!'

# 15

## AVA

As I put the finishing touches on tonight's chicken salad, my mind's still on what happened with Robyn, earlier. Try as I might, I haven't been able to get that blog out of my head all afternoon and, given work was so busy, we never got the chance to talk about it again.

*Then* about an hour ago I got that text through from Will.

Looking forward to our dinner tonight. Some interesting conversations came up in town, which I'm looking forward to talking through with you later! W x

The thought of tonight's dinner date with Will was already making me nervous enough. I've been heart-sick for the old, easy familiarity that was always there between us, hoping we could maybe recapture some of it tonight, and I have *no* idea who he's been chatting to. Hopefully not the local midwife? Still, with my doorbell already going it's too late for any speculation.

'Welcome!' I needn't have worried. Will's eyes light up on seeing me and there's not a trace of concern on his face.

'Wow,' he says, appreciatively. 'You're looking very lovely this evening, Ava!'

'Thanks.' I laugh, pleased he's noticed the effort. 'Did you find the place okay? Beach Cottage is a little off the beaten track and new postmen never find it too easily, either, some of them spend *years* wandering among the dunes and...'

'Oh, it was okay. I used my homing instinct.' He smiles.

'Did you?' I feel a stab of pleasure at that. Is he implying he knew his way back *home*?

He says, straight faced, 'Luckily, there were enough signs of civilisation about for me to take my cue from.' He turns, indicating Elsie's ample red knickers, which are, as ever, blowing merrily on the washing line next door.

'Though maybe those are a little... *family sized*, to fit you?'

'I'm glad you noticed!' I glance at the huge box of cakes from Bertrand's Patisserie in the town that he's brought with him.

'Though maybe after we've worked our way through those, it might be a different story?'

He smiles shyly.

'I couldn't choose between bringing dessert and flowers so I brought you both.'

'Who says you should never go for an indecisive man?'

He laughs, and I step back so he can come inside and, once he's safely set down the flowers and cake, he gives me a warm and lingering hug of greeting. Standing there swaying in his arms, I realise it's the first hug I've had from him, since... since he didn't know me any more. The thought fills me with both happiness and sadness. Sadness that he doesn't know me, happiness that he clearly *wants* to be here with me. He moves back after a bit.

'I couldn't decide what to wear, either, but seeing as *you've* made a real effort, I'm glad I went for this.'

He's looking handsome, dressed up in a smart suit, for me, tonight.

'You're looking *great,* Will. And I'm so happy that you've come. Thank you for the flowers.'

'You're more than welcome.' He glances curiously at the small, shell rimmed mirror in my hallway, the curving white bannisters that lead upstairs – does he recognise any of it? He won't, no, of course, but...

'I take it I've been here before?'

'Many times.'

'You want to do the tour? We've got...' I stop, correcting myself. '*I've* got two bedrooms upstairs, the second one's tiny, and a little work/study area where I do my sewing that looks out over a sea view, *if* you squint very hard and imagine that the trees aren't all there in the way...'

He nods. I see him take in a breath, bite his lip, and I realise I might have been talking a little fast.

'Sounds amazing.' He looks around briefly, taking in the place, but his eyes have come to rest on mine again. 'We've got *so* much to talk about, haven't we?'

'We do!' Is this about *those interesting conversations* he's been having in town? Whatever it is, we might as well get it over with.

I swallow. 'Dinner's ready whenever we are, but I've got some cold drinks chilling for us, first. Come right through.'

In the lounge, settling on our wide, comfy sofa, he chooses the exact same spot where he always sat. Looking so at home as he does, he might never have left. He's picked up the bottle I chose for us and now he's looking at the label closely.

'Is this one of our favourites?'

'It isn't, I'm afraid,' I admit. 'This bottle's non-alcoholic, and given that right now *neither* of us are meant to be...' I stop talking, and he shoots me a small, puzzled smile.

'Looks good.' Will pours us each a glass. 'I wondered if this was the kind of healthy cordial I'm into these days.' Taking a small sip, he shoots me a glance.

'Apparently, your neighbour, Elsie, managed to convince her husband that he liked liver and onions, once he lost his memory.'

I burst out laughing. 'Hell, he should've known *that* was a lie.'

'I guess he should.'

'So, you've already met Elsie, then?' I angle myself to face him a little better and the fluttery feeling in my stomach is back. He nods. I take a sip of my drink.

'You mentioned you had some interesting conversations in town today?'

'I did! I had the strangest conversations...' He's been gazing at me intently but now he breaks eye contact. 'I learned, for instance, that, *during the time I've forgotten*, I've somehow become friends with a man I've considered an arch enemy for most of my life.'

'Mule?'

He nods.

'He sends you some lovely goodies through at Christmas,' I tell him. 'Turkey and a big ham. He's a very appreciative guy.' Is this all he wanted to ask me about? I feel myself relaxing even though Will himself seems at a loss to know how to take the fact that his enemy is now his friend, though, in his own mind, he never made the journey to get there.

'Well, that's good to know.' Will's looking around the place again, his gaze alighting on the stone figurine I keep by the fireplace.

'Interesting piece.'

'You like it?'

'I like the colour. It's an unusual stone.'

'It's red Java marble.' I add, 'It caught your eye after you saw it in a pub when you were staying over in Bali with some of your mates. That would've been shortly after we met, I think.' He loved that thing! Does he not have any idea how much he wanted that figurine? What he was once prepared to pay for it?

'I've been to *Bali*?' he says, shaking his head, regretfully. 'Man, I can't believe I've been to Bali.'

'You can go again,' I offer. 'And it'll all be as wonderful and new to you this time as it was last time round.'

He laughs. 'That's a plus, then.'

'Definitely a plus.'

He catches my eye. 'What about you and me, then, Ava? I take it we know each other well?'

'I know *you* well,' I assure him. He knew me too. But, maybe to him,

I'll be like that figurine, hotly desired yesterday, but not so much any longer?

He tilts his head to one side questioningly.

'And my Bali figurine is sitting here adorning *your* fireplace because...?'

'Because,' I tell him carefully, 'you were living here with me, Will. For a long time, this was our place.'

'I see, so Elsie was right. We *had* split up. And you didn't think to tell me?'

Darn it. *So, someone did get in ahead of me, then?* I've got to tell him everything, tonight.

'It's true we were separated for a few months, though we'd already made up well before your operation. You were spending most of your free time back here with me, much of your gear was here anyway...'

He glances up the stairs. 'My stuff is here?'

I nod. 'Most of it, and you were *about* to move the rest of it back in. I'd have said, but when you woke up after your op it seemed like an unnecessary complication to bring up too soon.'

He leans back on the settee. 'So – you and I had been having problems? Any specific reasons I should know about?'

I'm silent for a while. 'Yes. And no.'

He waits.

'We'd been squabbling, under a lot of pressure because of... things that weren't going too well in our lives. Things that were beyond our control. After Christmas, you'd moved back out to your old place at DelRoy's.' I rub at my neck. I have to be careful here, and the less said, the better.

'But like I said...' I look straight at him. '... we got back together. Things were going really great between us, when...' I swallow. 'When we got wind that something might be wrong with you.'

He's taking me in intently. 'I see.'

'After that, it only took a little while, back and forth, before they confirmed that you'd need an operation. We'd have known even sooner if you'd gone to the doctor's straight away, only...' I finish hesitantly. 'You took a bit of persuading to go in and get things checked out.'

He doesn't look surprised at that. 'Runs in the family. Us Tylers are all a bit stubborn, that way. Hate hospitals, medical stuff, all that...'

'I get it. But sometimes we need them.'

He nods slightly. 'And... that's it?'

'Yes.' It took so much more than he might imagine to get him to see the doctors and he's asked me for total honesty, but... I can't go into any detail, can I? I push away the immediate pang of regret I feel at that but at least, after I've got this lie over and done with, it'll be the last.

'It's the *truth*, Will. It's how it happened.'

'It's okay,' he says. 'I believe you. If you didn't care about me, you'd never have stuck by me the way you have.'

I'm nodding. 'That's truer than you know.'

'Y'know,' he says, 'walking around town today, so much was the same and yet so much had changed, too, it's hard to describe.' He blinks. 'I got this sense that something very important was missing. At first, I put that down to Gil's Music shop not being there.' He pulls a rueful smile.

'Seeing it gone just about wrecked me for a while there, but then... I came to thinking maybe there was something else I was missing? Maybe it was *you*?' he offers. 'Maybe that's all that was missing?'

I give a low laugh. 'Probably.'

As his arm sneaks around the top of the settee and then closes comfortably around me, I snuggle in close. Close enough to feel the soft beating of Will's heart and the warmth of his breath on my cheek.

'If it's all right with you, I'd like to move back in some time soon,' he decides. 'I'd be happy to take the spare bedroom if you...'

'Oh, no,' I tell him hurriedly. 'You don't have to.'

'You sure?'

'Oh, I'm sure.'

He smiles and, *finally*, he leans in to span that last little bit of distance between us. For him, at least, it's our very first kiss.

I make sure it's a good one.

# 16

## WILL

What can I say? I'm happy. She's happy. I know this is what Ava's been hoping for ever since I woke up from the op.

'William.'

'Ava?'

'There's something I've been wanting to talk to you about.'

'Oh, yes?' She's nervous, I see, fingering the collar of her dress. I lean back, smiling.

'Something important, I take it?' After that kiss we shared, it must be. Why else would you interrupt a flow that was developing so beautifully into something *even more interesting*?

'Actually, yes. It's something... really important.' She sits up straighter, pushing her hair back. 'It wasn't anything I wanted to lay on you without knowing we'd have the possibility of a relationship, again. It didn't seem fair, otherwise. But, as you've already indicated you'd like to move back in...'

'Hey, whatever it is, it's okay.' Even from here, I can feel her heart racing. 'Let me guess?'

Ava's shaking her head. 'You *won't* guess.'

'No?' I laugh softly. 'This'll be about... our rules of engagement, right? If I move back in, there are certain things you want me to know about why our cohabiting didn't work, beforehand?'

She looks surprised as I pull a face.

'So, I'm thinking maybe... I didn't do my share of the housework?' She's shaking her head. 'Or maybe, I got too intensely involved with my work and didn't pay you enough attention at times?' That's a big one with women, I know. I've heard that plenty of times from friends, before.

'William,' she comes straight out and says. 'I'm *pregnant*.'

I jerk my head back. 'I'm sorry. *What?*' I grab hold of her arm. 'What did you...?'

'I'm expecting,' she says.

I must be staring like an idiot.

'A baby?'

She lets out a splutter of laughter, covering her mouth with her hands. A baby, of course that, what else? *A letter?* But so many questions are pushing their way to the front of my mind I hardly know which one to ask first.

'And... I knew that, before?'

She's nodding.

'I knew that you were expecting and I *split up* with you?'

'No!' Ava grabs hold of both my hands. 'You were over the moon about *that*. We were happy, we'd got...' She swallows hard, as if her throat has suddenly tightened with the memory. 'Will, it was all so sudden, like I said. We had the good news and then we had...' She motions towards my head. 'We had the not-so-good news.'

'One thing came on top of the other?'

'That's how it was. I think we had a week, at most, between learning about the baby and then the letter coming in, saying that you were sick...'

'Jeez.' I put my hands up to my head gingerly. I'm reeling. It's good news, of course, she could've honestly delivered no better news to me today, but still shocking. 'I'm going to be a dad?' The implications of it are only starting to trickle in. 'Looks like I've been busier than I knew in the last few years?' Euphoria is conquering my initial disbelief. 'Of all the things I've learned about myself since waking, this one piece of news makes it all worthwhile.'

She's smiling, looking relieved.

When I pull her in close to kiss her for the second time she melts into my arms. I sense she must have been dreading a different response.

'Hey... how come you didn't tell me all this before?'

She takes a moment before replying. 'I *wanted* to tell you before, believe me. Then, when you woke up from the operation and you were none too sure about being with me, I didn't want you to feel obliged...'

That stuns me into silence for a moment, and I realise how much she's been holding onto, not wanting to coerce me into anything.

'My God. But you must've *known* I'd always take my responsibilities towards any child of mine seriously, even if I wasn't with the mother?'

'I knew that. I just...'

'I get it. Hey, why are you...?' There are tears rolling down her face and I stroke her hair now. If they're tears of joy, why does she suddenly look so sad?

When I whisper softly, *'It's okay,'* Ava quickly turns her head away from me, wiping her eyes. Is it because she's had to keep this incredible news from me until I showed some willingness to commit to her? Is that it?

If it is, I feel bad about that. The feeling battles with the sheer pride that's swelling in my chest. It makes me wish I'd shown her a little more affection sooner, and it makes me all the more determined to make it up to her.

I know that I will.

When I come down from my shower on Monday morning, still yawning, getting dressed as I go, the sharp sound of rapping at the kitchen window is the last thing I want to hear. I only moved into Beach Cottage with Ava just over a week ago, and maybe that's how they do things around here, but why didn't *whoever it is* simply come around the front?

The sombre faced dude with the straight, shoulder length black hair who's appeared at the window looks as if he could be trouble. This man's got an intent, purposeful glint in his eye. He's tall, built like a state trooper and, by the way he's rattling the door handle, determined to enter one way or another. He probably doesn't even realise I'm in here.

'Who's there?' I call out. No answer. This place is relatively isolated, after all. If this bloke can't hear me, he'll imagine Ava's gone out or, if she's in, that she'll be no match for him. I feel a flash of anger at the thought.

Tracking back, I go and fetch the fire poker from the hearth, weighing it in one hand. If that geezer thinks he's breaking his way in here, he's got another think coming. To my dismay, not two seconds later, he's worked the back door open. *Security in this place is crap,* I'm thinking. *Just as well I'm here now to see to this kind of bother,* but first...

He's copped sight of me, with my metal stick, and his eyes go large as I brandish it towards him a fraction.

'Didn't expect anyone in this morning, I take it?'

He opens up his arms wide, palms facing me. The fringes on the arms of his black leather jacket are distracting. They look pretty cool, I'll admit. So does his belt buckle, a silver-coloured ram's head. He probably pays for all this radical gear by burgling other people's houses.

'I was...' he says cautiously, 'expecting *you.*'

He's got a very deep voice.

'No, you weren't.' I cough. Tough guy. He's not fooling anyone, but I'd have been happier if I'd managed to get my T-shirt on at least.

'Nice head wear,' he observes. His gaze slides over to my head, where I'm still sporting Ava's floral, pink shower cap. Not supposed to get the area too wet, am I? I resist the automatic urge to whip the thing off. He might be an intruder but do I really want him to see me in this women's-wear? What's worse – that, or him seeing the ugly, sore, shaved portion of my poor scalp? I swallow.

As if he's read my thoughts, he motions towards my head.

'That hurting you much, fella?' What's that supposed to mean?

'Look, I don't know who you are, but...' I make a lunge towards him, and his hands go up again. He takes one or two steps backwards, staving me off, laughing.

'You really *don't recognise me*, do you?'

'Should I?' My heart is thumping treacherously, but my head's going, *hold your horses a minute here, Will Tyler.*

'Who are you?' I say.

'I...' he comes in closer, pushing the metal poker away gently with the back of one hand, and picking up my T-shirt to hand me with the other '... am one of your closest and dearest friends.'

Dear God. I stare at him. What if he's right?

'You...' I clear my throat. 'What's your name, then? And why didn't I know you were coming? I'm pretty certain Ava would've warned me if...' Even as I'm saying it, I spy her note written in big letters, propped up against the toast rack on the breakfast table.

*Remember: I'm at a work meeting with my friend, Virginia, in London today. Your old mate, Toby, is coming here at 10 a.m. A xx*

The dude's eyebrows go up.

'You were saying?'

'So, you're... Toby?' I rub at the bridge of my nose. Put the poker down. 'I feel like a right wally.'

He's got a deep, musical laugh, eyes that twinkle in an '*all is forgiven*' kind of way and, whoever this fella is, I've got the feeling I already like him.

'Wally,' he says. 'An insult? That's a British thing, right?'

'Which you are clearly not?' I push one of the kitchen chairs out so he can take a seat. I can feel my shoulders sagging in relief, aware of a growing intrigue.

'Most certainly not, fella. Toby Myers, at your service. I hail from the Ozarks, Missouri.'

Wherever that is, he sounds pretty proud of it.

'Ava told me she'd leave the back door unlocked in case you were sleeping, so I let myself in. Hope I didn't scare you too bad?'

'Not at all,' I lie. 'Uh. Hold on one moment, please.' I leave him to go and look in the box Ava keeps in the hall. Dignity demands that I lose the shower cap, replace it with the red beanie. Any coloured beanie, just not... the shower cap.

'That is so much more *you*,' he approves as soon as I return. Then, leaning over the table the minute I sit down, he grasps my hands in a warm grip with both of his.

'William, I have been praying so hard for you, man.'

'Thank you.' I look at him curiously, feeling at a distinct disadvantage. 'You... uh... knew about my op, then?'

'I knew. Ava messaged me to say it had gone well. I'd have texted you myself but as I knew we had a meeting scheduled, I thought it might be better to wait to see you in person...'

I don't know why, but I love this dude's voice, his energy, his whole persona; it lifts my spirits to be around him.

'So, you and I had a meeting scheduled and – we're very good friends, you say?'

'Brothers in arms. Fellow adventurers on the wide and choppy open seas of creativity. Collaborators in the field of composing exciting, ground breaking music.'

'Ah, so you're a fellow musician?'

He looks slightly disappointed that I could've imagined anything else.

'And you...' he's looking at me bemusedly '... really *don't* remember anything?'

'I don't. Going back for the last seven years. Not even you.'

'Clearly not. You have no idea how strange that feels to me, dude.' *To him?* I give a short laugh. He leans back in his chair, stretching his long legs out in front of him.

'To be fair, it's what your girlfriend told me when I rang her this morning to remind you I was in your fair and beautiful country for a while and I'd be dropping by, but I wasn't entirely sure how much you'd...?'

'Nothing,' I tell him. 'I remember nothing of our collaboration, or our friendship.'

He gives me a long, considered look.

'You and I sure look to have got a lot to catch up on, fella,' he says. 'I think I could use a drink.'

I get up to put the kettle on. Meeting this man, I'm feeling distinctly more cheerful. So, I *do* still have friends in the music industry? All those unidentifiable names in my phone contacts list – maybe they'll turn out to be people I can totally relate to, like this dude? Who is pretty awesome.

I'm fetching us down some coffee mugs when he says, 'That's okay, I'll take it straight out of the bottle.'

He wants *beer*?

'Uh... sure.'

I hand him one, which, by Ava's prescience, I find in the fridge. I put the coffee mugs back, recalling I'm off it anyway, but with the realisation dawning that this guy could fill me in on *so many things*. This is really exciting!

'Toast?' I offer. I'd been about to make breakfast, I remember, and this could take a while. He shakes his head, *I'm good*.

'So please, tell me everything.' I sit down eagerly. 'Let's start at the beginning. Did we meet through the lads from the band? DelRoy?'

'Met them once or twice, courtesy of you,' he allows. 'Though I hear they've all gone their own ways?'

'So Ava said.' It hasn't quite sunk in yet. In my mind, they're all still out there somewhere, singing their songs, still touring Europe.

'So, you and I met... where?'

'In Stuttgart, in a cafe. You recognised me, I think.' *Which is more than I do now.* 'I was doing a lot of DJ-ing back then. You'd already split from the band. I think you were after some airtime for your own music.' He chuckles suddenly. '*Man,* you were annoying! You came and sat at the table behind me, playing this one track on your phone, over and over, long enough and loud enough that I'd notice.'

'I did that?' The toaster dings. I get up to fetch my breakfast, still riveted by his story, feeling pretty impressed with myself. 'And... you eventually came over to ask me about it?'

'I came over to tell you I was having a drink with this girl I'd been chasing for weeks and I couldn't hear my thoughts in my own head and if you didn't turn off that damn phone speaker, I would be forced, as you Brits quaintly like to put it, to *deck you one*.'

I laugh. 'Sounds like the start of a beautiful friendship.'

'Oh, it was,' he continues. 'We went on to take it outside.'

I took it outside *with him*? I'm impressing myself more with every minute.

'I'm not usually inclined to get into argy-bargy with people that easily.' I look at him, wonderingly. 'Am I?'

He motions towards the discarded poker. Then his face creases into a smile.

'Argy-bargy. Gotta *love* you British.'

But I'm still hooked. Did I get the shit beaten out of me or what? How did this all turn into the beautiful friendship he says we now have?

'So, we took it outside and, fortunately for you, while we were going out, this other song you had on your phone came up.' His eyes go over a little misty. 'And *then* you had me.' He opens up his hands. 'After that, you and I got to talking. My date got seriously pissed off and threatened to walk, but I liked your *chutzpah*!'

'Thank God for that one track...'

'Amen to that,' he tells me seriously. 'I went on to sell it to some big players and it's what's allowed us to concentrate on our collaboration.'

I smile at him, loving the sound of this story of my life more with every passing second. So, I've actually made some good money, songwriting? My heart skips a beat. Ava's hinted as much but there's been that problem with me getting into my bank account; I've not been able to check.

'So, you lost the girl and found me?'

'She left. Never called me back so you still owe me one, there.' He winks, taking a swig of his beer. I spread some honey on my toast, still taking all this in, feeling my appetite return properly for the first time in ages. He's saying, 'I expect you to organise a date with a lovely British lady for me one day, to make up for it.'

'Uh. You might have to take a rain check on that. I only appear to know one lovely British lady at the moment.'

'It'll keep.' He smiles. 'I'm glad to have caught you, man. I'm only in your neck of the woods for a few days this time around, but I'm back working in the UK in late summer for a longer stint.'

'So, you don't live here?'

'I travel, but I currently live in Missouri most of the year round. You and I collaborate over the Net.'

He's smiling, leaning in to pick up his mobile. 'And, if you don't know what you've been working on, these past few years, you're in for a surprise, my friend. A very big one.'

'Go on, then.' This is such exciting news.

He proceeds to play me one of *our* tracks over the speaker of his mobile. I lean back, closing my eyes, listening to it.

The sound is... it's like nothing I've ever heard before. It's piano and guitar like I'm familiar with, and a host of wind instruments and percussion, but *different* somehow. I can pick out themes to it, haunting and then, by turns, scary and wild and joyous. This music sounds big. It sounds... overwhelming.

'There are some small inflections there – some places at the end of that first stanza – that could do with being quieter...' he's saying and I find myself nodding, agreeing with him. Listening to it, I'm automatically logging the places where piano would more usefully replace the violins, less percussion, and so on, but on the whole...

'It's pretty bloody amazing,' I get out at last.

'It is,' he agrees. 'And it's our little project.'

Wow. Ours. I did that. With him, but still... where did all those emotions come from? I think, *how* did I write those songs, do that?

'It sounds like some background track to a big budget Hollywood production.'

It really does. Listening to it, I felt a huge flash of pride but that's been replaced almost immediately with something else that I don't like so much, something that feels more like worry.

He's still smiling at me. 'Feels good, huh?'

I tell him ruefully, 'It *feels* like the time I bribed some genius in the sixth form to write a school science assignment for me and then it all backfired when I was somehow awarded the school prize for it.' I lift my hands to massage my brow, reliving that. They'd asked me to go up onstage and talk about what I'd written. I couldn't do it, ended up fretting I'd be discovered as a cheat and a fraud.

It feels like that.

Because, if this is my work, how do I begin to connect with it? How can I continue working on something that I don't even know how I started? It doesn't *feel* like my work; it feels like someone else's work. Toby Myers' or... that other Will, the one I've had excised out of my brain. His work. Not mine.

Toby seems a little bemused at my reaction. I add, 'No question it's bloody amazing, though.'

I ladle another spoonful of honey over my toast. I'm about to sink my teeth into it when he says, a little alarmed, 'You *sure* you want to eat that, fella?'

I'm still blown away with what I've heard. Still trying to make sense of it all. I look at the toast.

'It's... breakfast.'

'Maybe, but, last I saw, you were allergic to honey. You came up in great big hives all over the place, real *nasty*.' He shakes his head sorrowfully and I look at the piece of toast I've slathered in the sweet, golden brown honey.

'You got stung by a bee and somehow it translated into an allergy to bee products. I'm sorry, I don't know how that works...'

I throw my toast back onto the plate, feeling gutted. How many other things don't I know? Could that many things change about a man's life in only seven years? I wipe my mouth with the edge of a tea cloth and then I see this slow, deliciously mischievous smile cross his face.

'Just kidding, brother.'

I sink my head into my hands. 'You have your fun,' I say, feeling a relieved grin breaking out, all the same. 'You go ahead.'

'Hey,' he says. 'You'd do the same for me, I promise you. So. You're going to be a daddy soon. How did that happen?'

'I wish I could remember.'

'You really don't?'

'How babies get made, yes. The act of making this one, no.'

He's smiling broadly. 'You woke up one day to a ready-made family, eh?'

'A ready-made life, it seems.'

'That must feel like some weird shit, man?'

'Pretty much.'

'People could rip you off all over the place. Like, our music,' he muses. 'I could've made off with it and you'd never have had any benefit?'

'Sorry,' I tell him. 'But I think you've missed that opportunity.'

'I know! I blame it on Pastor Williamson's Sunday morning bible classes.' Toby thumps the table, loudly. 'I could've been a rich man instead of an honest one.'

'Sounds like a good lyric...'

'Sounds like you've forgotten we already wrote it?'

'Did we?'

He thumps his head on the table, this time. 'Boy, I'm *really* gonna have some fun with you, aren't I?'

'Maybe,' I warn. 'I've still got mixed feelings about you, Toby from the Ozarks. I'm still deciding who I'll be keeping in my life, moving forward.'

'Hell, hang onto whoever'll tell you it like it is. That's what always works best for me.'

'And you?'

He raises his beer to me. 'Oh, I'll always tell it to you straight.'

'Pastor Williamson again?'

'Damn right. He's got a lot to answer for. Anyhow...' he puts his phone away '... we've got a potential offer on this one, just so y'know. A film producer I was talking to up Frisco way. He liked it. A lot. He wants us to finish it, so I'm hoping you're going to be up for doing that, soon as you're feeling recovered some?'

A big film producer is interested in our music?

'Pull the other one.' He looks puzzled. I explain. 'This another one of your little jokes?'

'Not on your life,' he says, dead serious. 'There are two things in life I never joke about, William, boy. Music is one of them.'

'And the other?'

'Ah, that. Stick around with me for long enough,' he promises, 'and maybe you'll find out.'

## 18

## AVA

Ginny curls up her legs on her elegant, seaweed green sofa, looking at me curiously.

'So... tell me *everything*. Does he still fancy you, do you still fancy him, and how's it all going back at your house?'

I smile softly. This last week tucked away with Will at Beach Cottage has been intense – exhausting both physically and mentally, but also cosy and fun.

'It's been kind of lovely, just the two of us.' It couldn't last, though. 'He's got one of his musician mates visiting today.'

She nods, approvingly. 'That's good.' Ginny pats the space beside her, invitingly. 'If he's ready to let the rest of the world in, I imagine that'll also help take the pressure off you?'

I look away, shrugging off my jacket. When I left Will this morning, I was happy his friend was coming over, but I couldn't help the slight cloud of worry in my mind, too.

'I guess. Will and Toby were always close collaboratively, but...' I pick up the *Catalogue of Medieval and Renaissance Costumes* she's been leafing through, looking for somewhere safe to put it while she unceremoniously dumps a pile of delicate velvet sample swatches onto the floor. I shoot her a sideways glance.

'D'you think... men ever talk about their private concerns in the same way that women do?'

'Why? You're not worried they might get chatting about anything in particular, are you?'

'No, but...'

She lets out a trumpet-like laugh. 'In any event, you *know* the answer to that one, honey! Since when did men ever talk about things the way we women do?'

'True.'

She says decisively, 'If he's got matters on his mind after the op, then you're the best person to deal with them.'

I sit, realising I've been chewing on my fingernails again, and make a deliberate effort to stop doing that. She's right, and besides, once Will and Toby get back into playing their guitars or whatever, they'll almost certainly get totally lost in that. Which means that *I* can safely lose myself in my own world of work for the next hour or so. I look up as the girl who let me into the office appears with a tray of drinks.

'Mango and lemongrass smoothies,' Ginny says. 'Yummy.' This'll be courtesy of Ginny being on a healthy 'dry' spell, because, knowing her as I do, I'm sure she'd prefer to be partaking of something a little stronger.

She adds, 'Meet Patsy, my new personal assistant.'

So, Ginny's got a PA, now? My old bestie from fashion college sure has gone up in the world – I hadn't appreciated quite how much. We mostly keep in touch by text, these days, though when we *do* reconnect it's as if no time at all has passed. She contacted me in the new year, offering to subcontract some very lucrative costume design and sewing work, and my trip up here today is partially in the hopes of reviving that offer.

Looking around us, I see the walls are covered with posters from big theatre productions Ginny's been involved with.

'Wow. Little wonder you need a *personal assistant*.' I smile at her. 'I knew you'd been taking on more clients, searching for bigger premises, but all this...?'

I turn and point to the office door, where she's even got her name 'Virginia Newfields: Film and Stage Theatrical Costume Design' embossed in gold lettering on the glass. This is everything Ginny dreamed of having and, in truth, I'm feeling both pleased and envious in equal measure.

'You never let on how big this whole operation was becoming, Gin?'

'Oh, this is all just work. Lovely work. But I want to hear about all *your* goss.' Ginny's eyes are sparkling. She leans in now, adding, sotto voce, 'What I'm really dying to know is, have you *told* him yet?'

I stiffen. Then shoot her a tight smile.

'You mean, about the...?'

'Yes, yes.' She does a little impatient gesture with her fingertips. 'The baby, Ava. What else?'

I rub at my throat, feeling my face going pink. 'He knows.'

*'And?'* She sits up, incredulous perhaps at finding me so tight lipped. 'How'd he take it?'

I swallow. 'He was over the moon, like you'd expect.' Shoot. I've got to stop feeling as if I'm going around with a glaring, neon 'I'm a Big Fat Liar' sign on my face every time the topic of the baby gets brought up because if I don't, I'll come a cropper before I know it.

I've got to... *forget it isn't his.* Bury that. Bury it as deep in me as it can go and never look at it again and get on with living my life.

Ginny's looking at me, puzzled.

'The truth is... I was so worried I didn't tell Will about the baby for days, because I was so scared that he wouldn't...'

Ginny puts her hand on my arm. 'Oh, hon! Who wouldn't feel that way? You found yourself in a totally impossible situation!'

I gulp, and she rushes on, 'Listen, you've risen to the challenge in a way only a real winner could and... I'm so *proud* of you, hon.' She's rubbing at my arm, eyes full of fellow feeling. 'I've no kids, but I don't believe there's a woman alive who wouldn't totally empathise with your situation.'

I clear the frog in my throat.

'Thank you.' Wishing that my face didn't feel so hot, wishing that I could be honest with her.

Ginny's still looking at me admiringly. 'I imagine you must've been terrified he'd wake up after his op and feel differently about wanting kiddies?' She gives a dramatic shiver. 'What if you'd suddenly found yourself stranded with the burden of having to bring this one up on your own, without him, after all that you two have been through?'

I nod, taking another sip though the drink tastes disgusting, *anything* rather than risk her seeing what's really on my face.

'Hon, you're a real heroine,' Ginny asserts, and then, leaning in quietly, she adds, 'If you ever need any help at all – be it with getting a job or help finding your feet, whatever, you always know where I am. We girls must stick together.'

I smile. 'Appreciated, Gin.'

'He took it well, though? That's got to have been a real weight off your shoulders?'

'It was,' I rally, keen to get her off the topic of *what a hero I am*. 'But then we also had the age difference hurdle,' I say ruefully. 'When I told him the other day I was thirty-one, he was honestly surprised. Told me he'd never gone out with an older woman before…'

'Ouch,' she laughs.

'He was also put out because apparently all these iconic musicians have died while he was… well, in the bit Will doesn't recall, and he's taken to scouring the Internet to find out who's still alive.'

Ginny balances her drink on her lap. 'You hear about these things happening. These operations. People seem to manage, somehow, but you always imagine it's got to change them in some way…' Her look manages to convey both sympathy and curiosity at the same time. '*Is* he the same, Ava, really?'

'He is to me,' I tell her quietly. 'To me he's still the same man I fell in love with. Only, with a lot of wrong assumptions in his head about the way things are now. And of course…' I look down, my fingertips running over a beautiful swatch of velvet samples I've still got in my hand '… he's also minus the memories of how much he once loved me.'

'Lord.' She leans back, taking that in for a moment. 'I can't even *imagine* what that must feel like,' she muses. 'If Ned even forgets our anniversary, I flip. I'm too insecure. If he didn't know me any more and we had to go through the whole courtship thing all over again, I'd... well, I think I'd freak out,' she tells me.

'What choice do I have, Ginny? I have to keep going, even if I'm only beginning to register to him.'

'Are you? Thank the Lord for that, at least.' Virginia's eyes are twinkling a little. 'So, go on, tell me all...'

I laugh.

'And, *pur-leese*...' she wags her finger '... don't do that thing you do and go all dark horse on me.'

Ginny's one of my oldest girlfriends. Ever since the first day we bumped into each other at college I've shared more with her than I have with anyone else, but this is one scenario where even she can't know it all.

I glance away, feeling a pang of regret. 'That's hardly fair, Gin. Besides, what's to tell, anyway?'

'Well, *you know*. How it's working out,' she prompts. 'Have you two...?'

I shake my head rapidly. 'Not yet. The op, you know, and... well, us getting to know each other. I'm sure it's on the cards soon, though.'

'I should hope!' She makes a face. '*He's got eyes*. And he's falling for you again, clearly?' Ginny's giving me a big thumbs-up sign.

'I like to think so.' I give an inner sigh, realising that even though I'd been looking forward to our catch-up, I can't be properly me, not like this, watching my every word. It's time I changed the subject. Ginny's generous with her time and we've had masses to catch up on, but the fact is I'm also here angling for that upcoming work project she's mentioned.

She's saying, 'Well, you need to keep all the different plates in your life spinning, hon. We've all got bills to pay...'

'I'm really grateful you thought of me for this project, Ginny...'

'I *always* think of you first, any time a project comes my way that I think you'd be able to fulfil, you know that.'

'Thank you.'

'Friendship aside, it's simply good business.' She brushes aside my gratitude. 'If I want a project brought in on time and within budget, with rigorous attention paid to costume details which are not only aesthetically pleasing but often stunning, you're always going to be my first port of call.'

'Flattery,' I laugh, 'will get you everywhere! Plus, with the baby coming, I need this work. I really do.'

Ginny sips at her smoothie thoughtfully. 'You needed the work I was offering you in the autumn,' she reminds me. 'And some of the preliminary sketches you were showing me back then were bang on target, too.'

I groan. 'I wanted that work, Gin!' Before Christmas, though, my mind was taken up by so many other things. The problems between Will and myself were coming to a head.

'I'd hoped to repair things at home before diving into a huge, busy work project, but in the end...'

Ginny nods. 'I understand, hon. You wanted to fix things so you sacrificed your work.'

I glance up at her, silent. Will and I had split up anyway.

'And look, after all that,' she finishes, 'things are working out between you again.'

I smile ruefully. 'I could've had my cake and eaten it, you mean?'

'I'm a great believer in eating cake whenever you get the opportunity, as you know.'

Ginny's always been great at making the most of whatever opportunities come her way, a talent which, as she's fond of reminding me, has not always been my forte.

'Talking of cake, come and stop by the gardens some time and I'll sort you out some lovely coffee and walnut slices. I know they're your favourites...'

'You're still at the tea rooms?' she mutters under her breath. 'Such a waste, Ava. If you'd only taken my advice a few years back…'

'Can't turn the clock back.' I suck in my lips. 'Not that I'd want to, either.'

We're both silent for a bit, then she says, 'Okay. *All that aside*, you're confident that things are stable enough at home for you to take on this new contract for me?'

'They have to be, don't they?' Quite apart from the occasional shifts I manage at the tea rooms, I still need some proper work. I tell her, 'Will's got some funds coming in, sure, but I can't rely on a man who feels he barely knows me.'

'True.' She adds, 'Listen, hon. I'll tell it to you straight. This production company I'm looking at is fairly new but early rumours are, they're going places. I'd like us to go with them. Everyone I take on has to pull their weight when competition for these opportunities is so fierce. You understand?'

I'm nodding like one of those ornamental bulldogs you used to see in the back of people's cars.

She's still looking at me intently. 'You mentioned over the phone that Will's moved back in, right? I take it, apart from getting re-acquainted, you're the one helping to look after him during recovery?'

I nod. She gives me a thumbs up for that one.

'I take it… he also knows *why* he moved out in the first place?'

Jeez. She had to ask that, didn't she?

'Will knows,' I say carefully, 'that we'd been having difficulties.'

'He must also know why, though?' She shifts in her chair, looking puzzled. 'You mean, you haven't told him *why*?'

I look away from her. 'I didn't see the need to drag it all up, Gin. I'm pregnant. It's not important any more, is it? Will doesn't need to know.'

More than that, he *can't*. I feel my stomach sinking again, wishing she would drop it. I never bargained with all this when I made Will that promise to keep things quiet from him – *for him* – I never realised how many people there were, still around us, who knew part of the picture, that could come back to haunt me.

'Best to leave all that in the past, Gin.'

A slow smile is spreading across Ginny's face.

'Well, well. I have to admit, there are one or two things I wish *I* could just... disappear out of my Ned's memory, if you get my drift. Can't really say I blame you, hon.'

I don't answer her. Ginny and I have always liked to share, yes, but I'm wishing now I'd never shared with her as much as I did.

'Okay, then,' she decides, when I don't elaborate any further. 'Welcome on board this project. I know you won't let me down, Ava.'

'I love my work. I love you,' I tell her, relieved to be back onto a safer topic. Besides, I need this. *Letting her down* on this is the last thing I'd ever do.

Now I only need to make sure she and Will don't ever get the chance to chat about things on a day when she's given up on the smoothies and she's had a tad too much to drink.

## 19

## WILL

'This is the one track we've been having problems with from the start.' Toby and I decamped back to DelRoy's flat three hours ago. It was the logical thing to do, given that's where all the musical equipment is. The front room coffee table's already got four empty beer bottles on it, never mind what time it is, and we've been having a blast jamming on the old honky-tonk piano, inventing some new riffs on the electric guitar.

'The melody wouldn't flow, the transitions weren't right but...' Toby swings around on the piano stool. 'I've been working on this one back home for a while. What d'you think of this?'

After he's played it a couple of times, 'Try... C major,' I suggest. 'Try shifting tempo before the break.'

An accomplished musician, he nods and, closing his eyes, plays it again, easily incorporating the changes along with a little improvisation of his own. A gentle, beaming smile spreads slowly across his face as he plays. It seems my instinctive suggestions were exactly what he was looking for.

'*Well, whaddya know?*' He reaches up to give me a high five, grasping my hand for a few seconds in a display of camaraderie and gratitude. 'I think we may have cracked it.'

It's a good feeling. Today, for the first time since I woke up from the op, I feel as if I'm reconnecting with something, finding my tribe.

'Apparently, we make a great team.'

'Sure do, son.'

I sit back, listening as Toby returns to the piano to segue onto a new tune, one that's as full of raw beauty as this sunny May morning.

'Now *that* one,' I tell him thickly, 'I love.'

He's smiling, still playing, still with his eyes closed. I get the feeling this piece must go towards the end of that film score he says we'd both been working on. It's the denouement. The bit where all the pieces come together in a satisfyingly moving, perfect climax.

'You're one hell of a talented songwriter.' When he's done, I get up to raise my glass to him. I've actually got a lump in my throat. 'That's got to be one of the most moving pieces I've ever heard anyone play.'

'You wrote it, man.'

'No.' I sink back into my chair. 'I wrote that?'

'It was shortly after you'd heard about the baby. You were so full of joy. This must've all spilled out.'

I wrote that music after I'd heard Ava was expecting? Feeling a prickling in the corners of my eyes I'd prefer this dude didn't see, I make a move to snatch up the empty beer bottles from the table.

'Refill?'

'Don't mind if I do.'

By the time I come back, a tad more composed, he's saying, 'When you wrote this, you had it all going on, dude.'

'It sure seems like it, doesn't it?' I'm still basking in the wonder of the piece he's played me. The one I wrote. I want to sit down at the piano and play it myself, but something holds me back.

He catches my gaze, perhaps hearing something in my voice.

'Having a little trouble believing it, fella?'

I bite my bottom lip. 'It feels to me that I fell asleep in a world that looked a lot greyer to me than this one does. I'd left the band to play the music my heart yearned to play but the record label hated it and dropped me. There was nobody out there who wanted to listen to it.' I look down, scrunching my eyes. 'I was broke, only keeping afloat because I was staying rent free at DelRoy's and, believe me, I had nothing that looked remotely like any loving girlfriend on the horizon.'

He nods. 'And then you wake up one day to find you must've rubbed an old oil lamp and let a genie out of a bottle because suddenly you're living the dream?'

I open up my hands. 'That's exactly it. Only...'

Toby tilts his head to one side. 'Only you had to have a brain op and – as it feels to you – lose seven years of your life to get here?'

'Yeah.' I push back the beanie hat to the edge of my hairline. My scalp is starting to itch again, like crazy, but it's an itch I'm not allowed to scratch. I have to distract myself. I stand up and walk over to pick up the Spanish guitar DelRoy keeps in the corner. It's always felt a little battered and old and maybe a little unloved.

'Something bugging you, fella?'

'The seven years lost bit is fine. I've made my peace with it. I'm glad to be alive, grateful for all the support I'm getting,' I say earnestly. 'I'm grateful to be feeling a little stronger with every passing day.'

'Only...?'

I sigh. I wasn't going to say this. 'Only, every day when I wake up, I'm still having trouble believing this really is my life.' I start strumming a few chords but something's wrong. I stop.

'Does this guitar sound *off* to you?'

'Don't think so.' He pulls a face as if he doesn't see any problem.

'It does to me. Hold on a minute...' I lean inwards, listening intently, my fingers automatically adjusting the keys at the top to tune it.

'When I was a kid,' I tell him apropos of nothing, 'I once found a fifty pound note flying down the road. Fifty. Can you believe that?'

'I've seen a few one hundred dollar notes...'

'Well, we didn't see too many fifties around. Still don't. The point is, I found it, but it wasn't mine. Everyone said, "Finders, keepers!" My mates wanted me to go and blow it all in the sweet shop, but...' I pull my beanie hat down a little.

'I know what Pastor Williamson would've said,' he murmurs in his deep voice. 'Though I reckon I wouldn't have told him.'

'No.' I laugh. 'Maybe the problem was, I was brought up to believe there's no such thing as a free lunch?' I smile ruefully. 'In the end, I handed the fifty over to my mum and she dropped it off at the police station.'

'You don't believe in good luck that comes out of the blue?'

'Oh, I do. But someone else must've done something to earn that money. Something about the whole idea of claiming that note felt wrong.' I add, 'I'm feeling a little bit like it now.'

'I'm sorry,' he says.

'There's so much of this new life I've come into that I can't *own*.' I shoot Toby a painful smile. 'I can't own all these songs I wrote that've apparently taken off and been such a success. I love them. I'm overjoyed to hear I wrote them. But in all honesty, it feels like you've handed these to me on a plate.'

Toby's deep brown eyes are locked onto mine.

'There's part of me that doesn't understand how I came to have this caring and beautiful girlfriend, along with our little family that's coming, either.' I take in a breath. 'Of course, I'm happy, I *must* be happy, I'm just...'

'You're not feeling it?'

I stare at him, my new friend – no, one of my *closest and dearest friends* – feeling a small sense of panic even admitting this out loud. 'I've been having moments when I'm finding it really hard to take it all in, can you comprehend that? It's hard,' I tell him. 'Not knowing, I don't even know *what* it is I don't know sometimes, I only feel it there. Under the surface. Something.'

'That's what we musicians do,' he agrees. 'We feel things we don't understand. And then we take those things and put into our music... all those things we can't express in any other way.'

Toby comes over and pats me on the shoulder.

'I'm sure any psychologist could explain the way you *feel* to you. All I can tell you for certain is this: you've grafted for every bit of your success. You didn't win it, and nobody handed it to you on any plate. Trust me when I tell you that whatever you've got, you earned it.'

He adds, 'Perhaps you're feeling pleasantly shocked and surprised in an "I just won a million on the lottery" kind of way?'

'Maybe.'

He throws me a look. 'Well, you might well win the professional lottery, if we can carry on getting this piece done at the pace we've been working at today. I know you've still got to be finding your feet, working out what your life's about, but the good news is, I'm meeting my Frisco contact in London later on this week.' Toby does a little flourish on the piano. 'He's super keen for us to complete this work. I'm hoping to tell him we'll have the full score to show him by the end of the summer – what d'you think?'

'Sounds good!'

Toby tells me, 'I'll be honest, I didn't know what to expect from you this morning, Will, but I am *so* happy I've come in and found you up for it. You can have no idea exactly how important this is...'

I'm rapidly getting the picture.

'I'm glad, too. Your turning up this morning is the best thing that could've happened.' It's true. Our jamming session has taken me into a whole different space. I indicate the room around us, the drum kit we've pulled out of the spare bedroom and set up, the discarded sheet music all over the floor, the amps and the pedals and the guitars.

'I *get* this. Music is something I've always felt comfortable with. I'm grateful, I've felt more like the me I recognise, this morning, than I have since I woke up after the op. Thank you so much.' Even aside from the amazing career news he's just landed on me, having him around has been a blast.

'As for Ava...' Toby adds after a bit. 'She's a sweetheart. You struck pure gold, there, William, and you deserve that, too.'

I smile and play a few gentle chords on the Spanish guitar. It's old and worn, but it's always had a warm, mellow sound I really like. I look up, still strumming.

'Nice. Now... what does this sound like to you? Sunshine on a warm beach?'

'Hits the spot,' he agrees. 'Like ice-cold beer on a hot day.'

'Nostalgic and beautiful... like an emerald cove full of ancient white fishing boats,' I murmur.

'Like hot, sirocco winds blowing in the night. A fulsome woman in your arms...' Toby winks at me. 'Any full-blooded man in your position would take the gifts of the life you've been given and run with them.'

'I know. And I'm grateful.' I am.

It will go away soon, this feeling. I'm sure it will. I strum some more on the old guitar, losing myself in the rhythm, enjoying the melodic sounds. And for now, they are like a balm, soothing the unquiet places in my soul, just as music has always done.

# 20

## AVA

'I've always loved this place, Ava. It's one of my favourite places in the world.'

I'm sitting with Will on the edge of the crumbling old sea wall at Holcombe Bay watching the fresh, fine sea mist that's been rolling in all morning; and he's looking so relaxed and happy. I've been feeling it, too.

'Is this really where your gramps taught you to fish?'

He shoots me a shy smile. 'I'm surprised I never told you about that before?'

'You haven't. But thank you for sharing it with me. And… for buying lunch.'

Will spears a fat, gloriously crispy, chip with a little wooden fork, proffering it into my mouth.

'You like chips, don't you?'

'Chips are the enemy,' I tell him, opening my mouth to scoff it anyway. 'But yes, what girl doesn't secretly enjoy sitting al fresco, eating chips?'

I pull my cardigan a little more firmly around me, determined to make the most of it. We've both been so busy all week – with him keen to get some work done while Toby's still around, and me cracking on with Ginny's commission – we've barely seen each other since the weekend.

'You sure?' He hides the smile that appears at the corners of his mouth. 'The last girl I recall bringing here complained rather a lot about her bum getting damp.'

I laugh. If that was his ex in one of her fabulous frocks I can well imagine. I hold out my hand, relishing the feel of the cold sea spray surging up to meet us.

'Sitting by the water, how can you avoid it?'

He glances ruefully at the box of chips. 'You must think me a real cheap date?'

'Not at all! I wouldn't have missed coming out here for the world.' I pause, wondering if maybe there's something else behind that comment – he still hasn't got his monetary affairs under control yet, has he? I venture, 'If you're worried about funds, Will, I'd be more than happy to stand us lunch.'

'Funds?'

'Well, if you're short of money?' I offer. 'Your appointment at the bank's not till tomorrow,' I run on, 'and until you're able to sort out your finances, I'm more than happy to stand you...'

'Thanks, but no way.' He shakes his head firmly. 'There's no problem with funds. It's some sort of administrative issue that'll be cleared up as soon as I see the manager. Anyway, I'm the one who buys lunch around here, not my girlfriend.'

There's the old Will resurfacing, right there, and did he just call me *his girlfriend?* I beam.

'You would say if you were too cold, wouldn't you?'

'I'm *fine*.' I don't care about the chill, I've been ignoring it, but Will's picked up my frozen hands and he's warming them now, in his own toasty ones.

'I'm always a little too hot or too cold these days. Don't know what's up with me, really – maybe it's just the hormones?'

To my surprise, Will leans in to pat my tummy.

'Does it feel strange, having someone living in there?'

I laugh. 'No!' While his head is bowed over my practically invisible bump, I stretch out my fingers to gently wipe away all the tiny water droplets on the surface of his red beanie hat. *God, you are so handsome, Will.* We sit there together for a few moments, very still and close and cosy. I'm letting my thoughts wander to how he might react if I kissed him, when he turns his face, catching me out.

'You okay, Ava?'

I clear my throat, tucking in a couple of the red-gold tendrils of his hair sticking out of the sides of the hat.

'I am very okay, thank you.'

'So, tell me.' He shifts position, leaning back easily on the sea wall, propped on his elbows. 'Given that we've been together for a while, did this pregnancy just *happen* or...' he smiles shyly '... had we been trying for it?'

'Oh, I'd say we'd been ready for it to happen.' I swallow as the memory of all our romantic trysts returns, aware that, at the moment, I am trying very hard not to gawp at his physique under that T-shirt he's wearing. He's been a lot more affectionate with me, ever since he agreed to move back in. There's been no actual intimacy yet, but then, quite apart from any other considerations, Will's still physically recovering. That part of it, they warned us from the start, would take a while.

'And, Ava, did we ever discuss...?' Will smiles at me again, melting my insides more than a guy has any right to do.

'Yes?' *Did we discuss marriage is what he's going to ask,* isn't he?

Finally! I've been waiting for him to ask about this. When I lean in a little, my head barely touching his chest, I can hear the thump, thump, thump of his heart, actually *feel* the heat of his body coming right through his T-shirt.

I smile at him encouragingly and he asks, 'Did we ever get around to discussing things like baby names?'

I blink.

'No.' I look away, down at the gravelled paving of the sea wall where we're sitting, feeling a tad disappointed.

'No?' He touches my arm softly. 'We didn't go looking up all the cutesy baby books for potential names? Isn't that unusual?'

Is it? I'm not sure what he means; maybe it is, maybe it isn't. *Too many things were happening all at the same time, Will!*

Too many things.

'I think maybe we had... one or two ideas.' God. *You wanted Rapunzel, for a girl*, I remember. Rapunzel. Like the princess with the long hair. *But if you don't remember that...*

'My mum's friend was going to dig out her old baby-name book. But then, so soon after we found out about the baby... the whole picture changed.'

He nods.

'It sure did.'

A couple of seagulls flap near us now, making a racket. They're after his chips and they won't go away till Will tips the rest of the packet down onto the shingle. We watch the two feathered furies diving onto it, tearing the packet apart, making off with our lunch, but he doesn't seem in too much of a hurry to move.

'This is so surreal, isn't it, Ava? You and me,' he says after a bit. 'It's like something out of a movie.'

'I can see why you'd feel that way. It'd make a great movie! I do a writing motion in the air. "The Story of Us" by Will and Ava.'

'It has a ring to it.' He laughs. 'We'd be a huge box office success, don't you think?'

I nudge his chest, angling my face to smile at him.

'I suppose all the blokes would want to know how it feels to wake up and learn you've got this hot girlfriend in your life who you never even had to woo...' I hint.

'Oh, definitely.' He grins. 'No doubt, all the girls would also be keen to know exactly how *you're* making the most of things, given you're with a partner who can't remember so much?'

'What do you...?'

'Oh, I know women. Women are nothing if not resourceful, no?'

I've stopped laughing but he's still smiling.

'Surely you've had *some* discussions with your girlfriends about how my not remembering anything could only work to your advantage?'

I sit up a little taller.

'I wouldn't ever take advantage of you, Will.'

'Oh, c'mon!' Will laughs. 'Say you happened to mention to me that I'm one of those dudes who "cleans the house" for relaxation?' He nudges me back. 'Say you convinced me I enjoy cooking too? That I cook us a roast every Sunday.'

'You don't...'

'Oh, and I always take you to the Cartier diamond shop to choose a gift every time our anniversary rolls around?'

I relax a little, cottoning on that he's teasing.

'Now *that* one does happen to be true.'

'Is it?'

I hoot with laughter.

'And... did I mention you always let me warm my feet on yours in bed at night if I'm feeling frozen?'

Will pulls a grimace.

'Not too sure about that one, Ava.' He breaks into a grin. 'Though I could probably think of one or two other ways to warm you up if that's what you needed...'

'I imagine you could. *Oh!*' I look up, shivering, as some spots of rain start falling. 'I think our al fresco lunch just got too *fresco.*'

'Here.' Still on his meds, he can't afford to catch a cold, but even as I'm shaking my head Will's shrugging off his quilted jacket.

'No,' I tell him.

'I didn't even have it zipped up. And you've got our littl'un to keep warm in there.' He hands me the jacket. 'Take it. Pretty please?'

I smile. 'Always such a gentleman.'

'Am I?'

We're both silent for a moment, then he says, 'I've never actually asked you before how things have been for *you*, have I? How you've been coping with all this?'

'I'm good.'

Our eyes lock.

'I'm sorry I've not been able to support you better. That I've been so wrapped up in my own recovery that I couldn't.'

'Hey, it's okay.' I open up my hands. 'I've had support. People have been very good to me, Will. At work, my sister and my friends. Everyone's been very kind and...' He just reached out to push back a lock of my hair. An old, familiar gesture, which has brought a lump to my throat.

'*You okay*, Ava?'

'Sure.' Sitting here beside the sea, Will's eyes have a grey-green tint to them, today. He has such beautiful eyes. Soulful eyes I fell in love with the moment I saw them; I always hoped for a baby with eyes like that. But this baby won't... *Oh, God.* I can't even look at him, now.

'You sure you're okay?'

'It's all just... going to take so long,' I breathe.

'The pregnancy?' he assumes I mean. 'Perhaps I might know a little brain op that would let you scroll right through the next few months and get you to the end a lot quicker?'

'Ha!'

'Just kidding. I wouldn't wish this on anyone, no matter what they were going through. *Hey.*' He pulls me in towards him for a hug. 'We're going to make it. You-me-and-baby-makes-three! It's gonna be all right, Ava, you do know that?'

I nod, trying to smile.

'Sure, I do.' But I've got a lump in my throat. I think, *I love you and I hate lying to you.*

If I could only wake up a year on from now and this baby was born and somehow – *even with knowing everything that you never wanted to know* – you still wanted me again.

It'd be a year well worth sacrificing.

## 21

## WILL

'So, Will.' Hannah, the occupational therapist who's just called me into her room, tilts her head to one side, seeming pleased to see me. 'From the way you've walked in here, I'd say you're making a very good recovery?'

'I hope so.' I sit down on the chair opposite her desk and fold one leg easily over the other.

'Seriously, you're looking well.'

'I've come from a very nice lunch.' I smile. 'With a very nice girl.'

'Your fiancée?'

I blink.

'Sort of,' I say. 'Soon, I hope.'

'Excellent,' she beams. 'That is really good news. Because, even though you and your girl have been together...' she glances at her notes '... three years, you didn't actually recall her, last time we spoke?'

Last time we spoke, shortly after the op, I'd barely wanted to stand, let alone discuss the strangers who'd suddenly presented themselves as the most important people in my life.

'I didn't remember Ava,' I agree. 'But, she's an easy person to fall in love with.' I open my hands. 'You going to ask me to do some of those horrible yoga poses again?'

She laughs. 'Not today.' She runs cursorily over the form I've filled in for her and then sits back, looking me up and down appraisingly.

'How've things been, Will?'

'Very good.'

'No headaches, blurry vision, flashing lights?' I shake my head, and she rattles off: 'Dizziness when bending, deep brain ache, soreness of the scalp?'

I shake my head.

'Exhaustion?'

'That one,' I am forced to admit. 'Yes.' It's only after meeting Toby a couple of days ago that I've attempted to do any real work, but it's been challenging to say the least. 'I want to do a lot more than I find I'm physically able to. It's frustrating,' I tell her. 'I feel okay, but as soon as I start doing anything, I quickly get tired. Also, everything I do attempt seems to be taking me a long time.'

'It's not been very long,' she says.

'No?'

'This could take months! Go easy on yourself. You should expect it to take that long before you begin to feel anything like normal again.' While I'm still chewing on that, she says, 'Oh. And I see you've logged a change of address, here?'

'I'm back living with my girlfriend.'

'Good man. So, keeping active, Will?'

'Too much,' I say ruefully. 'I did a lot of walking in the town one Saturday afternoon. A *lot*.' Just so she knows. 'I ended up having to spend most of Sunday in bed.'

'You probably overdid it,' Hannah says. 'What about hobbies and your usual activities? It says here you're a musician. You play the guitar, the piano and all sorts – very impressive! Also excellent for getting back all kinds of co-ordination and memory function.' She looks up. 'Have you been keeping up with any of that?'

I nod. 'I've been getting back into my music.'

'Notice anything different, when you're playing?'

I give a small laugh. 'Would you believe me if I said that I can hear music *in my head* that much more loudly? And the notes, the music, everything sounds so much clearer somehow, than it did before.'

'You're turning into Beethoven!' She laughs. 'Actually, enhanced auditory perception – especially if you're already a musician – is not unheard of.' She adds, 'It can also go the other way, but I'm glad in this case it's worked out for you. And how about your co-ordination, when you're actually playing the instruments?'

I think about that for a moment. 'No difference that I've noticed... is that something I need to look out for?'

'Not so much. All that uses a different memory circuit, but I have to ask. Anyhow, this is looking brilliant.' Hannah puts her pen down and looks up for a moment.

'And how would you rate your overall mood, post-op?' she wants to know. 'How've you been feeling *in yourself*?'

I shrug. 'Overall, I'm happy. Pretty happy.' I give a small laugh. 'I have every reason to be. Don't I?'

'True. But we don't always feel exactly what we expect to feel.'

'No?'

'Not always.'

'Okay, well. It's true my life feels... odd, in so many ways. I'm still trying to understand what's happened to me, where everyone's gone, what my place is in the...' I swallow; I won't say *in the world* '... in the scheme of things, but...' I shoot her a small smile now. 'I also recently learned that my girlfriend's expecting. Of all the news I could've woken up to hear, that's got to be the best.'

'It must be. Congratulations.' Her eyes crinkle softly. 'That's wonderful.' Then she seems to wake up, gathering her thoughts.

'So. Bathroom activities all normal, Will?'

'Bathroom...? Uh – yes.' Only because Andy gave me some syrupy concoction before I left the hospital, telling me things wouldn't quite work if I didn't have it.

'Really? Oh, well done!' She scribbles that down enthusiastically. I get the impression that's a *he's doing well* point.

Hannah stops writing again. 'You're really looking forward to this, I can tell.'

I blink. Looking forward to...?

'The baby,' she prompts.

'Ah, yes.' We're back to that.

'Planned, or a complete surprise?'

'The latter,' I tell her. Definitely the latter, to me at least. Even if Ava tells me we were ready for it.

'Something to keep you in good spirits though, eh? Your first child. Wonderful. I bet everyone around you is thrilled too?'

'They are.' I laugh quietly. 'I called my mum to share the great news, Saturday night, and... "Oh, good," she said. "So, we're telling people now? Thank goodness, it's been killing me keeping quiet." She already knew.'

'Well, she would,' Hannah says. 'As did you, before.'

'It still felt odd, Mum knowing about it before I did. It kind of stole my thunder a little bit.'

'I can imagine.' She grins. 'Consider for a moment those poor souls before you who've woken up from their op to the reality of a houseful of hormonal teenagers they have no recollection about...'

'That sounds really... horrible.'

She looks back at her note pad, apparently getting through her list of questions at a satisfactory rate.

'And, how about the journalling? Have you managed to do any? I won't ask to see it unless you specifically want to share, it's for you, but, believe me, it *will* be a great help to you, further down the line.'

'It's coming along,' I tell her. Hannah jots that down, too, and then shakes out her hand, as if she's finished doing a timed exam, and says, 'Well, then, I think that's all we need.' Glancing at her watch, 'Any questions for me, Will?'

'Not really, only...' Now that she's mentioning stuff that'll help me *further down the line*, I'm wondering why I didn't leave more instructions on how to sync back into my own life than I did.

Just the thought of some of my upcoming tasks, like, for instance, my meeting tomorrow with the bank who've kindly locked me out of their systems, is enough to give me a *deep brain ache*.

I might not always be the best organised person, but I need to know I'm solvent, how my finances are going to be over the next few weeks and months.

'I wish I'd made better preparation for this, beforehand,' I muse. 'It would've been very handy to have some more clues about what to do, *what to expect*, in this phase.'

Sure, I did leave myself some pre-op thoughts. Ava showed me some things I'd written down, about *where I wanted to live* and such. There was that small snippet of me on Ava's phone, talking about the op. Also, that other segment she showed me where I clearly knew we were expecting. It didn't feel like a lot to have left myself, though. It didn't feel like *enough*.

'We usually recommend it, if at all possible.' Hannah nods. 'Some clinicians will even help you with it – we have some special forms. If you had completed any of that with my other colleague who saw you pre-op, she'd have sent a copy home to you, though. You'd already have had sight of it.'

Which I haven't.

She adds, 'We suggest writing down all the things you think you're going to need to let yourself know. It can be very hard to take it all in, otherwise.'

I say ruefully, 'I'm guessing there was probably little time for it, between the diagnosis and my op?'

Hannah frowns. 'No, I don't *think* that's so.' She goes back to read through my file. 'You had ample time to have left yourself some useful instructions if you'd had a mind to.'

'You think I might have been too shocked, maybe?' Too taken up with so much news coming in all at once that I simply never got my head in gear, never managed to get organised?

She's gone quiet. 'Some patients simply can't take in what's happening to them at the time,' Hannah says gently after a bit. 'I *have* known patients who never made any provisions for future reference because they'd already made up their mind they weren't going to need them.'

'How so?'

She hesitates for a moment, stacking the papers on her desk in a neat pile. Then she says, 'Some people do refuse this operation. Believe me, it does happen.'

'Not me,' I tell her.

But she's looking at me very strangely.

'Has no one actually spoken to you about any of this... what your state of mind was, before you decided to have this operation, Will?'

'My state of mind?'

'It indicates here in your notes that you were... highly depressed.'

'Me?' I give a small, uncertain laugh. 'Must have got the wrong person, Hannah!' Toby told me himself, didn't he, *how happy I was*, when he rang and I'd told him Ava and I were expecting? And then I'd written all that beautiful music...

'I don't think that could have been me.'

'Okay, well.' She shuts my file and it doesn't occur to me in time to ask if I could look at the notes, before she's already up and opening the door for me.

'You seem very happy now, and that's all that matters, right?'

'Sure,' I say. Her next patient is waiting. Whoever wrote those last notes must've got it all wrong. I wasn't depressed before this op. I was cock-a-hoop!

There must be some other reason why I never made myself any post-operative instruction notes.

But as I walk down the hospital corridor her last words, for some reason, won't stop echoing in my head.

## 22

## AVA

Robyn's saying, 'So, what *did* you two talk about, over your cosy lunch?'

'He didn't ask me to marry him, if that's what you're driving at!' I dump the contents of one entire drawer onto the floor where my sister and I have been sitting for the past hour, and the small remaining visible patch of carpet in my spare room disappears under a pile of folders.

'You sure?' she persists. 'I definitely got the impression you were a little cheerier when I saw you walk through that door earlier on.'

'Was I?' I hide my smile. 'I guess I was, then.'

'Go on,' she says.

I relent. 'Will wanted to know if we'd been trying very long, for the baby.' I glance up at her.

'Oh, yeah?' A wide grin crosses her face. She's at that age. I pull her thoughts back.

'Yeah. He asked if we'd thought of any baby names, all that kind of stuff.' I hand her a fat, battered looking folder to direct her mind back onto task. I need to retrieve some dress designs I sketched out a while back. Ones that I'm hoping Ginny might be interested in. *Strike while the iron's hot*, she always says, so I've been working flat out on potential costumes ever since our meeting at her offices on Monday. Robyn's here to assist.

'We're looking for a green, long sleeved princess dress, with back eyelets and cording closure and a short train,' I remind her. 'The belt, as I recall, had a suede trim.'

'He's certainly still keen, then?' Robyn's not listening. 'On the idea of the baby, at any rate. How about you two? Any flirting going on...?'

'Definitely.' I add, 'We kissed when we went our separate ways after the restaurant.' I smile, remembering it. 'It was a very nice kiss.'

She's looking at me slightly enviously. 'Lucky you!'

I close the folder I'm working on, recalling that Robyn's not had fantastic luck so far when it comes to finding herself a man.

'It was... nice. Being with him. We went through some of the usual social media pics so he got a look at some of our friends. He was also keen to know who all the contacts in his phone were.'

I put on my version of Will's voice, 'There's this dude in here called Red Sphynx. I have a friend called RED SPHYNX!'

Robyn doubles over. 'So, he didn't know...'

'That it's the name of the music production company he works with...?' I grin. 'He thought it might be some creepy nightclub owner, or some other dubious character – don't ask!'

She chuckles. Then, a little more thoughtful, she adds, 'I take it you didn't talk about...' She opens her hands out to take the folder I'm holding. 'You know. Anything controversial, then?'

'No,' I tell her. 'We didn't.'

'He really doesn't remember *anything*?'

'Like they said.'

'Well, good,' she asserts. 'Leave the past in the past, right?'

'That's probably the best place for it.'

I bite my lip.

My sister puts her head down, rifling through her pile quickly and pulling out a picture of a green dress. 'This one any good?'

I shake my head.

'Just so you know,' she adds quietly, 'I got Carenza to take down those photos off her blog like you requested.'

I carefully don't look up. 'Thank you. Much appreciated, Robbie.' It's one thing less to worry about. But Robyn hasn't let it go quite yet.

'She wasn't thrilled but she did as I asked.' My sister adds, '*Some* of the pics of you that you wanted removed happened to also be the best ones of the birthday cake and her other mate, who made it, was keen for the exposure, even if...' Robyn pauses slightly '... you weren't.'

I let out a silent breath. 'They can crop the cake and still use the pics, I'm sure.'

She shrugs.

'Hey, sis, I totally understand why you wanted those pics taken down, and that's fine, but... it wasn't really such a big deal, was it? After all, you did nothing wrong.'

'No.' I look away uneasily.

'You *didn't*, Ava.'

'I know I didn't,' I say slowly, aware that *it's happening again* – me having to lie to someone who I care about because it's the only way I can keep this thing going. And I hate, *hate* having to lie to people. Especially my sister.

She's still looking at me curiously, so I explain again.

'Listen, the only reason it's a big deal is because of the place William finds himself in, currently.' She knows all this. 'He doesn't recognise himself any more. He doesn't know us, what we were to each other. He doesn't *know* that me going to your party wasn't a big deal. I don't want to have any photos hanging around that could fuel any doubts, that's all.'

'It's okay,' she says. 'I get it.'

We stare at each other for a bit and, finally, Robyn looks away.

'About this little spare room of yours,' she changes the subject at last. 'The Butterfly Gardens is such a short walk from here, if only you guys would agree to let me come and stay here in this little room, it would be *so* much more convenient for work.'

I frown slightly, recalling I once promised her that if she ever did any summer work at the tea rooms, she could come stay at ours, only now the picture's changed.

'The trouble is...'

'Plus,' she adds, eyes sparkling, 'whenever I wasn't working, I'd always be around.'

Precisely. While I'm happy for her to drop by, Robyn can't come and live with us. I already told her, things are still too delicate between me and Will. Three's a crowd and, besides, let's face it, my sister's not exactly a quiet, tactful person. She'd be bound to bring up something I don't want mentioned, and I simply can't afford to risk it.

'It's not for long, though – you'll be back at uni soon?'

As I push the empty drawer back in place to get it out of the way, she drops in casually, 'I'm not sure any more that I'm cut out for doing this marketing course though, Ava. I've been getting horrible grades. I might just... drop it.'

'What?' I stop what I'm doing. I knew she wasn't happy with her grades, but she's a clever girl, a capable girl, and there's a good reason why her grades have been so low. I remind her, 'Hey – what if you gave up on it and you end up living at home with our parents, permanently?'

She gives a shudder and I laugh.

'Hon, have you never thought that if you'd maybe spent a little less time socialising and a little more time actually *working* on your course assignments, you might make it work?'

She gives a tiny shrug, admitting, 'I think it might be too late for that. Besides, it was so *hard*.'

When I don't answer, she changes tack.

'Everyone on my course was a mature student and it wasn't till after I met Carenza and her crowd that things picked up.' She adds wistfully, 'There she was, always surrounded by so many fun people from her drama course and they always seemed to be having such a good time...'

She's lonely, is the problem. And, right now, aimless.

'Can't I please stay here? I'll be gone by the time the baby arrives...'

'Sweetie, *you can't*.'

Robyn hunches over, examining her fingernails miserably.

'Hey,' I remind her. 'You're not a child and... you've got friends. Ask someone to stay with you while Mum and Dad are away,' I put in. 'Why don't you?' I'm also thinking, having one of her uni friends around might be all the encouragement she needs not to leave her course.

The suggestion seems to cheer her. 'I might just do that.'

I smile. 'Now – let's crack on and find this princess dress, shall we?'

The box file she's currently got open doesn't look too promising. She's about to pull some of the papers out, when I hear her laugh. 'Don't think I'll find too much that's of any use in *this* one.' She's right. It's a miscellaneous bunch of utility bills, old birthday cards and general paperwork that nobody was prepared to either file or throw away at the time. Robyn's plucked out one of Will's old band promo photos. 'Cute!' She's grinning. 'Your boyfriend would've been no more than my age at the time.'

'Oh, my!' She's right. I take it from her, my eyebrows going up as another picture slips out from behind the first one.

'And... who's *she*?' Robyn crowds in curiously over my shoulder. 'Some groupie?'

'His ex, actually. She was their assistant tour manager at the time.'

'Hmm.' Robyn's silent for a bit. She might at times be the most annoying sister in the world but she's nothing if not loyal. 'I think she's ugly.'

I laugh. 'She's not *ugly*, Robyn.' We both examine the picture of the long haired, long legged brunette.

Robyn comments, 'I think she is. Too much slap on. He must've forgotten to chuck that one away.'

'Will is *rubbish* at throwing things away,' I point out. It's true. He's got the habit of keeping everything. I reach for my scrunchie to re-secure my ponytail, pushing back the surge of unease I'm feeling. The spectre of his ex has been a pain in my side but I don't like to think of myself as the jealous type.

'Still...' My sister's looking at me closely, putting two and two together. 'Is she the same woman you told me about, who was trying to worm her way back into his life the moment she found out that you two had separated for a bit?'

*Did I tell her about that?*

'Um...' I stare at Robyn, uncomfortably.

She adds, 'The one with the ridiculous name: She-she?'

'That's not her real name.' Which matters not one jot, of course. I put my head down, still trying to get on with my search for the elusive design, but it's no good, the happy image of Will and his pouting ex standing so comfortably close together has already etched itself indelibly onto my mind's eye. *If only I could forget everything, like you have, Will.*

*You have no idea how much I sometimes wish that I, too, could forget.*

# 23

## AVA

I slide the old photo with Will and his ex back into its folder but it's no good, I can't focus.

Was it really only February when I turned up at DelRoy's flat with Will's leather biker gloves in hand? The temperatures had dropped that low, there were icicles sparkling in the trees. *If I close my eyes, I can still smell the cold.* I'd found Will's gloves in the wooden box in my hall, knew he'd be missing them, told myself I only wanted to return his belongings, but... in reality, the visit was an excuse to see Will.

Would he want to see me, though? We'd split after Christmas, following weeks of stupid, pointless arguing. We'd been at the point where neither of us knew what we wanted any more, except, once without him, I knew only that I felt utterly bereft. I wanted him back, but did he want the same? How long did I wait at the door of his flat before summoning up the courage to ring his doorbell? I waited, even though I still had his spare key!

*Ages*, I stood there, my nose getting redder and more numb with the cold, not daring to ring it, watching the wind shiver through the vacant, icy little cobweb lacing the corner of his flat door, dreading the worst. Now that we were no longer together – what if he'd left, returned to his family up north? My plans to blithely post the gloves through Will's letterbox and scarper evaporated. Instead, I stood there till my toes went numb, realising that there was no way I could leave without seeing him.

When I finally rang the bell, Will opened up so quickly it was as if he'd been standing there on the other side of it, waiting for me. I can still recall the blue long sleeved shirt he was wearing, the thin leather strip around his neck that he always wore, the one I'd given him. And his huge, sad, smile – *filled with relief* – to see me standing there. Something happened inside me, then. Everything melted away, all the cross words and the recriminations and the heated disappointments of the last few months. All I knew was that I loved him. I could see in Will's eyes that he loved me too. It had been a mistake, nothing but a huge mistake, us splitting up.

And then... I heard *her* voice, ChiChi, calling him back into the sitting room.

The expression on his face immediately changed, as if she'd broken a spell – or maybe she had cast one?

*'Hey.'* I can hear Robyn's voice, coming from somewhere far away. She's been talking about my costume designs, how pretty they all are, prattling merrily away like she used to when we were both kids and I'd make dresses for her dolls.

*'You okay?'*

'I'm fine.'

*It's all going to work out.* William told me that, on the sea wall, didn't he? He said it again, when we were eating our lunch. How he very much hoped that we'd grow close, become a couple, again. I know he's starting to fancy me; it's obvious every time he looks at me. It's *me* he wants, not...

I shuffle some papers through my hands, trying to look purposeful for my sister, but the truth is I'm not seeing a single thing that's in front of my eyes right now.

Had Will asked me into the flat, that day I turned up unexpectedly, or had I gone in to see for myself? That bit I don't remember.

I *do* remember walking into the sitting room to the shock of finding

ChiChi already sitting there, long legs up, all comfy, with a large coffee mug cradled in her hands.

'We're... having some coffee,' he said to me. His voice cracked. There was a bottle of some creamy liqueur out on the coffee table, too. Her drink. She'd have brought that one. Will cleared his throat. 'Would you like...?'

'Yes,' I told him. Contrary cow that I am. Had I interrupted something? If I had, it was going to be a good, long interruption, I'd make sure of that. I settled onto the middle of the sofa, eyes locked onto her huge, luminous ones. She seemed almost amused. I turned to him.

'I'd *love* some coffee, Will.'

When he went to the kitchen area to fetch it, 'He's been sharing his troubles,' ChiChi said to me. 'With an old friend. This *is* okay, isn't it?' She fluttered her eyelashes innocently. 'You don't mind? I believe you two are currently split up, yes?'

I did mind. *So what* if Will and I weren't together? We hadn't properly let go of each other yet, had we? I hadn't. I didn't want to. Did he?

He answered for me, coming back from the kitchen.

'We're... on a break.'

His ex sipped her drink, still gloating in my direction.

Will said, 'Thank you for bringing me the gloves, Ava.' When he put the coffee down beside me, I got the impression there was so much else he wanted to say. But then she chipped in, eyes sparkling.

'Lucky thing for me, eh?' As if the gloves had never been mentioned, her mind still on his availability.

My sister calls me more forcefully back to her. 'Um, Ava... there's *this*, too.'

I look up. 'Sorry, sis. My mind went off somewhere there for a bit. Looking at all this old stuff...' I clear my throat. 'What's that you've got there?'

I take it from her, distracted. The white envelope with Will's name and address handwritten on the front looks fairly innocuous.

'That looks like a woman's handwriting and it's not yours.' Robyn's looking at me closely. 'From her?'

'What?' My thoughts are still in DelRoy's flat, but I need to get my head back in gear. Then I give an uncertain laugh. Robyn's always had the uncanniest ability to read my mind at times. It's a pain.

'That is *most* unlikely.' I turn the envelope over, but don't open it. The letter is quite thin. 'It's only some... small thing, feels like some old passport photos,' I tell her.

I hand Robyn a safe, thin pink folder that I'm fairly sure contains only dress designs.

'Leave that other, old miscellaneous folder to one side, for now, will you?'

My sister remains unconvinced. 'You're not going to look?'

'It won't be anything important, Robbie. After we split, some of Will's stuff inevitably got left behind and I must've stowed his things all over the place.' Whatever it is, it's his, anyway, not mine.

She doesn't move. To oblige her, I open up the thin envelope. A narrow strip of photos – taken, as I'd imagined, in a photo booth – falls into my hand. Photos of Will and his ex, clowning around, all taken long before Will and I ever met, I know, and yet the fact that *he's still kept all this...* it stings, deeply. Especially after... I look away, deliberately keeping my voice bright.

'Gosh, he looks young in these, doesn't he? Even younger than he thinks he is now!'

'I'd chuck all that out if I were you,' Robyn's muttering. 'It belongs in the past he's lost and it needs to stay there.'

'I wish,' I tell her. 'Only he hasn't lost that bit. He remembered his ex well enough from a picture on the wall in DelRoy's flat the other day.' I look at the floor. At the mess I've made, looking for one, single sketch, and I suddenly feel very, very weary. As if my energy just drained out of me faster than the air in a punctured tyre.

'Besides, I can't just throw Will's things out, Robbie.' I force a smile at her. 'I'll ask him later on what he wants to do with them.'

She doesn't return my smile. 'Why?' she wants to know. 'Why can't you chuck those pictures away? They've clearly upset you, and he probably doesn't even know any longer that they exist...'

'No,' I tell her.

After a few moments, she says, 'Is *this* the princess dress you were looking for?'

'Aha! The very one.' I give her a quick hug, glad that we've found it but, at the same time, deeply perplexed at how put out I'm still feeling. How those stupid, old goofing-around photos of Will with his ex haven't quite left my thoughts yet.

I lean in surreptitiously to pick them up.

'What's wrong now?' Robyn mutters.

'Nothing. It's a little hot in here, that's all...'

'Sis?'

I'm up on my feet, feeling my legs trembling, pretending I'm fumbling with the blinds, adjusting the amount of sunlight streaming in, but I'm actually taking in some deep, deep breaths of air. These pictures are ancient and I shouldn't care so much only it's *hard* for me to remain nonchalant about it all; hard for me to dismiss Will's relationship with his ex and these fading, forgotten photos in the way I know I should, when... *that woman* is at the root of so much of the dilemma I now find myself in.

Did Will mean to keep them, or is this just typical of him? Whatever his thinking was they can't *be* here. In my house. I know what I said to Robyn about not chucking away his property, but still...

My back turned to her, I crumple the photo strip into a ball, stuffing it into my pocket. I'll dispose of it quietly, later on. There's no need for Robyn to know how much it's really affected me. I will keep it in the quiet place where I hold that other thing I'm keeping, and nobody needs to know.

Nobody ever shall.

Outside, high up in the blue sky, some small grey clouds are forming, marching our way, squalls coming. The seabirds are circling; they know it. I know it.

# 24

# WILL

'Oh, you're in *here*, Will?' Ava's dashed into the bedroom unbuttoning her wet coat, but she's just stopped abruptly. 'I'm sorry – I came in to make sure the windows were all closed. I didn't mean to barge in on you.' I pat the space beside me. She drapes her coat over the back of a chair and then, pushing back damp hair, comes and sits on the edge of the bed.

I smile. 'I had a shower and, when I came out, I went to lie down for what I thought would be five minutes and it's somehow turned into...' The daylight coming through the window behind her has all but faded, whatever was left of it swallowed by dark rain clouds a while ago. I glance at the bedside clock... 'Three *hours*? Jeez.'

She laughs quietly, her eyes flickering over me. I lean back easily with my hands behind my head.

'Cold, out?'

'A bit!' When she drops her gaze, stretching out her limbs, I'm mesmerised. The light from the hallway picks up all the droplets of rain on her hair, turning them into a myriad of little golden lights.

'Did you have a productive afternoon after we parted post-lunch?'

'Busy!' she breathes. 'I got caught up in town and the traffic coming home was *horrible* and I was worried about the...' She stops, looking apologetic. 'I did shoot you a text, to say I'd be in a little late.'

'So you did.'

'I was worried you might not get it.' Ava's distracted, today, though doing her best to hide it. 'We don't always get the best signal down here.'

'As I've picked up.'

A flash of light at the window elicits an intake of breath. Ava kicks off her shoes and climbs onto the bed beside me. Maybe she's feeling cold, because I can see she's shivering a little.

'It's going to be a close one,' she says. Out here at Beach Cottage, as I'm learning, when the weather comes in, we get the full force of it. 'One, two, three, four...' The light flash is followed rapidly by a loud crack of thunder. I see her eyebrows go up.

'Four miles,' I say.

She leans back, flat on the bed, crossing her arms over her stomach. I'm here. Right here, beside her, but she's quiet again. She came in that way, didn't she?

'You seem a little sad today.'

'I'm just really tired.'

'Doing too much?' She's had to run around after me, because of this tiredness I've had, and I get a flash of guilt. According to the baby book I was reading, she should be resting up, too.

'I noticed, when I went in looking for my guitar, that you'd even been clearing out the spare room.'

'Ah, yes.' Her eyes open up wide as if she's been caught out, somehow. 'Me and Robyn were in there earlier, looking for a folder with some of my designs.'

'You found it?'

'What?'

'The folder.'

'We did.' There's a long pause before she adds, 'That's what I went into town to buy fabric for. I'm planning to do a mock-up of that dress tomorrow, and...' She looks at me strangely, her voice flat. 'We also found... lots of... your old papers that'll need sorting out at some point, but they're not important.'

'You *have* been busy.' I add softly, 'That's a heavy sigh.'

'I'm sorry, Will.' She rolls over onto her side to face me. 'I'm a little preoccupied, it's true, but...' she reaches out to touch my arm lightly '... the best and nicest bit of all of today was the time I spent with you.'

'It was absolutely the best part of my day, too!' I catch hold of her hand and when she smiles, the tension lines furrowing her brow disappear.

'About lunch,' I add. 'Don't think I won't reimburse you when I get through to my bank tomorrow.'

She laughs.

'No need. We're good, Will!'

'If you won't let me pay for our lunch, then I'll have to think of something even better to repay you with.'

She pushes back her hair, smiling softly. 'Oh, yes? Like what?'

'You'll have to let me take you on some European city break. Paris for the weekend. Or... Venice? Would you like that?'

'Ooh la-la!' The dimples come out now. 'This is all sounding dangerously close to being *romantic*, Will.'

'Well, it's supposed to.' I smile, even though I feel a bit sheepish saying it out loud. 'I'm wooing you, aren't I?'

'Are you?'

'Yeah, I'm wooing you all over again, like a man would who's just met a girl he likes and wants to get to know her better. And... I really would like to get to know you better.'

'I'm glad.'

There's that sigh again.

'What about your day?' Ava attempts to inject a little enthusiasm into her voice for me. 'Did you hear anything back from the bank?'

'Only a text confirming my appointment with them first thing tomorrow.'

'Oh, and how did the OT visit go?' She remembers suddenly.

'It went great! I think I answered her questions just fine.'

'Yay!' Ava jiggles her arms in the air, a celebratory gesture that does nothing to belie how low her energy is tonight. 'You're making a great recovery, Will.'

'So it seems. There was one question she couldn't answer for me, though.'

'What's that?'

I hesitate. 'It was the whole issue of why I never left myself more instructions for what to expect, post-op. For instance, this whole problem I've got to sort with the bank tomorrow could've been avoided if only I'd done so.'

Ava's silent so I press, 'Hannah tells me I refused the operation, initially? That I was *depressed*.' I turn round, facing her full on. 'I don't get how that could've been true, though? I was overjoyed about the baby – how could I have been so down?'

'Will. It *is* true.' Ava's busy tracing the embroidered whorl pattern on our duvet cover with her finger, round and round, her voice very quiet. 'It's true, though it's also true that you were overjoyed about the baby.'

I take that in for a moment, recognising that there must've been more going on for me, before the op, than meets the eye.

'So... *why*, then?'

'Why?' She lets out a long, uneven breath. 'Because shortly after learning about the pregnancy, we also had the letter through that indicated there might be something wrong with you.' She hesitates. 'You were reluctant to do anything about it initially. By the time you booked a doctor's appointment and they'd redone the blood tests and then you had a CT scan that led to an MRI and we'd realised you had something very bad going on...'

Her voice catches.

'We went from being overjoyed to the news that you might not have very long to live, after all.'

I frown, still trying to understand.

'I get that, but – *why* wouldn't I have jumped at the chance of this life-saving operation?'

'You didn't, because...' She looks down, swallowing. *'Because*, they had such a small window of time to make an effective surgical intervention. There was so little time to process anything, Will! You needed that operation asap or you knew it would kill you in the long run only... you also knew you'd lose a large chunk of your memory. You were saying things like, "I've just got my life together – if I lose it all, what's the point?" And yes, without the op...' she bites her lip '... they couldn't guarantee how long you'd have left.'

My mouth has fallen open. 'That's it? So, I was still hoping I could beat this thing without having an op, because I didn't want to lose my memory?'

'You didn't want to lose who you *were*, Will. Your sense of you. Your music. That's what was scaring you. It was a horrendous decision to make. And you didn't have very long to make it.'

'And then, I suppose,' I say slowly, 'there was always the risk of the op going horribly wrong?' My old nightmare returns to haunt me. 'With me ending up all...' I do a shimmering motion with my fingers, over my head '... like Maracas Man?'

She nods, agreeing softly. 'There was always that.'

I tell her, 'I know it must sound crazy but that *terrible film* about a mad scientist who went around pulling buskers off the streets, tampering with their brains and turning them all into zombies... it's never left me.'

Hearing her sad laugh, I say, 'I always thought that must be the worst fate for any street musician! Maracas Man was unknown but still talented, someone with big dreams, who could've *been* someone, until...' My voice gets tangled in my throat and Ava finishes for me.

'Until the scientist altered him and he ended up a zombie?'

I ask, feeling a little bemused, 'You think maybe part of my thought process could've been influenced by that old film?'

She lifts her shoulders. She doesn't know, but it makes some sense to me.

'He lost it all, Ava. Only in his case...' I frown softly '... there'd been a part of him that never let go of his music, see. He still *wanted* to play. Only, he couldn't. Nothing except the maracas.'

In the end, that became his signature. When people from the town would hear his maracas, they'd run for the hills in terror, knowing he was coming.

'Maracas Man,' I say, 'was a zombie *who knew what he was*, what he'd lost.'

'You mean... he knew he'd never be able to fulfil his creative potential?'

'That's exactly it.' I shoot her a glance. She does understand, it seems. 'And that's what I was scared of?'

'That was part of it, Will.'

We're both silent for a while, and I get a sinking feeling. This is surely something it would've been important for me to know and the fact Ava didn't see it is disappointing. Has she forgotten our agreement? She's promised to be open with me. Always. I look at her sideways.

'Were you ever going to tell me? Even if I felt that way before the op, you do realise that, after I came out of it feeling as well and as whole as I did, that might have been a good time to explain?'

She makes a strangled noise in her throat, shakes her head – *what am I missing? Am I not seeing something blindingly obvious?* And suddenly it dawns on me.

'Oh, my word. You were *scared*, weren't you?'

'What?' Ava sits up in the bed, pulls her knees up to her chest and her skin is covered in goosebumps. I can see them on her arms, each time a flash of lightning comes through the blinds.

'I imagine it must have scared *you*, too?' I say softly. 'You must have been terrified I'd end up unable to be of any use to you either as a partner or as a father to our child.'

Her chin lifts slightly.

'My parents brought me and Robyn up to be strong, competent women. I knew I'd cope, whatever came.' Her voice goes a little quieter. 'The only one thing I was ever scared about was... *Oh!*'

A huge flash of light, together with an ear shattering clap of thunder, breaks directly overhead, and she jumps right out of her side of the bed and straight into my arms.

'How much longer is this going to go on for?' She's covering her face with her hands. Despite what we've been speaking about I can't help laughing out loud.

'Not that much that scares you, eh?' Outside, the wooden shutters on the other side of the house must have partially broken loose because we can hear the wind whipping them to and fro, bang, bang, *bang*. It's wild out here tonight. Beyond the dunes behind our house, I know the storm waves will be crashing on the dark beach. Elemental. Fierce. When I draw Ava in close towards me, she's trembling. She pulls the duvet right up to our chins.

'So, what's the one thing that you get scared about, Mrs Strong and Competent – thunder and lightning storms?'

She doesn't answer me for a few long moments. Then she turns her face up towards mine. 'I was scared of *losing you*, Will. I wanted you to live, I needed you to live, and you… you didn't want to.'

That gets me somehow, right here in the chest.

'I'm sorry I put you through that.' What else is there for me to say? The Will who put her through that wasn't *me* though. I don't know him. 'I wouldn't do that to you,' I assure her. She has been through a lot, this girl, for the first time I am starting to appreciate how much, but I am here. I am going to be here.

The thunder cracks overhead again. I bend my head down, my lips brushing softly against hers. If this were any other time in my life – if my poor, beleaguered body were up for it – I know exactly where this would be headed but, as I've already discovered on a couple of occasions since my op, it is not to be. Not yet.

'Thank you for being honest with me tonight, Ava. Please, always know that you can be.' Her head still buried in my chest, her answer is a muffled blur.

We lie there for over an hour, listening to the storm battering against the windowpanes, whipping the pampas grass in the garden, rattling at the shutters and against the back door. So much rain. She falls asleep long before I do and I lie awake for a long time, holding her.

Afterwards, when I roll her gently onto one side so I can take some rest, there's a cold spot where her face was lying against me, the breast pocket of my T-shirt all wet.

'You won't believe what she said.' The metal bench where we're sitting, just outside the bank, is still damp from last night's storm. I stretch out my legs, the bottom of my jeans still soaked from the run-off on the road. Toby's smiling at me.

'Go on, then.'

'The last bank representative I spoke to over the phone actually used these words: "I am afraid, Mr Tyler, that you do not exist."'

'You don't, huh?' Toby's dark eyebrows point straight downwards in a cartoon-style '*that's bad*' expression.

'According to the bank, I am nowhere on their system, and so I don't exist.' I kick at an empty can that has rolled near my foot, under the bench, and ham it up. 'If they prick me, will I not bleed?' I say. 'If they tickle me, will I not laugh?'

'Apparently not.' Toby rolls his eyes. 'Though I'd take care before allowing any of these banking types near you with a feather duster. Some of 'em can get a little kinky, I hear.'

'Funny.' But it is not really. *How* can I be nowhere on their system, at either of the addresses I've given them? How can my own bank claim not to know who I am? Even though I've explained the situation, over and over, each time to a more senior 'supervisor', and I'm told that, unless I can provide a whole bunch of codes and pin numbers and passwords – none of which I have – they will decline to speak to me, further. In the interests of security, they say. I'm dead to them.

'If I get no joy today, I'm gonna have to up the ante...' I mutter.

'Try going in packing a Nef 929, son, and see how soon folks turn all friendly and reasonable. My uncle Dilbert once had a beef with—'

'A *what* 929?' I pull a bored frown. 'Is that the ice cream with a chocolate flake on the top?'

'That's a Flake 99,' he corrects. 'One of the first – and most important – local details I learned upon entering your quaint country. A Nef is a little larger, a little heavier and, when it goes off, a little louder. Though of course...' he winks at me '... I'm fully aware you Brits generally prefer to *protest most strenuously* and fill in a bunch of complaint forms, first.'

'Your suggestion may have some merit,' I tell him. 'A little size, a little weight and a little more noise. It's taken me long enough even to set this meeting up, given that they've been reluctant to accept that I have an account with them in the first place.'

He frowns. 'You've got to wonder about things like identity theft and so on, don't you? If they don't think you're you... then who *do* they think is you?'

'No one.' I look up. 'I don't exist, remember?'

'Bizarre. Still... once you get this money business sorted out, you'll hopefully be able to devote your full attention to the matter of our *magnum opus*. Eh?'

'I sure hope so, Toby.' I've had this tune running in my head ever since I awoke this morning, and I'm hankering to get to our session, as I know he is. Sitting here in my beanie hat and wet jeans with the plastic bag full of my papers Ava hurriedly sorted out for me this morning on my lap, I don't feel much like a professional. I feel more like the nothing-to-his-name twenty-seven year old I woke up thinking I was. The guy who hadn't got his shit sorted out yet. Him.

'I've not been making a huge deal of it to anyone else, but this whole situation with my money, it stinks, man. It's been getting me down, a bit.'

'I understand.' He slaps me gently on the arm. 'You know, if you need anything, I'd always be more than willing...'

'Appreciate it.' I grimace. 'Let's hope by the time I join you at DelRoy's place later, this is all sorted. I'll need to be providing for a family, soon...'

'Talking of the family,' he segues artfully, 'all going well with you and little Mama, I take it?'

I laugh. 'She'd be horrified to hear you call her that, but yes.' I smile. 'Our relationship's growing, day on day. She's... sweet and loving and kind,' I say shyly. 'I'm getting comfortable with her.'

'Hallelujah!'

I glance up at him, feeling a touch of guilt. 'Even though I still get the feeling that she's a little sad, at times. She puts it down to the baby hormones.'

'That could be true.' Toby brings a harmonica out of his pocket and plays a catchy riff. His tune and the tune playing in my head compete for a little while. A police siren blasts by. Some other customers, also waiting, start talking to each other loudly and eventually the song my brain has been playing drops out. I groan, rubbing my face with my hands.

'It could be hormones or maybe it's about me,' I admit reluctantly. 'Maybe it's because of some of the things I learned about yesterday, like, how I never even wanted to have this operation, how I apparently *initially refused it*?'

Toby stops playing his harmonica. Wipes the mouthpiece carefully on his sleeve and his deep, baritone voice is soft now.

'That was a very sad week in my life, brother.'

'You knew?' I blink, feeling a little stunned. 'You *knew* that I'd refused it?'

'I knew.'

Okay, so he knew. We were friends, after all.

'*Why*, though?' I lean in a little. Sure, Ava explained it all to me last night and there were plausible reasons, but still. 'They tell me I'd got so down I didn't even want to...?' I open up my hands and Toby shoots me a painful look.

'I can't even imagine what you've gone through, bud.'

'It feels so... *odd*, though, not remembering any of it.' In some ways, I'm still going through it. *It* – whatever this is – feels like hacking my way through the briars of a dark, overgrown forest. I'm still trying to find my way back to something that feels like a starting place I can recognise.

'It's crap, hearing about all this, what I was feeling, what I did, what I didn't do – and not to be able to connect with any of it. How I could have felt so strongly that life wasn't worth it...' I swallow. 'Especially given she was expecting. It honestly doesn't sound like me, Toby.' Not like the man I know myself to be.

'No.' Toby's dark eyes suddenly look very luminous. He turns away for a moment and wipes his face with his jacket sleeve.

I press, 'I just wish I knew *why*.'

He looks down, brushing back his long, straight hair in an automatic gesture.

'I can't tell you for certain, bud. We spoke over the phone a few times. I knew that shortly after getting your wonderful news you then got the *bad* news.'

He pauses, then admits, 'There was a stretch of time when you weren't composing, you were having all these tests and your heart wasn't in it. And then, there were some things your consultant said, I think, that upset you.'

My ears prick up.

'What things?'

'Dude, you were never...' He opens up his arms, apologetically. 'I was in a country far away and you were going through a lot and we weren't having long drawn-out discussions over the phone about it. I'm sorry. I only know you were desperately worried that you and I would never get to complete what we'd started.'

'Is that so?' I get up, unable to sit still any longer. One of the unsmiling bank staff gestures me to come on in, and the narrative in my head about *how things were* shifts and settles a little. So – I was worried I wouldn't be able to finish what we were working on… because we wouldn't have time? Because I wouldn't be the same man and I wouldn't be able to?

Because… Maracas Man?

God knows.

I pick up the plastic bag Ava cobbled together this morning with my passport and my driving licence and my photo-id sports centre entry card.

'Right,' I say. 'I'm off to persuade these intransigent bank people that I do still exist. Whatever their infallible computer system might be telling them.'

'Remember not to let any of them near enough to tickle you,' he says with a deadpan face.

But I am not in an easily amused mood, this morning. Toby's confirmed what Ava and the OT told me yesterday but I still feel that, every time I speak to people about what happened before, I end up feeling more confused and not less.

Added to which, the seat of my jeans has soaked up way too much of the rain on the bench. Now I've got to go in and have an argument with the bank manager, like this, with a wet backside.

# WILL

'I apologise for the delay.' The Holcombe bank employee who saw me in a good twenty minutes ago pops her head around the door. 'Mr de Bruce was seeing to a problem with the... erm... but he'll be happy to see you now,' she says crisply. 'If you can wait here, he'll be with you in another couple of minutes.'

'Here?' I assumed this was the waiting area. I look around at the little box of an 'office' with its red, zigzaggy carpet and clear Perspex walls and realise with some surprise that this is it, the bank manager's office. Where are the old studded red-leather chairs I recall from previous visits? More to the point, I clutch my plastic bag full of identification documents a little closer to my chest, wondering – how do people manage to conduct private, in depth conversations about their monetary affairs in a room where the see-through walls don't quite reach up to the ceiling?

'Is that okay?'

'Uh. Sure.' I come back to her. 'I was wondering if you'd had any luck locating my...?'

'Ah, here's Mr de Bruce to see you now.'

'Mr *Tyler*.' The young blond dude with the slightly snug navy suit who walks in gives my hand a studied shake before seating himself in the plastic chair opposite me.

'Sorry to have kept you waiting,' he says cheerfully. Right now, I'm mainly feeling thrown by how *young* this guy is. I was definitely expecting someone older.

'So. You're here about your missing bank account?'

I nod, clearing my throat. 'I don't seem to be able to get into it.'

'Let's see what we've got here, then.' He's got all the pertinent details on a piece of paper in front of him, taps a few things in. Shifting a little on my plastic chair, I can feel where the seat of my jeans hasn't quite dried out yet.

When he glances up, I look over, grimly hopeful.

'Find anything?'

'Hmmm. Here's the strange thing, Mr Tyler.' He pulls a smile at me. 'We've looked into this. It would appear the problem is...' He leans back in, folding his hands confidently in front of him. '*The problem is* that you don't actually appear to have an account with us.'

I feel my stomach sink. 'No. There must be some mistake. This is why I physically came in, today.' I lean in, earnestly. 'I thought if I came here in person, you'd be able to sort it out.'

'I must be honest, Mr Tyler, we have no record of you, whatsoever.'

'I *have* an account with you,' I tell him slowly, 'which has all my money in it. All of it. I came here and opened it way back when I was eighteen, at my grandad's insistence.' I add, 'You gave me a free Railcard for a year and a plastic pig money box.'

I still have that pig, somewhere.

'It is a mystery,' he agrees. 'Your details simply don't tally up with anything on our computer.'

I look at him tentatively.

'I just feel... it can't be *right* that...'

He's tapping his forehead thoughtfully, like a shrink.

'Sorry, but I have to tell you that I'm satisfied that the checks we've run have been as thorough as they need to be. You're not a customer here.'

I swallow. 'Mr de Bruce, please appreciate, I can't buy anything. I can't pay my bills. I can't do anything or have anything. I'm being forced to live off the charity of everyone around me. Without my bank account, it's as if I've become a complete *persona non grata*.'

He gives a long sigh, looking uneasy, and I realise what I must look like to him. Me with my beanie hat and my damp jeans and my plastic bag full of papers.

'With respect, are you *100 per cent sure*...' he gives me a significant look '... that the identity documents you've supplied to us are genuine, and that you weren't previously operating under – shall we say – an assumed identity?'

'No!' I rub at my neck, suddenly feeling hot. Am I under suspicion here? Lord, what have I been up to in the past few years? How can I be certain?

'I mean, yes. My documents are genuine.' *What's he on about?* 'I am Will Tyler,' I say. 'I have always been Will Tyler, even if your systems don't recognise me any more.'

'The problem is, I honestly don't think we're going to be of any help to you today, Mr Tyler.' He's half got up off his seat, pausing for me to follow suit, but I don't. I can't, because his words have resonated with something deep inside me.

'I'm sorry?' I say, shakily.

'I honestly don't think—'

'No, Mr de Bruce, you will help me. You must. Please. My girlfriend's expecting our first child and I need... I need you to help me get to the bottom of this.' I hold out my hand and maybe he sees something in my face because he hesitates. There's a moment where it's, like, fifty-fifty whether or not he calls security and gets me chucked off the premises, but he must have a moment of compassion because he doesn't do that.

'Okay. Let me... go check something else out.' He gets up and leaves the room with no real walls and I take the opportunity to go and sit by the door, gasping for some fresher air.

While I wait, I rifle idly through the papers and documentation that Ava sorted out for me earlier. No bank statements, since I apparently went paperless, but there is one, very old, letter from the bank, which they must have sent me over three years ago, saying...

I do a double take, feeling my heart thumping a little harder.

Dear Mr Tyler,

We are sorry to learn that you've decided to switch banks from Holcombe City to New Amstell Banking Inc.

New Amstell?
My eyes skim over that bit again then run on.

If there is anything we can do to help out and encourage you to switch back again, please let us know. In the meantime, all your direct debits, etc, etc are being forwarded to your new bank with effect of the 1st April...etc, etc...

My arm drops and I let out a loud, shaky laugh. Good Lord, I'm a prize idiot! I've been barking up the wrong tree, all along...

And now, Mr de Bruce is back, with a computer printout in his hand, looking pleased with himself.

'I think we may have got to the bottom of it for you, Mr Tyler.'

'Uh. Yes.' I hold up the crumpled document in my hand, feeling sheepish, and he folds his arms, looking both relieved and vindicated. I don't know how they wouldn't have kept the records of their past customers for this short length of time but hey – computers sometimes have blips; life doesn't always work as we expect it to. Either way, this morning I feel as if I've had a huge reprieve.

'I won't take up any more of your time, then.'

It looks as if – finally – Will Tyler is back.

# AVA

A bright pinprick of blood has just appeared on the fabric in my hands, which feels too fine, too slippery this morning, as if my fingers are made of big rubbery balloons that won't allow me to do my work properly. I want to do my sewing today. I *need* to do it. But the needle-prick on my index finger is stinging like mad. It won't stop even when I stick it into the warmth of my mouth, and, when I check, the bloodstain on the fabric has already spread into the size of a small coin.

I drop the ruined material onto the table, aware of a growing dull ache in my back that was not there before. And the *tick-tick-tick* of the kitchen clock sounds far too loud. I stare up at it, pushing my hair back and feeling confused. I don't remember it ever being that loud before. I want it to stop. I wish that the time would stop being so noisy.

God, what's happening to me?

The day outside, bright and sunny when Will left earlier, has dulled. I get up to put on the overhead light, but find myself leaning against the wall instead, my heart swelling in sadness and disappointment. I'm not sure at what.

And now there's somebody at my front door; I can hear it being pushed open.

'*Halloooo?* Anyone in?'

I rub at my eyes, aware, above everything, of the need to *pull myself together*, and the next thing I know Robyn's skipped into my kitchen looking cheery. She's all dressed in pink today, gives me a warm hug coming in, but now she's holding me at arm's length.

*'Hey.'* She's looking at me, concerned. 'Is everything all right today, sis?'

'Yup.'

'You don't look as if everything's all right.'

'Uh!' I force out a small laugh. There's a piece of kitchen roll on the table and I pick it up. Wipe my face and blow my nose, pretending I'm coming down with a bit of a cold, but I'm not fooling Robyn.

'Not really, Robbie.'

'What is it?' She ushers me back into my chair. 'It's not the baby, is it?' Her voice goes up a notch, her alarm catching. *Am I looking that awful?*

'Ava, let me call the doctor for you and get you seen straight away.' She's already whipped out her phone. 'They won't have any appointments at this hour, but if it's the baby...'

'No.' I lay my hand on her arm, wishing she'd just stop talking for a minute. Everything's going so fast. I can't... 'It's not the baby, Robyn. Everything with the baby is just... *fine!*'

'It's fine?' She sits down on the chair beside me and now I feel her hands wrap comfortingly around my shoulders. 'You really aren't looking all that fine, hon.'

She pauses.

'Is it Will?' My sister's got her head up, scanning the place now. 'Where is he, anyway?'

'At the bank. He went off with his mate, Toby,' I get out. 'Robbie, this is *nothing to do* with William.'

She drops her arm, her face still creased with concern. 'What's going on, then?'

I let out a breath, feeling as if I've got the weight of the world on my shoulders. 'I've made a mistake, Robyn. A really, big...' I stop for a moment, clutching my hand to my chest.

My sister waits. 'This?' I see her glance cursorily over the bits of material and pattern I've got laid out on the kitchen table. 'The princess dress?'

I stare at it. 'It's ruined. Ginny's expecting me to deliver the dress. I *promised...*'

Robyn picks up the bloodstained front panel and now she's examining it minutely. She eventually puts it back down gently on the table.

'We can't always keep all our promises,' she concedes.

I push down the panic threatening to rise when she says that.

'What d'you mean?'

'Well,' she says reasonably, 'she'll understand. We can't *always* keep our—'

'I have to, though!'

She doesn't reply and I hear myself saying, 'I planned to spend today assembling it. I've even got a courier booked in to pick it up tomorrow lunchtime. If I can't wash that bloodstain out, I'll have to dash back into town and get some—'

'Ava,' she says softly. 'It's not the end of the world.'

'It *is*.' Even I can appreciate I'm overreacting. 'I can't believe I made a rookie mistake like this,' I tell her now. 'Not when I'm trying so desperately hard to get this commission in for Ginny and it matters. It really *matters*.'

My sister's silent, waiting for me to finish. When I do, she pats me gently on the knee and I gulp.

'I'm sorry. Everything just seems to be getting on top of me at the moment.' I wipe at my face. 'These baby hormones have probably got a lot more to answer for than I'm crediting them with.'

'I think you're right about that.' She shoots me a reassuring smile. 'Even without the *baby hormones*, you've had a stupid amount on your plate, you'll agree?'

I shrug.

'With the worry about the op and then looking after Will?' She pulls a face at me. 'C'mon, sis. You've had it all going on. Cut yourself a little slack, will you?'

'You could be right.'

She gets up and goes to fix us both a sweet hot chocolate, *à la Robyn,* and I examine my fingers while I wait. They're only a tiny bit swollen, really. They're not the huge sausages they felt like before. The pinprick on my index finger's still looking sore and unhappy but I'm starting to thaw. I don't know what came over me, but I woke up not feeling quite *right* today.

Robyn's back.

'You need to chill out, and stop trying to do it all.' She places our drinks down on the table. 'One thing less for you to worry about, at least – I have some good news!'

'Oh, yes?' I pull a smile, wanting to be pleased for her.

'Turns out I don't need to come and stay here with you guys any more.'

She's been a godsend to me this morning, but that's still a relief. I lift my mug to my lips, taking a sip of the warm drink.

'You don't?'

'No. I've solved that problem by asking Carenza over to stay with me.'

'Ah!' The girl with the blog. That bit is not so good. Before I can comment, she adds, 'And afterwards, she and I are planning a holiday in Greece for a month!'

That gets my attention.

'You're going to Greece for a month?' *With Carenza?*

She's nodding happily.

'I am *so* made up about that. She's got some relatives out in Kos who live in the hugest house, right by this golden beach. And her uncle's some sort of cultural attaché. They hold these lavish parties where it's useful for them to have native English-speaking people around and she's hinted that it might even lead to some work opportunities if...' She lets out a breath. 'Ava, it's all going to be *wonderful.*'

'Wow.' I'm struggling to keep up.

'In exchange, Carenza only wants me to organise some work experience at the Butterfly Gardens for her, because of the amazing photo opportunities for her blog, which is great by Phyllis, too. *Plus*, she's got a car, so we'd have no trouble at all, getting into work.'

Uh... *wait, what*?

I look at her, startled, but, perhaps to forestall me giving my opinion on that, Robyn's already jumped up, hugging me goodbye.

'I really gotta go now. We'll talk more later... oh, and your post's just arrived,' she calls out before banging the front door behind her.

I'm scarcely paying attention. We've only just got rid of the blog-post problem. Having her friend down to stay in Holcombe Bay – especially working at the gardens, where she's bound to come across us at Beach Cottage – it's just... not going to be the most helpful thing to me right now. But there's nothing I can do about it.

The little notch of tightness at the base of my neck has started to pulse again. This new piece of information just accentuates the fact that I can't keep the whole world and everyone in it away from Will, forever. Little wonder I am so stressed.

Padding over to check out the post, I see there's a strangely familiar, thick white envelope addressed to *Mr William Tyler* waiting on the mat. I bend to retrieve it, my unease deepening further. If this is what I think it is, then I have seen one exactly like it, before. I got rid of the last one ages ago, but what're these people doing, contacting him again? I stifle a dismayed moan.

Is this *never* going to end?

# 28

# AVA

Taking the letter into the living room, I sit down on the chair by the window and open it, even though it isn't addressed to me, allowing myself to skim over the unwelcome words one more time.

Dear Mr Tyler,

Thank you for choosing to visit us at our clinic at Men First Fertility, in February this year. I trust you were happy with the attention you received at the time.

I note from our records that we were unable to pinpoint the exact cause of your azoospermia and the initial prognosis was that, unfortunately, you would be unable to achieve conception in your current condition.

I pause there for a moment, biting back the tears that I've been holding onto for weeks, resting my hands lightly on my stomach that is only now starting to show the beginnings of the longed-for bump.

However, our review of your blood results also indicated an abnormally high white blood cell count. As these can be indicators of more serious causes for male infertility – including testicular or brain cancer – you were advised at the time to book a follow-up appointment with your GP as soon as possible. I was concerned to note we have not heard anything back from you.

I would stress that – with confidentiality being a paramount patient concern – we would not usually undertake to contact NHS doctors on your behalf unless specifically requested by you to do so. If you have not done so already, I would therefore like to encourage you to make an appointment with your own doctor, as soon as you can.

If we at Men First Fertility can be of any further assistance etc, etc...

The letter crumples in my lap. *Why hadn't I wanted the operation?* Will asked me last night. How could I tell him it was because of this? I'd promised him he would never know. I thought it would be as simple as that – me keeping quiet – but the truth seems to want to keep coming at him.

Perhaps it's because Will never replied to them at the time, went straight to his own GP, that they've sent it back again?

I'll have to ring them, I guess, let them know it's all being dealt with. Tell them they don't need to send him any more letters, only... it's shocking to think how easily he could've picked this up off the mat, instead of me! The ache in my back turns into something sharper, *real pain*. No matter how much I rub at it with the heel of my hand, it won't go away.

How many hazards like this might there still be lurking out there, waiting to trip me up? How many more potential disasters like Carenza's blog or *her impending visit* am I going to have to keep batting away?

I push back my hair and take out a tissue to wipe my nose, feeling, for the first time, today, very bloated and weepy and *pregnant*. Undeniably pregnant, only in the place of the joy I want so much to feel there is only sadness. In the dull light of my empty house this morning, the tears flow silently like a river. I wish that I could call back my sister. I wish I could call Ginny, or someone, *anyone*, because this feels much too hard to bear alone.

But no one can know.

At last, I take the letter and tear it up into a hundred tiny little bits of paper. To minimise the risk, I won't bin these in the house. I'll take them well away from here so there can be not the smallest chance of anyone piecing them back together again.

*For you* – I rub gently at the bump under my jumper. Because ever since that letter first arrived, I haven't been able to celebrate you properly in my heart the way you deserve to be celebrated.

For Will. For me. Because this bad dream I keep waking up to, all alone, every morning – it's real. It's the truth of how it is, no matter how much I've been trying to deny it.

I stay there for a good long while with the torn letter in my lap, watching the wind pushing the trees to and fro outside, staring at the thin ragged clouds, trying to find some way to square *what is* with *what I would like to be true*. I can't do it and I can't imagine a time when I will be able to.

And yet... I still have to find some way to make this go away.

# 29

# AVA

Pulling my jacket a little tighter around me, I'm hurrying down to the Butterfly Gardens, the only place I can think of where I'll be able to collect myself and stop panicking.

Finding a private little nook where I can be alone, I sit down on a bench for what feels like ages, feeling the hundred little pieces of telltale paper that're still in my pocket, desperately telling myself that *I have to be able to think*, or there's no way I'm getting myself out of this hole. Coming down. Slowly. In the one space in the world where it's possible for me to do this. Little by little. And, after a while, it comes to me, that all I need to do right now is deal with these pieces of paper. It is still only a letter. One that's been torn into pieces at that.

I can deal with that.

For the sake of everything that's still wonderful and good in my life, I can. And I will.

These little shreds of paper need to be gone. Completely gone. I push them out, and the wind picks them up and rolls them along the gravelled path and into the furrowed herbaceous border, reminding me of so many little white flakes of snow.

That image catches in my mind for a second, taking me back to the last time the snow fell; to what was happening to me and Will back then, to what's led to where we are now.

It catches, and then, like a snowflake, disappears, because I am not there any more, I am here. And I am not alone either.

Old Harry's arrived.

'We're closed at the moment,' Harry calls out the moment he sees me.

I think on my feet. 'Oh.' I tell him. 'I've only popped by to see Phyllis.'

'We're not taking on any new volunteers at the moment,' he says kindly. 'She'll tell you that herself, soon as she turns up.'

I hesitate for a second, glancing at the flower beds – did he see what I did with all those bits of paper? He doesn't appear to have as he makes no mention of it, and I calm down a little, debating whether to go through the usual charade of explaining to Harry once again how '*I've been working here for years*'. Because he won't recall it. He never will.

'Phyllis called me earlier,' I tell him quietly. I sit down on the edge of the low garden wall, unable to look away as he picks up a fork and begins automatically turning the soil over – right by the dahlia bushes – innocently incorporating all the little white bits I've discarded.

'You know Phyllis?' He looks up suddenly, catching me watching him.

'I...' I blink, gathering myself. 'Yes, I know her, Harry,' I add, 'and you, too.'

'This variety of dahlia here is called Harry's Gold,' he tells me, apropos of nothing. 'Developed it myself, you see. It took me many long years of breeding to get them this colour.'

I say politely, 'The flowers are gold?' Perhaps I should leave? I already did what I came to do. I've buried what I had to, come to terms with it – just a blip – and there's no need to linger.

'Have I made your acquaintance yet, young lady?' He stops for a moment to scrutinise me a little more closely. 'Because I don't believe we've ever...'

'Harry, my name is Ava!' I breathe. 'You know me. I let you have your favourite raspberry-and-chocolate-chip cookies, which you're not supposed to have because your wife always keeps you to a strict diet, but we sneak them in anyway, and then, every time we meet, you think I'm a volunteer.'

*How can you even live like this?* I think. *How can you keep going when half of what you know, you don't know, any more?*

'Is that so?'

'It is.' A pang of sadness washes over me. It must be *so easy* for folk to pull the wool over Harry's eyes. He's turned away and is back at his work, busy tethering some luxuriously leafy dahlias to some tall stakes with a bit of garden twine.

I glance at him tentatively.

'Harry – do you ever get a funny feeling that you're not being told the whole truth about things?'

'Sometimes.'

'And...' I swallow '... that doesn't bother you?'

'Not any more.' He smiles, securing his precious plants, pushing down the soil around the cloches.

'That's probably just as well.' I come and kneel down beside him, helping him pat it all down.

He smiles. 'Besides, I don't always need to know *everything*. I manage okay, don't I?'

It's a heartening thought.

Together, we work silently for a bit, pushing down the dark earth around the base of his plants.

'You're right,' I agree slowly. 'Sometimes things might have happened in a person's past that they don't need to know about; not if there's nothing they can do about it. Not if... *knowing it* would ruin everything good they've currently got going, don't you think?'

'I don't think about it too much,' he comes back eventually. 'Besides, I am old, Ava. I've come to realise that truth is... you could say, it's a little like my dahlias here.'

I look up.

'Truth is like a dahlia?'

'Like everything in life, it seeks the sun. And so...' He straightens for a moment, brushing over the many unopened buds of Harry's Gold with the tips of his fingers in expectant joy.

'In its own time, the truth must always unfurl.'

Does it, though? Does it *always?* I look away, feeling my resolve hardening because it seems to me that not all truths are equal, not all can or even should, come to light. Sometimes you need to be the guardian of the truth if you want to protect someone.

How would me *coming clean with Will* serve our happiness and our life? It wouldn't, and it is not going to happen.

On my knees beside Harry, working my fingers deep into the rich soil, I push the last remaining shreds of the letter further down. When the rain comes, they'll go into a mulch and feed the plants. The words that were once written there will be gone, forever.

And so will the wretched *truth*.

## 30

## AVA

'Y'know, I've heard more than my fair share of awesome sounds in my life but, I promise you, *that* has to be the most beautiful thing I ever heard.'

I laugh.

'Still thinking about the baby's heartbeat?'

When I asked Will, on a whim, if he'd like to tag along for my routine midwife appointment this morning, I had no idea how blown away he'd be. How happy.

'That's got to be the coolest sound. Da-da voom, *da-da voom.*' He plays some air-drums with his free hand, echoing the beat. Our midwife visit has made the pregnancy real for him in a tangible way that maybe it wasn't before. Like getting through to the bank and finding out he isn't a pauper, it's made a real difference to his mood.

Straight after, we came down to watch the practice for the upcoming kite festival. Nothing's really got under way yet, but as I walk along with Will's arm resting companionably around my shoulders, there's a gentle breeze blowing along the shore of Holcombe Bay this morning; a crunch in the sand and a warm glow over the sea that's already whispering, *Summer's coming.* I get the sense that even the spectacle of kites flying on a blue-sky morning couldn't bring me any more contentment than I already feel.

'170 beats per minute, the midwife said,' Will muses. 'What's the little blighter even doing in there, for its heart to be going so fast?'

I laugh.

Drinking him in for a moment, all I'm thinking is, Will has no idea what him standing so close to me does to *my* heart-rate, does he? Tall and lean, wearing skinny jeans and a T-shirt that shows off his pecs, Will's looking pretty hot today in that effortless way he has. More than one person passing us has done a double take, I know that. Both men and women. That's just him. With only a bandana to cover the head wound, and his curly, red-gold hair blowing back in the breeze, *shining like a lion's mane*, I think, Lord knows, he's beautiful and I love him, but I'd love him whatever he looked like.

In the last few weeks, I've also been happy to discover he's the same skilful, considerate lover he always was, he hasn't lost his touch.

'*What?*' He laughs.

'I'm sorry?' I can feel myself going pink. *Was I staring?*

'Penny for your thoughts?' He stops now, pulls me down easily onto the sand after him. I push my hair away from my face, feeling warm.

'My thoughts?'

He bites his lower lip, hiding a smile. I *know* he caught me looking at him but I'm not admitting to that.

'Uh. Well. I was wondering...' I smile easily at him '... whether what you'd *really* brought me out here to talk about was the surprise you've been busy planning.'

'What surprise?'

'C'mon.' I push his shoulder gently. 'You know I *know* you're plotting something.'

'Plotting, is it now? Not planning, any more?'

'Plotting, planning, cooking up... you've got something in the works that you're not telling me about. I know you do because every time I come up behind you, you shut down your computer or minimise the screen.'

He grins. 'You sure there couldn't be any other explanation for my secrecy?'

I fold my arms. 'Like what? You're having an affair?'

He throws back his head, bursting into delicious laughter at the thought of that.

'Look,' I say. 'I know it's not that, so why else would you be so concerned if I saw what you were—?'

'Okay.' He holds up his hands. 'You've got me. I'm planning a surprise. But I can't tell you.'

'Why?' I beg, leaning in a little, but he just shakes his head.

'Because...' he taps my nose gently '... it's a *surprise*.'

Darn it. I hate surprises. He's probably forgotten that. *Of course, he's forgotten it.* Perhaps I should remind him?

But Will's attention has already been captured elsewhere. '*Awww.* Poor little soul.'

'Who? What?' I frown, looking in the direction of his gaze, not entirely convinced this isn't a ruse to push me off track. But it isn't.

'Look at him.' Will scrambles to sit up. A young lad, about six, is running desperately after his kite that's got caught up in a breeze, and is bounding free along the shore.

'He must've been hoping to get it going up alongside those professional ones.'

'Probably.'

From here, a little crowd has already gathered to watch 'Billie the Blue Beluga Whale' and the 'Sugarloaf Mountain' monster kites being launched, but this kid's little diamond shaped kite isn't going anywhere. Except maybe in the sea.

And he's sobbing.

'Oh, *no*...' It's exactly the kind of scenario that breaks my soft-hearted, hard-working boyfriend's heart.

'Here comes the boy's dad,' I point out. We watch as Dad manages to rescue the kite from the water's edge, only to fail in every subsequent attempt to get it airborne. After a few more minutes of us watching this, I'm done, but it's clear that Will's still riveted.

'He can do it.' Will's fretting. 'All that man needs is some simple, basic instruction, that's all.'

'Please don't tell me you're tempted to go over and instruct the man on how to get it up?'

'Ignoring that innuendo, which I am sure was *purely unintentional*...'

'Purely intentional, actually...'

Will shoots me a sidelong glance. 'Ignoring that. I just might.'

'That's very civic-minded of you, Will, but...' I sigh.

Perhaps we should've walked straight home after that midwife appointment after all? Giving me a quick, apologetic hug, Will's already run over to demonstrate to the guy exactly how things should be done. I remain sitting where I am, pushing a pile of dry sand into a mound, and it doesn't take long before the father and son duo have got the little toy kite fluttering merrily. Will's pleased. I can see it on his face. Maybe he's thinking this'll be him and our child, one of these days?

I hug my knees to me, feeling my heart swell a little with pride, and now the breeze carries hints and wisps of their conversation to my ears. One minute they're talking about *wind shadows and lift and the importance of the kite's tail*. The next, right as I'm thinking their exchange will soon be over, Will and the bloke seem to be high-fiving and giving each other bear hugs as if they've realised they already know one another...

I prick up my ears.

'Gil... left the area years ago... come along?'

I screw up my eyes to see, but I don't recognise the man. It must be a friend of his from before, and one he seems very happy to be reacquainted with. I don't want to barge in on them, so I remain patiently where I am.

About ten minutes later, Will appears, out of breath from jogging back.

'Sorry, sorry...' Will lowers himself down onto the sand alongside me. 'I bumped into Mel... used to know him from Gil's Music store. Apparently, that store closed *five years* back.'

'It did.' I brush the sand off the palms of my hands, looking at him curiously.

'Turns out Gil's moved to the next town, but he still holds musician reunions. All welcome, and there's one coming up this weekend, Mel tells me.' Will's eyes are shining eagerly.

'DelRoy might be there too. I said I'd go. Would you like to come?'

'Uh...'

'Girlfriends very welcome, Mel said. You wouldn't be the only girl there.'

'Perhaps I'd better, then?' *Especially if DelRoy and his girlfriend will be.* I draw in a breath. Am I ready for us to go back out into the world as a couple? I don't know, but I knew it had to happen, sooner or later.

Will sits still for a moment, catching his breath back.

'Man, did you *see* that kite go?'

I nod.

'Mel was clueless. And they'd got the ideal weather conditions. They needed to stand with the wind behind them, that was all.'

'Like so much in life,' I say drily. '*It's where you stand that counts...*'

Will laughs.

'That's exactly what Grandpa Jeff used to say!'

I know. I smile at him coyly.

'So, now that my hero boyfriend has solved all the world's problems... will you *please* tell me what that surprise you're planning is all about?'

Will considers for a moment.

'I will only tell you this: be sure to leave the last weekend of the month, and the whole of the week that follows, free, to be with me.'

I lean in, anticipating that a little more detail must naturally follow, but no.

'That's it?' When I bow my head, I feel him lean in to kiss me, softly.

'That's your lot, I'm afraid.'

He smiles mysteriously. I clap my hands together, suddenly ridiculously excited. He's booked us a whole week somewhere? Just him and me.

For now, that'll have to be enough.

# 31

# WILL

'Wow, look at *you*.' The large, clean shaven man with the 'I'm the Head Cook' apron puts down his BBQ tongs and says again, *'Look at you!'*

I laugh, jovially. I'm getting used to this. People who I don't know any more knowing me.

The guy's come right over to give me a good, proper hug, so I hug him back. Ava's standing in the doorway, smiling faintly, but she's not catching my silent plea – *give me a hint, who is this guy?* Given that we're here at Gil's for his musician's-reunion thing, there's no question I've already met a lot of these dudes before. Trouble is, I honestly expected to recognise most of them. That was the whole point.

'So... um... it's been a while,' I say to the large guy. 'How've you been?'

He indicates the house and garden about us, proudly. 'Settling into domestic bliss, as you can see.'

This is his house? *Gil?* Lord, how didn't I recognise him? I gulp, indicating the front of my face.

'I see you've lost your...'

'Oh, yes. Had to lose the lady tickler when I gave up the shop and went for that computer repair job, didn't I?' He sounds a little sad. Gil's repairing computers now? What happened there? Indicating for a younger man to come and take over his cooking task, Gil's ushering me eagerly over to one side. 'But you, William Tyler... I've been saving this one for you.' He pours out a generous measure from a bottle of fine malt whisky that looks very old and very expensive, and places the glass solicitously in my hands. '*You've* gone from strength to strength, I hear?'

'In some respects.' I glance towards the door but Ava's already talking to some women she's met; she's doing just fine. And I can too. I've been so looking forward to reuniting with my old friends. Literally, for weeks, ever since I first woke up from the op and found I didn't know anyone.

Only, it occurs to me for the first time, how many of these people are actually aware of what's happened to me? They're friends, true, but from the distant past. Mel didn't mention anything about my operation when I ran into him on the beach last week and I didn't clue him in. Maybe I should've said something then?

'I heard you left DelRoy's band and never looked back?' Gil's eyes narrow curiously. 'I left town after what happened to the shop, but then, you'll know all about that...'

'Uh.' I stare at my whisky glass for a second. I don't know, not any more. 'I was really sorry to see it was gone, man. We had such good times. Your music shop,' I tell him feelingly, 'was once the making of me.'

'True.' He looks a little teary eyed. Ava and I arrived an hour into the proceedings, so if he's had one or two beers already, that's only to be expected. 'And you... you've filled out some, man!' He looks at me admiringly. 'When you first walked into my store you were... what... twelve?'

'I was thirteen. Sent down to spend the summer with my grandad in Holcombe. I'd never picked up a musical instrument till the day I walked into your shop, Gil. You will never know how much I appreciated you letting me hang out.'

I swirl Gil's whisky around in my glass and he smiles.

'I did, didn't I, squirt?' His bushy brows knit together as he recalls,

'You were this pale, skinny little kid, desperate to hang out with the big boys, the *real* musicians, and now...'

I was actually desperate to get away from Mule and his mates, the first time I ducked into Gil's Music store, but we'll leave that to history. Gil grabs hold of another passing dude by his shirt tail.

'Rambo, will you look-see who we've got here today?'

'*Whoa!*' The lean, olive skinned bloke who greets me by grabbing hold of my arm with his own muscular one is one person I do recognise straight off. Rambo the psycho. Best drummer and craziest guy I ever met in my life. 'We are honoured...' he shoots me a gap-toothed grin '... to have you in our presence again.'

'Good to see you, man.' I grin back, recalling how he'd always generously let me have a go on his drum kit – which he called *his sacred drums* – whenever he wasn't using it. He had a bass guitar too, which he called Binky. That must've been even more sacred because he never let me or anyone else touch that.

'Your musical prowess,' he says, in the strangely formal way he always had, 'has us in awe, my friend.'

'We all heard about your deal with the Red Sphynx label.' I'm not sure if that's pride or envy now in Gil's voice. Maybe a little of both? He's got no clue I've only recently *heard* about that myself, has he? I had to look them up, too. They weren't around as a label seven years ago, even if they're currently hot.

'I'm flattered that you've kept up with me, to be honest. I've been a little...'

I glance around, aware of a few more musicians, people I vaguely recognise from my youth, gathering about. I once loved and admired all these dudes, *so much*. How did I let them all slip out of my life?

'I've been, like you say, working with Red Sphynx,' I end lamely. I've been putting off getting in touch with my contact at the label, till I feel well and truly ready to get back in there. What would be the point of letting everyone cotton on to how debilitated I've been feeling? But maybe it's time I did something about that?

'Some of us have got demo-discs.' A guy with a silver-white ponytail pushes forward. 'Some tracks you might be interested to hear. *If you have the time, at some point? Always good to share contacts,*' he adds meaningfully, in case I hadn't got his drift.

'I'll let you know.'

'Don't crowd the man, Rafe.' Someone else laughs, coming in to shake my hand. 'Give him a chance to get to know us, again. It's *Dave,*' he says to my blank look. 'Keyboard and piano. Though I do a lot more besides, these days. Finances and stuff – I tried to help Gil out when he was going bankrupt, you know.'

'Of course. Dave.' So that's what happened to Gil. Poor Gil. But, 'Yes, I know you.' Actually, it's the mullet I recognise. Dave – like a lot of them – still has the same hairstyle he had back when I was in my teens. As if they've all got stuck in some sort of time warp.

The irony of which doesn't escape me.

I glance about, wondering where Ava is. She already reassured me, coming down here: *you get on with reconnecting with your friends, don't worry about sticking with me*, but I still like to know she's okay. I have to assume she is because I can't see her, but the next familiar face I do see comes as a shock, almost makes me want to weep.

'Oh, *man.*' Unlike everyone else, DelRoy looks *exactly* the same as he did when I saw him last. With his big, shaggy hair and eyes that always reminded me of an old, wise angel, how could he ever change? When he draws me in tight for a long, very overdue embrace, he even smells the same – *woodbines and sandalwood* – he *feels* the same.

'Hey,' he says softly. 'You okay?'

For a moment, I don't speak. I just get a tight sadness in my throat; a *'where've you been since all of this that's happened to me, dude?'* moment. And I realise I needed him there when I woke up. All those weeks back. He should've been there. I swallow.

'Do you even know,' I get out, 'what's happened to me?' Maybe he doesn't know? Maybe he's like everyone else here, clueless. The other guys obligingly melt away, giving us our space, and DelRoy and I walk over to the one tiny free area left, in a dark corner of Gil's garden. I lean up against the old oak I find there, glad of its support, and we stare at each other for a while.

'I do know,' he admits after a bit. 'I knew.'

*'Why in heaven's name, then...?'* I temper my first response, leaning in a little closer. 'Why did you never come to see me, DR? Why've you made no contact at all? I left voicemail messages, man. I left you about half a dozen! D'you have the first idea what it's been like for me? Waking up to...' I swallow, painfully, wondering where the heck *all these emotions* have suddenly welled up from, because I was feeling 100 per cent okay until I saw him. 'Waking up to a world where everyone's felt like a stranger. Everyone. Even...' Even the woman who's carrying my baby. I don't say it.

He's looking at me, sorrowfully. DelRoy's always had the most expressive eyes. He feels bad, I can see it. But that doesn't explain it. Why he left me...

'Even one little text message to say that you were thinking of me, that would've made all the difference. Didn't you know, I've even been staying in your flat?'

'I'm so sorry,' is all he says. 'I'm sorry that I couldn't.'

I crinkle up my eyes.

'Couldn't?'

He doesn't break eye contact with me. No. DelRoy never does.

'That is how it was. I heard from Gil you were coming here tonight though, so I came. For you. I hope that'll be enough, for us to...?'

I sigh, feeling my throat hurting, aware of all sorts of things going on inside that I have no idea how to put together, yet.

'I've missed you,' I get out. Because, no matter how much I want to feel mad at him, that much is also true.

'I know, little brother.' He clasps my hand in his own, his use of that old name turning my puzzled anger back into sadness again.

'I just... don't understand so much.' I sink down onto the grass, my back against the gnarled old tree. 'I've lost so much,' I tell him painfully. 'Seven years, DelRoy.'

'*Seven*, is it?' He didn't know that much, then, even if he knew I'd had the op?

I hold my head in my hands. 'How much do you know, then? In fact, *when did we last speak*, you and I?'

He doesn't answer for a moment. Then he crouches down beside me. 'It was a while back, Will. Too long. And I wish that it had not been so.'

I look at him painfully.

'*Why?*' I say.

'You won't remember it, but...' He bows his head. 'You didn't forgive me too easily when I started going out with your ex.'

I'm shaking my head, feeling more puzzled than ever.

'I'd already broken up with her, hadn't I?'

'Yes.' He gives a broken laugh. 'It was still painful for you, though. I understand that, my man. I understand it. And you didn't want to see me.'

'But we were *still friends*?' I insist. 'I broke up with her years ago, surely? Look. I stayed in your flat... even recently...'

'You still had my key. You knew I'd always let you use it if you needed to, and you knew...' he says quietly, 'that I wouldn't be there.'

'Are we not friends any more?'

'In my heart, always,' he says quietly. 'I hope, in yours, too?'

I stare at him.

'Delroy. I don't remember us ever arguing. I only remember the good times. I love you, man. I always have done and I always will.'

He makes a strange noise in his throat.

'I let you down,' he says. 'I could've chosen any other girl, but I chose—'

'I don't care,' I say over him. 'I don't care who you're going out with. Really. I'm with Ava now, and she's...' I hesitate, and then I say it. 'She's expecting our first child, DelRoy.'

A look of pure joy crosses his face.

'That much, I didn't know. Congratulations, William.'

'Thank you.' I take him in sadly. We'd fought, him and me, and *I never knew*. I can't believe I did that. I didn't even want ChiChi back. At least, I don't think so.

And if I ever did, I don't, any more.

'Who told you, then? About my op, I mean?'

'Would you believe it, it was Sylvie?'

I give a short laugh. My *mum*?

'Apparently, when she was visiting you at the hospital you kept asking for me...'

'I was. I wondered why nobody had turned up for me. The staff said that only close family were allowed, so as not to overwhelm and so on... but then, even after I got home, the only people who came were all strangers...'

He's shaking his head sadly.

'I'd have come sooner, except I thought you might not actually want to see me.'

'That's crazy.'

He breaks into a smile.

'Seems like it now, doesn't it?' He makes a whistling sound through his teeth. 'So, you really don't remember?'

I shake my head. 'Seven years. Imagine that? That's why I wanted to connect with all these dudes tonight.'

'Wonderful. You enjoying it?'

I admit, 'It's been cool, but the truth is, I barely recognise most of them. When did they all get so old?'

He laughs warmly.

'About the same time *you* turned into a successful musician and songwriter and put all the rest of us into the shade?' He adds, 'And you... I hear you're working with Toby Myers?'

'I am.' I smile. 'We're collaborating on something that we're both very excited about. Him especially, because at some point we're down to meet some film people he thinks might be interested in a score we've written.'

His eyebrows go up.

'You'd love him,' I enthuse. 'He says he's met you once before, but I'll introduce you again, if you like. Such a down-to-earth bloke.'

My old friend is rubbing at his face. 'Have you actually gone online and looked him up, yet?'

'Online, no. Should I have? He appeared at the door one day. I thought he was an intruder and nearly thrashed him with the fire poker...' I laugh. 'One of the great disadvantages of forgetting all the people you've met in the past seven years.'

Delroy just put a hand on my shoulder. 'Toby Myers is mega in our industry, William. *Mega*.'

'Well, whadd'ya know?' I get a shot of pleasure in my belly. 'I had no idea.'

DelRoy's busy retrieving Gil's deep amber whisky, which I'd set down on the grass. *Go ahead*, I motion.

He pours a little of it into his own, empty glass and says, 'I'm happy for you, old friend. You deserve it. You really do.'

This is exactly what Toby said, isn't it? Maybe it's even true? Judging by the way all the guys from Gil's Music store have been acting around me, they could be right. Maybe I didn't waste those seven lost years, after all? Maybe I really do deserve all the good luck I currently seem to be enjoying?

I hesitate before picking up the fine single malt he's proffered, swirling it around in its glass for a moment. Then I sit back and bask. The luscious scents which waft upwards seem to me to be magnified a hundredfold. A rush of smoky air follows a waft of citrus and exotic fruits; then a sweet earthiness, chased by a long, creamy finish...

'To the many joys we've been blessed with in our lives. May we always be prepared to love and appreciate them!'

DelRoy takes his first sip of Gil's malt and I watch as an expression of pure contentment spreads across his face. It brings back welcome memories. We used to do this all the time, after our gigs. Pool together to buy ourselves a bottle of the best booze we could afford, give ourselves a congratulatory toast and then just *celebrate*.

'And now, your cup truly runneth over, brother.'

I smile at him.

'To all the joys...' When I finally knock it back, my own drink doesn't taste exactly how I was imagining, though. The smokiness is charcoal, the citrus, burnt fruit; it burns my throat all the way down, leaving me with a quiet sense of unease, and then, echoes of some long-forgotten disappointment. An emptiness I wasn't expecting.

'Good?' he enquires to my sudden silence.

'*My cup...*' I rub at my throat, coughing quietly. I don't know what else to say. '*... runneth over.*' He beams at me and I add, 'Doth it not?'

'Yeth, it doth.'

We both laugh.

I get to my feet, the sense of hollowness I was feeling turning into a strange sensation of nausea in my belly. I wanted so much to celebrate, but I shouldn't have drunk that fine malt, maybe? I don't know. I just feel... inexplicably bereft, as if I've been robbed of something.

When I look around to find Ava, I spy her straight off, still standing in the same place where she's been all along. This time, though, she doesn't look over at me the minute I look her way because she's deep in her own conversation. She isn't smiling. A little jolt of unease pulses through me now, as I clock who she's with.

She's talking to ChiChi.

# 32

# AVA

'So, the two of you got back together in the end?' ChiChi smooths down her tight-fitting white dress and smiles. 'Well done!'

*Well done?* What's that supposed to mean? She was there in snowy February, of course, consoling Will when he was at DelRoy's flat. A fact she's clearly not going to let me forget easily. But, I've been enjoying my time at Gil's so far, chatting to the girls. There is no way I'm letting this woman get under my skin.

I give her a curt nod and she adds, in her husky voice, 'William looks well, by the way. How's he been?'

I look at her unsurely. 'You mean...?'

'After the op? I heard all about it, but don't worry, I understand it's not common knowledge in these circles and I'll keep my mouth shut till William decides to let people know in his own time. To be frank...' she leans in, confidential-like '... after having had such a major procedure, he appears one helluva lot better than I'd imagined he was going to... In fact, he looks much the same.' She takes me in curiously. '*Is* he?'

I put my orange juice to my mouth and take a deliberate sip.

'Hey, go talk to him in a bit, and you'll see for yourself,' I say at last. 'I'm sure he'll remember you from the past.' *Dim and distant,* I don't add.

'Men do tend to,' she replies, looking around. Is she looking for Will? I saw him with her boyfriend, DelRoy, a few moments ago. They were huddled in close conversation by the tree, but she can discover that much by herself. I feel a flash of heat come to my face. I don't know what she's after. If she and Will ever *did* get anything going after Christmas, she's going to be disappointed because he won't remember it.

No matter how unforgettable she thinks she is.

There again, I doubt anything happened. Whatever residual feelings Will might still have had for *her*, I know he'd never have done anything to wrong DelRoy. He just wouldn't. And she and DelRoy have been together for years, they were *still* together in the new year – so, she can hint away all she likes, but I'm not biting.

We're standing by the patio doors out to Gil's garden, but, not finding who she's been scanning for, ChiChi turns back to me now.

'Not you, though, Ava?'

'I'm sorry?'

'I heard he didn't remember *you*?'

I blink. How much does this woman know?

'Oh.' I force a laugh. 'Who've you been talking to, ChiChi?'

'William's mum, Sylvie, rang us a few weeks back...'

'Ah. Of course.' I know Sylvie always adored both DelRoy and ChiChi. As they were formerly important people in Will's life, I can see why she'd have thought to have let them know. Especially as she's not been able to be around too much herself. But I wish she hadn't.

'That must've been something, though – going in after that op, to find your boyfriend of a few years doesn't even *know* you?' ChiChi pursues with a little shudder. 'My word, what must that have felt like for you?'

'It's felt...' I hesitate, remembering that, no matter how concerned she might appear, this woman has never been a friend. Then I look her square in the eyes.

'It has felt like having someone fall in love with you, all over again.'

'Nice.'

One of Gil's kids, dressed as Spiderman, goes by with some crudités and dip, and ChiChi picks at one, delicately. I'm not sure if that *nice* comment was meant for me or the kid. Not that I care.

'No one wants to take any of mine.' Spiderman sounds totally fed up, lifting his tray a little higher. 'They all just want the pastries. My sister's tray is *nearly empty*.'

So, I take two carrot sticks and a piece of celery, neither of which I have any appetite for, just to help him along.

ChiChi comments, crunching on her morsel in a manner designed to remove the least amount of lipstick, 'You'll be feeling blessed that Will's been prepared to give you another chance, I imagine, Ava?'

Another chance, in what way?

'We're both happier than you could possibly imagine,' I tell her. We are, but I don't want to stand here having this conversation with this woman, I realise. Practically everything she says feels to me laced with some *double entendre* that she may or may not mean, depending on how much she actually knows. And ChiChi's always been good at that. Getting you to say more than you meant to say.

It's a game I don't want to play tonight.

'Well, it's been nice to see you, ChiChi...' But before I can follow through and step away, Gil's wife, Hayley, comes by now with two expensively dressed girlfriends in tow.

'Congratulations!' she says. 'I just *heard*.'

ChiChi immediately shoots me an incredulous look, but Hayley's leaving no one in any doubt.

'When's it due?'

'Early November.'

'*What?*' ChiChi says, annoyed. 'You're actually *pregnant*?'

But Hayley's still got the floor. She's telling her friends enthusiastically, 'This girl, you absolutely have to meet! Ava's the woman I was telling you about who designed and hand-made the bridesmaids' dresses for two of my dearest friends. She is *stunningly* talented and you'll definitely want a word with her before you go to anyone else.'

'Aw. Recommendations always appreciated.' I smile. 'Thanks,

Hayley.' I chat to the other two, both brides-to-be, for a bit and direct them to my website. ChiChi chips in with the name of her own couturier, just for good measure, but I can see the news has got to her.

Once the others have gone, 'So – your news.' She breathes. 'I take it... William's happy about it?'

'Of course.' I feel my face going pinker, glad of the darkening evening about us. 'He's *very* happy,' I assure her. 'Very. You know how he's always felt about having kids.'

She knows. I don't have to rub it in.

'Well, congrats, then. That's... *wonderful*.' She sucks in her lips. She doesn't sound as if she thinks it's wonderful, but she adds, 'I hope you're both very happy. I hope that his... memory loss doesn't get between you, and you're able to make it together again.'

'So do I, ChiChi. The thing is, even if he's forgotten me, he's still the same old Will, underneath.'

'*Is* he, though?'

'I believe so. People don't change, deep underneath, do they? He's still the same guy I fell for three years ago, even if he doesn't quite know it yet.'

She takes a long, measured sip of her cocktail, moving the little paper umbrella delicately out of the way before smiling sweetly at me.

'I think,' she says before she leaves me, 'you must be a much braver woman than me.'

When she takes her leave, it feels as if she's managed to disturb something deep inside me that I don't quite want to look at.

That I can't.

So, I stand there on the patio by myself, nursing my drink, smiling at people that go by. And I breathe. Slowly. In and out, and let the waves of sadness that I feel wash over me, until they subside, because I miss him. Will's the only one who could make me feel better, right now. If only I could tell him the truth. But I can't. I need to be strong. We're a team. That's how it's meant to be. I glance around, realising it's been a while. Is he looking for me? I wonder.

But, when I finally look over to the place where he's been chatting with DelRoy all along, Will has gone.

# 33

# WILL

Gil's back.

'I knew I'd been saving that fine malt for a reason.'

*He's got more?* There's a part of my brain that's telling me that might not be a very good idea. Alcohol only makes maudlin feelings get worse, doesn't it? On the other hand, it would be churlish to interrupt the flow... He proffers a burly hand, helping me up from where I've been sitting by the tree.

'Hayley's told me your good news! Take a swig of that, my lad.'

I obligingly take a swallow from the glass he's handed me but weirdly, just like before, I can't taste much.

'Uh... good stuff.' I nod at him.

DelRoy stands with me, grinning.

'This really *is* your year, isn't it?'

I take another swallow from the glass, making a monumental effort to get my shit together, because all those inexplicable feelings I was having a few minutes ago of *grief*, they have no place in my life. They might be a side effect of the meds or maybe the op itself. *Wherever they came from,* I think fiercely, *they better get back in their box.*

I tell the guys, 'I guess it is.'

Gil insists that we follow him through into the music room upstairs.

'Here's where I keep all the essential equipment *and*,' he says with a flourish, 'the good booze.'

Plenty of the other guys have already congregated up there for a jamming session. Rambo on the drums, a couple on electric guitars and a bass player, but Gil interrupts them to propose they all join him in a toast to 'our long-lost friend', which is the cause of a lot of loud hooting and toasting. After a good half hour, Gil remembers to come back with another toast for *'our long-lost friend's good news because his wife, Ava, is expecting...'*

Cue more cheering, hearty shouts of congratulations and an impressive solo fanfare on a Jupiter 378 series tuba. All followed by more of Gil's special malt, of which he fortunately appears to have saved more than one bottle.

'Is she?' DelRoy nudges me, the moment we move on to the quieter space on the balcony outside to carry on our conversation.

'Pregnant, yes. My wife...' I look at him, starting to feel slightly woozy. 'No. Not yet, anyway.' I tip what's left of the whisky in my glass into his – disappointingly, it's still not tasting as good as I'm expecting it to, *bitter*, somehow – and pick up a nearby glass of water.

*Where's Ava gone, anyway?* She popped her head into the music room a while back, to tell me she was going to help Hayley with clearing up the kitchen. She seemed pleased when she saw I was still with DelRoy and I got the impression she was only making sure I was okay. I sit down on one of the wrought-iron chairs by the metal table on the balcony and wait for the room to stop gently going round and round.

I lean over to poke Delroy in the sleeve of his very nice white shirt. He's got some lovely buttons on that shirt. Why that feels relevant now I don't know, but anyway...

'Did I tell you that I don't remember why I went through a phase of *refusing to have a life-saving operation*? Imagine that, if you will.'

His deep, dark eyes look pained.

'You've really been through it, haven't you? Why didn't you reach out to me, beforehand, man? Why didn't you say?'

'I don't remember.' I blink. 'You tell me. Why didn't I?'

'Will,' he says quietly. 'Last time we met you told me if I ever tried to contact you again, you'd stick my best guitar in a most unmentionable place.'

'Was I really such an ass?'

He sucks in a breath through his teeth. 'You are many things, Will Tyler, but I'd never call you that.'

I laugh.

'Truth is, I've got no idea about *so many things*,' I muse. 'I'm still coming to terms with the fact that maybe I never will.'

We're both quiet for a bit.

The evening is drawing in, the warmth of the June day beginning to turn slightly chill, but I welcome it. The feeling of cold on my face. The scent of newly mown grass wafting up to us from Gil's lawn. The feeling of damp on the breeze and all the tiny raindrops that seem to shimmer like gold dust in the air. I hold out my hands and welcome it. Because it's life. I don't know why I once refused that op, but I'm glad in my very bones, tonight, that I did have it. Glad of the chance to be alive.

The lull in our conversation lengthens as we pause to take in the sight of the women who've come out, throwing off their shoes to enjoy a little dancing on the lawn, beneath us. We're not the only ones to notice. The heavier beat of the rock music coming from the adjacent, upstairs room has changed abruptly to a jollier dance tune. DelRoy leans forward, drawing my attention to one particular couple.

'I think you might have some competition, my friend.'

And there's my Ava on the grass, laughing, boogying with a mini Spiderman. He's got fluorescent red slippers on, standing on her feet as she sways them to and fro to the music. She glances up immediately, sensing me looking, gesturing *come on down*.

I smile, indicating up at the clouds, and it doesn't take long before a soft shower sends most of the women running back inside, shrieking and laughing. Not her, though. She pushes back wet hair.

*Music's still playing,* she mouths up at me.

So, I get up, tucking in my shirt behind me, taking my leave of DelRoy. Outside, before I can get to Ava, Spiderman's sister – all of maybe seven years old – claims my hand.

'You are *my* partner now,' she tells me.

I glance over to the women standing quietly by the edge of the lawn and her mum gives me an encouraging nod.

So the girl places her feet on mine, exactly like Spidey with Ava, and she smiles boldly into my eyes while we dance.

'You're my favouritest of them all, William Tyler,' she says. She knows my name.

'I am?' I play along. 'Why's that?'

'*Because* I like your music the best.'

'Well, thank you.' I'm glancing towards the balcony, fully expecting a crowd of my old mates to be falling over themselves laughing at this obvious set-up. But to my surprise, there's no one there. This child actually knows my music? Just another one of the wonders of this world I'm living in that I've got to get used to.

When I glance towards a silently chuckling Ava, she's gesturing over the child's head: *I think she's a little in love with you.*

*I think* he's *in love with you,* I motion in turn towards Spidey. *And, I think I'm in love with you, too.* But, turning to hand her damp, sleepy partner over to his mum, Ava missed that bit.

Just as well, perhaps. My own tiny dancer is making a fuss as her mum pulls her away too, but my mind is elsewhere. Did I mean it? Love is a big word.

A very big word. I glance over at Ava.

I came here tonight to remember who I was. Who I *still am*. I push away the tightness in my chest that threatens to overwhelm me. There's no place for that here tonight. And I'm starting to see that, even if there is so much I still don't understand, maybe there are some deeper truths to our lives that hold? They always hold. It's come as something of a shock to me to recognise it but I'm seeing now...

The fact that I love Ava – that much is still true.

# 34

# AVA

'So, what d'you reckon? *These?*' I place a pair of hiking boots down on the patio table in front of Will. 'Or, these?' I dangle the elegant pair of heels I'm holding in my other hand.

He opens one eye, lazily.

'Uh. Either, maybe. Both?' The sun is shining off his face, turning the short, fair hairs of his beard a reddish gold. I can't resist reaching out to touch his cheeks. He looks up for a kiss and we lean in together close, enjoying the moment.

'Okay,' I say at last, settling on the chair beside him. I need to get down to business. 'Can you at least tell me if I should be packing my passport?'

A small smile appears at the corners of his mouth. 'That much,' he tells me, 'I can confirm.'

*Ha.* I get a zing of excitement in my belly. *Thought as much.*

'Wonderful.' It's the Austrian mountains, then? Either that, or Santorini. Could be either, 'cos I glimpsed guidebooks for both of those locations artfully hidden amongst the pile of books he keeps downstairs. I only need to narrow it down a little. Without appearing to, naturally, but a girl being whisked away for a romantic break by her partner does need to be prepared.

'Beautiful morning,' I murmur.

'It is,' he answers lazily.

'I wonder if it'll be quite as warm where we're going?'

'It's likely.'

'No need for jackets, then, you reckon?'

'I'd take one, anyway.' He's leaned back in his chair again, shutting his eyes.

'Smart or... more functional, d'you think?' I don't know what the Austrian alps will be like in July, but, 'I imagine the higher up you go, the colder it gets,' I say casually. 'There again, if you're near water, it can also get chilly at night.' I pause, biting my lip as I realise his face has taken on that same peaceful, faraway look he gets when he's composing.

'Will?'

'Uh?' He blinks his eyes open again.

'You don't seem very... concerned, given that we're off today?'

'Why should I be concerned?'

'Because...' I breathe out. 'We'll be flying out of the country in a few hours' time and I still have no clue what to pack!'

'Okay,' he relents. 'Seeing as we're so near to leaving, I will give you three clues, Ava Morley. But, only three. Will you be satisfied with that?'

'Three clues?' I sit up. 'Definitely.'

'Fine. First clue.' He strokes his chin for a moment. '*First* clue is that this is a place you're definitely going to enjoy, whatever you end up packing, so you don't need to worry and that's an absolute promise.'

I nod, hoping the next clue will be a little more informative.

'Second clue, there's an important thing about this location that both you and the place have in common.'

'Me and the place? Ooh.' I can feel my smile widening, racking my brains, trying to imagine what on earth that could possibly be. 'An important thing, you say, like, what... a name? Like... Avila? That's a place in Spain, isn't it?' I think some friends of mine went to a place called something like that a few years back. 'Are we going to Spain?'

He shrugs, not letting on.

'Third clue,' he says solemnly, 'what happens on this holiday will be something that you're *never* going to forget.'

'My word.' I beam. 'You're really building all this up, Will.'

'It's going to be good!'

I shoot him a look, recalling that I heard him use that exact same phrase once before, when he took me on one of our very early dates a few years back, and it turned out to be a camping holiday. I remember him setting his alarm for 4 a.m. so we could both be awake to see the sunrise together. I felt like an actual ice block but *he* thought it was the most romantic thing ever. I swallow down my disappointment as it dawns on me that my boyfriend doesn't have the air about him of anyone about to undertake international travel...

He's way too chilled.

Now I think on it, Will put a wash on earlier, too. I reckon half of his favourite T-shirts are still going around in the machine. I'd sneakily hoped to be able to garner some clues from whatever Will put away in his own suitcase, but he's not even started sorting out his luggage yet, has he? And he's told me to be ready for 3 p.m.?

I feel my shoulders slump. 'I hope you're not playing me, with the whole *needing your passport* thing, and we end up going camping to Slapton Ley again?'

'Where?'

'Never mind.' I stand up. 'I'm off to finish packing. Time waits for no man,' I hint heavily.

Will opens out his arms. 'I packed my case while you were taking a shower, earlier. I've booked us the taxi for this afternoon, and I've already asked Elsie to put the rubbish out for us, Monday morning, so it doesn't sit there all week.'

I blink. 'Oh. You already took care of all that?' When I glance over to the clothes line, for the first time I notice he's got the washing hung out, as well.

He follows my gaze. 'It's okay. Rain's forecast, but Elsie's promised to take that down for us, too.'

'Uh. Right.'

'Ready to put your faith in me yet, Ava?'

Like he's had to do with me, he means? I guess I am. Blowing him a kiss, I run off to get on with my packing.

After all, I'm about to be whisked off on a surprise holiday that *I'm never going to forget.*

# 35

# AVA

'Oh, my!' Coming out of the cool, white-painted lobby, I notice the cobbled street outside our hotel has been freshly rain washed during the night.

'Look,' I say. 'Look at *that.*' Shining out of the puddle of water in front of us is the perfect reflection of a medieval cherub carved out of stone. It's sitting nonchalantly, high up on the façade of our hotel. Everywhere you go in this city, there are gems just like it. 'This is so *not* what I was expecting.'

The hotel Will's brought me to is stunning but there's a natural beauty to this place that trumps even that. Lit up by the morning sun, the pavement in front of us is so steeply bathed in gold, I need to put a hand up to shield my eyes.

'When I first spotted our destination at the airport gate, *Florence*, I imagined that it'd be a stop-over flight to somewhere else, like...'

Will nudges me gently. 'To somewhere like Santorini or the Austrian Alps?'

I turn to stare at him, feeling my face flush. 'You knew I thought that?'

'Oh, I think I'm getting the measure of you.'

'You are?' I bite my bottom lip, the realisation dawning. 'William, you deliberately "hid" those other guide books in amongst the pile, didn't you?'

'No. I did originally consider those other two places,' he admits easily. 'I just deliberately didn't remove the books.'

'Because you knew I'd find them?' I want to be annoyed but I can't help breaking into a smile. 'I'm not sure who's the sneakier of the two of us... or would you say that we're evenly matched?'

'I honestly don't know. But, all *sneakiness* aside...' he looks at me hopefully '... are you happy with my choice of holiday destination?'

'Very happy. Florence is the perfect place to have brought me.' I add after a bit, 'Like the unexpected breakfast in bed you ordered for us this morning. Very rock and roll.'

He smiles.

'Not sure that's how the Red Sphynx people would describe me, but I hoped you'd enjoy it. Sorry it wasn't the champagne breakfast...' He looks towards my bump, meaningfully. Across the narrow road, he leans against the old stone wall that runs alongside the river's length and unfurls the city map they handed us at Reception.

'Only, according to this guide, it says, *"The Ponte Vecchio is best appreciated through the eyes of those intoxicated..."*'

'"... the eyes of those intoxicated with the magic of true *love*,"' I read out. 'Not champagne! D'you think we qualify?'

He stretches one arm behind his head, grinning.

'Maybe if the hotel's fire alarm hadn't gone off last night at the most crucial moment...' he says softly.

'Bad timing,' I agree. 'The smoky candles from that lady who was trying to have a romantic candle-lit bath kind of ruined the moment for us a bit, didn't it?'

We'd all had to troop out into the hotel courtyard while the fire brigade located the source of the smoke.

'I'm sure there'll be other moments like it.'

'Maybe.' I look away swiftly, hiding my smile. 'If you're lucky.'

I lock my arm through his and we walk on down for a further hundred yards or so. Here, a right turn takes us directly onto the cobbled, medieval street over the Ponte Vecchio. It's quiet, this early. Peaceful and deserted of most tourists. All the high-end jewellery and trinket shops lining the bridge are shut but an ornate lattice-work heart pendant in a shop window leaps out at me.

'Oh, my. Some of these pieces are going to be *perfect* for incorporating into costume design ideas, later on,' I tell him, excited. He waits patiently while I go through all the window displays, taking photos.

Then, I want some pictures of the two of us. Firstly, we're in dark shadow and then, in the middle where there's a break in the row of buildings further down, we're lit up by bright sunlight. I get some shots of us with the wide green river flowing behind and the fairy-tale setting of pretty houses in the distance. Then some pictures of the statue of a famous goldsmith named Cellini, by the ornate metal railings. The railings, intriguingly, appear to have *hundreds* of old, weathered padlocks attached to them and we stop to wonder at them for a bit.

'What could these be for?' Will bends to examine them a little more closely. 'They're much too small to be any use for bicycles, but... ah!' He's got our trusty, annotated hotel tourist map out again.

'Interesting. According to this, *"Legend has it that if lovers attach a padlock to any place on this bridge then throw away the key into the Arno, their love will last for all eternity."*'

'Really?' I run my fingers lightly along the top of them all. 'For all eternity?'

'Apparently.'

'Wouldn't that be something, though? If people could always remember how they felt about each other, when...' I swallow, glancing over at him a little sadly. 'When they were in the first throes of their love? That would be a real bit of magic, wouldn't it?'

'I guess it would.' He comes up behind me, putting his arms protectively around my shoulders. We peer over the wall, lost in our own thoughts, scanning the choppy, fast flowing river Arno as it streams past. Being carried along with it this morning are two families of ducks, three swans and some unidentifiable brown bird that's trying its level best to swim in the opposite direction. Will watches the bird for a bit, shoulders shaking.

*'Forget it.'* He cups his hand to his mouth. 'Give up, little brown bird, and go with the flow. Your life will be that much easier.'

'Is that your most considered advice?'

'Hell, no.' He turns to lean against the wall, facing me. 'If I were *really* giving him some advice, I'd tell him to swim in whatever darn direction his little heart pulled him in. We'd all end up on the same shore, otherwise, and what's the point of that?'

I smile at him curiously. 'Is that how you felt the day you decided to leave DelRoy's band, to write your own kind of music?'

'I guess I did.' He goes quiet for a moment, perhaps reliving that decision. 'I've always needed to do my own thing, creatively at least. Not always what's expected of me.' He adds ruefully, 'But... you probably already know that?'

'I know it, Will.' I add, 'It's part of what I love about you.'

A new thought occurs to him. 'Ava, we haven't... I mean, *you and I*, we haven't been here already, have we? Like... you told me I went to Bali and I had no idea of it.'

'We've never been here before,' I say.

'Well, I'm glad, you know that?'

'You're glad?'

'I'm glad that you're the one standing on this bridge with me on this beautiful morning, Ava. Watching that brown duck, breathing in this fresh air and enjoying the river. I'm glad that the first person I'm ever experiencing this magical place with is *you*.' He reaches out his hand to catch hold of mine.

'Likewise.'

'Hey,' he offers now. 'How about I attach one of those eternal love padlocks up there for you and me, Ava? I could do it, y'know.'

I laugh. 'No, you can't.'

'Oh, yes, I can.' In what feels like one beautiful, serendipitous moment, he remembers the little padlock he detached from his suitcase when we got to the hotel last night. One minute he's feeling for it in his pocket and then, 'Look.' He's holding it aloft for me to see, key and all.

I shake my head at him. 'William, *we can't...*'

'Who's to tell us that we can't?'

'Well, him, for starters.' I motion towards the unsmiling policeman who's walked past us, hands behind his back. 'And... then there's that.' I point out the sign placed prominently on a wall nearby, that Will doesn't seem to have noticed yet. Written in Italian, the import is clear enough.

A hefty penalty or even a prison stay might be involved, if anyone attempts to attach a padlock up here.

We've moved away from the railings to allay the policeman's suspicions, but he's stopped walking, and is standing nearby, watching us.

'He doesn't want us getting up to any mischief.' I laugh under my breath.

'What about eternal love, though?'

'What about the hefty penalty or prison stay?'

'The heck with that. Hey.' Will suddenly moves back nearer to the railings, jumping onto the back of Cellini's statue, waving his arms about. '*Take a picture of me*, Ava!'

Our policeman saunters over again, suddenly vigilant.

'Take some good ones,' Will calls to me. 'For my Instagram feed.'

'You don't have an Instagram feed.'

'Take some anyway...' He pulls a few funny faces, changing his pose, and I carry on snapping away. Eventually, some people come along asking the policeman for directions, which divides his attention. In the same moment, I see Will jump down off the statue, snapping his little padlock directly onto another one that's already up on the railings. It takes him all of ten seconds flat and for about two of those seconds, he looks pretty triumphant, until we spot that the policeman is already marching towards us, scowling.

I say to Will, 'D'you think there's a CCTV up here?'

'Christ.'

The policeman calls out. 'Hey!'

That's when I feel Will take hold of my hand.

*'Run.'*

I don't need telling twice. We both dash blindly like street urchins back the way we came, over the bridge, until an immediate turn to our right takes us out onto a long, sunlit, arching walkway. At the end of it, bumping into Will, breathless, I see him stop to toss the key into the river even while our pursuer is still calling angrily, 'Eh! *You two, stop!'*

'Oh, Lord,' I say. 'Now where to?'

'Anywhere.' Will looks over his shoulder determinedly. 'Just keep going...' A bit further on, I'm hoping, we'll be nearer the city centre. Other tourists are already up and roaming around and with any luck we'll get lost in amongst them. Or the policeman will.

Several minutes later, 'Boy, for a stocky dude, he really doesn't give up too easily.'

'Anyone would think he was apprehending people on commission.' I puff. 'Just imagine how many people could've attached their padlocks to the bridge in the time he's been busy chasing us!'

'We're doing all the lovers of Florence a favour.' Will turns back to wave at him cheerily. 'He'll return to a mountain of padlocks and serve him right...'

'Stop *making me laugh,*' I gasp. 'I can't run and laugh at the same time.' The policeman manages to hang onto our tail for a few minutes more but, finally, veering left into the cool darkness of the Piazza degli Uffizi, we're able to merge in with a bus load of tourists and lose him. Out of breath and doubled up with laughter, we collapse on some ancient stone steps opposite the mausoleum-like giant statues that line the entrance way to the galleria.

'William. You are seriously *crazy,*' I tell him, shivering. *'Pazzo!'* It's so much darker in here, more sombre, as if we've entered a graveyard.

'And you... I never knew you could sprint like that,' he says admiringly, rubbing at my arms.

'I never want to have to, again!'

'What, even for the promise of eternal love?'

'Even for that.'

I can't stop glancing towards the place where we came in. 'What if he's still waiting for us when we go back out onto the road?'

'You,' he reminds me, 'didn't do anything.'

'I was an accessory, distracting him with taking photos, wasn't I?'

'I suppose you were. My partner in crime. Hey, we make a good team though, you and I, you must admit?'

'We always have,' I tell him, and he smiles softly at me. Is he starting to believe it?

'Ava and Will,' he says. 'Has a ring to it, you agree? Like...' He leans back on the cold grey steps, searching for inspiration. 'Like... Bonnie and Clyde?'

I laugh. 'Definitely not!'

'Tristan and Isolde, then?' he offers, but I'm still shaking my head. '*Romeo and Juliet?* No? Not even...?'

'They all ended tragically, Will.'

'Ah, I see.'

'And that's not how it's going to be, for us.'

'No. Never,' he says solemnly. 'Speaking of which, did you work out what it is that you have in common with Florence yet?'

I lean in, intrigued.

'You're both *hopelessly romantic*.' He grins.

'Hah!'

Leaning in to take hold of my face, ever so gently, he adds, 'Don't look now, but our policeman has entered the area.'

'Oh, my word...'

My heart's thumping again, but Will's laughing quietly. 'If anything happens and we end up separated... I promise I'll wait for you,' he says gallantly.

'I guess you'd have to now.' I look at him through spread fingers. 'What with that *padlock* up there and all...'

'I guess I would.' He pulls me in closer to him, still laughing, burying his face in my hair. 'How about you, Ava – would you wait for me?'

'For all eternity,' I tell him quietly. 'I'd wait that long for you, William. But then, you already knew that, didn't you?'

# 36

# WILL

I've been trying to work my way up to this, all week, and I am not leaving Florence with it in my suitcase...

'Ava Morley...' I drop to one knee on the shiny cobblestones, just as a light shower comes pattering down onto our heads. Ava looks up, and then, quickly, back down at me.

'Ava Morley, will you do me the great honour of becoming my wife?'

'Will!' She gives a delighted peal of laughter but she's fumbling so much, I have to open up the little box for her, retrieve the shiny ring that's inside, and slip it onto her finger. It's diamond and white gold, fashioned into the shape of a heart, with a large sparkling gem in the middle that matches the heart pendant she was so keen to photograph in the window of the jeweller's on the bridge, that first day.

'When did you...?' She gulps.

'I nipped out and bought it when you went for a little nap at the hotel one afternoon.'

'But you never left the hotel, William?' She's shaking her head in disbelief. 'At least, I never heard you...'

'No,' I say softly. 'You weren't meant to.'

'Oh, my word. I can't believe that you...'

I smile at her. The people sitting at both of the adjacent tables have cottoned on, the moment lengthening as they all turn to look our way expectantly and, I realise, she hasn't given me an answer yet.

'Yes? No?' I prompt. *'Maybe?'*

Ava's looking completely overwhelmed, like I haven't seen her before. She stares at me for a moment, then, throwing her arms around my neck, she buries her face.

'God. *Yes,*' she whispers hoarsely. 'A thousand, thousand times, yes.'

A loud cheer goes up from the surrounding tables, warming my heart. This is what I've longed for. I can feel it, in my bones. Something I've wanted for a very long time. I hug Ava tight, laughing. She holds onto me for so long that when she finally lifts her head, I'm surprised to feel my neck is cold and wet.

'So sad?' I pull a rueful smile.

'Not sad,' she says gruffly. 'I'm crying because I'm *so happy*.'

'You sure you're happy?' This *'tears of joy'* thing that women do, I'm never sure I'm totally comfortable with it.

'I am happier at this moment than I've ever been in my life.'

I rub at her arms affectionately, recognising with a shot of sadness that what my girlfriend actually sounds like is *very relieved*. And understandably so.

'I'm only sorry it's taken me a little while to get to this point,' I begin.

'*Don't*, Will.' She strokes my fingers. It's starting to sink in now. What's happened. Where this leaves the two of us. 'In all honesty...' she motions towards the glittering diamond on her hand, adding '... this is probably a much quicker proposal than any girl has a right to hope for.'

I smile. 'This is the weirdest thing, isn't it?'

'Very weird.'

'Ava, did we never actually talk about getting married?' I glance at her curiously. 'Before all this happened, I mean?' We were together three years, and with a baby on the way, how come we never...?

'We might've spoken about it a couple of times.' She's dabbing at her face with a tissue. 'But you only ever brought it up in your usual jokey way, y'know, Will. I was never sure if what you really wanted was...' She stops.

'I *do* want,' I say, holding her gaze. 'I very much want.'

She smiles, but I can see tears glittering in her eyes again. 'You've no idea how long I've waited for you to say that.'

'Forever?'

She shoots me a pained look and I put up one hand. Okay. No more jesting, not for tonight. Ava takes a long drink of the lemonade she's been sipping all evening. Then, putting her damp tissues away in her handbag, she says apologetically, 'Oh, my gosh, Will, I'm *so* sorry but I really need to go visit the Ladies again...'

'No need to apologise, babe...'

It dawns on me now, she's a little shell-shocked. Was this all too much, done without any warning and maybe too publicly? I thought it'd be romantic and I promised her a holiday she would never forget so I thought she'd be excited and happy.

I think she is.

She accepted my proposal, didn't she? She must be happy.

As Ava goes off, her shoulders slightly hunched, wobbling slightly on the damp cobblestones, I fight the urge to run after her and hold her hand, make sure she gets there and back safely, but while I'm still dithering a new message from Toby pings in.

Meeting with Tom Redwick from the film company set up and confirmed for last week in Sept – details below (Hallelujah and all the saints be praised, as Pastor Williamson would've said). Can you confirm your end?

Oh, man. So Toby's actually done it! I feel a leap of excitement, doing a joyous fist-in-the-air, beaming into my phone. Now that I appreciate exactly what it will have taken for him to set this up, and *who these people are*, what they could potentially do for my career, the feeling that all the stars are aligned for me just got stronger.

Wild horses wouldn't keep me away, I text him back. Plus, Ava's just agreed to marry me!

A string of celebratory emojis ping straight back from him. My head's reeling. I sit back, smiling to myself, and the kindly Italian man sitting at the next table plants a small glass of something celebratory, which looks like limoncello, in front of me. These people love family, I remember. They appreciate and honour the bonds of love, wherever they may be, and touchingly, even though they don't know us from Adam, he and his wife seem to want to be in on the celebration. He does a *'drink it'* motion, beaming.

*To the many joys we've been blessed with in our lives.* DelRoy's toast returns to me, and I have had many. Ava even had her ultrasound scan last week and all is well with the baby. They told us it's a boy! I happily oblige the old gent.

'*Prego.*'

'She is very, very happy.' He leans in to assure me. 'You are too lucky, eh?'

I am. Oh, yes, I am.

*Lucky* and… I stare up at the sky, palms upturned as yet another sprinkling of summer rain begins to fall gently across the piazza. I muse, in the heat of this afternoon, sightseeing, this would've been such a relief. Only when did the evening turn so chilly?

I didn't notice it. I didn't notice the lights slowly being turned off around the square, either. When I look around me now, I get the strangest sense something's slowly turning off inside me too. Something I can't explain and the experience leaves me feeling puzzled and also a little troubled.

*C'mon, Will! With* all the many joys you've been blessed with… *I swear, you should be feeling lit up inside like a bloody Christmas tree.*

I want to. I knock back the drink the old gent's poured for me, generously, from his own bottle, accepting the warm handshake he extends to me, his smile enshrining all the happiness that's present in the moment. And I long to feel all that, truly. But the drink goes down as bitter as Gil's fine malt whisky. And this time, I can't pretend to myself that it's my altered sense of taste.

So, *what the heck...?*

I clench my fists under the table, frustrated at myself for not feeling the sheer happiness I was expecting to feel. In its place, there's only a dark puddle, like the one that's forming in the middle of the piazza. A puddle of water that's reflecting nothing back, none of the statues; none of the architecture; none of the beauty of this place, because it's all got too dark.

I realise with a scary sense of emptiness that I can't actually feel the happiness that I want to feel. That I surely deserve to feel.

I can't.

I don't.

# 37

# AVA

Ginny's taking forever. Sitting on one of the elegant reception chairs outside her office, I'm practically squirming with excitement. She doesn't know about the engagement yet! I've deliberately kept it under wraps, savouring the anticipation, just so I could see the look on her face when I tell her. Last time I was with her, Will had barely got out of hospital, so she's going to be gobsmacked at how I've turned this around – I'm feeling pretty proud of myself.

I sit up, hearing her office door open. *Finally.* But she is not alone.

'The money we've received from your organisation has been a real game-changer...' Ginny's smiling gratefully at the smartly dressed, middle-aged woman she's just accompanied out. Glimpsing me waiting, she stiffens a little. Had she forgotten I was coming today? I see her motion silently, now, *Be with you in five!*

'The trustees at the Venus Sanctuary Outreach are going to be delighted with my report on your progress.' The woman's shaking her hand warmly. 'Money well spent, for sure – this enterprise is a real showcase for what women can achieve.' She stops for a meaningful pause. 'Especially unfortunate women who've found themselves in the same unhappy position you were once in.'

'Thank you, Margaret.' Ginny rapidly hands the woman her coat.

'I'm very happy you think so.' The minute she leaves, Ginny leans back against the door, making a show of wiping her brow.

'Phew!'

I smile.

'Who was *that*?' Whoever she is, I'm glad she's gone.

'Uh! Margaret's on the board of a grant-giving trust, nothing exciting, just someone I need to schmooze every so often.' My friend motions me into the privacy of her office and closes the door with a loud exhalation of breath.

'*You*, however, I am always delighted to see.' She pauses to give me an appraising once-over now, her gaze lingering on my increasing girth.

'Or should I say, you two?'

I give a small laugh.

Then, almost immediately, she says, 'Oh, my actual giddy aunt! What's that bloody great rock doing on your finger?'

I hold up my hand, jiggling my ring finger so she can better see my shiny sparkler.

'He *never*?'

'He did!' I laugh. 'Will proposed to me while we were in Florence.'

'But that was...' she stops the expletive that's about to explode from her lips, changing it to '... a whole friggin month ago, Ava!'

We both sit down and she looks at me incredulously.

'And you've kept it *quiet*?'

'I *have* been doing my level best to catch up with you ever since we got back...'

'You have, true.' She does a waving motion with her hands. 'I've been so ridiculously busy, dealing with clients, and I've also had some unexpected...' she falters a bit here '... potential upsets to plans. Which is, sort of, what Margaret was here about.'

'I picked up you were looking a little...' I don't quite say the word *fraught*. I've been dying to meet up with my bestie ever since Florence, but this sounds like a bit of a bummer. 'Things haven't been too bad, I hope?' When she doesn't reply, I ask politely, 'What's up with this Venus Sanctuary Outreach, anyway?'

'Eh?' She stares blankly at me for a moment. 'Oh, it's a... women's shelter enterprise, Ava. Part of the boring business side of things, and honestly nothing you need concern yourself about.'

Just as well. We've far more exciting things to talk about today! I see my friend taking in a deep breath.

'So... how was Florence?' She plumps up the cushion in her lap, giving me her full attention for the moment.

'Amazing!' I sit up, beaming. 'I can't tell you how much we loved it.'

'Did you get to see the exhibition of medieval fabrics they've got on at the leather market just now?'

'Ah...' I'm forced to admit, 'We only really crammed our sightseeing into the last two days.' I smile. 'Too busy... *you know*.'

'Lucky you!' Her eyes narrow a little. 'I wish things were going so well in that department for me and Ned. Still...' She leans over to top up the glass of sauvignon blanc she's already got going on the coffee table, leaving me to pour my own soda water.

'It must be a huge relief,' she muses. 'With everything getting back to normal with Will, and such?'

I shoot her a puzzled glance. She's saying all the right words, but she's not really present.

'He's even got that fabulous project going with Toby Myers, no? You mentioned they met up with some film people?'

'Sure.' I pause, surprised she's even remembered that.

'Well, fantastic!' She chinks her glass against mine. 'If his film contacts need any help at all in the costume departments...?'

I nod, putting down my soda. She hasn't even asked me if we've started having any venue ideas or making any wedding plans, yet! She hasn't made any comment about how she's – *obviously* – going to be one of my maids of honour. It's like... my wedding's not even happening! This is so not like Gin. I imagined this'd be all we'd talk about today, but she's not in the slightest bit curious – doesn't she even care?

Her phone beeps and she can't resist glancing at it.

'So, anyway.' Texting done, she leans in and pats my knee suddenly. 'How about all those lovely costumes you've brought in for me to see?'

I give a slightly disappointed laugh.

'You sure you want to look at them right *now*?' I brought them in because she asked me, but they're hardly the focus of my trip here today. It's as if she wants to talk about anything and everything that *isn't* to do with my news. What's up with her today? Feeling distinctly put out, I lean over to retrieve my bag as she's asked, shaking out the first of the garments, and she exclaims loudly.

'Oh, excellent! This is exactly what my clients were looking for.' I hand her the dress, and watch as she examines it minutely, her eagle eye taking in every seam and every stitch.

'Thank you so much!' She's muttering, 'And... sorry for keeping you waiting, earlier.'

'Hey, we're all good.'

'Margaret took up *far* too much of my time this morning and just when we've got a rush job on, that's not good.'

I shoot her a polite smile. Ginny never wastes her time with people she doesn't want to be with, I know that much.

'I'm guessing it was important you dealt with her, if she handles all the funds allocated by the trust?'

Ginny nods. There's no doubt much of her uptightness is down to stress over their meeting. As soon as I get her out of the office and into some lovely bistro I reckon I'll have her talking flowers and churches and castle-on-the-hill venues in no time.

'She was saying lovely things, and she's clearly got the measure of you,' I reassure her. 'Apart from that one strange comment about... *unfortunate women who've found themselves in the same unhappy position you were once in* – what was that about?'

She looks up and I give a little shrug.

'Well, you never *were* in that kind of position, yourself, were you?'

'How'd you mean?'

I can feel my eyes widening in surprise. I spell it out. 'You weren't ever forced to seek refuge in a women's shelter?'

'Well, no.'

'That's what I meant, then.' This is weird. How did we even get onto this topic?

I delve into my bag, keen to get the costumes over with, and Ginny adds, a little defensively, 'She might think that, but I never actually said so, on any occasion.'

'You wouldn't have.'

'No.' She's busy pulling at the seams of the costume I've handed her, holding the material up to the light, but her mouth is doing something strange. I lean in, feeling a little worried.

'You *didn't*, did you – have to spend some time in a women's shelter, I mean? Ginny, if there are some things about your early life I never knew about and I've made some wrong assumptions...'

'Yeah, you're pretty good at doing that, sometimes, aren't you?' The cutting edge in her voice is unmistakeable.

'I'm sorry?'

She puts my garment down. 'I know everything's going great in your life right now, but maybe you've forgotten what a cut-throat business we work in? You don't get this level of success handed to you on a plate. You have to work your backside off, accept help wherever it's offered, *including* this kind of grant.'

I sit back, feeling a little startled. Where has all this come from?

'I-I get that,' I stutter. 'And it's totally okay that you applied for a grant if you needed it.'

Whatever's eating at Ginny, she's not done yet. 'You *knew*,' she says, eyes glittering, 'about the grant! I told you it was what helped me get this business off the ground in the first place.'

I open up my arms. 'Gin... it's okay.' She might've mentioned something. I had a lot going on in my own life back then.

'Of course, I *was* involved with one of those shelters myself at one time,' she says solicitously. 'Otherwise I wouldn't have been eligible to apply.'

I look away, feeling sad for her. Ginny takes a big slug of her drink. 'It was every Saturday afternoon, y'know, for a whole year. I used to go up with some other girls from school and we'd help entertain their children, so the women at the shelter could have a little free time.'

I sit back. 'Now, I am confused.'

She's twiddling her empty glass in between her fingers. 'Okay. Between you and me, I might have egged the pudding a little, when it came to filling in my grant application form...'

The penny has finally dropped. I stifle a gasp. 'Ginny, you...?'

She's saying defensively, 'It was a genuine error. I didn't deliberately set out to deceive anyone. I hope you don't think that I did? By the time I found out that maybe, possibly, this grant hadn't been set up for the likes of me, well, it was all a little too late. The money had been spent. Or allocated.'

I stare at her.

'Oh, c'mon! How d'you think I landed the film production clients I did?' She's looking a little bleary eyed. 'The ones who *you're* employed to work for now? That all costs money, y'know. Making contacts. Being in the right place at the right time...'

I really don't know what to say.

She's staring at me defensively. 'You think I don't deserve it?'

'Hell, Ginny. You deserve a grant, yes. Only, surely not this one, not if it was intended to go to women who...?'

She gives a loud laugh. I watch as Ginny puts her wine glass deliberately back down on the table.

'You really *don't have a clue*, do you?'

I sit back, letting this sink in. Now, she just sounds guilty as hell. I reckon she *knows* what she's doing is wrong, and is just wishing she hadn't let it slip to me.

'You didn't have a clue before, and you still don't...' She growls, 'If you had any idea how this game is played, you'd still be in it. Someone as talented as you, you'd have been feeding *me* the work, not the other way around. If you're not in that place now, that's only because of...'

I shoot her a warning look. 'Because of what?' If she's bringing up my past now, it's only because she feels caught out on something *she's* done wrong. She's folded her arms.

'I'm only saying that *in life*, you sometimes have to tell people what they want to hear and that way you get what you want. Everyone's happy and there's no harm done.'

No harm? I roll my eyes. 'Whatever you put on that grant application form, it was your choice, Ginny.'

She narrows her eyes at me. 'Sometimes we all have to make difficult choices in what we say or don't say to people, you do understand that, don't you?' She adds quietly, 'I know that you do.'

I flush. 'If you're still banging on about why I left my job in the fashion industry...?'

'I'm not,' she says softly. 'I'm talking about Will.'

I stare at her, shocked.

'Oh, you're always so careful not to open up to anyone – not even your best friends!' she taunts. 'But I'd lay good money on it – Will still doesn't know all there is to know, does he?'

'What are you even *talking* about, Ginny?' She doesn't know a thing about it. She's just... reaching, because she's feeling miffed, but we're supposed to be friends, has she forgotten that? And her words feel hurtful. I pick up my sample garments, shoving them back into my bag.

'Listen. I think we're done here for today, don't you?'

For one hopeful moment, I think she's going to break into one of her infectious laughs, change the subject and suggest we head off to have our lunch. I'm not entirely sure I even want to, any more. I came in here today feeling so carefree and happy. How did our conversation veer so swiftly into something that feels as venomous as this? We need to pull things back together, but Ginny's saying coolly, 'See you soon, then, honey.'

I stand up, feeling wobbly. She doesn't even care that I'm leaving like this? She obviously feels I've somehow insulted her, challenged her choices, and she's hit back where it hurts. Heading for the Tube station, I am completely gutted but also glad to be homebound. Whatever's going on for Gin, I don't feel strong enough to cope with her reaction today.

Only lost and deeply confused.

# 38

# AVA

Robyn slides wearily into the chair across the table from me, her eyelids actually *drooping*. August is always busy but her friend's blog has caused an explosion of interest in the gardens this summer, and Robyn's taken on extra hours, here, working hard and saving up like mad for her Kos holiday. I smile, glad to see her. It's been ages since she and I caught up, and I have come, by way of reparation, bearing gifts. I place a small shopping bag down on the metal table between us and she opens one eye.

'What's this?'

'These,' I tell her, 'are the sparkly heels and the top you were admiring from the photo I sent you of my last night in Florence.'

A small smile crosses her lips. 'I also greatly admired the ring, don't forget.'

'That item's not up for loan, even for you.'

'No.' She takes up my finger and examines it more closely. 'It's a real stunner.' She adds a little quietly, 'I imagine Mum nearly fell out of her chair when you sent her a picture of it?'

'Pretty much. They'll have been thinking it's about time, no doubt.' I smile, feeling a little sentimental. *Finally*, what I want to do with my life is coinciding with what our parents would like me to do...'

Perhaps it's the wrong thing to say because, unusually for her, she doesn't come back with a quip. I glance curiously at Robyn. Is this because she's not looking forward to telling them about quitting uni?

'You been overdoing it, hon?'

'What?' She's taken my items out of the bag and she is lost, admiring the sparkly silver heels of my shoes, turning them this way and that in the sunshine.

'I mean... with all the extra hours here, and then all those house parties with Carenza's mates that you've been telling me about...?' I smile at my sister, but she's still subdued.

'I *guess*.' She puts my shoe carefully down on the table. 'These are lovely, Ava. Thanks for bringing them.' She takes in a breath. 'I shan't be needing them any more, though.'

'Oh?' She's just turned her face away. '*What?*' I tap her arm gently, feeling a little alarmed. 'What's going on?'

'I'm not going anywhere, that's all.' She swallows. 'Me and Carenza had a falling out. And I'm not going.'

'You two had a falling out?' I stare at her, trying to take this in. 'Since when?'

'Since... she packed up her things and left, a week ago,' she finally admits.

'She *left*?' I blink. 'Why ever haven't you rung me? You haven't said?'

'No.'

'But...' I shake her arm a little, seeing her eyes glittering. '*Why*, Robyn?'

'Why did I not say, or why has Carenza left?'

'Either. Both.' I open up my arms, feeling more distressed by her sadness than surprised. Carenza was always a car crash waiting to happen. 'Listen, I thought you'd been such bosom buddies, having a ball working here at the gardens together and everything?' A touch of guilt hits me, recalling how all my initial reservations about her uni mate turning up and somehow saying all the wrong things to my fiancé had never materialised. In the end, her friend and her blog seem to have been a force for the good.

When she doesn't answer me, I prompt, 'You two were having such fun. And wasn't she teaching you all the tricks of the trade, how to monetise a blog and so on?'

'Yes, we did start doing that.' My sister's back stroking the sparkly bits on my shoes. 'And we *were* having fun. Carenza knows a lot of people,' my sister says in a croaky voice. I'm aware, all of the last month, I've been receiving photos of the two of them from all over the place.

I look at her, concerned. 'So, what's gone so terribly wrong?'

Robyn pushes back her hair. 'That's just it,' she gets out. 'There wasn't any one, really big thing. And I'm not actually sure *how* it happened.' She casts her eyes over towards me. 'I'd been keeping quiet about a load of things, y'know, Ava. Just... little things. Because living with her wasn't as easy as you might imagine.'

I hide my smile. 'I didn't imagine.'

'No. Well. It wasn't, anyway, because despite the fact there was only us two girls, you'd think there was an army of people living in the house. She'd leave stuff lying around everywhere and then she'd never lift a finger. She said it was because of all the extra work she had, teaching *me* stuff for the blog, which of course I understood. So, I cleared up after her myself.'

I nod. So far, it sounds like the kind of typical stuff two girls might get into, nothing major. Robyn hasn't finished though.

'But then, there were other things... like, groceries. I'd be the one getting in all the staples, like bathroom stuff and then bread and milk and cereal and... everyday food.'

I grimace. 'Is there anything left?'

'For Carenza, yes, because she'd go out every so often and splurge on some really extravagant champagne, or, like, one time we went into Harrods food hall, and she came away with some truffles and caviar, to treat us, she said.'

Oh, dear.

'She ended up cross with me because I *didn't appreciate her treat* and scoffed it all herself! And then, if I'd ever mention her contributing to the everyday groceries, she'd bring up the truffles, as if that made up for it, somehow...'

It's all beginning to add up... what happened to their beautiful relationship.

'So, you fell out over the household stuff?'

Robyn shakes her head. 'Not exactly *fell out*. I didn't want to rock the boat. She was my friend and she was my guest, and I was also having a good time because of her. But then one day she mentioned that she'd changed her flight so she was flying out to Kos a few days *ahead* of me. For a wedding, she said. Which was *fine* by me, I understood that. She has a lot of relatives, I don't expect to hitch a ride on every single invite she gets, but...'

I lift my cup and take a sip of tea, waiting patiently while Robyn picks up her own, but she doesn't drink, only stares into it. I'm getting the sense we're coming to the crux of the matter.

'I thought it was really odd that she has some special shoes... a bit like *these*... that she wears for every glam occasion, but she wasn't packing them. When I mentioned it, she got all shirty. Accused me of *prying*, and said I was being rude.' Robyn gulps. 'When I really wasn't.'

'No. Oh, Robbie!'

'And *then*, it turned out she was going away with some other friends, not to a wedding at all, and she didn't say because she didn't want to invite me. Because – get this – I might bring up the un-classy subject of money, she said. Like, not wanting to go equal shares with all her buddies after they'd had a hard night of drinking and I'd been sipping one orange juice all evening. And *that* comment made me really cross, because that only ever happened once, and with her mates who all have high-flying jobs in the city when *they know* I'm relatively broke. It seemed so unfair, and I told her so.'

She's been hanging out with people who're older and wealthier than her. There had to be a reality check of sorts at some point, but seeing my sister this upset really bugs me. I lean in and give her a hug.

'Hey, at least you were able to tell her how you felt?'

'Yes, but *that's* when she...' Robyn's eyes go even more round and sad. 'She completely flipped on me. Told me she'd put up with my ways for long enough and she'd been feeling for a while that we weren't well suited to being friends and then she left.'

'Oh. I'm so sorry, Robbie.' My sister's dissolved into tears. Ginny and I had parted with an awkward hug last time we'd met, but... it's over, I know it is. And I'm only too aware how much it hurts, how Robbie's going to miss her best friend like crazy. I know for sure that I've been missing mine.

'Sometimes...' I open up my arms. 'Sometimes friendships only work well for both parties for a little while, hon.'

But Robbie's still distraught. 'I thought she'd be back, y'know, because she hadn't packed anything, but then this morning I got a text through saying she'd like me to pack everything up and send it on by courier for her.'

I hold the thought that perhaps she should stick it all in the dump. 'So,' I pull myself up, getting back to the matter at hand. 'You've been at home alone since she left, and now there's no holiday in Kos, either?'

My sister gives a small shake of her head. 'Turns out you were completely right about Carenza.'

I'm about to tell her how much I wish I had been wrong when a bright yellow butterfly lands on a jasmine flower by Robbie's ear and despite everything she manages a smile.

'Hey, that's the type of butterfly Old Harry showed me when I first came here.' She tells me quietly, 'He said it's one of the most difficult to breed, in this climate, he's never had any success with it at all, and I told him I had a feeling that he'd make it, this year...'

'He'll be very happy, then, *if he remembers*.'

She nods. 'It's an achievement. Even if he doesn't remember. He'll be happy to see it – he deserves it after being so persevering.' She says, turning to me now, 'Like *you*, Ava. You always persevere, don't you?'

I give a surprised laugh. 'Do I?'

'It's how you make it through everything, isn't it?' She's still looking sad. 'Y'know, when you contacted me from Florence that night, I was sitting with a load of Carenza's friends on a gorgeous barge in the middle of the Thames.'

'I remember.' I give her a soft nudge. 'It was a balmy evening and you were being treated to some outrageously expensive cocktails.'

'I was.' She gulps. 'And all I could think was... none of this fills me up, none of it makes me smile the way you were smiling that night, because I don't have anyone who loves me like Will loves you.'

I give a sad laugh. 'I love you, you big Dodo!'

'Not the same thing.'

I put my hand firmly on her arm. 'You'll get there, Robyn.'

She says, her voice trembling, 'I hope so. You're the one who's always had all the big dreams, always gone right after whatever it was you wanted. First, with your fashion career, then with Will. You persevere and at the same time you're always so... unapologetically *you* and I wish... *I* could be more like that.'

Her words come as a warm surprise but also go some way towards healing the sore place inside that's taken a hit since my falling out with Ginny.

'Well, then,' I tell her fondly. 'What's stopping you?'

My sister gives a small shrug. 'I told Carenza how I felt and look where it got me. What is it they say about *the truth shall set you free*?' she mutters. 'Well, it's not always the case. It hasn't done much for me, has it?'

'The truth,' I admit, 'can sometimes be overrated.'

We both know the truth, on this occasion, has cost her a friend. *Whereas,* the memory flits back, *there can be no question that Ginny's lies have benefitted her enormously.*

Robyn's still looking troubled and forlorn. 'You think maybe I should never have said anything to her? I'd have still had it all going on, wouldn't I? The lifts into work in her cute little sports car. The holiday, the friends, the potential Greek job...' She looks at me regretfully. 'Would *you* have told her, Ava?'

I take a moment before answering my sister, because I have told my fair share of lies and had the benefit of them, too. Only, I reflect – unlike Ginny, my lies never hurt anyone. And – despite anything my old mate might believe – I never set out to tell them for my own benefit. How else could I have kept Will alive?

I swallow. 'I think you did what you had to do.'

The white, star shaped jasmine flowers beside us are giving off a heady perfume, and for a few moments we just sit, drinking our tea, basking in the dappled shade. We watch the yellow butterfly as it hovers around for a bit, sipping from each flower, a little here and a little there.

'Simple pleasures, eh?' Robyn's gutted at her change of circumstance, trying to put on a brave face. She sighs. 'I think you're right.' She gets up, rubbing at her eyes. 'And I think maybe what I gotta do *now* is get some rest. Mind if we finish this chat a little later, sis?'

'Sure, we can. Robyn, if there's anything you need...?'

I'm thinking the spare room at the cottage is still free, if she wants it. She's had a big setback, maybe she needs some TLC, but she says, 'Thank you. I'll ask you if I need anything, but I've a feeling I'll come back stronger from this if I... I find my own way. You do understand, don't you?'

I nod.

I've been there so very recently, haven't I? I understand completely. The thought of moving away from working for Ginny and starting afresh on my own has been a scary one and I'm still skirting around it.

The yellow butterfly's still there five minutes later when I see Robyn go out of the front gate of the tea rooms wheeling a rusty old bike. When she gets on it, wobbling like mad up the road, I have to hold in a sad laugh because of the memories that seeing her brings back. She never did learn how to ride a bike as a kid, my little sister. She was never too fond of the feeling of falling off. I can still see her, screwing up big, round eyes, wailing, *'The ground is too far away, it's such a long, long way down! If I fall down there it's going to hurt and I'm never going to get up again. Never!'*

I know exactly how she feels. I've got a sense she's willing to risk it this time round, though. She has to.

Maybe we both do?

# 39

# AVA

*Hey, I thought you'd be dressed already...* I'm about to walk into the bedroom bearing a couple of large mugs of tea but something about the way Will's sitting so quietly on the edge of the bed pulls me up short. So instead, I pause outside for a moment. It's mid-morning. The love of my life is still wearing nothing but his PJ bottoms and he's strumming, ever so softly, on the guitar in his lap. Looking at him with his head down, eyes closed and his thick, wavy hair already grown back over the wound, there's nothing to say there was anything ever amiss. Nothing to say that we had ever...

'Hello.' He opens his eyes and looks directly at me.

'Oh!' I laugh, coming in. 'You had that faraway look you get when you're composing and I didn't want to interrupt.'

He indicates his well-honed bod, a wry smile on his face. 'You sure you weren't just ogling *this*?'

'I wasn't.' Which is not entirely true. 'Though it's well worth ogling, as I'm sure you'll agree.' I set our mugs down on the nightstand and he reaches out to stroke my arm as I pass.

'I'd rather ogle yours, beloved.'

'You already availed yourself of *that* chance last night.' Our still-tousled bed sheets can testify to that much. 'And besides...' I look at him fondly. 'Weren't you meant to be getting up early for an online composing session with Toby this morning?'

He looks away, not answering that, and instead plays another few chords on his guitar. Not anything I recognise.

'Not going too well?'

'Sorry?'

'The composing. It's proving a little elusive?'

'It's not. I wasn't... this is an old song, Ava.' He's smiling affectionately and yet, it seems to me there's something troubling him this morning.

'An old song,' I say. 'That you're having difficulty with?'

He sighs quietly.

'An old song I used to love, that doesn't sound the same.'

I sit down carefully on the edge of the bed. 'You mean because you're hearing things differently?' Has Will's auditory sense, like his olfactory one, also altered? He never complains at all, never says much about what he's going through, but how strange this must all be, for him. I can't even imagine what it must be like. I pull my knees up a little and he puts his guitar to one side, making space for me.

'Or perhaps...' his hand goes up to cup softly around one of my earlobes '... I'm hearing things with different ears.'

'Different ears?' I kiss his cheek affectionately. 'Ever since the op, you mean?'

He shakes his head, ever so slightly.

'In a sensory way? Do you mean, like your sense of smell?' I scooch in closer. 'Like, the day you came running down to the Butterfly Gardens looking for me to give me back Lucky Troll and, after, you told me the scent of the lavender beds was the nearest you'd ever got to sensing heaven?'

He laughs sadly. 'It's something like that, only... the opposite. Because I can't...' He breathes out, and I get the sense he's suddenly too full to speak.

'Hey, *Will*, what's...?'

He's shut his eyes, pulling my face so close to his that our foreheads touch, not answering me. I can feel him trembling, and so full of reservation that he's scaring me.

'I can't reach... I don't... I just don't get the sense that there's too much heaven in the world, lately.'

'Why d'you say that?' My heart shrinks. 'What does that even *mean*, Will?'

'*Will?*'

'Babe. I need to tell you something and I'm not sure how best to say it.'

I swallow. 'Okay.'

'We promised we'd be honest and open with each other and I owe you that much. I'm... honestly experiencing the whole world very differently, right now.'

I wait, and he says, 'Ever since we came back from Florence, I've been thinking that... something's not quite right.'

I breathe in slowly, desperate not to let him see how scary this is for me. In all the weeks that have passed since our holiday, he's not said anything. We've been busy, each in our own ways and what with planning the wedding and stuff. He's never said. Have some of his symptoms returned?

'You're not feeling physically unwell in any way, are you? You *promise* you'd tell me if anything was...?'

'No, not that.'

'Then, what is it?'

'I wish I knew, babe.' He looks at me, pained. 'I don't know. I don't know what it is...'

I sit back a little, watching him. 'You *feel* it?'

He shakes his head sadly. 'No. That's precisely it. I'm not feeling it. What I'm expecting to feel, about... everything. My music. The bloody amazing contract with Toby's film producer. You, me...'

'You're unhappy with *us*? Last night, everything was fine, we were in bed together and you never showed any sign that...' My voice gets stuck in my throat.

'Not just us, babe! Everything. Every... little thing. Even...' He looks at my baby-bump, significantly, and the crushing sense of unhappiness I'm feeling dives even lower.

*Even that?*

I look at him, feeling shocked. 'Are you saying that you don't want...?'

He looks alarmed. 'Babe, please try and understand, this isn't about you *or* our baby. It's about... how there's something wrong with how I'm feeling, inside. In my head, I'm happy. I know that I should be happy – everything's perfect, isn't it? All as I'd wish for it to be, and yet...'

*Where did this all come from?*

A shiver of panic and sadness presses, in the shape of a memory, bleak and cold as the snow clouds that were still hanging over us in the spring. Will's starting to sound like he did back when he was still refusing the operation. Back then, his heart had closed down in sadness and shock. He wasn't himself, couldn't think, couldn't feel. He was suffering from everything that started the terrible day that letter came, only...

He doesn't *know* about what it said in that letter any more. He can't know. I look at him covertly, the deep and uncomfortable thought starting to take root, inside. This can't be some sort of reprise of everything he was feeling back then, surely? What Harry said – the heart remembers...? It can't be that.

No. I push the thought away. It *can't* be.

'I'm trying to understand. I *want* to understand what's happening to me. I want you to be patient, and to help me. Will you do that?'

I gulp. 'I'll do what I can, Will.' But at the same time, I'm feeling my own despair trickling in now because what more can I do, to help him? Other than what I have already promised to do: keep the truth from him?

Nothing. I can do nothing.

'Do you remember when this *feeling* came on?'

'It first started when we were at Gil's party,' he says slowly. 'It started when I realised I couldn't properly appreciate his fine malt whisky.'

'You couldn't taste...?'

'Oh, no, I could *taste* it, all right. I simply couldn't appreciate it. I felt like a lemon with all the juice sucked out of it. When I drank Gil's fine malt, there was simply nothing there, of what I'd expected to feel...'

My heart sinks.

It *is* happening then, just like before. This malaise he's describing... I recognise it. I shake my head, desperately not wanting to think that way, because there may yet be other explanations, more logical explanations.

'And then...?' I breathe.

He looks at me, deeply apologetic – *is it because he doesn't want to hurt me?*

'Then there was the night I proposed to you in Florence.'

Okay, that *does* hurt. I blink, putting my hand to my throat.

'You honestly didn't feel *anything*, then?' That can't be true. I know it's not true...

'Oh, I did. For a few minutes, I felt it. When you smiled at me that way, and I realised how much I loved you, that spending my life with you was what I wanted more than anything else, but afterwards...'

He goes silent. I lean in to stroke his back and he stares into his lap.

'Then, the moment you'd gone,' he says at last, 'I looked around me and all I could see was *how dark* it all was. All I was aware of was that spark of joy I wanted so desperately to share with you – it wasn't there.' He looks up. 'And it should have been there and I keep getting this sense that something's not how it should be. Something's not right in...' He motions towards his heart. 'I don't know what.'

I'm silent for a bit, willing away the tight band of sadness around my chest. Then I ask him, 'Are you feeling depressed, Will?'

'I don't know. It makes no sense, does it?' He's looking at me, desperately wanting answers, and his suffering feels like a knife sliding into me. 'It doesn't, to me, babe. Can *you* make any sense of it?'

'Me?' I pull away from him now, standing up, because it's all too much to bear.

I go over and pick up my tea mug, cradling it to my chest because I can't answer him – *I can't tell him anything.*

'Do you think maybe I need to see a shrink?'

'A shrink? *No!*' I sit down by him again, setting down the mug. Rubbing his hands, I'm wanting and wishing for something, anything, I could tell him that'd make all this go away.

'Maybe it's delayed shock or some other side effect from the meds and maybe it's a normal part of recovery from this?' I stop, because my voice has gone high pitched. Calm myself. Because, if I carry on down this route, I might end up telling him all sorts of things I don't want to. All the things that I have sworn to protect him from because he can't take it and *he might not want to live* and... he's already been through enough. I take in a deep breath.

'Babe, you're seeing Mr Tripoli and the OT soon, aren't you? Can't you ask them? Maybe they'll have some answers for you?' I'm hoping and praying that this will be the case. That this is not... what Old Harry said.

He looks at me unsurely.

'I'm not due to see the doc for a few weeks.'

'We'll ask to see someone sooner, then! We'll get help with this, Will, you're not... you're not alone.'

'No.' Then he asks quietly, 'Would you come with me when I go for that appointment?'

'Of course, I'll come!' I reach in to hug him tight. 'I'd do anything to help you, you know that and... Oh!'

With perfect timing, as I lean down, I feel something in my belly. A tiny, little kick. For a moment no longer than a breath, like the fluttering of wings, it's a reminder of what matters, what all this is about, and a flash of excitement goes through me, despite everything.

'God, Will.' I pick up his hand and place it gently on my belly. 'He's *moving.*' After all these weeks when Will's been trying to catch the moment and he's missed it, every time. 'Can you feel him?'

'I can feel him.' Will's smile is genuine enough. I stand still for a few moments while he puts his head to my belly, listening. Is this enough, to pierce through the deep nothingness, the black well of emptiness he's been feeling in his heart? *Lord, if this isn't enough, I don't know what ever could be.*

Will admits quietly, 'It's not the first time. I felt him last night, while you were sleeping.'

I gawp at him.

'You did?' I gulp. 'How come you never...?'

'I did try.' He smiles quietly. 'Look. I put my hand *here*.' He places his hands on either side of my bump. 'The little guy was beating a military tattoo, from the sounds of it. I thought he'd be bound to wake you.'

His soft laugh is like a spring breeze, bright, but laden with the promise of rain. 'Hell, I thought he'd wake Elsie next door!'

'You should've woken me.' I'm holding back my disappointment. I'd so looked forward to seeing Will's face, the first time he felt this baby moving. 'You should've said.'

'I called your name. I rubbed your arm, like *this*. But nothing he or I could do would stir you.' He catches my eye, and the sadness I see reflected in his own cuts me to the quick, because it has no place in this moment.

'I tried, but you just...' He swallows. 'You wouldn't wake up, Ava. Somehow, you kept on sleeping.'

# 40

# WILL

'I wanted to live... I had every reason to... and waking up potentially like a zombie was a price I was prepared to pay.'

Jeez, what must that've felt like? I'm trying to imagine the place I must've been in before I went for the op. The huge risk I took, to save my life...

Ava nudges my elbow.

'Will, I think that's you.'

'Uh?'

'The nurse has called your name.'

I close down the video snippet she forwarded onto my phone, weeks ago. Me before my op. Me then explaining to me now, what I was thinking, what I was feeling. I can see how terrified I must've been of what must have felt a very real potential outcome. And... maybe that fear got stuck in there, somehow, and it hasn't gone away yet, even though it's all worked out fine?

The nurse is saying, 'All right, Mr Tyler?'

I shoot her a curt nod and Ava stands with me, slipping her hand into mine.

My stomach contracts as I follow Mr Tripoli's nurse into his office.

Does part of me remember this? Remember the dismay and fear I imagine I must have experienced, hearing the news, in this very office?

'Mr Tyler.' My consultant half stands, extending his hand to shake mine the minute we walk in. He's taller than I remember him from the hospital. And congenial.

'Sit, sit.' He indicates Ava, smiling. 'Brought some moral support with you, today, eh?'

We both laugh politely.

'So.' He glances at his notes. 'You're here for your scheduled follow up?'

I swallow. 'That's right.'

'And you were initially seen by our staff at...' he scans the computer screen again '... roughly three weeks? Apparently, the initial OT assessment found you to be in excellent recovery at the time and in a good overall state of mind.' He runs his eyes over me.

'It says here you reported some concerns recently and a colleague of mine was able to see you in advance of this appointment?'

'Dr Mason. Yes, I...' I glance at Ava. The doctor had run some extensive tests and asked me lots of questions. 'She confirmed that I'm in good physical health, Doctor.' I pause. She had not, however, been able to provide any explanation for how increasingly down I've been feeling, even though Ava's remained hopeful that my consultant might prove more help on that score.

'Excellent. Back at work, yet?' He folds his hands together in front of him.

'I'm a musician. And yes, I'm back composing.' He seems to be waiting for more, so I say, 'I'm working on a film score with a colleague.'

Mr Tripoli looks pleased.

'Wonderful. You were a songwriter, of course, I remember that now. And having some very exciting successes too, you told me?' He adds, to no one in particular, 'Never could learn my scales as a child. Failed my grade one piano four times before my mother gave up and sold the piano to buy me the bally microscope I wanted.' He's up and at my side now, running lithe fingers lightly over the scar tissue.

'We did a neat little job there. You see...' he turns to Ava '... where the hairline is, we run the incision parallel, alongside it, these days. Heals so much faster and more completely.'

'It hardly even shows,' she agrees.

'Rather proud of that. So...' He turns back to me. 'No headaches, unusual visual or auditory sensations, palpitations, tingling in extremities?'

'None.'

'Sleeping well and eating well, taking some exercise?' He's back at his desk, taking notes.

'Yes.'

He looks up. 'What exercise are you taking?'

'I've taken up running, again.' I tell him, ruefully, 'We had a little break in Florence and it made me realise how much even walking took out of me. So, I go down to the beach front each morning and run the length of it before the sun comes up.' I see Ava's eyelids flicker slightly as I add, 'Sometimes twice.' She doesn't say anything.

'Gently does it,' he murmurs. 'But you'd say you were generally in good working order?' he asks. 'All normal sexual functions re-established?'

Ava and I exchange a look.

'Uh, it's all good, Mr Tripoli.' Still one thing I want to ask him about, though... I've been waiting for the right moment.

He's drumming his fingers on the top of his desk, turning back to look at his computer screen. 'The good news is that all post-op indicators are extremely positive, young man.'

'That is good news.'

'You must have an extremely good support system in place because, it seems, you are disgustingly healthy.'

I let out a breath and Ava gives a little laugh.

'When's baby due?' he asks her.

'November 10th.'

'Well, congratulations to you both! In fact...' he looks back at me '... it's been shown, time and again, that patients who have the most compelling, joyful reasons to recover are the same ones who make the best recovery.' He opens up his hands. 'No surprise there really, is there?'

'None at all.' I hesitate. 'Doctor, there was one other thing I needed to ask you about.'

'Fire away.'

'It's about...' I glance at Ava and she shoots me an encouraging nod. 'It's about how I've been feeling, lately.'

'Yes?'

I hesitate. 'Everything in my life's going great, like we said, but I've not been feeling all that great. It's as though... I can't connect with all the good things going on around me, any more. Like, all the colour's been sucked out of everything.'

My consultant looks surprised. And a little puzzled.

'I was hoping you'd tell me this was a normal side effect of having this kind of op?'

He thinks about this for a bit.

'Well, I do sometimes see people who're taking longer than they hoped to recover. They can't get on with their lives in a physical sense, and that's a problem. You, however...' he indicates towards me with an elegant wave of his hand '... appear to have everything going for you?'

'I do.' God, what kind of an ungrateful tyke must I look like to him? 'I have everything and more than I could've ever hoped for. I find I just can't... feel it like I should.'

Mr Tripoli shoots a glance at Ava. Then he looks back at me.

I say, 'It's not a side effect of one of the meds I was on, then?'

'I wouldn't usually expect that to be the case.'

That's disappointing. I'd been kind of hoping that he'd tell me a different story from Dr Mason. Because now I'm off the meds, I thought maybe the colour would start to trickle back.

'If it's not the after effects of the operation itself, or the meds...' My heart's started beating very fast all of a sudden. 'I can only put it down to all the dire warnings I must've been given before consenting to have this op?' I shoot him a weak smile. 'About what could go wrong. I've long held this irrational fear of... ending up like a zombie, you see.'

He blinks. 'Pardon me?'

'Like a... Maracas Man.'

He gives a short laugh. 'That takes me back! But, Mr Tyler, please. We are all professionals. I don't think anyone here would've encouraged that particular notion.

'No.' I can feel my face going pink. It's mortifying. I frown, deepening my voice. 'No, but it's a high-risk procedure, right? Cutting someone's skull open and going in with a scalpel and...'

He's shaking his head, still looking vaguely bemused.

'The thing is, I've got a video clip where I'm clearly...' I stop. The words I'd been about to say freeze in my throat. He's got his hands steepled thoughtfully.

'I promise you, we weren't, at any juncture, concerned that you'd end up like a zombie after this operation, Mr Tyler.'

'You weren't?'

'No. The discrete location of the tumour was such, we knew exactly what we were going in to remove. We fully expected to be able to safely achieve that, and for there to be a reasonable chance you'd regain all normal functions.'

'So, there wasn't any...?'

'Brain surgery is an inherently risky endeavour, as I'm sure you'll appreciate. But this one was well within the parameters of acceptable risk.' He pauses for a moment, adding gravely, 'The only absolutely certain risk to yourself was that of death within a relatively short time, had you chosen to forgo the procedure.'

'But I...' I look from one to the other of them. 'I didn't choose to have it, did I, Mr Tripoli? Not at the beginning, anyway, I know that much. There was a period where I refused to have it...'

His eyes look straight into mine.

'I believe that is correct.'

'But...' I choke. 'Why, though? That doesn't make sense, if what you're telling me is the outcome was fairly predictable either way. Why wouldn't I have gone for it?'

The question – which Dr Mason ducked – hangs in the air like a piece of bread that, once swallowed, stubbornly won't go down. One of them knows something. They must do. I glance from him to Ava, and she's fiddling with her ring, maddeningly.

I clear my throat. 'Can someone please tell me – if it wasn't for the fear of ending up a zombie – why I initially refused?'

Mr Tripoli is looking at Ava again. As if he expects her, somehow, to come up with some answer. But, she can't.

He's rubbing his chin.

'It's not within my remit to take guesses at why my patients make the choices they do,' he's saying gently. 'As the saying goes, "The heart has reasons which reason cannot know." But, Mr Tyler, I can only note that when you first came to me, you mentioned a huge burst of creative activity you'd recently experienced. At the time, we did explore the possibility that this might be down to the effects of the growing tumour.'

So, my creative activity might have been connected with the brain tumour? My mouth drops open.

'Nobody ever... I didn't know that, Mr Tripoli.'

'I can promise you, before you had the op, you did know it. Given the degree of professional success you were having at the time, you understandably expressed concerns that your creative flow might be interrupted.'

I put my hands up to the sides of my head, looking towards Ava.

'Is that true?'

'It's true that you'd begun composing at a much faster rate.' She gulps. 'Songs you were very happy with...'

All those songs Toby and I have been working on, polishing, ever since? Great songs. Wonderful compositions, but...

'Surely,' I say faintly, 'that wouldn't have been enough to make me risk my life?'

'You were certainly distressed at the time. Who knows why?' He shrugs gently. 'Who knows what goes through a man's mind when he's faced with his own mortality? I see many different reactions in this office every day, and they're not always the ones you'd expect. However, what I can tell you is...' Mr Tripoli taps his screen lightly with his ball-point pen '... you appear to be perfectly healthy now and there's no reason to think you will have a relapse. You have everything to live for. And if there's anything getting in the way of that...' Here he turns to look pointedly at Ava for one last time. I follow his gaze and she's breathing ever so fast; she seems so... unhappy?

'If there is, then maybe a little gentle counselling or therapy might be in order. I deal only with the hard-wiring of the brain here, I'm afraid.' Mr Tripoli shoots me a rueful, self-deprecating smile. 'As for all the other, more delicate aspects of the psyche and the soul, I leave that to others far more skilled than me...'

# 41

# AVA

A little gentle counselling...

Oh, Lord, but how can that hope to fix something that has been so badly broken? Coming away from Mr Tripoli's office, Will and I are both silent on the way home. He says nothing, staring out of the window. Could he be, like me, suffering from déjà vu?

The month after the letter exploded into our lives, the heating broke down at the cottage. One morning I woke up early, my feet frozen, to a thin film of ice on the inside of our bedroom window. I woke up alone. Will had taken to sleeping on the couch – he was wounded and I understood. Apart from the news about the baby, we'd only just begun to grasp how truly bad was the situation with his health.

But waking up that day... for a few chilling seconds of sheer, dark, emptiness, I had the strongest sense that that was it.

Will was gone. Not just from the cottage, not just from my life, but from the world. That he was gone forever.

For that one, terrible sliver of time, I felt my heart crushed right down to nothing. The beat and pulse of my life stopped, in shock and grief and disbelief. How could he be gone? And how could I go on and live my own life without him...?

When I got up and ran into the sitting room and saw him still lying there, asleep on the sofa, the fear that'd gripped my heart didn't go. Even when I tiptoed right over to him and stood for a while in the early morning half-light, checking, ever so carefully, for the rise and fall of his chest, even when I put my hand over the tear stains on his cheeks and felt for myself the living heat of his skin... the fear didn't go. It stayed with me, pulsing and growing slowly in the small space where my heart had been.

It stayed with me like a presence, warning me, and I knew... I knew... that even though the doctors were warning us he needed an operation, something had already closed down in him. His will to life, like a vital organ, had shut down. Was it because of his grief, learning about the baby? I knew that if I didn't do something, take some action, persuade Will somehow to follow their advice, he wouldn't live.

And then... later on that day, after I found the strength to tackle him, we had come to our plan.

The promise I made Will was so simple and solved everything; he agreed to have the operation, and he's recovered and he's even fallen in love with me again. It has soothed away all our sorrows and all the pain.

But how could I have foreseen that, like the analgesic it was, it would eventually wear off? How could I have known our trouble would come back?

But it has.

Will did not get the answers he hoped for today. Driving home, I catch glimpses of it on the bright sunlight flickering over every disappointed line on Will's face; I can hear it in the strangely echoing silence between us in the car; I can feel it, the despondence in him that has returned in force, only...

This time, I have no sleight-of-hand tricks up my sleeve to make it go away. This time, I don't even have Will on board with me; I have no one.

I am back to the beginning, not knowing what to do or what to say to make things better.

All I know is, the dread fear in my heart has come back. Maybe, this time, there is nothing left?

# 42

# WILL

'Does the running help?'

Standing here by the front door, it's dark, with only the porchlight to see by, but I get the impression Ava was waiting for me.

'Sure.' I bend, securing my shoelaces, pulling them tight.

I've done less than ten minutes tonight. I only swung back round for my water bottle, don't mean to stay, but, 'How?' She stays my arm as I straighten. 'How does it help, Will?'

'I'm sorry?'

*'How does...?'* She swallows and in the back of my mind I know she's desperate for me not to go. She's saying quietly, 'It's getting worse, isn't it?'

'What is?'

'What you're feeling. It's not getting any better.' A gust of cold wind blows right across us and she pulls her cardigan in tighter about her. 'Ever since we saw Mr Tripoli and he assured you that his operation was never going to turn you into a zombie – it's true, isn't it?' she accuses. 'You've been feeling steadily *worse*...'

I give a small laugh, shaking my head.

'I have not been feeling anything,' I tell her. That is both true and not true. Since the consultant's appointment, my whole body and mind have felt as if they're slowly being encased in a dense fog, one that is blissfully numbing at the same time as it cuts me off from the source of all light. I long for some end to this darkness and yet, when Ava flung open the curtains this morning, the sunlight felt like a piercing dagger. I dived back under the covers.

Not like me. *So* not like me.

'No?' Ava says. 'Why all the running, then? You started off at one mile, then three, then five, do you realise? When will it be enough? What are you running from?'

'*From?* Nothing.' I frown, pulling on my hat, itching to go and wishing she would let me.

'Is it because you're depressed?' She rubs at her arms. 'Is it because you can't feel anything any more?'

'I run,' I tell her slowly, 'because when I run, it's one of the few times I actually *can* feel anything.'

'Do you, Will?' She steps closer to me, her breath coming a little faster. She looks so sad. I don't want her to feel that way. But why must we have this conversation *now*, when the desire to run is rising in me, as inexorable as the moon coming over the horizon? I can't stop it. She can't stop it. It's going to happen.

'When I run, I can feel the pavement,' I explain. 'I can feel the rhythm of my feet, hitting the ground.' I pause. 'And it helps me know that there *is* a ground.' I look directly at her, wanting her to see what that feels like, to be so far removed from the centre of your own life that you're not even sure the ground will be there, when you put your feet down every morning.

She tilts her head to one side, quiet for a moment. Then, 'You realise – you haven't even told me yet, how the big meeting went today?'

I stare at her.

'The meeting?' I bend again, pulling up my socks, checking the tightness of my shoelaces though there is no need.

'The one with Toby and that big-shot film producer.'

Though I'm moving off, Ava's begun walking after me.

'Oh, that.' Unlatching the gate at the front, I've quickened my pace but she follows me still as I walk down the lane, not letting me take off.

'Will?'

I can't leave her, heavily pregnant with our child, walking out with a cardigan but no coat in this biting wind.

'That... we decided to rearrange that one, in the end.'

Her intake of breath doesn't escape me.

'They did... or *you* did?'

'Me, them? What does it matter? It's going to be rearranged, hon.'

'Even though Toby will no longer be in the UK and that film guy will probably have moved on too and heaven knows when...?'

We've reached the path that leads to the dunes. From here, a smooth, unlit, straight three mile run beckons me. I can see the dark edge of the sea, hear it as it crashes comfortingly on the shore only a few yards away. I've never been a fan of the sea. It's vicious, cruel. The sea can sweep you away in an instant and I have always thought that must be... the worst death, and yet, on my runs lately, I've come to think of it as my companion. Even a friend. In a moment I will be on my way, enveloped in the dark, because the clouds have already covered the moonlight tonight. It's where I want to be but she's still following me.

'Why are you doing this, William?'

'Doing what, babe?'

*'Throwing everything away?'*

'I'm not.' But seeing her face so pinched and white, I feel a pang of sadness grip me. I stop to envelop her in a hug. 'You're turning into a popsicle! Go back. Please, babe.'

'No. I'm frightened where this'll all end!'

'Hey,' I say, feeling weary. 'I'm only going for a—'

'You can't pretend to me...' She gulps. 'Things aren't right, are they? You've already admitted you cancelled one of the most important meetings of your career today and going out *running* isn't going to help. Things aren't right and you can't keep on running away from them.'

'No,' I admit at last. 'Things aren't right. But I no longer know what to do about that.' I feel so tired and heavy. I want her with our child to be home and safe and in the warm. I want her to feel the happiness I know she deserves to feel even if I can't feel it, myself.

My throat closes as I tell her, 'I've come to the conclusion there must be something very badly wrong with me.'

'Wrong?' She gasps. 'What do you mean, Will? You saw the counsellor last week, didn't you? She said you could keep on going if…'

I shake my head. 'She didn't help. She couldn't. She kept on asking me if I knew where things had gone wrong and what could I tell her? My life's perfect, isn't it? So that only leaves something being wrong with me. And it is, you know, hon.' I lean closer to stroke her face for a moment. 'I don't feel any *happiness,* any more. D'you know what that feels like? Can you imagine what it is, to feel numbed to your core when everything in your world's opened up like the oyster with the biggest pearl, and every dream you've ever had has come true? *Can you imagine that?*'

When I hug her, I can feel her shuddering in my arms.

'I am so sorry, babe. I go out running so I won't have to sit at home and let you see it. So that I'll feel better for a little while, but it doesn't last…' I motion towards my head. 'Something's *gone.* I don't know how or where or when, but it's gone, and I've been putting off facing it. I am not the man you think I am.'

'Will,' she's saying in a strangled voice. 'You *are*…'

'I'm not, Ava.' It's costing me everything to say this. How can I let her down? But she's seen right through me, hasn't she? My arm about her waist, I start walking her back. 'I want to be, believe me. I wanted so much to be a good dad to our child and a good husband to you. But I promised you that I'd be honest with you and… truthfully, I don't believe any more that I can be that man.'

Her mouth twists in disbelief. 'You mean, you no longer want us to…?'

'*I want*, yes,' I tell her desperately. 'I want you and our child. But what good am I going to be to you when I can't even…?' I trail off, seeing her tears. 'I don't know how to make this better, babe.' It's not as if I don't already have it all. For me, there is nothing left to hope for, is there?

'Something's got broken deep inside me. I don't know what it is and I don't know how to fix it.'

She's staring at me, wild-eyed. It's a big shock for her, as I knew that it would be. Any minute now she's going to try and persuade me I'm wrong, tell me that she knows me better than anyone and say she loves me and that I'm perfect as I am.

But she doesn't. As we walk back towards Beach Cottage, I can feel her, desperately sad and her silence is deafening.

At last, she says, 'I think... I *do* know what's broken, Will.'

'Do you?' I look her straight in the eye, surprised. She so desperately wants to put this right for me, doesn't she? She can't, though. There is no way. When she hangs her head, I can hear the tears in her voice.

'I've known it all along. And I think perhaps it's time that you knew it, too.'

# 43

## AVA

Will's voice is low, devoid of any expectation.

'If there's anything you could tell me that'd help, I'd be grateful to hear it.'

I swallow hard.

'I do,' I tell him. 'I think, maybe I do.' When he hears what I have to say, he won't be as grateful as he thinks, but at least I've stopped him in his tracks. I knew when I followed him out here tonight that I was going to have to come clean. His running was starting to feel too desperate. Dangerous. God, I've seen him in this place before, *I know*. I haven't forgotten. I grab hold of his arm.

'I think this might be about something that happened during the time that you can't remember.'

'Oh, yes?' Will's gone very still and attentive and quiet.

'Babe, I think this might be about...' My teeth have started juddering so hard I can barely even speak.

'Let's get ourselves back into the warm,' he suggests. 'First things first, eh?'

I nod, feeling sick, knowing how he's going to take what I have to say next, but clear that I *have to*, because I've run out of road; focussing now only on how best to put it to him. At least we're walking back.

And now the light streaming through the cottage door, which I left open as I ran out, looks so cosy and inviting. *Our home,* I think; the place around which we've spun so many hopes and dreams. So many. And he... I glance at him as we walk back, arm in arm – *will his heart still remember* all that we've meant to each other, once I've said what I'm about to say?

Will he understand that I'm doing this only for love, though every other consideration would suggest I'd do better to hold my tongue?

'This is better.' Inside, pulling on a hoodie over his running vest, Will shoots me a curious smile, sitting down beside me on the sofa.

'So. You've got some ideas for me, babe?'

'Yes. This is about...' I clear my throat, feeling very hot. 'Old Harry told me something, once. He said the heart always remembers, even when the mind's forgotten.' I pause.

He nods, attentive, examining the ends of his fingers.

'Something we haven't spoken about, yet, I take it?'

'We haven't. At least, not this side of your operation...' I look at him unhappily. 'It was something that upset you so badly at the time that you almost didn't have the op...'

He looks up sharply.

'There *was* a reason for that, then?'

'There was.'

'You think the way I'm feeling might be linked to... what?' His eyes look directly into mine.

I swallow, hard.

'I think it might be linked to something that you've always known, in your deepest heart of hearts, has always mattered to you the most.'

*Go on,* he motions.

'Something which mattered so much, you were even willing to let go of a previous girlfriend, over it, because you two weren't on the same page...'

'ChiChi?' He looks a little puzzled. 'This is about her?'

'No,' I say rapidly. 'Not *about* her, more about the reason why you split up with her.'

He opens up his hands. 'Because she didn't want to have any kids?'
'And you did.'

'Yes.'

'You always wanted them. Always.'

His brow is furrowing. 'I did.' He puts out a hand to pat my belly affectionately. 'And now, I have one.'

My eyes close for a brief second at that and he says, 'So – what've I forgotten?'

I say softly, 'Will, you've forgotten... there was a time when you believed you might not ever be able to have any.'

'I thought that?'

I nod.

He lets out a puzzled laugh.

'Why – because we'd been having problems conceiving, is that it? Ava, you already told me this, we spoke about this before...' He gives me a sideways glance. 'Are you suggesting this depression might be linked to the time when you and I weren't having any success conceiving?'

'I think it's linked.'

He's silent for a moment, puzzling it out. *God, Will.* His blue-grey eyes are all at sea tonight and my throat is filling with sobs. *How am I going to tell you?*

He leans back on the sofa, pushing back his hair, trying to connect with the memories, but failing.

'Because we'd split up for a while, you mean? Is it that I became very sad, and you think this is maybe somehow a reprise of that?'

'A reprise of *that*, no.' My voice has gone quiet and croaky. 'Will, I'm no psychologist, but I've come to think that maybe, once our emotional upsets are resolved, we don't *get* a reprise of them.'

'If they're resolved, we don't? And we'd already got back together?'

'Yes.'

He's half frowning, half smiling, trying to keep up with me. 'So it wasn't that. Are you trying to tell me there was some emotional upset that *didn't* get resolved?'

I nod. Rub at my face, and when I look up, he's still waiting, patiently.

I say quietly, 'Will, we've never discussed how it was we found out about the tumour in the first place, have we?'

'No.' He considers this for a bit. 'I assumed I'd been having migraines or some other symptoms? I must've gone to see my GP, and it went from there?'

'No,' I say carefully. 'This tumour was completely symptomless. You went to see a doctor for something else, and, in the end, it was only the elevated levels of white blood cells in your test results that alerted them to the tumour.'

'Really?' He seems grateful. 'A blessing in disguise, then?'

'I...' I hang my head. 'In one way, it was. Only...' I shoot him a pained look. 'This blessing came in a particularly upsetting disguise.'

He blinks.

'More upsetting than learning I had a *brain tumour*?'

'At the time, I think you took it that way.'

He frowns, taking that in. I go on.

'Babe, you know about the fact that we'd spent some time apart, after Christmas. What you don't know is that, while we were apart, you decided to have some fertility tests done...'

'Did I?' He looks uneasy. 'Things were that bad, eh?'

I nod rapidly and he glances at my belly, shrugging.

'But I guess they must've all come back good, though, if—?'

'No,' I cut across him. 'They didn't.'

He stares at me.

'They... *Will*,' I breathe. 'I'm afraid they all came back negative.'

His body is inching back, on the sofa.

'They came back...' My heart's pounding in my throat but *I have to keep going, I have to say it.* 'I'm so sorry, my love, but they all came back saying that you had zero chance of conceiving a child. You couldn't...' I grind to a halt, catching the horrified look of disbelief on his face.

'The tests came back saying I can't have any children?'

'They came back...' I say gently, 'and you couldn't, no. And they also flagged up the other problem that we then, almost immediately, had to deal with, which was the...'

But now he's saying, in a very low voice, 'How d'you mean, *zero chance*, if you were already pregnant?'

'Yes,' I breathe. 'I was.'

'I don't understand.'

'I was...' I force myself to say it. 'We were on a break, after Christmas, Will.'

He starts, his eyes narrowing as the terrible realisation is beginning to dawn.

'You mean...' He blinks, still not quite believing it. 'You...?'

'We weren't together, Will!' I desperately want to move, to get up and get away from here and the thing that I did – *a mistake, it was one mistake!* One I'd hoped to avoid telling him at all costs, but it's far too late. He has to know the truth. All of it.

'We went on a break and you straight away found yourself another...?'

'No!' It wasn't like that. I get out, 'I thought you were dating ChiChi again, and—'

'I wasn't dating ChiChi.'

'We were apart, William! We'd *been* apart since before the New Year. When I went back, hoping to see you at your flat and *she* was there, I thought that meant it was really over between you and me for good, and I thought...'

His voice is strangled.

'You thought what?'

Oh, God, I *so deeply* regret the burning hurt I see in Will's eyes. I was wrong about ChiChi, I believe that, now, but at the time...

'I went to Robyn's party that night. Please believe that I never meant for anything to happen. My ex, Max, was there, but I never meant to even dance with...'

Now he sees it.

'Oh, my G—' The grief in his voice cuts right through me. He's stood up now and turned away. He can't even look at me.

Half standing, I plead to his back, 'Will... you have to believe, this came as a huge shock to me too!' But my legs won't hold my weight any more and I have to sit back down.

'You and me got back together straight after Robyn's party,' I'm muttering, more to myself than to him because I'm not even sure he's listening. 'Me and Max never even spoke again after. We've had no contact. In the beginning, honestly...' I gulp. 'I *never imagined* this baby could be anyone's other than yours, Will.

'It wasn't till those fertility results came back negative that I realised and I was totally shocked. I didn't want it to be anyone else's. I always wanted it to be yours...'

*You wanted?* I'm waiting for him to turn round and reproach. *Why and how could you do that to me, Ava? Pass off this child as mine when...?*

But he doesn't turn to face me. Why won't he say something? I bite my lip.

'Will, I get how much it must hurt, to learn that our child was fathered by another man, but I swear we could get past this if you would only...' I falter as he goes to lean by the window, his hand on his stomach as if he's been kicked.

'This could be *our* baby, don't you see? In every way except biologically, ours. It doesn't really change...' I gulp.

*But you were only too willing to pass this child off as mine and deceive me,* he's saying in my head. It's what he'll be thinking, because he surely can't be thinking anything else. *I'm not the father. I was relying on you to tell me the truth. We had an agreement and you've broken that.*

'You weren't going to tell me?' Will's head drops still further. He's got his fist to his heart.

'I wasn't, but...' It's what we agreed. But seeing as now I'm telling him and he's feeling so angry and so betrayed by me, he might as well know he had his part in it, as well.

He has to know the truth. All of it.

## 44

## AVA

'You're right. I wasn't going to say, but there *were* good reasons why, Will, and there's a reason why I've told you now...'

For a while, neither of us speak. The only sounds are those of the wind, rattling at the front door latch, howling through the trees in the garden, a horrible sound, which turns into a deep, guttural keening that I have to acknowledge, at last, is coming from him. The sight of his stooped shoulders is almost too painful to bear. I want to go and comfort him, but I can't. I can't get to my feet, feel frozen to the chair.

'Can't you see...? I've been witness every single day to what the hurt inside must be doing to you. How you've been so unhappy, unable to connect with anything and how there must've been a part of you that still knew it, anyway. I've told you the truth about the baby now because...' I gulp '... I really think, in the end, it'll help you become whole again.'

He's silently shaking his head. He doesn't want to hear it, does he? I clutch at my chest, realising that what I'm about to tell him next is going to *sound* like the lamest excuse: like me trying to get out of the blame for doing something terrible, when I've already done him the greatest wrong! But I've still got to find a way to say it.

'Having this baby mattered more to you than anything. You knew that as well as I did. And... after this happened, there was no need for you to know it...'

'No *need*?' When he turns very slowly to look at me, his expression is a mixture of sadness and contempt.

'So, you did it all for me?'

'For you?' I gulp. 'Yes, of course, I did! Will, and the truth is you actually *wanted* me to...'

But he's not listening, is he?

'Will, please listen to me. I wasn't the only one who decided...'

'*And this is why*,' he says slowly, 'I almost didn't have the operation?'

I nod, feeling a mixture of sadness and fear coursing through me, realising that the way he's blocking me out now is just what he did to DelRoy when his old mate came around trying to apologise for getting with his ex. He didn't want to hear him out then, either. He chucked him out. He can't chuck *me* out, but... 'You're going to leave, aren't you?

He blinks his eyes closed for a second.

'Is that what you've been most afraid of, Ava?'

'Afraid, yes! *Of course*, I've been afraid of that, but it was never the reason why I kept this from you. I did it to protect you, Will.' He was in this same terrible state when he found out about the baby first time around. It's what I've been dreading.

'And now...' a sob catches in my throat '... I've told you the truth for the very same reason.'

He's still not listening. Just like with DelRoy. He's made up his mind he can't trust me, hasn't he?

'At least, you know. And...' I gulp, reaching for courage because the look on his face is enough to stop me in my tracks. 'The rest of it is that *you and I agreed—*'

He cuts right across me now. 'It doesn't matter, does it?'

'*Will...*'

He turns away again, not hearing, and I can only watch, my heart breaking, as his hand closes in a claw up against the wall, his back turned once more to me.

'This child isn't mine, Ava, and... now, no child ever can be.'

## 45

## AVA

Will...!

I pull up against the sofa, willing myself to my feet as Will silently walks over to unlock one of the patio doors, sliding it open. But I can't get up. Like a huge, beached whale my body has become uncooperative and frozen.

*Where are you...?* I can't even get the words out, but something in me follows him outside, nonetheless. *This isn't what was meant to happen, Will. You shouldn't be reacting like this; you were meant to...* I swallow as a blast of pure cold floods in, carrying with it something of the raw darkness I'm feeling inside, a flurry of crumpled leaves.

I thought you'd get angry, and we'd have it out and then... you'd understand.

The door shuts behind him, with a firm *click*.

The room is so empty. I look around trying, but unable, to fathom it. How could a room be this much emptier, with only one less person in it? It feels like a death, like a...

*Will, don't...*

Sinking deeper into the cushions of the chair, I cover my face with my hands with the dawning horror of the huge mistake I've made.

A mistake that there is no coming back from.

Oh, my God. What have I just done?

I have made things so much worse for him. For us. And I never meant... I rub at my belly, vaguely aware of the sudden flurry of kicking that's coming from inside... I only meant to make things better. *For you, Will*, if not for me. Telling you the truth was never going to make things better for me. I knew it when I decided to tell you, that I was making a dangerous sacrifice. But it was for you...

The Truth.

It was meant to have helped.

The pain in the back of my throat is unbearable.

Because it hasn't helped, has it?

I sit where I am, glaring at the swirly pattern on the arm of the settee, and as I trace it round and around with my finger the whole world slowly closes in. All there is, is the dim light about me in a room that's lost all its pretence of cosiness and feels muted and airless; it's hard for me to even catch a single breath. All I can think about is the look of utter horror I saw in your eyes.

Not pain and disappointment. Not anger or sadness or reproach, none of the things that I expected. None of the things I hoped might help build the bridge you need to build inside to take you back to *you* again.

Just... horror.

As if I'd told you that your life was over, even though it isn't.

*It isn't*, Will. I rub at the back of my neck and the swirly pattern on the armrest grows wide and then shrinks to a dot as I keep staring at it, willing him to still hear my thoughts even if he won't hear me out. You've survived. Even if our relationship can't, you're still here, Will. You'll go on, can't you see that?

By a sheer act of determination, I push myself to my feet. Heavy and dizzy, I stand there, swaying lightly for a bit, rubbing my belly till the sensation of kicking from inside stops. Then I edge over to peer through the patio door. The wind's whipping up a storm of leaves in the garden but he's still out there. I can see the shadowy shape of him standing by the fence with his hand resting on the gate and his face upturned to the sky, but the relief I so desperately want to feel does not come. Will's here. He has not left. But I know, *I can tell*, that if I call out to him, he won't respond.

Because he doesn't care any more.

The Truth didn't work.

Something deeper than I can see in him has snapped.

And my sacrifice has all been for nothing.

# 46

# WILL

I have to get out of here. I can't listen to Ava any more. No more words, no more excuses, no more anything, I need some air.

I can't...I'll never... have any children of my own? *All I ever really wanted, ripped away from me in a...* It can't be true.

I close my eyes and the deep, salt smell of the sea fills my nostrils. As much as I want to disbelieve Ava, I know that it is true.

And I so desperately want to get away. *Run.* Like I've been doing every day. I *need* to do that, only it feels now as if there's nowhere to go. My feet won't take me, and when I turn to look to the left and the right of me all paths look the same; I can't work out the way.

I shake my head, feeling confused and numbed. No way out of this. *Trapped*, like...

Maracas Man.

I've felt this before, I know that much. I've been here before. I clutch at the fence a little harder, feeling it sway precariously beneath my grasp...

I rub at my eyes, knowing only that I have to find my way back to a place where things make sense...

When I stare up at the sky, there are no stars tonight, no moon.

Nothing to navigate by, not even Ava.

Nothing.

Only the unbearable pain that seems to be coming and going, pulsing right through my chest. That remains.

It is the one thing that I know for sure right now is *real*.

# 47

# AVA

It's been two days already. Why won't he come out and *talk to me*?

From here, pegging my clothes up on the line, I can see that Will's still got the spare room blinds drawn. Is he even up yet? I can't tell. Since I told him what I had to, he's no longer sharing either my bed or my life. Maybe stupidly, I'm taking some small heart from the fact that he hasn't left, yet. *Maybe he won't leave?* Maybe we can still...?

I feel my heart constrict at the thought. Being without him feels so desperately lonely. Each time I've tried to say something – spying him in the kitchen and then another time in the hallway – he only shook his head at me, wouldn't engage. He's *here*, but at the same time, he isn't. And the look in his eyes was so... strange.

I don't know what to do. I've been so desperate to talk to someone and yet who to turn to, when everything still feels so raw? Ginny and Robyn are out, for now, and this is so personal, there's no one else I'd feel comfortable bringing it up with. It's Will I need to talk to and he can't. He won't.

Not yet.

As a distraction, I've been laundering all the tiny, first-stage baby clothes friends have donated. Phyllis from the tea rooms brought in a bag from her daughter-in-law. Elsie next door did likewise, and the girls at my dance fit class have also come up trumps. I have enough clothes to kit out quads! I peg the last Babygro up on the line and stand back a little, inhaling the scent of fresh laundry. It's a clear day but there's already a soft bite in the autumn air, the faint smell of burning wood wafting over from one of the other cottages further down, the sense of a sea change coming in.

The whole summer has gone so fast and, soon, my baby's coming. Despite everything that's happened, even thinking about that still gives me a small flush of excitement. Over and above the deep sadness I feel over Will, the soft, fine fabric of the baby clothes beneath my fingers stirs something in me, I can't deny it.

This little boy that Will and I have been so excited about. The one he's now so sad about. He's still coming into our world. *My* world. And I've got to be ready.

The phone in my pocket is buzzing, and I feel a shot of hope. Robyn, maybe? I texted her, late last night, yearning for some contact with *someone*, even though she's been so tied up with her own life she barely gets back to my texts with anything other than emojis these days.

But it's not Robyn.

'Ava, is that you?'

I frown softly. *'Ginny?'*

'Oh, thank goodness,' she breathes. 'I was beginning to think you'd had the baby early or something.'

'No.' Ever since she and I had our last conversation at her office things haven't been the same and yet here she is ringing me up like nothing has changed. I put the phone on speaker and stare at the screen, feeling a little bemused. 'Why would you think that?'

'Why?' She gives a high laugh. 'Because you... you haven't been answering any of my texts or emails, that's why!'

I blink.

'I'm sure I did.' I answered her last email, but I see there are a couple of messages that've come in recently that might have gone unanswered. They were about some work she needs doing and, as I'd already told her I wasn't available, I assumed they must be general call outs.

Ginny's saying, 'Is everything okay, hon?'

'Sure, I...' Can she tell? Is there something in my voice giving away how *not okay* everything is, even when I'm doing my best to cover it? I throw the last of my pegs into the laundry basket, musing how great it would be if only... things could go back to how they used to be between us. If only I could tell her everything. Would she roll up in her jazzy bright green convertible and whisk me away for a consolatory high tea in some posh London hotel?

After all, it was Ginny who took me to that wine bar after the disastrous break-up I had with my first important boyfriend. She ordered – and we drank – two whole bottles of prosecco and ate too many *tapas* and then we went out dancing somewhere and all I remember about that is staggering out of a nightclub in Soho with her, somewhere in the early hours, feeling...

Feeling *better* because at least somebody knew and understood what I was going through. Somebody cared enough to want to do something about it. Would she still be that way with me now? I wish so much that I could just share the disaster that's occurred, with Ginny...

'Uh... I'm getting there,' I say cautiously. 'I'm currently doing baby-prep stuff, while I have the chance.'

'Nice.'

I'd been about to go on, tempted to say a little more, but something in her tone alerts me.

'How about you? All good your end?'

'Well, not exactly,' she comes back crisply. 'Two of my Polish girls have jumped ship, my PA has gone back to the States and *you've* been ignoring all of my emails...'

'That's not true...' I stop. She's having some problems, clearly. I don't want to be unsympathetic. 'Ginny, the truth is, we've been having a few hiccups here. I won't go into it more than that, but...'

'Baby's okay, though?' Her voice is strained.

'Baby's fine, please don't worry,' I tell her. When she doesn't come back immediately, I reassure. 'I saw the midwife earlier this week and she says everything's going perfectly, so—'

She cuts through me. 'What, then? Will's not sick again, is he?'

'No.' I pause. Not sick, but...

A couple of raindrops just landed on my cheeks. I stick out my free hand, palm upturned, wondering if I'm going to need to bring all the clothes in again as she says, 'Listen, Ava. I know the way we left things at our last meeting was a little strained, but we *have* been friends for a long time.'

'True,' I concede. The fact is, if only we could sit down and have a proper conversation, maybe we'd both feel a lot better?

'We have,' Ginny's saying quietly. 'And I've helped you out more than once.' Pause. 'Like, when you were stranded at home with your parents for months doing that killer bore of a job at the bank your dad shoehorned you into before I came along and offered you some designer work?'

'You basically saved my life,' I admit. The money she paid allowed me to rent Beach Cottage, to get away from the stifling atmosphere at home and also fulfil my dream of living by the sea.

She adds, 'It was enough for you not to need to work every hour of the day, to be able to spend time at your precious Butterfly Gardens, and I know how much that meant to you.'

'It did,' I say slowly. More than she will ever know.

'Thing is...' she comes back, plaintively. 'I'd like to have thought you'd have been here for me too, when I needed you.'

Steady on a moment. She'd been happy enough to have me on board at the time, I recall. She'd scratched my back and I'd scratched hers, so no charity effort.

'Gin—'

'*Instead of which*, all I've had from you in response to my requests for help is almost complete radio silence.' She sounds reproachful. 'The samples you showed me were perfect. I told you that at the time, and I naturally expected you to follow through on making the orders. I've got the film people breathing down my neck... and you seem to have unilaterally pulled out. You promised me, Ava, you'd be reliable!'

I snap my hand shut, feeling confused.

'I'm so sorry if you thought I'd promised you anything,' I tell her. 'I'm not sure how come you did, though. My commitment was to producing those designs for you but not beyond that.' Ginny's been let down by a few of her workers, that's clear, but not by me.

'I told you, Ginny, I sent you a text after we met last time. I even said that you could go ahead and use all my designs if you wanted.' I swallow. That last offer hadn't been made lightly, either, but had seemed only fair under the circumstances.

'I *also* said I wouldn't be making any more of the garments for you, myself.'

I hear a disbelieving noise at her end.

'Look, when you sent your emails offering me further commissions, I was clear. I declined them.'

Pause.

'I declined them, Ginny.'

'But we both knew you didn't mean it!' Her voice has gone up a notch. 'You're having a baby. You need the work – my pay is great and... and this gig is perfect for you!'

'I did mean it.'

'*Why?*'

'Because...' I say carefully. 'The situation has changed.'

'Oh, my word!' The penny drops. 'This is about... it's about Margaret, isn't it?'

I wasn't going to bring that up but if she really wants to go there...

'Partly, it is, yes. I was really uncomfortable with what you told me about accepting that grant from the Venus Sanctuary Outreach, and I won't deny it.'

Ginny makes a disbelieving *ptff* noise.

'Have you *any* idea how this business is actually run, honey?'

I don't answer her.

'No, I forgot, of course you don't,' she's hissing. 'If you did, you'd never have got into the hot water you did before you ran away from the *very desirable job* you once had in the industry, isn't that so?'

Here we go again! I am so not in the mood for this today. If she had any idea what's been happening with Will, how gutted I've been, how alone I've felt, she wouldn't be doing this to me, twisting this knife.

I say wearily, 'I didn't run away from my job, Gin. I *left* it. I left it because a colleague who I'd considered a friend, who *should've* been assisting me on a very important project, was actually only there to steal the designs I'd worked on for months...'

'Ava,' Ginny says quietly. 'Don't overdramatise – Billie just took the general direction you'd shown her and ran with it...'

'She took the entire collection, from the actual designs and fabric I'd chosen right down to the exact and precise colours, right before a major fashion week event, and tried to pass it off as her own!'

'Oh, it's a competitive industry, and you were the one with all the good ideas,' she comes back. 'The girl probably didn't want to be bested. Imitation is the sincerest form of—'

'Glad you can see it all so clearly from her point of view, Ginny!' When we'd both produced a virtually identical folder to show our boss, Lukas, Billie had landed me in it with him, big time. Somehow, he'd been reluctant to publicly disbelieve her, and when push came to shove he didn't take any action to support me, even when she tried it again, a few months later...

I pick up my laundry basket and stalk back into the house.

'I thought I had a really good working relationship with Lukas but, in the end, he didn't trust me enough to know when I was telling him the truth, did he?'

'Or perhaps,' she suggests, 'as thirty years her senior, he was having way too much fun with that particular intern to care too much whose designs they really were?'

I can almost see Ginny shrugging from here. 'Like it or loathe it. It's how the game is played, hon.'

'Like with your dealings with Margaret, you mean?'

She's silent for a fraction of a second before replying. 'Just so.'

'Which is why,' I tell her quietly, 'I'm out of it.'

'Ava,' she's saying plaintively. 'Please reconsider. I'm telling you this for your own good, not only for mine. You've a baby on the way. Are you really prepared to throw all your independence away like this?'

She's right about that much at least. She has no idea but, even if I wanted to, I couldn't give up work, not with Will being in the place he's at; I doubt he'll be offering to pay for a cotton bud.

'I am really sorry, but I can't help you any more.' I'm done with pretending. I'm *done* with having to go along with great, big, whopping lies, only to get to somewhere I'm not sure I want to go.

'For so many reasons, I can't.'

Her voice is distinctly cooler when she comes back, this time.

'Beggars can't be choosers.' She sounds angry as hell, angry that she can't force me to do what she wants. 'Why are you so determined to ruin my life, so you can run away to your *one foot in the grave* butterfly tea rooms?'

'I don't want to ruin your life. This isn't about you.'

'Why are you so willing to ruin your career when I'm offering you so much?' She carries on over me. 'Just tell me why?'

'Because... I don't trust you any more!' I tell her simply. At the other end of the line, I hear her sharp intake of breath and the shining, gossamer thread that once held together the friendship between us snags and breaks.

For a few minutes after she slams the phone down, ending our call, I stand there in the garden, hugging my arms to my chest while a soft sprinkling of autumn rain patters down around me. I can scarcely believe that Ginny and I are ending like this. It's heartbreaking to see how much we've grown apart. But we have.

Just like that, all our years of friendship go swirling away down the pan.

# 48

## WILL

When I open my eyes, the image fades instantly. It's gone. Flown like a moth flurrying out of the corners of my mind, but whatever it was woke me up and my heart's still pounding.

That thing. That thing I can't remember...

I sit bolt upright on the too-small spare bed where I've been sleeping for the past week, trying to bring it back. It felt like a refrain to some forgotten piece of music. It felt like it might be an *answer* of some sort...

And I need some answers, God knows. I need some *something* that is not... this.

I kick my frozen feet back under the covers and the stack of crockery and notes that've been accumulating on the floor beside the bed topples over, hitting the edge of my guitar. Groaning, I force myself out of bed to check, praying that it's okay. And also – I glance towards the wall, feeling a stab of guilt – hoping that I haven't woken Ava.

A couple of plates have been cracked but, most importantly, my guitar is unscathed. I pick it up tenderly, strumming very, very quietly. Breathing out. It's okay, *it's okay*. The song is not one I've heard before and I wonder... was it this I was dreaming about?

I don't know. I sit for a while, caressing the neck, reassuring myself that the guitar's fine, but there's still the rest of the mess to deal with.

I curse softly, retrieving the journal I've spent so much time poring over and writing in over the past week, now soaked in yesterday's coffee dregs. The first words I see as I pick it up resonate deeply.

*Woke up gripped with the strongest sense that I've been trapped in a nightmare for the past week...*

The date, unbelievably, is Weds, 9th May.

All those months ago! I rub the heel of my hand into my eyes. All those months since my op and since Ava came into my life and for all of those months, with every triumph I've felt at my recovering body, with every bit of joy I've discovered in my new life, there's also been *this*, lying dormant underneath it all.

This kaleidoscope of numbness and confusion and sorrow, it has been there, I know it. Because this isn't anything new to me, is it?

I stop what I'm doing, dabbing at what's left of the journal with a sock. It's cold. I need to pull on some clothes and I don't, in all honesty, care a damn about the journal. The OT may have been very earnest in her opinion that *it's really important you write things down, William,* but I'm starting to see she was wrong about that. These notes aren't getting me anywhere, they're only making me feel worse.

All these thoughts I've been spilling onto the page, they aren't helping me out of this space I've gone to, in my head; none of it is getting me back to myself. Or... back to Ava. I wanted them to, I hoped, but I've not even been able to *talk* to her.

I pick up the soggy mess and drop the lot into the overflowing bin by the window where I pause for a moment, trying to figure out, did I even open up these blinds at all, yesterday? Or the day before? I must've spent more time in here than I thought, playing my guitar, sleeping, lost in those notes, because I don't recall doing so.

When I tug at the cord, the blinds making a *snap* noise, lifting. The first signs of daybreak over the horizon catch me by surprise – so late already? Another day started and me no further along than I was at the beginning of the week? I drum my fingers on the windowsill, realising the truth of it. No progress made, because I feel no better, no... *answers*?

I once believed the answers to every trouble life could bring would lie here, in Holcombe Bay. I thought, as long as I had this place to come home to, nothing too bad could ever happen. I'd be all right, and it used to be so, but...

Not any more. I stand for a bit, glued to the sight of dunnocks flitting in and out amongst the pampas grass, envying them their unbroken connection to life. Without thinking, I bend to retrieve my trainers from under the bed, pulling them on. *How can even the birds outside be so full of purpose*, when I... I feel so very empty? I don't know how.

All I know is, the answers don't lie in here.

## 49

## WILL

At the top of the dunes, the wind is blustering around my cheeks, my ears, my neck. Turning my face skywards, I close my eyes and let it all wash over me: cold air, cloud and yellow-grey, mottled autumn light. The crunch of sand and stone and sea-vetch beneath my feet. The crisp, overpoweringly salty smell of the sea. All of it. Everything I sense I'll soon be saying goodbye to. Even... I open my eyes abruptly, recognising that the place where I've come to stop is exactly where Ava caught up with me a week ago and turned me round...

Even *her?*

It hurts, to think that, so I don't dwell on it. Concentrate instead on kicking up the half-buried pebbles beneath my feet. Some of them are stubborn and don't want to move, but *I* do want them to. Everything's got to get moving again. All the things that've been stuck for such a long time. Even these. I kick at them, hard, with the heel of my foot, watching with some satisfaction as a load of 'em go bouncing and spinning off down the scarp.

Then I stop, a little horrified, spying the father and son walking along the beach, directly below. *Christ.* As the man instinctively shields his child and the stones bounce harmlessly around them, I'm simultaneously aware of two things. One, sheer relief that nothing hit them, and... second, much less comfortably, the pure envy I can feel bubbling up inside me. Watching that bloke as he crouches so tenderly to brush the sand off his startled kid, and his simple act of doing up the last button on the little guy's duffle coat, all I can think is, *he's* got the one thing I'm never going to have.

When he looks up to see where the stones rained down from, the man's scowl seems disturbingly familiar. I stiffen.

'Oh, it's *you*?' Mule's gaze softens instantly. 'Hey there, Tyler.'

'Uh... sorry about that!' I manage. 'The shingle must've worked a bit loose, up here...'

'Storms would've done that,' he notes amicably. He stands. Just as I remember him, he's a huge bloke, a solid mass of fat and muscle, but it's almost shocking to see how much more... *mature* he looks. So much more, at any rate, than I currently feel. Is it having a kid of your own that does that to you?

'How're you doing, mate?'

'*Good,*' I lie, jumping down reluctantly to join them. 'All good. You?' I can barely tear my eyes away from the kid.

'Yeah.' When he smiles, the creases around his eyes are those of a contented man. 'We're only out here waiting for the missus to give birth.'

'Oh, is she...?' He nods, clearly nervous and excited, and the knot in the centre of my stomach tightens a little more. I think, not happy with one child, he's about to have another one. Just because he can.

'You know Jacob, of course.'

Jacob. I swallow my sadness.

'You've forgotten?' Mule picks up in a heartbeat.

'Afraid I have.'

'Well, he won't ever forget *you*,' he tells me. 'We keep a big photo of the two of you in the sitting room, so he'll never forget how you jumped into the water to save his life.'

'Hey, look, it was nothing...' Literally, nothing to me, because I have no recollection of it, but Mule's already waving away my vague attempt at modesty.

'You're his hero, ain't you, Tyler?'

I point towards myself. *Me?*

Jacob's nodding in rapid agreement with his dad. I'm this kid's hero? That feels weird. Gratifying, in a strange way, but still weird.

'He sends you a piece of his birthday cake every year, to remind you.'

*Aww.* 'That's sweet.'

I crouch down beside him. 'Listen, kiddo. Maybe I saved you on *that* particular day, but a boy's dad is always his first and best hero, right? I know mine always was.'

I have no idea why I brought that up. Haven't spoken about my dad for as long as I can remember. It feels... strange.

*'Hey,'* I add, to cover my embarrassment. 'Want to see a special trick that my old man once showed me?'

Jacob nods, dark eyes sparkling, and I bend to retrieve some of the flat, rounded pebbles I inadvertently showered on them. Taking wide aim, I skim the first stone across the choppy grey surface of the water and it obligingly bounces, once, twice, and then – miraculously – three times. *Heeey,* I think, hearing their roar of approval. Haven't lost my touch, have I? And Jacob has found his tongue.

'Again!'

I laugh, pretty impressed with myself. 'I'll try.' I'm not sure I can reproduce the feat, but I do it anyway. This one manages only two and a half bounces but it travels even further before sinking beneath the waves.

'Cool.' Mule's shaking his head. He bends to pick up a flat pebble of his own, but palms it, looking unsure. 'You using some special kind of technique or summat?'

'For sure.' My next one sails out so far none of us are even certain where it's dropped. Mule looks at me in astonishment.

'Your go, Dad!' His son turns to him expectantly, but – maybe luckily for his old man – the sound of his mobile going saves the day. Mule looks at me, a little panic-stricken.

'Hey, mate, mind keeping an eye on him for me, while I take this?'

'No problem.'

He turns away, so nervous he's struggling to even get his phone out, and now that small, impatient tug I'm feeling at the back of my jacket is Jacob.

'Again?' His excitement is strangely catching. He reminds me, in fact, of me at his age.

'You sure?'

'Again, again!' He's jumping up and down, the bright red bobble on the top of his too-big woollen hat bobbing back and forth with him. The more he jumps, the more the hat falls down over his eyes, till it's suddenly slipped, covering his whole face. With his thickly gloved fingers, he can't do a thing about it, either. Despite myself, I can't help grinning. He looks ridiculous!

'Can't see!' He turns round and round now, like a spinning top. I give a deep belly laugh, pulling the offending hat out of his eyes.

'Again.' He adds, as an afterthought, *'Pweese.'*

I give it another go, but a wave gets in the way of this one, cutting the pebble's trajectory short.

'Can't win 'em all.' I smile. To preserve my reputation, I say, 'It's your turn.'

Jacob bends to pick up a handful of silt and gravel. As he turns to hurl it, it hits the back of his dad's jacket with a silent *thonk*. His hands go up to his mouth in horror, but – deep in his phone conversation – Mule hasn't even noticed. Jacob and I exchange a conspiratorial look as his dad starts walking back towards us.

I call out, 'Baby here yet?'

'Nah. False alarm.' Mule's crouching to pick up his own selection of pebbles. 'Your dad really the one who showed you how to skim those stones, Tyler?'

'Sure, he was. Why?'

'Just imagined it might have been your gramps, that's all.'

'Don't know why you'd have thought that.'

He's distracted, and his first pebble's fallen short. 'Because... when you first came down to Holcombe Bay, he'd take you anywhere, do anything for you, wouldn't he?'

'I guess he must've felt sorry for me after I lost my dad.'

'Oh, yeah?' He's nodding towards the water with some dissatisfaction. His second pebble has also sunk without trace. He glances at me for a moment.

'That why you came down here, Tyler?'

'Not exactly.' I shrug. After all these years, I'm not sure why we're even having this conversation, but... what does it matter now? 'I came down to Holcombe Bay when I was thirteen because... I chose to do that.' I add, 'I *could've* stayed on in Leeds, Mum always wanted me to, but then...' I lean back, skimming a further stone. This one falls disappointingly short.

Mule says thoughtfully, 'You probably thought I was a right little shit to you, back then, didn't you?'

'Little?'

'Hey, you had *everything*, man.' He turns to skim a run of about five or six stones across the waves, saying evenly, 'Why wouldn't I hate you?'

My mouth has fallen open in astonishment. 'I didn't have everything. I just told you... I didn't have my dad, did I?'

He shrugs. 'There was still your mum.'

'You think?' I frown. Jacob's found a dead fish and he's staring at it, both fascinated and horrified, so we can both stop skimming stones.

'After Dad passed away, my mum took up with a new man, didn't she?' I frown, recalling it. 'Did it within a year of my dad's death. Worse than that, she tried to pass it off as being all for *my* benefit.'

'Oh, women will do that,' he agrees.

'Mum went around telling everyone that *a boy needs a dad*.' As if she'd done it for me! Well, her new bloke, Joe, wasn't ever going to be that. I fold my arms, feeling the resurfacing of an old grievance. Surprisingly strongly, too. Where'd all this come from? I have no idea.

'But,' I say to Mule, 'there was no way I'd ever need or want anything from *him*.'

'That's because you still had your gramps.' Mule is rubbing his hands together, blowing on them briskly. 'Remember how he spent all that time with you, teaching you stuff like how to fly those kites?' He adds regretfully, 'Only thing I ever got taught by anyone was the proper way to cut up a ham hock...'

'A life skill,' I give him. 'I personally have no idea how to cut up a ham hock.'

'No?' He glances at me sideways. 'You wanna stop by the shop some time, I'll show you.'

'Maybe.' We both glance over to where Jacob's begun prodding the dead fish with a bit of driftwood, pushing it back towards the water's edge.

'He thinks if he puts it back in the water it'll come alive and swim off,' Mule scoffs tenderly.

'If only it were that easy, eh?'

He's already steering his boy away, distracting him onto something less unwholesome than the rotting fish. The tenderness I see between them is giving me a sore feeling in my throat, my envy at his good luck bobbing up again, along with a side serving of sorrow.

Hell. I stick my hands deep in my pockets.

'Having kids must change a man,' I prod. 'You were never so soft.'

He nods. 'Sure, it does, Tyler. It does make you soft in some ways. Stronger in others.' He glances at a text that's come in on his phone. Sighs. 'Apparently she's still got a good while to go, yet.'

'After waiting nine months... I guess a few more hours won't hurt, eh?'

'I guess.'

'And...' the sadness in my throat is threatening to swamp me '... you'll have been through it all before, anyway?'

'What's that?' He's looking at me, distracted. The whites of his eyes are actually showing. I think, this is the first time in my life I have ever seen this dude looking terrified.

'You'll have been through all the waiting before,' I repeat patiently, nodding towards Jacob. 'With him.'

'Nah.' He's shaking his head. 'When I met Chrissy, he was already eighteen months old, wasn't he?'

My mouth drops open.

'So, he's not...?'

'Oh, *he's mine*.' He's scooped his boy up, placing him easily atop his ample shoulders. Jacob peers down at him, adoringly, the sheer affection between the two undeniable. Mule says firmly, 'Adopted him when I wed his mum, closed records, and there's nothing more ever needs to be said about *that*.'

'No.' The tight space in my belly just stopped hurting, for some reason. There is nothing more that needs to be said about it.

'See ya soon, then, bro?'

I nod, and after they walk off, Jacob waving from his dad's shoulders till they've climbed up the dunes at the very end, I turn back to watch the waves crashing down in little cascades and it's as if I'm seeing them for the very first time. It feels, momentarily, as if the day's opened up a crack and some sunlight has started pouring in from somewhere.

Just for a brief moment.

But it's something.

# 50

# AVA

'William not here with you today?' My midwife, Terry, offers me her arm, helping me down off the couch.

'Your partner doesn't normally miss an appointment, does he?'

'Uh, no.' I'm glad she can't see my face. Head down, pulling my top back into place, I make up, 'He had some... er, work commitments.'

The words stick in my throat. The truth is, I don't know where Will is. He's gone out, but he's not telling me where, these days. He's not asking me where I'm going, either.

'I'll bet, with so little time to go, he'll be excited, though?'

'Sure. He's excited.'

Terry leans in, admitting with a little smile, 'Y'know, we get to see a lot of daddies-to-be at this surgery, but Will's always our favourite.'

'Oh, yeah?'

I get my water bottle out of my bag. Raising it up to my lips, I'm thankful she's putting her gear away, still commenting cheerily, 'He is. Will always seems so... devoted. It's a truly lovely thing to see and he's going to make the best dad. You're one lucky girl, Ava!'

I was holding it together so well, but I can feel my face crumpling.

'Oh!' she says now. 'Oh... is everything all right, Ava? Everything okay?'

I'm nodding, but, to my embarrassment, I've dissolved into tears, right there, in the middle of Terry's consulting room. She's calmly handing me a pile of tissues.

'*Yes*,' I get out. 'It's only that...'

She waits, patiently. And I say, 'Nothing.'

'You sure?' she says. 'I know the change in hormones can sometimes do that to you.'

'Yes,' I gulp, half laughing. I've been blaming hormones for *everything*, these past few months, haven't I? 'That's what it is.' Because I can't tell her what I want to tell her, that, no, everything is not all right. Everything is very definitely not okay.

Everything is... very bad, indeed.

Will is getting himself ready to leave me, I know he is; even if he hasn't said anything, I can feel it.

I can feel it, and I can't tell anyone. Not Ginny, since my break-up with her. Robyn's gone away for a few days' break with another friend, after Carenza cancelled their Greek holiday, so I can't lean on her, either.

And I have felt so alone. I blow my nose with the tissues and Terry says, 'If there's anything you need at all... if you feel you need someone to talk to?'

'*Sure*,' I say. 'Thanks so much.' When she waves me out, she's sympathetic but she still thinks I'm the luckiest girl in the world; I can see it on her face. I won't be the one to tell her any different.

As I leave the surgery it's on my mind to go home, but somehow, before I know it, I've driven down to the Butterfly Gardens and, buying a large pot of tea for two, collared Old Harry, who was coming onto his break. Maybe I was hoping for a little comfort and peace?

Only – now I'm here, sitting at one of the tables outside with him and feeling chilly, I can see there isn't any solace to be found here today, either. Thanks to Carenza's blog posts drawing in a whole new demographic of visitors, the owners have decided to 'modernise' and the tea rooms have been getting noisy and disrupted, of late.

I pour us out some tea and Harry's saying unhappily, 'They've already torn down my wonderful, huge cottage roses that were growing over the old stone wall by the entrance.' When he picks up the dainty teacup I've pushed towards him, his hands are trembling. 'I can't for the life of me see how these "improvements" are going to work out, can you?'

'No, me neither.'

'All I'm saying is, if this new glass and chrome layout that's emerging is anything to go by, this whole place will soon be changed beyond recognition.'

'I'm sorry, Harry, what?' *If the drilling doesn't stop soon, this'll have been an entirely wasted trip.* Because I can't think, like this.

'It's all changing,' he says forlornly.

'True.' The gardens have been the same for the last thirty years, barely a thing altered from how they've always been, how he remembers it, and suddenly – all this. I put my teacup down on the table, looking around with a growing sense of unease and disappointment because he's right, this place is changing, vastly. And when it does, then where will I go when I need my place of sanctuary?

'When I came in this morning and saw what they'd been up to, I could've wept.' Harry draws up his shoulders, tall. 'Not that I'm allowed the luxury of *that*. Us men have to handle things a bit differently, don't we?'

I nod, reflecting; I've long run out of map when it comes to understanding Will's coping mechanisms.

'So... how *do* men cope when they're feeling overwhelmed, Harry?'

'Eh?'

'Do you go all silent? Or...' I stir in a lump of sugar, watching it dissolve slowly. 'Do you just avoid the person you're cross with?'

He's looking a little bemused.

'I'm only asking because... I've recently had this situation develop in my life,' I offer by way of explanation. '*It's Will*, Harry. I told him something and he's upset with me, but I get the feeling he won't be staying with me too much longer.'

'No?'

'No. I... *feel* it, in the air.' I suck in my lips, holding in the heaviness in my chest.

'I feel it every morning when I get up and he's not there having breakfast with me. He's... around, in his room, in the kitchen, and then, sometimes, walking out, but always alone. And every time I hear his guitar being played it's like, I can feel his resolve growing stronger, somehow, d'you see?'

He blinks. He won't even remember who Will is, but he's a trooper. 'Have you spoken to him yet?' he asks mildly.

'Oh, we've spoken, yes. In a very superficial, run-of-the-mill, here's-some-mail-that-arrived-for-you kind of way. Will's clearly not feeling as shocked, but something else has taken its place. It's as if he can't bear to be around me too much, and he's only working his way up to the point where he can...' I wipe away the tears that gather in the corners of my eyes the minute I mention it.

Just like the midwife, Terry, did, he's looking at me so sympathetically that it makes it all the harder to...

'Ah, *difficult*.'

'Yes, it's been... very difficult.' I look at Harry, desperately. 'I'm sorry to land this on you, but the truth is, I don't know what else to do, who else to talk to and I've been doing my best not to say anything, but... other people are starting to notice that things aren't right.'

'They are?'

'Yes, like, the midwife I saw this morning. She realised something was off, and kept asking me...'

There's a brief pause, then he says, 'Did you tell her?'

'Oh, God. I didn't say anything to her, no.' I pick up my cup and put it down again. 'I knew I wouldn't be able to keep it together if I did, but since... since I told *Will* the truth, I think the last few weeks have been among the saddest of my life.'

'I am very sorry to hear that,' he says solicitously.

'And I don't understand why he's...' I bring out a tissue and wipe my eyes and blow my nose but it's no good, I still can't see and I still can't breathe.

'Hmmm.' Harry folds his arms. Sitting opposite me with that dainty teacup in front of him, he looks out of his depth. I realise, he'd much rather be mulching the roses. He'd rather be sanding down and repainting the fence or tending to his caterpillars. Only... I need him to sit here and listen to me.

'I mean, I get it. *I do.* When I told Will the truth... it must have been a real shock. Will feels let down but, honestly, I'd hoped... after he had it out with me, maybe he'd settle down and get used to the idea, and we'd be able to get over that and move on.'

'And that hasn't happened?'

'No, because he never even got angry at me, Harry! He's never given us a chance to put it right.'

'He didn't get angry?'

'He didn't, and... that would be normal, right?' I hesitate, then I come out and say it. '*You'd* have been angry when you were younger if your girlfriend was expecting and you found out later that it wasn't yours, wouldn't you, Harry?'

'I should say!' Harry looks at me, frowning slightly, and I feel my face colouring. Is the poor old gent shocked? I bet he is. I bet he's thinking all sorts of things, even if he's too polite to say them to my face.

'Ah,' he says. 'Will's not the father and he thought that he was?'

I say miserably, 'It's been terrible, keeping that from him. But then, he didn't remember me and I was trying to get him to fall in love with me again, and what would he have thought of me, if... *surely you must see*, why I'd have to keep it under wraps?'

'The less people who know it, the better?'

'Yes,' I breathe.

'Which is why you're telling me?'

I nod, feeling absolutely terrible and wishing that things could be different. Harry goes quiet for a while, mulling all of this over.

'I need to understand...' I blow my nose again '... why he won't... *engage* with me, why he's gone so cold.'

But Harry doesn't have any answers. 'My dear,' he says eventually. 'I think you're right. You really do need to find someone to speak to about all this.'

I stare at him. 'I just did!' I say. Has he any notion of the number of times I've picked up the phone to ring someone – anyone – because I needed to tell someone so badly? 'I'm speaking to you, Harry. I'm telling the one person I can really trust...'

'I'm flattered, my dear. But no.' He shakes his head sadly. 'You must speak to someone else.'

'I can't!'

'You must,' he says firmly. 'For the sake of your own mental well-being, and that of your child. It's too much to be holding onto something so huge, all by yourself. You need to tell someone else because... well, I don't count, do I?'

'Of course, you do!' I take a big swallow of my tea, which has gone cold while I've sat here with him looking increasingly bewildered.

'I think... what you really need to do, is, to tell someone who knows you,' he says delicately.

'Harry...'

'And I don't. Before we sat down here to have this delightful chat together, my dear, I'm afraid I had never seen you before in my life.'

## 51

## WILL

This tune I began composing after unexpectedly coming across Mule and his son Jacob is going to be a special one. I can feel it. There's already something there, a thread running through it, promising to make this song joyful and uplifting... I close down the keyboard in front of me. *If I could finish it,* I think ruefully, *it might even turn out to be the best thing I've ever written.* Only, I've been at it for well over a week now and something's still not working. I get up and walk over to the window, easing out the muscles in my back. Something's still missing, and I can't connect with it, just like... like I can't connect with *her*.

Ava was outside my door this morning. She stopped for a good long while at the top of the stairs and when I came out, she said, 'Can we talk, please? I know you've been upset and you've been working, but I really need to talk to you.'

'Some time,' I told her. 'But not now.'

I know she's missing me. I could see it in her eyes and in the way she hung her head and in every fibre of her and I miss her, too.

Only, I also don't...!

Hell, I rub at my neck, feeling a familiar, real, bad-boy shoulder ache coming on. I miss... *what I thought we had.* I miss how I imagined we were. How we even *might* have been, if she hadn't tried to hide all the inconvenient, uncomfortable bits so we could both ride off into the sunset and play happy families.

*She lied.*

And every time I think of that, it makes me feel...

Reaching into my pocket for some painkillers, I shake my head, still caught between the desire to go back to her and my very real conviction that there's no way we're ever putting this one right. Because it's an undeniable fact that my memories are, and always will be, compromised. There are months and years of my life that're never coming back; I'll only ever know them second-hand. Ava took advantage of that, and if I can't trust the woman I love to be honest with me... We could patch up, yes, carry on *as if...* but deep beneath the surface there'll still always be this.

'Ugh!' No painkillers left, I realise. I ran out of them yesterday morning.

I've got to get out of here, before I drive myself crazy.

Outside, the light's so bright this morning, I'm squinting in pain. By the time I walk into the pharmacy for some tablets, everything around me – even Mr Huang's white hair – is a strange shade of yellow.

'Ah, our *time-traveller* has returned.'

I pull a grimace, rubbing at my shoulder. 'I have. I'm afraid today I've got the mother of all...'

He does a *hold-up there* motion to me, while he finishes serving his first customer.

While I wait, the tantalising aroma of roasting potatoes and gravy coming from upstairs, where his family live, puts me in touch with something else. *Did I even remember to eat anything yesterday?*

A roast like this one would've been the first thing I ever cooked for Ava. Impressed her no end, and it was my gramps who taught me how to make one.

As a former navvy, he was also the one who showed me how to sew a button on a shirt and the proper way to iron a crease in a pair of trousers. I smile. Ever since my conversation with Mule, little things like this have been coming back to me in snippets. Things I haven't really given any thought to, for years.

While I wait for Mr Huang, I reminisce about how I imagined my mum would be so impressed with my new-found skills. She was always banging on about how kids needed to become independent, but when I returned home and tried to use her iron, she was horrified! She insisted on taking it off me and wouldn't let me have a go.

Strange how my mum always expressed disapproval of Gramps and many of his ideas on how to bring up kids, and yet the day I announced I was leaving home, telling her I'd rather live down here with him, than with her and Joe – she didn't have too much to say about it. That never made too much sense to me, either.

Sure, she was a bit teary eyed but she also seemed relieved, never put up too much of a fight. Not as I recall. Jeez. I turn away from Mr Huang, grimacing to myself as the memory streams back and I can't stop it. All that pretence about Mum getting with Joe *mainly for my benefit* all went out of the window, didn't it? It was never for my benefit. Mum had done what she'd wanted to do and then she'd lied about it. Simple as.

She'd lied, just as Ava has done. At the time, it felt to me as if I'd lost both my dad and then my mum within the space of a year. I did. I lost 'em both and Mum never even had the decency to admit how well my arrangement with Gramps suited her.

And now… she won't stop messaging me. She wants me to go up to Leeds to visit Auntie Doris on her deathbed or something – even though I have enough shit of my own to deal with and, frankly, I barely even *know* Doris, but those texts keep on coming.

The band of sore muscles in my back tightens perceptibly.

*'Ouch.'*

Mr Huang's back. 'Okay, young man. How can I help?'

'I've got some bad neck and shoulder muscle pain,' I tell him through gritted teeth. 'You got any recommendations?'

'You might consider some acupuncture.'

'Really?'

'It's good for relieving anger,' he tells me, smiling. 'Which is often a major cause of pain.'

I stare at him. 'Do I *look* angry?'

'Ah. Yes. Big...' he motions to the space between my eyebrows '... frown gives it away.'

'So, that'll be the *big pain* I'm in.'

He nods. 'I see that.'

'It's probably because I've been up for the last two nights working on a melody. I've had no sleep. I'm probably dehydrated as well.'

'Ah,' he says, a little more sympathetically, handing me a bottle of water and a lavender bag. 'In that case, these might help.'

I decline the lavender bag and offer of acupuncture, take the water, some paracetamol and some heat-release pain pads, but the longer I've stayed out here, thinking about things, the less convinced I am that any of these purchases are going to help.

Because what's really bugging me is that the two most important women in my life have lied to me badly. And I don't know how to fix that. I don't think those things can ever be fixed.

As I walk back home, it's dawning on me finally that – like the situation with Mum and Joe – no matter what it costs me to lose Ava, I'm going to have to face it.

Very soon, it'll be time for me to move on.

# 52

# AVA

Robyn just sat down at my kitchen table.

'Everything okay?' Coming here today and finding me in this sorry state is probably the last thing Robyn expected but I'm done with pretending.

'Um...'

'No?'

'Oh, Robbie...' I've been trying so hard to keep it all together and I... can't... 'I feel as if I'm losing everything!' I get out. 'Everything that matters.' I swallow down a gulp of water, feeling as if I'm about to choke.

'Steady on, sis!' She shifts over rapidly to the chair beside mine, placing a firm arm about my shoulders. 'What's going on? Are we talking about work, here?'

We've already had text exchanges about the upset with Ginny – I saw no point in keeping that from her, at least – so, of course, she imagines it's that. I rub at my eyes.

'This isn't about work, Robbie.' I shake my head. 'It's far worse than that. It's about... me and Will and... the baby.'

Her eyes widen in alarm. 'Lord, is everything okay with Will? He's not sick again, is he?'

'What? No.' I force myself to say it. 'This isn't about anybody's health. It's about how unhappy I've been, and how bad things have got between us...'

I see her lean back a fraction. 'How'd you mean? You're the happiest woman I know! I mean – you should be... you've got everything you were hoping for, haven't you? What the heck's happened?'

I rub at my temples, unable to immediately find the right words. 'Will doesn't... he doesn't want to be with me any more.'

'Ava.' Her hand twists round to grab hold of mine. 'What are you talking about? Will's crazy about you!'

'He isn't. Not any more.'

'Why? What've you...?' She stops talking, looking at me a little horrified, and I don't want to tell her but *I have to*. I'm done keeping this secret. Harry was right: it has to come out or I'll drive myself mad with it.

'Things *were* going well, yes. We were happy together, but then I had to...'

She's waiting.

'I had to tell him something that was really difficult for him to hear.' I swallow. 'I had to tell Will that this wasn't his baby.'

Robyn's hands fly immediately to her mouth. 'No!'

Painful as it is, I hold her gaze. 'It's true, Robbie.'

'But what? *How...?*'

I can't bear it. I have to look away, but her eyes are still on mine, imploring.

'Ava...'

Her hand closes a little tighter on my arm. 'You're totally sure? I mean, how... could that happen?' Pause. 'Oh. Was it when you were...?'

'Separated, yes.'

'But you weren't even going out with anyone else,' she wails. 'You were pining over Will so badly you refused to see anyone for ages and... and I remember I had to practically drag you out of here even to come to my...'

She stops. 'Oh. Oh... *no?*'

My face is feeling really, really hot. 'Yep.'

'That's where it happened? At my party? But you weren't even with anyone. I mean, the only person you spent any time at all with was Max.' The realisations are dawning on her thick and fast. 'Oh, God. Not Max, Ava? We all knew you two were dancing but we never imagined...'

I don't even have to answer that; she can see it on my face.

'Bloody hell! And Will didn't know?'

I remind her, dully, 'Will didn't remember *anything*, did he?'

She stops talking for a moment.

'But...' She half stands up, and then, not sure what to do with herself, she sits back down again.

'Did *you* even know?'

I tell her slowly, 'I never suspected at first. Why would I? Will and I had been trying for so long to have a baby...'

She's nodding. 'So, when you found out you were expecting it was the most natural thing in the world to imagine it was his?'

I blink away big, fat tears.

'We both did, until...' I clear my throat. 'Will got some test results back that showed he couldn't have any kids and... that's when we realised.'

'What? Will can't actually *have* kids?' She sucks in her lips. 'A double whammy for him, then? Poor guy, he must've been so...'

I'm wringing my hands, staring down but not seeing them, reliving the expression of horror on his face when I told him, seeing only the pure betrayal he felt.

'He was utterly devastated,' I tell her. 'He still is.'

'And...' she shoots me a rueful glance '... you've been holding onto this all by yourself all this time? I mean – how could you not have said anything, never even breathed a word to me?'

'You can't understand *why*?'

'Ugh!' She flings back her hair. 'No wonder you're feeling like you do, Ava. It must've been driving you crazy. Ok-ay...' She tilts her head up. 'Okay, so, Will can't have any kids, but he's always been so desperate to be a dad, so surely, if you found out you were expecting anyway, that could be seen as a bit of a godsend?'

I shake my head.

'He was jealous and couldn't handle it?' She's nodding slowly. 'His reaction is totally understandable, if you think about it.'

It is. But, 'We weren't together, Robyn!' I add, 'I didn't want Max back. I wasn't thinking straight that night, that's all. I'd gone to see Will and found ChiChi there, acting as if they might be back together and then, when you came round for me later that day...'

She's nodding, understanding.

'I get it. You didn't mean to get pregnant that night.'

'No!' Never. I didn't mean to go to her party, or to get with Max, or for any of those things to happen, but they did and then Will got sick on top of it all and we are where we are...

'But the fact that you *did* get pregnant...' she brings us back round to the main matter '... that's still good news because you wanted a baby in the first place.'

'True.'

Robyn's looking thoughtful.

'But I can still see why Will might be jealous.'

'Yeah.' I mutter quietly, 'He was like it when he found out DelRoy was going out with his ex, too, didn't speak to his old mate for *ages*.'

My sister hands me a wodge of tissues for my nose.

'Listen, hon, under the circumstances, there are plenty of women who never would have said anything.' Pause. 'Sleeping dogs, y'know. I think it's admirable that you felt you *could* tell him.'

'Only, I didn't.' I pick up my water glass and gulp some more down. 'I *didn't* feel I could, Robbie, which is why I didn't tell him anything. Not at first. Not until it became so obvious to me how badly he was suffering.'

I glance at my sister, who's frowning, trying desperately to keep up with me. 'If you'd made up your mind not to say anything,' she says slowly, 'then why...?'

I throw open my hands. 'He was getting incredibly depressed and sad. Even though all Will's memories have been wiped, something Old Harry said stuck with me. He told me the heart always remembers, even when the mind forgets.'

She's frowning, nodding slowly.

'Like nothing gets lost? Things that've happened are always stored somewhere, even if we don't remember them?'

'Exactly, and when Will started having so many difficulties, I thought – maybe that's it? I thought, if only he could remember *why* he was feeling the way he did, we could work our way through it and then he'd feel better again.'

My sister's looking sceptical. 'D'you think that's even possible?'

'Maybe! Maybe it's a bit like the time when you were four and you crashed through the pane of glass in our kitchen door and ended up in A and E? They spent hours picking out all the glass but even years after it was all healed over, you used to complain about that shooting pain you'd sometimes get in your hand. Then, one day when you were about eight,' I say, breathless, 'that last shard of glass finally worked its way up to the surface.'

'It did,' she recalls. '*It did*, and after that I never got the pain again.' Her eyebrows narrow. 'And you think it's like, something similar?'

'I'd hoped so,' I tell her miserably. 'He was hurting but he couldn't remember how or why. He was starting to think he was going mad with it all and he wouldn't stop running and running and I was worried...'

She's nodding. 'I see.'

'Except...' I say, breathless, 'the night I told Will the truth about the baby, he never even got angry at me, like he did with DelRoy. So, if this *was* about him feeling jealous...'

'Eh?' She's got her elbow on the table, stroking the side of her face. I know she's been following me up to here, trying to understand how it makes sense, but here's where it doesn't make sense! Not to her and not to me either. I need her to help me make sense of it!

'I thought you said...?'

'Robbie, I was hoping that knowing the truth – painful as it was – would help him.'

'The truth,' she reminds me, 'is often vastly overrated.'

I groan.

'The truth has made things so much worse! Ever since I told Will, he's barely even spoken to me, and if he won't listen to me I know he's going to end up leaving and *then* what will I do...?'

'Take it easy, sis.'

I look at her, all my feelings of desperation surfacing like that shard of glass in her hand that remained buried for so many years. Everything is changing, right at a time when I most need a little peace and calm.

'Where will I go? I can't afford to rent this place on my own – not without Ginny's work coming through or at least something like it – and, apart from all the financial implications, *I don't even care about them*, it's him I care about... How will I manage, without him?' I rub at my throat.

'I miss him, Robbie! He's here but he's not here, and I miss him so much...'

She leans in to hug me, tight.

'You've always got us. You've still got yourself,' she says staunchly. 'You want to talk but Will's working through his own feelings of sadness, the only way he knows how. I guess he usually puts all his feelings into his songs and stuff, doesn't he?' We've run out of tissues so she hands me a paper napkin and I blow my nose, loudly. Sure, I've got my family, but I'm going to have this baby soon, and I need Will to be here for me.

'The night I told him...' I gulp. 'I kept trying to make him see that this needn't be a tragedy, but all he said was that *none of that mattered*, because the child wasn't his. And that now, no child ever would be.'

'Which is all true,' she soothes. 'And very sad, for him, too.' She muses, 'I guess it must've been really tough for him, finding out those two things at once.'

'It must've been devastating.' I stop blowing my nose, a new thought dawning on me. What if Will's reaction to what I told him *wasn't* about the one-night stand? What if he was reacting to the other thing he'd learned about on the same night – his infertility?

That might make sense.

'You think maybe he's just feeling *sad* rather than angry?'

She shrugs. 'Is he writing his songs again?'

'He is...' I stop talking as things start adding up. If he's sad it explains why he never really got angry; why he's spending so much time alone in his room with his guitar, trying to work his feelings through, because this is Will. This is what he does.

Oh, God – my heart has started pounding – could it be true?

It explains why Will's still here; why he's not left.

I say faintly, 'I think you might have just helped me understand something that I really couldn't see, Robbie.'

Her eyes light up a little. 'I did?'

A small relief floods through me – a hope, as Robyn pulls me in close for a warm, sisterly hug.

'Thank you so much. I never expected this, but sharing my troubles with you has left me feeling so much better, Robbie.'

She says, smiling sadly, 'Y'know, I think I've been waiting my whole life for you to tell me that.'

# 53

# AVA

'Ava – what are you doing?'

My arms laden with some heavy, freshly washed curtains I've come out to peg onto the line, I sweep round to look at Will. He's run out of the house to relieve me of my burden, shaking his head reprovingly.

'What?' I stand back, surprised but glad to see him.

'These're too heavy,' he says. 'You shouldn't be...' Pegging them up smartly himself, he turns back to me, saying more softly, 'Why are you even doing all this?'

'Washing curtains?' I give him an uncertain smile – you're speaking to me again? – feeling a rush of gladness. Seeing him properly for the first time in so many days, I think he looks pale, but, even if he's only come out here to tell me off, Will still wants to make sure I'm all right; he still cares.

'All this.'

He motions towards the sagging washing line, already laden with sheets and pillow cases and towels, and I admit, 'I don't know, really. I've been getting this... This overwhelming urge to clean everything, get everything fresh and ready for when...' I grind to a stop, not wanting to mention anything that'll cause him to walk away again.

There's a slight pause, while he takes me in, and I wonder what he's thinking, what's changed, and why he's out here talking to me. Whatever the reason, I'm deliriously happy that he is.

'You're nesting,' he says quietly.

'I'm sorry – what?' I give a little laugh but stop when his eyes look into mine, and there's still so much sadness.

'It's something women do when they're getting ready to give birth.'

I nod. He's the one who's read all the pregnancy books; he's been one step ahead of me, all the way.

'Hormones, again?' I move a smidgeon closer to him, pretending to pull the curtains a little straighter.

'I guess.'

'Not long to go,' I breathe.

'No.'

Oh, God, Will. There are so many things I want to say, so many things, but my heart's filled right up to the brim and I'm scared if I say the wrong things he won't stay and then I'll never get the chance...

He glances at me. 'You all packed and ready, yet?'

'What?' I blink back the tears that threaten to come. Without my work from Ginny, I can't afford to keep on this place without him, and I know we'll soon be going our separate ways, but he and I haven't even...

'Your hospital bag. Have you packed it?'

'Oh. I see.' I gulp. 'I've begun to pack some things. Some baby clothes and some toiletries, but, somehow...' I shoot him a sideways glance. 'My heart's not been in it.'

'Nonetheless, you'll need to,' he urges. 'And soon.'

'Yes.'

He hasn't moved away yet.

'Will...'

He says, 'I'll be needing to make a move some time soon, myself. I thought you'd want to know.'

'Soon?' I lift my chin. 'Are you leaving me, then?'

He looks a little surprised. 'I'm off to Leeds. Auntie Doris. She's in the ICU...'

'Oh.' I blink. 'I'm so sorry.'

He says, in a pained voice, 'I hardly knew her, Ava. I'm only going up because they're putting pressure on me to do so, but in all honesty I'd rather not go.'

'No.' I'm shaking my head understandingly, but it's not at all clear to me whether this is because he's decided he'd rather stay here and sort things out with me.

Darn it. 'Will...' I get out. 'Don't think that I don't know, that I can't understand how you're feeling – what you must be going through...'

'Can you?'

'I didn't understand,' I admit. 'I thought you were giving me the cold shoulder because you were angry at me for getting pregnant by Max, and, fine, I get that, too, but then I spoke to Robyn and she gave me a different perspective on it.'

How strangely he's looking at me, stepping back a little; his blue-grey-green eyes are all the different colours of a turbulent, storm washed sea and I sense whatever I've stirred up for him here runs deep.

He's saying softly, 'That was deeply shocking to hear, I'll admit. The idea that this child might not actually have been mine never occurred to me. Not even in my wildest dreams.'

'You trusted me, so why would it?'

He looks at the hand I've placed, ever so tentatively, on his arm, his mouth creasing unhappily.

'God, Will! I haven't wanted to be the first to speak because I've been waiting for you to, but I'm not waiting to say it any longer! I am so sorry for the hurt I've caused you. And for misunderstanding how much you've been suffering, for not getting how really sad you were...' I tell him desperately. 'Because you couldn't... because you'd never have any biological children of your own.'

'I won't, no.' He's shaking his head, pained. 'Then again, recently I saw an old... ' He stops himself, then starts up again. 'An old friend. He was with his stepson and I could plainly see that the two of them had as close and loving a bond as any father-child could ever hope to have.'

'Did you?' I smile. If only he could feel that way himself, about this child I'm carrying. It's what I've dreamed of, more than anything. Is he finally seeing that it's at least possible? 'Did it make you think maybe...?'

He glances at me uneasily.

'It made me realise that, yes, I could love another man's child as my own, if I brought them up. I could have that too, what he had...'

'Oh, yes?' I let out a shuddering breath. If he's realised that, it's... it's huge. It means that all the fears I've had about him not accepting this child as his own, us never being able to be a couple again... they could be unfounded.

I take a step closer to him, dare to reach my arms up and about his neck. Pull his face a little closer to my own, slowly, bit by bit, and he doesn't pull away. And when at last our foreheads touch, it's all I can do not to cry out – in relief, because I thought I'd lost him for good; in sadness, because I have missed him so much.

'D'you maybe think you could ever feel that way about this baby?' I swallow. 'I appreciate it's going to take some work, but, do you think you and I could ever be a couple again, and put all this behind us?'

'Oh, Ava.' His voice comes from deep within his throat. I feel the kiss of his mouth on my forehead, light as a feather, and for a few brief moments I feel delirious with happiness. To be this close to him, almost in the warmth of his arms again after so long and yet... I pull away a little, looking under my eyelashes at him, and he's still looking at me, heartbroken.

'Will?' And it's dawning on me how tense he feels beneath my arms. 'D'you think we could...?'

'No,' he says. 'I wish we could, but... no.'

'Why?' My voice comes out like a plea and I hate myself for wanting him so badly that I'd beg him to take me back. For needing him so much that I can't let him go, even when he's clearly done with me. 'I know I made you sad. I know... I can't undo... but, you clearly care about me too, so why can't you forgive and forget and move on?'

'I hope I will never forget you,' he says feelingly. 'And I do forgive you...'

'Then why?' I gasp. 'Why won't you take me back, Will?'

He pulls my arms away from his neck, gently and sadly.

'I won't. Because I relied on you to tell me the truth like you promised you would. I relied on you, Ava. And now... no matter what you say, no matter how much you protest that you meant it for the best...'

'But...'

Oh, God. I close my eyes, realising that we've come to it at last. What I tried to tell him before; the last bit of the truth, which he didn't want to hear.

'Will...' I begin. 'There's something else you need to know.'

'Something else?' He's shaking his head, backing away. Again? I stare at him in disbelief. He's not in the same angry place now so why won't he let me speak?

But he's saying, 'No. No more secrets, Ava. No more lies.'

'What? Please, let me...' But I see with a sinking heart that he still doesn't want to hear it. Just like the day he woke up from his operation and he didn't want to see his advance wishes, didn't want to take on board anything that I might have said, because I was no one to him.

And I see that it's too late. I will never get to say it.

The one thing left that might have changed Will's mind.

## 54

## AVA

Standing on the lawn for a good few minutes after Will goes, I feel my heart fill with sorrow and I am left without words. Without breath. After a while, the sound of Will's taxi breaks through, pulling up sharply on the gravel outside. The front door opens and then it closes; the crunch of his footsteps walking out to the car echoes loudly in my head. I know he's leaving but there's nothing I can do; my feet have been swallowed by the grass. And now, as I grasp at the bed sheets for support, they're billowing up on the line, only wrestling with me. I can't help this sense that I'm falling, all the while my heart's still pounding with grief and shock in my chest; *he's going* and there is nothing I can do to stop him.

And now there's only silence from out front. He's gone.

This time I know, deep in my heart, that I will never see him again. He'll disappear right off the radar and I will be cut off, like his mum once was.

The sheer and utter emptiness of that is like the huge, dark mouth of the raging sea reaching up to swallow me. It feels exactly like a death. Blundering back into the house, numbed and confused, I want to curl up in a dark room.

I want to stop... being.

I go over to stand by the old wooden mantelpiece. The place where he stood. I know I will never forget his face, the night I told him the truth; he had the same look of pain I'd seen the first time round, what I'd tried to wipe away at all costs. And I feel it, bubbling up in my throat; that sometimes, no matter how hard we try, we can't wipe it all away.

Bent over double in grief, I force myself to straighten, to remember. Will is at least alive, I achieved that much. I did *something* right, even if I did so much wrong and the time for reckoning has come. I always knew when I agreed to our Faustian pact that this might be the price I'd have to pay, but I also know I won't be bouncing back from this one. My heart's too sore and bruised and I'm not dreaming of anything any more.

Bending to pull his ring off my finger, I place it gently on the shelf, because... all I know is, it's not for me; I can't keep it.

My finger feels strangely bare and empty without it. Like a boat set adrift. When I look about me, the whole cottage is different, the light inside is greyer, darker somehow; it no longer feels like home. This new world without Will is a strange new, unwanted territory. A land lonely and uncharted. Deep in my bones, I am weary and empty.

And yet there's a small quiet voice, still tugging at my heart; it whispers to me that there's someone coming soon who'll have no option but to rely on me. There is still this. I can't stop it and I can't deny it and I can't just... fall to pieces.

Sweeping my hair back, struggling to fix my falling ponytail, I remind myself, my child is coming even if Will no longer wants to be with me. He's coming even if Ginny's not my friend any more and I no longer have a job. He's coming even if I can no longer afford to live in the home I love and I haven't the first idea how I'm going to support us both.

No matter how much I'm hurting and whatever else is happening in the world around me, this child will be arriving soon. And I have to be ready.

When I turn back to look over again at the beautiful symbol of everything that I'd hoped for, Will's ring sits there silently, twinkling back at me from the shelf. I don't pick it up.

Go love again, my darling. I wish you all the love in the world. Even though that girl won't be me.

Whoever she is, I hope it's someone who deserves you.

'You going straight back down after this?' It's more of a statement than a question. When I look over at Mum's stocky, square-set, salt-of-the-earth husband, Joe, I can't help noticing he looks so weary to the bone that I almost feel sorry for him. Almost.

'Back down...?' Is he asking if I'll go from the ICU at Leeds General straight back to the hotel I've booked for the night? Mum's the one stalwart out of all of them who's not left Auntie's side, yet. I doubt she will now, either, but – is he enquiring if I'm coming back to have dinner with him tonight?

'Back down to Holcombe.' He leans in and adds quietly in my ear. 'After the funeral, I mean.'

I jerk my head back. What's he saying? Doris isn't dead yet. Granted, the family waiting to see her are lined up in this corridor like footie fans waiting outside Elland Road stadium for a home match. But... I gulp... that doesn't mean anything, does it? She was a popular lady, my dad's sister. That question seems in such bad taste.

I turn my head away from him. 'I've got no plans beyond saying hello to Auntie Doris.'

'Any of us will be lucky to do that now, lad.'

I blink, slowly, feeling a small tic going in my jaw. He means nothing by it, I know, but – where does this bloke get off, calling me *lad*? That bugged me enough as a kid, but now, really?

Joe says, 'We got the word through last night Auntie's time was nigh and... they tend to be pretty accurate 'bout these things, the nurses.'

'Yes.' Mum's panicked call had caught me in the bath this morning. Lying in the tub, not relaxing very much but wrestling with a load of mixed-up, tangled feelings about Ava and myself, I'd picked up the call without thinking and regretted it immediately.

'Sylvie thought you'd want to see Auntie before... you know,' Joe's saying. 'She's been tryin' her best to get hold of you, lad.'

'I know.' I fold my arms, sighing quietly under my breath. Do they imagine I don't have a life of my own – *troubles enough of my own* – to see to? I glance at the queue of relatives – going down slowly as they're only allowing in two at a time – and wonder where all this lot were when I was having *my* op.

Joe's saying, 'Your Auntie Doris always thought the world of you, and all.'

'Sure.'

'Out of all of 'em, she always said it were you who reminded her most of your dad, that's why.'

'Well, he *was* my dad.' I shoot Joe a sharp glance. I only ever acknowledged the one.

'That he was.' Joe bows his head, acknowledging humbly. 'And a nicer, kinder, braver man I never met.'

'I'll bet you didn't.' They were good mates, once, this man and my father. After Dad passed away, he came around often, didn't he, making sure the family were okay, wanted for nothing, comforting Mum? And also trying, but not succeeding, to comfort me too, with cinema trips and go-kart racing and stuff. Trying to bribe me to love him, as I saw it at the time, but that was never going to work.

I sit back, arms tucked under my armpits, feeling stiff and hot in my shirt and smart jeans, wishing I could be back in the peace and quiet of my own hotel and this visit would be over with. I might come back and visit Auntie again in the morning when all this lot have gone back to their jobs and families. If we could have a little, private chat, that might feel a bit more meaningful than this cattle-call. I didn't know her too well, as I said to Ava, I left here too young for that, but she was close to my father as a boy. Maybe there are some little anecdotes she could tell me?

Joe's saying sorrowfully, 'You never got to see *him*, before he passed, did you? That rankled with you, I know.'

I turn my body away from Joe, more annoyed than I should be that he's brought that up.

'Sylvie knew it. That's why she was so keen for you to come.'

*God, does the man never stop talking?*

Staring up at the blinking fluorescent light in the hospital corridor, I wonder why on earth he would bring that up about me not getting to see my dad at the end. I didn't get to see Dad when he lay dying in his hospital bed, no. Nobody let me. That's partially why I've made the trek up.

But what's the use mentioning it – *is the man completely devoid of an empathic bone in his body?*

The ache I've felt in my heart since leaving Ava this morning just grew a little deeper and wider. Should I have brought her with me, for this one trip?

But, no. I did the right thing by making sure to pack enough of a suitcase so I could stay away for as long as I need to be able to get my thinking straight. I couldn't do it at Beach Cottage, in the place where she was. It hurt too much. Wanting to go to her and tell her what she was longing to hear; to say everything was all right.

I clench my fists. But that wouldn't have been true, comforting to both of us as it might've been. Everything is as far from all right as it could get. Me missing her doesn't change that.

'You'll be next,' Joe's saying.

*'Sorry?'*

He motions towards his watch and I recall how the thick, wiry hairs on his arms always freaked me out as a kid.

'You'll be going in to her next.'

'Oh. Good.' The door to the private room opens a fraction and everyone looks towards it, expectantly. We can all see the nurse standing inside, still talking to someone, and I find myself, like the rest of them, straining to hear what she's saying. Wondering what I'm going to say to the old lady when I go in, whether she'll recognise me or be so medicated that she won't know who I am.

'Who's next?'

I stand up as the door opens up a little wider, automatically tucking myself in at the back, and the nurse says, a little distractedly, 'Please wait one moment.'

I wait, aware of all the relatives looking at me, curiously, but my eyes are fixed on that half open white door. Mum'll be in there, I know. The minute she sees me she'll want to know about Ava and the baby. I won't tell her anything. Not now. I'm here for Doris, after all. Mum will prattle on about how excited she is to be a grandma, and how babies always bring new hope, and stuff like that, to make herself feel better.

'Which one is William?' the nurse says. I nod, grateful when she beckons me in, closing the door quickly before anyone else can enter. When I try and look past her to the bed, she's blocking my view. There's a slight pause before she says quietly, 'I'm very sorry, William, your Auntie Doris passed away peacefully a couple of minutes ago...'

When I look over, Mum's sitting there with her face crumpled, nodding.

'*No*, that's...' I fall back a couple of steps, feeling as if someone's punched me in the gut. I swallow. 'She's gone already? You sure?' Realising how stupid that sounds, even to my own ears.

'She is. I'm sorry.' The nurse is prompting me forward, to go join my mum, but I don't want to do that. They've removed Auntie's breathing mask, removed all the tubes, and from here she looks as if she might just be sleeping.

I've been away a long time and we weren't close, but I came up here to say goodbye to Auntie, because for some reason it felt as if it mattered. And now, totally out of the blue, a rush of heat comes to my head, and I recognise it as the pure, unremitting anger that it is. Anger that I didn't get to do what I came here to do.

The next instant, my heart folds, shrinks right down to a dot.

I've been cheated. *Robbed.*

I didn't get to say goodbye.

# 56

# AVA

'I still can't believe you're giving all this away!' Elsie selects a large stuffed bear from the pile of toys I've placed on my kitchen table and hugs him in her lap, looking desolate.

'Why now, when you're...?' She motions towards my belly. I keep pulling more stuff out of the black sack I've brought down from what would've been my baby's nursery. We both look down in dismay. So many lovely barely used things, even... even Bubs, the plush brown rabbit I had sitting at the end of the cot, who was the very first item I ran out and purchased the day I first got the news.

My neighbour's shaking her head, plainly puzzled.

'You're still going to have this baby, aren't you? You'll still need all this.'

'Please, I've already put by what I need,' I tell her quietly. 'Where I'm going, there isn't going to be the space.'

Elsie puts the bear down, jaw dropping. 'You're leaving?'

I nod.

'Soon. Before the end of the month.' I gather my hair back, tie it in a businesslike bun in an attempt to make myself look more in control, but the truth is I am barely staving off the urge to fall apart. 'I'm planning on moving back in with my parents for a bit.'

The one thing I was never gonna do. I swallow.

'Will and I are... we aren't together any more.'

'Oh, my dear, I'm so sorry...' She adds quietly, 'I missed seeing him, y'know, the past few weeks after, all those times when he was out walking alone – never with you, the spare bedroom curtains always drawn, as if there'd been some upset and now...?'

'He's *gone*, Elsie.' I look up at her, swallowing. 'But it's okay.'

It is not okay. *It's the least okay thing that could've happened in the world.* I've had a while to try and come to terms with it but, still, it all feels so wrong. I close my eyes, squeezing Bubs the brown bunny to my chest. I thought I was all cried out, but in the face of Elsie's sympathy my tears have started flowing again.

'Surely, he'll come to his senses and be back, though, love, he's bound to. He did last time, didn't he?'

'No,' I say out loud, eventually. 'This time he won't be returning.'

'Are you absolutely sure?'

To convince her, I pick up the note he left me, propped up against the toaster the day he left, handing it to her to read.

*Ava,*

*I have to leave and I imagine after Leeds I'll be moving on to somewhere else. We'll sort out the finer details of this when I return but please don't worry about me. I will be OK. I know you won't feel this way now but, please believe me, in the long run you will know it's for the best, too.*

*Will x*

*(Ps. under the circumstances, I feel it would be wrong of me to stop paying the rent on this place, so you'll be able to continue to live here for the time being.) W x*

'Oh,' she says. *'Oh.'*

'Believe me now?'

'What happened?' she asks gently. 'Would it be very intrusive of me to ask?'

I shoot her a pained look.

'He left after... after I let him believe some things that weren't entirely true. Things that *mattered*.'

Elsie contemplates this for a bit. She doesn't ask what.

'Listen, I've done the same, love – what woman hasn't? We do what we have to do to keep the family running smoothly, to keep things sweet.'

I don't answer that and she runs on.

'I always looked at you two and thought you were the finest little couple I ever did see. Something special, like this place.' She looks around regretfully. 'Once you let it go you won't find another place like it too soon. Why the hurry to leave, though?'

'I can't stay,' I say. It doesn't make logical sense, I know. I should stay here, at least till after the baby comes, wait till I can sort myself out with some new private commissions and hope that somehow, maybe, one day I'll be able to afford this cottage on my own, but...

'It doesn't feel right.'

I turn my head away, wishing all the things I've got to dispose of could magically disappear; wishing Beach Cottage didn't mean as much to me as it does.

'Does it feel right to *go*?'

'No.' I give a sad smile. 'You know, when I first left my parents' place and came out here to be by the sea and near the Butterfly Gardens – I thought I was the happiest woman alive.'

'And then you met Will.'

'And then I really *was* the happiest woman...'

My neighbour looks very sad. She glances towards my belly. '*Why* did you feel you had to tell him, my dear?'

I groan, rub at my face with my hands. 'I realised that what he didn't know *was* hurting him. So, I told him.' I look Elsie directly in the face now. 'I told him and I don't regret it, even if he's left me over it. Will was relying on me to tell him what was what after the op. I let him down and maybe I should've known it, because the time I've had Will in my life has been when my life's felt the sweetest and the most real.'

She's nodding sadly. 'It sounds as if you were trying to do your best by him. Surely if you only explained?'

'I did, *I tried*, but...' I stare down at my empty hands. I still don't know how I will ever find a way to glue myself back together into enough of a person to go on and deal with everything that's coming next, but I know that I have to.

'I know that this is something I've got to find a way to see through on my own, without Will's help. I have to go.'

She's saying, sorrowfully, 'Of course. If you're not working for your friend these days, I imagine your next job would also have to be more central, a little more nine-to-five?'

She's right about the job, too. I admit reluctantly, 'I've already made some queries regarding getting my old bank teller job back.'

'Oh.'

Did I show what I was really feeling on my face? I need to do better.

'Yes.' The one I had when I was living at my parents' place after losing my dream job at Lukas and Co. The bank job I was so bored at, I once swore I'd rather pick up rubbish than go back to it.

'My priorities have shifted,' I tell her. 'I'd prefer to see me and my child comfortable and I'd be grateful to have it.'

'In that case, I am sorry, my dear. I really am.' She pats my arm consolingly. My energy's deserted me and there's nothing left to be said. Perhaps needing some distraction, she's spied something else she wants to rescue from the big plastic bag we were filling.

'And this?' She fishes out Lucky Troll. 'Didn't you win this in some fashion magazine competition you entered?'

'I did!' Years ago. I was meant to be cramming for exams, instead of which I'd been dreaming of winning some tickets to Paris fashion week. I take it from her, pulling his green plastic hair into a point with my fingertips.

'I only got the consolation prize, but I still took it as some sort of sign!' I give a short laugh, reminiscing on my own pig-headedness. 'I decided it meant I was supposed to be designing clothes for a living...

no matter how many obstacles everyone else foresaw in my path! I've kept him by me for good luck, ever since.'

'Well, then,' she asserts. 'You should keep him. He's only tiny.'

He's tiny and he's huge at the same time.

'He's got to go.' I drop him back into the bag. 'I can't keep on relying on him. It's about time I took charge of my own luck, Elsie.'

In reply, she only pats my arm. When we're done with the packing 'Maybe you can give all these things to your daughter-in-law?' I tell her.

'No,' Elsie says decisively. 'Maybe I'll put them by for you at mine for a little while – who knows how things will turn out, yet?'

I'm about to refuse but, touched by her kindness, I can only nod.

I've got a whole new little person on the way to think about now and it's like she said – we do whatever we have to do, to keep things together.

# 57

# WILL

'You sure you won't join the rest of us at The Golden Plough, lamb?'

I close my eyes briefly, aware that the quiet moment I'd planned at the graveside has been ruined.

Without turning, I shake my head at Mum. She pauses for a respectful moment, muttering an *Ave*, before finally trundling off, disconsolate. She's never liked to spend too long in this place. Her silent plea to Joe behind me, *to try and make the lad see sense*, is something I can feel more than see. Well, he can try.

Joe bends to arrange some red carnations in a vase by the grave, and I step out of his way, feeling annoyed. I should've brought some flowers of my own to place here, but I didn't. A little further down, a group of our other relatives are still saying their last farewells to Doris, moving off in small groups and arranging shared car lifts back to The Golden Plough.

Joe indicates Dad's grave. 'Got his sister there with him now,' he says.

I nod.

'Golden Plough was always your dad's favourite watering hole,' he observes quietly. 'Always said there was no place else in the world where they'd serve you a Guinness to match it.'

'I won't be going,' I tell him.

'I understand, lad.' He takes a step back, respectful. 'Coming back here makes you feel sad and... you're not in a mood to mingle.'

I turn my head to the side, aware of my own grimace at that. It hasn't made me feel sad. None of it. Not the priest's moving speech about Auntie that had everyone else in tears. Not the beautiful choir music Mum asked me to organise, that's taken up the best part of the last two weeks to arrange; nor the tributes that've been pouring in from relatives and friends near and far, including the video-collage my dad's cousin, Dick, made from old photos of Auntie with my dad and Mum and the rest of their family, throughout their lives. They had that showing up on a screen at the funeral. Dick had synched it to some of my music, which led to me getting a lot of comments, after. It made me realise – some of these people really are proud of me, of what I've achieved.

Even if I've been away so long, I barely know their names. Even if I don't feel like one of them any more – and I suspect that has more to do with the way I've lived my life than any memory wipe that's happened as a result of an operation – they're *proud of me*, as fond of me as they were of my dad. But I still don't feel anything.

'You're right,' I tell Joe, who seems to be waiting, 'I'm not in any mood to mingle.'

'Right you are,' he says, disappointed. 'Well – you know where we'll be.'

'Yep.' *Consuming beer and egg sandwiches in my dad's favourite watering hole;* the place he always said he'd take me one day to sample my first Guinness, soon as I was old enough, father-son style. So, no. I won't be joining them. I'd rather get on the first train home, if truth be told, but I still need to retrieve my stuff. I left the hotel a week ago – they were fully booked up – and moved into Mum and Joe's place. *Might as well,* they'd coaxed. *You could help us organise the funeral and it's so good to see you home.*

All that guilt-trip stuff parents do, only – this isn't my home; it hasn't been for a very long time. I stayed because we were all waiting to ɔury Auntie and I wasn't clear what else I was going to do and ɔecause... I couldn't go back to my real home again. I didn't contact Ava.

She didn't contact me.

Two roads up from the cemetery there's a cafe with a good Wi-Fi ɔonnection. I order a coffee and make the video-call to Toby that I've ɔeen putting off for too long. He's not going to be happy with me, that's for sure.

'Hey, man! Been a while?' He picks up straight away and the sight of him, sitting there in a comfy oversized T-shirt with his favourite Les Paul on his lap, is achingly familiar. I swallow.

'I know. I... It's been a little... difficult here.' I'm not in the mood to apologise. I pause. 'You get the music I sent over?'

He pushes back his hair, frowning slightly. 'Sure, I did, William. But... where *are* you, man?' He's miffed. He's not saying anything yet, ɔut I can tell. Fair dos. I've been hellishly unreliable.

'And what's happened to your accent?'

'What accent?' I throw back. 'I don't have any accent.'

'Sure do,' he says.

I give an inward groan. This always happens when I get with my relatives. Pause.

'I'm in Leeds. At my aunt's funeral,' I say. Toby bows his head. 'I've ɔeen up here for a bit, helping them to—'

He cuts across me.

'Sorry, I thought you were just being a dick, not answering my messages.'

'Did you?' I give a short, humourless laugh. 'Why, is that what I'm like, Toby? You've known me for years, you say – that the person you've always known me to be?'

He gives the slightest shrug. 'Sometimes.'

'Oh, yeah?'

Toby says, a little hurt, 'Were you also in Leeds with your relatives when you blew me out over that big meeting with Redwick, the film guy?'

I blink. 'No. I was with... I was with Ava, then.' I stretch my arm out, rubbing at the back of my head. I let him down, I know. But I push back. 'I've been going through... some real bad times with her, man.'

Toby's silent, waiting. His dark eyebrows are pointed slightly downwards. I go on.

'She's been filling me in on some things that were going on between us before, that've... they've given me some cause to reassess the whole relationship.'

Toby's nodding, sombre. 'That happens, with partners. Every so often you've got to stop and assess where you're going, right?'

The waitress brings the coffee I've ordered and I look away, saying, 'Nowhere, man. We're going nowhere, Ava and I.'

'That bad?'

'You can't imagine. Look...' My throat is actually hurting from having to say that out loud. 'Let's just...'

'No – go on, try me.'

I shake my head. What am I gonna say? The whole tawdry truth?

'Ava *lied* to me, man. Big time. How can you ever trust a woman again once she's done that?'

'I don't know.' He pauses for a moment, thinking about this as if it weren't a blindingly obvious rhetorical question. 'Did she have a good reason?'

I pull a face, starting to feel angry at him, too. I've come out of a memory-wipe op, for Pete's sake – *has he forgotten that?*

'There *is* no good reason to do that, man.'

'Well – did she?'

I stare at the phone screen. 'Whose side are you on, anyway?'

Toby stops gently strumming his guitar and looks up, slightly hurt. 'I told you once, there are two things I don't mess around with: one's my music and the other – if you haven't figured it out yet – is my friends. And I am your friend. I'm on your side, William. *Your side.* Even if that means sometimes saying things to your face that you don't want to hear. Even if that means sometimes questioning your truth.'

'I've just lost my aunt! And my girlfriend! I've just visited my dad's grave for the first time in forever and my heart's torn in two and *you're fucking questioning my truth?'*

'You bet I fucking am.' He's strumming, again. 'You will too, once you've calmed down enough to see there'll be more than one side to this.'

'Hey – sure there is.' My voice goes up a notch. I know it because the waitress looks over at me sharply and the two people sitting at the table beside me have stopped talking.

'Two sides to every disagreement. Every time. Always? Because no one ever just does anyone any wrong in this world, do they?'

'Hell, *you're* sure as hell feeling wronged, aren't you?'

'You think I'm feeling...?' I stand now, draining the coffee cup, and the thick dark liquid is bitter in my throat. 'Y'know what, Toby – *fuck you too!'*

Was I yelling? I think I heard the waitress gasp.

Ending the call, I've stormed back out into the biting wind on the road. Too late, I see that I've left my jacket behind, but I don't care. No way I'm going back in there. Not after that grand exit.

What am I doing? I didn't intend to get mad at Toby. He's done nothing; it's been me who's been behaving like a dick. *What am I even doing?*

Twenty minutes up the road and – still jacketless – I'm freezing my balls off. The wind's whipping up a fury this afternoon and the usually heaving Milton Green is empty apart from a solitary dog walker and a couple of ten year olds arguing over their constantly crashing kite. I don't want to be here. In dispute with Toby and Ava and Mum and Joe. I don't want to be alone on the afternoon of Auntie's funeral. And I don't want to be... Hands deep in my pocket, I stand there for a bit, feeling my nose running, and watching the kite flyers fail, over and over. I'm tempted to walk off, but something pulls me back. *Didn't anyone ever teach these kids the proper way to fly a kite?*

'Gotta stand with your back to the wind,' I call out.

'What?'

'Stand with your...'

'Which way is *back to the wind*?' They look at each other, puzzled.

'Change where you're standing!' I do an about-turn motion with my finger. 'You need to move. It's all about where you're standing...'

They don't believe me, I can tell. So, I go over and show them. Five minutes later, their kite has caught the breeze, its tail shimmying a zigzag pattern right over the treeline and it's sailing up, up and away. They pause there with their mouths wide open for a bit and then they're laughing, taking it in turns to hold onto the handle with me, hanging on with all their might as it climbs.

And for a little while, their kite is like a living, breathing thing. The wind buffets us, almost pushing us over, but when I close my eyes, I can sense what I couldn't feel at the cemetery... *my father*, standing by my shoulders, steadying my hands, steadying their hands. *God, I miss you, Dad. I miss you and they never let me see you at the end and I never got to say all the...* I didn't. I couldn't.

The warm tears that're streaming down my face get lost instantly in the wind, but it doesn't matter because I can feel his feet, planted so strong on the earth behind me, reliable and loving and strong. Anchoring me to the earth. Helping me shake off the first sting of sleet on my face, shake off the heaviness and the sadness that've settled around me like a cloak.

It's all over in seconds.

As the wind eases off, I hand their kite back over to them and the boys take off. They've already run to the edge of the green, calling and laughing, and they don't even look back.

I stand there for a moment, swaying slightly. Looking upwards, their kite is a stairway to heaven, cracking open the clouds and letting a ray of light shine through, and I'm left feeling...

Different, somehow.

# 58

# WILL

Back at The Golden Plough, Joe's sitting by himself at the bar when I walk in.

'Décor's changed a little since I was last in here,' I say.

'It would do,' he says. 'Been a few years?'

'Quite a few.'

Joe doesn't say anything else, just pushes a full pint of Guinness towards me. It's gone a little flat on the top, and I get the impression it might have been waiting here a while. For me? I hesitate, looking around a bit, noticing the much-admired photo-collage has made a reappearance. This time it's up on a board by the corner.

The one of Auntie holding up my twelfth birthday cake while Mum blows out all the candles – I'd refused – looks particularly poignant to me; I'm looking surly as hell while Mum looks so unhappy. *Happy times, eh?* I give a snort.

'I never wanted a party that year and I said so.'

'You didn't,' he agrees.

'What I wanted was for them all to bugger off and leave me alone.'

'True.'

I shoot him a significant glance. '*You* most of all.'

He winces slightly.

'I know it was wrong to be mad at you,' I admit, 'but it made me so mad. How she never left enough time after Dad died, only wanted to pick up and carry on as if nothing had happened, and, every time I've thought about how she was lying to me all those years...'

'You thought she was *lying*?'

We both turn to look at the women of the family at the other end of the pub who've started up a little jig. Mum too. She catches my eye, and, seeing me sitting with Joe, her whole face turns into a beaming smile.

I look at my hands.

'All that business about... you being my new dad, and how I'd see it one day if only I gave you a...'

'She was never lying to you about that. I wanted to be that man...'

Joe's shaking his head, sadly.

'She never wanted you to be left all alone, William.'

'No.' I never wanted that, either, but I felt it. After she married him. And for such a long time, after going to Grandad's down in Holcombe Bay, till I discovered music, made friends, I felt so alone, but... maybe she *wasn't* lying about things in the way I thought she was? My throat has closed up. For the briefest second there, I thought I caught a whiff of one of Dad's favourite cigars.

I don't want to be alone now, either.

Joe raises his drink. 'To all the Tylers who've loved us in this life-time,' he says.

I blow my nose, loudly. Then I reach out to retrieve the tall glass he's been keeping by for me.

'To all the Tylers,' I say. My first taste of Guinness is as I'd always imagined it. Slightly flat and dark and malty and... something that brings me to the brink of manhood that's so long eluded me.

'To all the Tylers. And, also, to *us*.'

# 59

# AVA

*'It's a very brave thing that you are doing, Ava.'* As I pull up onto my parents' drive, Robyn's words from our last telephone conversation come echoing back to me. I couldn't figure out yesterday evening why she said it. What's so brave about returning to a loving home when you're at your lowest ebb and you need some support? When I phoned Mum and Dad to fill them in before coming down here – paving the way for the help I'll need to ask of them – they were surprised. From their voices, maybe even a little shocked. They must have imagined my star was in the ascendant, so to learn how far I've fallen...

I swallow, shielding my eyes from the bright morning sun, feeling sorry that I'm putting them through all this. They're good, hard-working people and they've worked years for the retirement they were hoping to enjoy together. I know spending time abroad was something they saw on the horizon. Though they're looking forward to their first grandchild, me returning home is going to scupper the travel plans, for sure. But I already knew all I had to do was hold out my hand to ask and I'd never be turned away.

Where's the bravery in that?

No bravery, just reality, that's all. The reality that I'm going to need to take my head out of the clouds and face the life that I've *made* for myself. Even if that no longer includes my dreams of designing beautiful clothes, even if it doesn't include me riding off into the sunset with the man I love. I have to face it.

When I finally make myself get out of the car, I find the front door is already left open for me. There are fresh flowers on the table in the hallway and the faint, warm smell of baking coming from the kitchen opens up gentle memories of older times: of cupcakes and loose-leaf tea out of an ornate, old-style teapot – like they do at the Butterfly Gardens – when me and Mum and Robyn would sit and chat for a while, settling back into the house, and I'd feel as if I'd come *home*.

It doesn't feel quite like that today, though. Peering through the kitchen window at my parents, I can see they're animated, chatting to the neighbours, regaling them with 'Tales from the Spanish Restaurant'. It's not that warm but they're both wearing short sleeves, showing off their tans, and Mum's sporting a chic, surprisingly modern, hairdo. She turns around and spots me. With a whoop of greeting, she puts off the neighbours and hurries back inside.

'Ava!' Mum comes over and gives me a concerned hug. Then it's Dad's turn.

'Welcome back, stranger!'

'I'm not the one who went away,' I remind them. Though in a sense, we all know that I am.

'My, but you've grown some!' Mum breathes, patting my tummy. She and Dad exchange a glance. After our phone call last night, they'll be bursting to have some answers, they must be, but I'm happy they're taking their time, not rushing to bombard me with questions.

'Tea?' Dad offers.

'Of course.' I give him a weak smile.

'Listen.' Mum sits me down at the kitchen table while Dad goes about the task of warming the teapot. 'You need to know that we're here for you, love. Whatever's gone wrong. Whatever time you need, to sort yourself out again, me and Dad have decided, you and the baby come first.'

'I know. Thank you.'

She's running on earnestly. 'The minute we heard about your troubles last night, we went straight up to have a look at your old bedroom to check out the state of it.'

I rub at my eyes. Last time I left home, I was so thrilled to get the chance to leave, I got my things out of here on the same day Ginny's call came, never looking back! Back then, returning home would only have meant a failure of everything I ever set out to achieve, a shameful admission of defeat.

I could never have foreseen how grateful I'd feel for the safety net my parents are offering me and my child now.

Mum smiles reassuringly. 'The old pink rosebud wallpaper you chose ages ago is looking a little tired,' she tells me, 'but that's no problem because I imagine you'll be wanting a fresher look for yourself and the little one, anyway?'

'There's no rush,' I tell her slowly. 'But thank you.'

'It's no trouble. We're back home, so me and your dad can get onto that, no worries.'

They're going out of their way to make things okay again and yet I rub at my neck, realising with a sinking heart that her reassuring words aren't hitting the spot. And maybe... this time, they can't? Maybe this time the sadness in me runs too deep and no amount of kindness is going to help?

'That's... very kind of you.'

Dad's back with the warmed cups and teapot, setting them all down carefully on the table.

'Obviously we don't know if you've got any plans for work, yet, but...'

'I'll be looking for work properly, soon,' I tell them. 'I thought, one thing at a time, though; sort out where we're going to be living, first, and then...'

Mum glances at Dad and I think I know what's coming.

'Yes.' He clears his throat. 'I've spoken to old Clarkson at the bank and if that was the sort of thing you were looking for, he might still be able to pull a few strings.'

I know Dad means for the best, but they're doing enough for me already. I didn't want him to fix me up with a job as well. My throat is starting to feel clammed up.

'Though, what with all the human resources nonsense they've got to sign up for these days, that mightn't be *quite* as straightforward. Still.' Dad straightens. 'He's said he'll do what he can for you.'

I take a sip of my tea, again, feeling vaguely put out. 'Good of you to ask him, Dad, but... please don't feel you have to sort out *all* my problems for me.'

'Not at all,' he says. 'You know we'll help you any way we can.'

'I know. I just need to take on the responsibility for some things myself.'

'Of course, you do! And...' Mum says, very casually, 'if you and Will ever decide that some counselling would be of any help, my friend Jennifer—'

'No.' I look her directly in the eye. 'There's no counselling to be done here, Mum. There's no coming back from what's gone wrong for us.' Neither of them have actually asked what that was, and I'm grateful they haven't.

Mum splutters, 'I know you feel that way now, but...'

Dad lays his hand quietly over hers, patting her into silence. For the moment, at least.

'Well, in the meantime – just so you know – anything that you want to do or need to do, we'll be there to take care of baby once he comes. Even night times, if you've got to get up early for work.'

I must be frowning slightly because Dad says, '*If* that helps?'

'Yes. Although,' I add carefully, 'that probably won't be necessary.'

'Oh, it's no problem. I'm quite looking forward to it, really!' Mum's voice suddenly goes into cheerful mode. Ever the pragmatist, she's seen the silver lining to this cloud.

'She's taken up knitting,' Dad mutters, pouring out more tea with slightly shaking hands. 'Going to some sort of class for it, aren't you Sadie?'

Mum smiles. 'I wasn't going to say, but yes. He's a winter baby. I thought for our trips down to the duck pond and so on...'

She's painting a vivid picture. I push my tea away as it dawns on me, slowly, how it will be, them taking my son for outings in his pushchair, while I work. Them getting up at night to bottle feed him while I sleep.

Them stepping in gallantly, and – *with all the love in the world* – doing all the many, myriad things for my child that I was so looking forward to doing. Taking the photos, snapping his first smile. Echoing back his first word. All that. They'll give me all the help and support I've come here to ask of them, and in return I'll hand over the one last precious dream that I had left – the time I was going to spend with my own child.

I rub at my brow with the heel of my hand.

'You're offering to do a lot for me,' I say. 'Too much, perhaps. I really couldn't have asked for more.'

'This is your *home*, love,' Dad says quietly. 'You know we'll always stand by our girls, as long as you need us to.'

It's what I came here wanting. For them to take me back in, not to question too much, but he's just said the magic word – home.

A deep, longing homesickness for the wild, sweet freshness of my cottage by the sea hits me and I swallow, feeling sad and lost.

Even though it's taking me a while to figure out why, I'm slowly realising there *is* no coming back to this house. If I do that, I stop being me, living the life I was meant to live, however tenuous and strewn with uncertainties that may be. If I come back, I risk getting swallowed up forever. The day I stood up and told Will the truth – that was the day I found out how brave I truly was. I'm going to have to find the courage to tell them, too: that I'm not going to be spending my evenings helping them strip down the ancient rosebud wallpaper in my old bedroom, or reconfiguring my childhood room as a space for the baby. There'll be no coming back from brisk walks to the park to the aroma of fresh home baking, and no high fives from Dad for climbing the job ladder at the local bank. The last time I left home, it was for the final time.

I don't know what I'm going to do, but the tangled, half formed plan I had of returning here just collapsed right in front of me.

'Mum, Dad, the thing is...'

The way they're looking at each other, I sense they already know what's coming.

'It's okay,' I say to their shocked faces. 'I know what I said over the phone, but you don't need to worry about me because I've got other plans.'

Mum's eyes have gone very round and shiny, pulling at the guilt strings in my heart. Dad's put his arm about her shoulder in support.

'What plans?' he wants to know, looking worried. 'What are you going to do? Where are you going to go? We can't let you... camp out on the streets, Ava!'

I shake my head, softly. 'Who said I was going to do that?'

'Bob, you've got to talk some sense into her!'

My dad's sitting there looking helpless and very old, all of a sudden. I stand up straight, despite the slow, painful ache in my lower back.

'Trust me,' I tell them, getting up. 'I'll be okay. I'll be around in a few days and fill you both in on all my plans, so please don't worry about me.'

Dad frowns. 'You're leaving now? Are you... are you *sure*?'

I nod at him. I *am* sure. I don't know how. And I don't know why, but something magical and big just shifted deep in the core fabric of me, *I felt it*, and somehow, I know I'll be fine. Me and my child, together. Even without my beloved William. I wish him – and them – all the love in the world. I know that, each in their own way, they've all loved me the best they can.

But this last bit, I must do on my own.

Standing for a moment, catching the brief sunshine on the drive and stretching cramped limbs, I let that sink in: I've already moved on much too far in my own life and I will not be coming back here.

And that feels... so deeply sad and scary, but it's also liberating. It is a beautiful thing. Like some rare and fragile butterfly emerging from its chrysalis; I know that it is time.

You're leaving so soon... Tomorrow?' London St Pancras is crowded this morning. Our table at the dimly lit breakfast-and-pastry bar is uncomfortably cheek-by-jowl with that of our neighbours and this unwelcome bit of news hits my stomach like a burned piece of toast.

'Sure am.' Toby waves his fork at me. In front of him, an overflowing plate of mushrooms, bacon, eggs and beans sits waiting to be demolished. 'You want some of this?'

I shake my head, pushing away the Danish pastry he insisted on buying for me.

'Not had much of an appetite since Auntie's funeral, somehow.'

'It's all the loss.' His straight dark eyebrows go up, sympathetically. 'You've had a few of those, recently.'

'True.' I look away, pretend I need to concentrate hard on stirring the froth on the top of my coffee, but he doesn't avert his gaze and I soon run out of an excuse to keep stirring.

'I've had some losses and... out of the ashes of those, maybe, some gains, too.'

'Oh, yeah?' He sips at his own coffee.

'I've been spending a bit more time than usual with my folks around the funeral.' A lot more time, if truth be told. Joe and I have

been out to The Golden Plough a couple more times since the funeral,
we've shared a lot of home truths. He's a much more decent bloke than
I ever took him to be and Mum... well, she's never been too keen on
conflict of any kind, so I haven't had the same level of candid conversation with her as with Joe but, still, there's been a healing of sorts.

'I've... kinda come to some better terms with them as a result.'

He nods, dead serious. 'I'm happy for you, bro.'

'And listen,' I add uncomfortably. 'I'm sorry for... all the things I
said to you, man. The day I told you *where to go*, I didn't really mean...'

'No,' he says. 'I know that.'

'I was...' I look around at the teeming rail concourse – so many
people, all in such a hurry. Lord knows why, where they've got to get to,
and why it matters so much; *nothing matters that much...* 'I was hurting
too badly, being a dick, when you were only trying to help me.'

He nods, understanding. 'We're all good. And, speaking of home...'
His eyes light up and I remember he's going back to Missouri in less
than twenty-four hours. I get a real pang of sorrow at the thought.
Another loss, for me, and I don't know if I can cope with too many
more of those.

'Hey, I'll miss you, man.'

He bows his head in acknowledgement. 'We'll continue our collaboration like we were doing before, Will, never fear, but... I was referring
to *your* home.'

'Ugh, that!' I bury my head in my hands, feeling lost and – despite
my new-found ties with my family – strangely disconnected. DelRoy
was back in contact only recently, asking if I'd like to join him for part
of this tour of Ireland his new band's doing, kicking off before
Christmas at Killarney. I'll admit I was slightly tempted, but, 'Maybe I
should come over to Missouri with you for a few months – finish the
work we're doing and then go on to travel for a bit?'

'You could...' His eyebrows just met in a stern 'v' in the middle. 'But,
what about...?'

I stare at my own fingertips, drumming on the table in front of us,
for a bit, then I tell him, my voice thick, 'Didn't I mention, Ava and I

aren't together, now? There's no longer anywhere that feels like home to me.' If I'm doing my best to convince him, my words are dripping off my tongue about as easily as treacle off a tablespoon, gloopy and slow.

'*Home...*' Toby lifts his fist to the centre of his chest '... is always where the heart is, no?'

'I'd have agreed with you once, but now...' Who wants to get in touch with a heart that's been broken into a million pieces? 'No,' I say firmly. 'I need a new start, a new... *life*, somewhere else, preferably far away from everything here that'll only serve to remind me too painfully of—'

'You mean – like you did when you left everything and everyone behind in your home town to go and live down in Holcombe?'

'*Exactly* like...' I stop. Stare at him, brows furrowing, but he's busy tucking into his breakfast again, smiling at the waitress who's bringing him over a fresh cup of coffee; just an innocent old friend, reminding me about my past as old friends are wont to do.

When we leave St Pancras an hour later, hugging hard, promising to remain in touch, his words are still echoing in my ears, though.

Echoing in my ears and reverberating in my messed up, broken heart.

# 61

# AVA

'Oh, my. We'll be so very sorry to see you go.' Standing outside Phyllis's office once we've said our goodbyes, I'm sad to think I won't be back to enjoy the peace and beauty of this place, not for a long time, and by then – how much of all that I've loved about it will remain?

'Me too.' I tell her, 'Only, the flat I've got lined up to move into is going to be that bit too far to travel, once the baby arrives.'

She smiles, sympathetic.

'You've definitely decided against your parents' place, then?'

I nod.

'I know it doesn't make sense, in so many ways, and I know they're disappointed, only... I *need* this, Phyllis.'

I look at her, frowning softly. It wasn't the easiest decision to make.

'They'll understand,' she says. 'We all need to make the break some time or other.' It feels heartening to hear her say it. She laughs, patting my elbow. 'And – even if you don't know it yet – I suspect you already made yours some time back!'

I smile.

She asks, 'And... your sister?'

'Doing great.' I already mentioned to Phyllis that I can't dally. I'm meeting up with her shortly, for my final hospital visit this afternoon.

'Be sure to send Robyn our regards, will you? All that extra work she did to help us with our website was phenomenal – if we can ever tempt her back in to work for a stint, let us know?'

I give Phyllis a thumbs up.

'She'll be pleased to hear it, but she's unlikely to be back soon.' Robyn's got herself a new boyfriend recently and he's persuaded her to retake her last year at uni. I tell Phyllis, 'Her spare time's even more precious, these days, so I won't keep her waiting.'

I've also had a dull ache going low in my belly for the last half hour. This baby isn't due yet and I've been trying to ignore it, but something is niggling at me. I'll be glad to get it checked out.

'Only one last person to say goodbye to, then?' Phyllis says and I nod, feeling sad, now that we've come to it.

'Is he in?' I glance about us. 'I didn't spot him pottering around as usual when I first came in.'

Phyllis isn't entirely sure. They've got a new, younger guy in to help out with the gardening and butterfly breeding side of the business, these days. Harry's in less often, and coming and going pretty much as he pleases. I'll need to take a good look around if I want to find him.

Today, paper lanterns are hanging from every tree, the walkways lined with ornamental pumpkins of burnt orange and sienna and golden cider brown, for Halloween. Shielding my eyes as I go, feeling the warm, late October sunlight hitting my face, I realise how... simply *glad* I am to be here.

From somewhere over one of the walled gardens, a gentle breeze is blowing over the scent of burning wood and compost, a comforting, earthy smell. Following it, I finally find Harry by his dahlia bed, scratching his head in wonder at the huge, late blossoming tangerine flower heads.

'What're these doing here?' he wants to know, the minute he sees me. 'These something new? You the new gardener here, miss?'

'No.' I smile softly. 'I'm Ava Morley, an old friend of yours, and these,' I remind him, 'are Harry's Gold.'

He shakes his head, bemused.

'They are!' I take a step closer. 'They're named after you, Harry. You bred them and you planted them here, yourself. I know it because I was here with you the day you dug them into the ground.'

'You sure?'

I nod rapidly, recalling the day I'd flung all the little pieces of Will's Men First Fertility letter into the earth.

'I'll never forget it because we were talking about something... something confidential that was very close to my heart. I needed some advice and there was no one else I could turn to except you and you told me...'

His faded eyes look into mine, only mildly curious.

'You told me the truth is like a dahlia.' I run on, 'Like everything in life, you said, it seeks the sun, and you told me that in its own time truth would always unfurl, and it made me realise some things, it made me...'

He waits, patiently.

*Does he even care?* I wonder. He doesn't know me. He barely knows anyone... I stare at him, willing him to recall something that he won't. He can't, because...

It's gone, isn't it? All gone.

And soon, I will be gone. Gone from here and gone from his mind and it'll be as if he and I never, ever spoke... The thought chokes me a little.

'I know that you don't know it now,' I tell him, 'but you helped me see the matter clearly at a time when I couldn't see it.'

'That... the truth is like a dahlia?'

I laugh, sadly. 'It is, though! You were right. You see... my boyfriend, Will Tyler, is a bit like you. There are things he's forgotten, including, in his case, some truths that he once desperately wanted to forget.' I rub at my stomach, to settle the baby's kicking.

'Speaking to you made me question whether we ever do really forget anything – or if somehow, somewhere, even in some small squashed place inside our hearts, we remember it all.'

Harry nods, silent, and now all the rest of the unhappy thoughts

I've been longing to be able to share with another human being come spilling out in the one safe place I have.

'It was you who helped me to understand the double-bind I'd got myself into, Harry. You see... we learned this baby I'm carrying isn't his because he... he can't have any. He'd got really depressed about that.' I take in a deep breath. 'To convince Will to go ahead with the operation that'd save his life, I promised him I'd always keep that from him and then...' I gulp. 'One of the first things he did when he awoke from that operation, with his memories gone, was ask me to promise that I'd *never* keep any secrets from him!'

'That does indeed sound like a double-bind,' he agrees. 'Very tough.'

Robyn's calling. I can hear my phone going in my pocket and I know it's her, waiting, because I said I'd be outside by this time. The dull pains haven't gone away. If anything, they're getting sharper. I've got to be on my way, but this might be the last time I ever see my dear old friend. He's failing, isn't he? Next time I come, several months from hence, he won't be here any more, I'm sure of it.

And he is the only person alive apart from myself who knows the whole truth.

I tell him, 'I knew I had to make a choice.'

He's asking mildly, 'Which of your two promises did you keep, in the end?'

I wipe at my eyes with the back of my hand. I'd like to know that Old Harry approves of my choices because there've been so many times recently when I've questioned them myself.

'I kept the one that left me feeling the most whole, Harry.'

He doesn't ask which one that was.

'Ah.' Harry straightens and I see his solemn face breaking slowly into a gentle smile. 'In that case, young lady, I think you definitely did the right thing.'

# 62

# WILL

Lifting the latch at the garden gate, I'm slowly becoming aware of the deep silence all around me. Was it a mistake to come back here?

I could've gone anywhere. The rest of my life's still waiting for me, a myriad of exciting possibilities calling. I've come away from Leeds sadder and wiser but also refreshed, as if some invisible, heavy burden has been lifted. I came away realising Mum and Joe may have made some mistakes, but none of what they did was because they didn't *care* for me. Some of it might even have been because they did.

And all it took for me to see it was that advice I got from my gramps... Like those kids flying their kite in the park that windy day, I needed to change where I was standing. All that grief I've pushed down, it's been holding me back, I see that now. When I left Toby earlier and bought my ticket to come back down to Holcombe, maybe it was because I wanted to have a proper goodbye with Ava, too?

I know now that we both deserve a proper ending. I hoped we might get one tonight, only... I've arrived to find not a single light is turned on at the cottage, no hint of welcoming warmth beckoning from the inside. At the front door, no one's answering when I ring the bell. I still have the key but it's early evening and she might be asleep already. I don't want to startle her. When I go and rap on the kitchen window like Toby did, so many months back, there's no answer there, either.

Giving in at last, I'm feeling nervous, and have to fumble for an age with the key in the lock. Stepping into the hall, eventually, I'm immediately struck by the *emptiness* that hits me.

Ava's not here.

I know it before I hit the stairs, checking rapidly in the bedrooms, flinging the bathroom door open wide. Taking the time to look more carefully – checking out the precious little that's been left in the wardrobes, the cupboards, all the spaces that we shared – I become painfully aware that everything's gone. The rug in the hall is gone; the floorboards are bare. The shell mirror above the hall table that she laughed at, called tacky, that's disappeared too. Everything that made it lovely is gone, though I know none of those things are what really made the difference. It was always *her* that made this place a home.

I pause in the hallway. This place has come to feel like my home, and I can't help the sense that the ground's been pulled from under my feet, when I wasn't looking.

I am too late to say goodbye.

Like I was with Auntie Doris. Like I was with my dad.

*Why does this keep on happening to me?* Why didn't I at least text Ava to let her know I was coming? I should have done that, only there was a small part of me worrying that she might've said *don't bother*.

Getting out my phone, my fingers feel thick. I shoot her a text.

Ava, I'm back at Beach Cottage. Please get back if you can. Really need to speak to you. Will x

I kick back and wait patiently a good while for notification that she's even received it but nothing comes. The reception in this place has always been horrible but where is she? Is her phone even on?

Scratching my head, not wanting to feel my own despair, I tell myself it makes sense – with the baby due soon, she'll have left to go somewhere where she won't be alone. Is her sister, Robyn, still about?

Are Ava's parents even back – could she have gone over to theirs for a bit? Could she have gone over to that other friend she often mentioned *what was her name, Ginny*?

I wish that I'd been paying more attention to what Ava was always telling me about all the little things going on in her life. I wish that I'd been more present for her, but I wasn't fully there for myself at the time, was I?

I couldn't fully appreciate all the things she did for me, everything she was trying to do for me. Even the painful truth about the baby that she'd have preferred I didn't know. She confessed that in the end only to help me. I see that.

I see a lot of things now that I couldn't see before.

I rub at my neck, sorrowfully. I came back here because I didn't want us to end the memory of everything good and lovely that we had as enemies. I appreciate she needs to get on with her own life and I need to move on, too, but I'd rather not leave things between us like this.

Where've you gone, Ava?

Hey, you could've at least left me a note, babe. You could've left me something. It's not as if I even have your parents' number to contact them. Do you imagine that I do? Or Robyn's. I have no number but...

As I sit on the bottom step, something twinkling on the mantelpiece catches my eye for the first time.

Seeing it is like a punch in the gut. I get to my feet to go and retrieve it. She left my ring behind, then? Of course, she did.

In the middle of my chest, a deep and widening chasm is opening up, filling the space that she once filled with nothing but sadness. I can't stay in this empty house any longer. She's gone and I should go, too.

As I lock up it's cold, and already dark. I'm torn between heading to the railway station to make my way back to Mum and Joe's or making my way over to DelRoy's for the night, but neither of them appeal. I'd sooner head straight to Heathrow to get on the next flight out to join Toby in Missouri. He'd welcome it, I know. I need to get out of this own and preferably out of this country. Anything would be better than staying in Holcombe, feeling like this.

Feeling, for the first time, my own deep sorrow at the knowledge that the woman I loved has moved on and now we'll never get to say goodbye.

# 63

# WILL

I don't go with any of those choices. In the end, I run down to the one place I can think of where someone might still know where Ava's gone to.

At the Butterfly Gardens – miraculously still open because it's Halloween – none of the students on duty seem to be familiar with any of the regular staff. Trying to locate anyone who's even heard of Ava, I spend a good while stumbling past lanterns and pumpkins and stepping over their apple dunking tubs, until I come across an older man wearing a staff lanyard, sitting quietly in a corner by himself.

'Hey.' I stand there for a moment, bending over slightly, panting. 'Hello.'

'Good evening, sir.'

'My name is...' I sit down on the wall nearby him. 'My name's Will and I'm looking for my...' I take in a long, deep breath. 'I'm looking for my girlfriend, who works here, Ava Morley.'

'Oh, yes?'

'D'you know her, by any chance?'

'Ava Morley.' He nods slowly. 'It rings a bell, certainly.'

'Does it?' I clear my throat. 'She's about five foot four, longish auburn hair, and about...' I glance at him '... eight and a half months pregnant, you really couldn't miss her.'

'Ah, yes.' He smiles. 'I do know her.'

'You do?' *Thank God.* 'Do you happen to know where she...?' I trail off as his vigilant gaze follows a couple of zombies walking past.

'Got to make sure none of them stray into the herb garden section,' he tells me. 'I've got some delicates in there, otherwise I wouldn't even be here at this hour.'

'Oh. Right.' I look back at him. 'Is Ava here, tonight, d'you know?'

He stares at me blankly.

'Ava Morley,' I say. 'You mentioned you knew her. She works here...' He does work here too, doesn't he?

'Yes.' He suddenly comes back. 'Spoke to her not so long ago, as it happens. She told me she was leaving. I reckon that would've been, one... maybe two...'

So, it's true, then? My heart constricts. *Was this one week, two weeks ago, soon after I left her?*

Leaning in a little closer, I read off his badge: 'My name is Harry...'

'Listen, Harry...'

He looks back at me, smiling softly. 'I take it *you* must be her boyfriend, Will, then?'

I nod, a little confused. I already told him my name was Will, but...

'She's spoken to you about me?'

'Oh, yes. You two split up, recently, she said?'

'She mentioned that?' I mutter unhappily.

He gives a soft laugh. 'She told me lots of things.'

'Like...' I prompt. 'Where she'd be heading out to?'

'Not that.' Harry twists the piece of twine he's holding in his hand and makes a satisfied grunt. 'The knots these get into can be real buggers if you're not careful. Got to sort them out, quickly, you see.'

'I can imagine. So, look, are you sure she didn't... she didn't give you any indication at all where she was going?'

Harry lifts his lanyard up for me to see better, pointing at one sentence in particular.

'"Due to a medical condition,"' I read out slowly, '"I am a forgetful man. Please do not take offence if we have spoken before and I do not know you."'

Is he saying he doesn't recall?

I swallow. How useful this dude is really going to be to me is becoming a little hazy. Just like his memory.

'It's okay.' I look about, making ready to get up and go.

Then he adds, 'No, we talked about... you and her, mostly.' He glances up at me, kindly. 'The things she wanted to talk about.'

'Oh, yeah?' I sit back down again. I should get on with trying to find her, but my curiosity is getting the better of me. 'What'd she say?'

'She was wondering if people ever really forget anything or if the most important events of our lives – however painful – always get stored, here.' He touches his heart, reminding me of Toby's earlier gesture.

'It's Halloween tonight, Harry. Not Valentine's.'

He goes on, 'She still loves you, though.'

I give a wry smile. 'You reckon?'

He shoots me a glance. 'She seemed pretty heartbroken that you'd left her.'

I stick my hands in my pockets, getting a stab of guilt. 'Listen, she's about to have a baby...'

'Too right about that.' He smiles. 'Last time we spoke she was with her sister, heading off to the hospital...'

I stare at him, feeling dumbfounded. Already? *So soon – and not even a word to me?* Again, I get the sense of having been left behind. Of course, she wouldn't have told me, not after how we left things.

I tell him, 'Listen, I left Holcombe and I know how it looks to others seeing it from the outside, but... our relationship is... it's complex.' I add, man to man, 'Make no mistake, it's had more knots in it than that piece of twine you've been busy untangling.'

'I know,' he says, his face inscrutable in the dark evening.

'*What* do you know?' I have no idea why I'm even sitting here having this conversation with him. It's all over. She's had the baby and he's gone. But I can't seem to tear myself away.

'I know that you asked her to keep a big secret for you once, Will Tyler.'

I look at him. Has she told him what she told me – about the baby and about my inability to have any? Surely, she wouldn't have...?

'You asked her to keep something quiet and I believe she agreed because...' He looks directly into my eyes. 'She agreed because she felt that was the only way she could persuade you, at the time, to have the operation you needed.'

'I'm sorry?' I give a dry laugh, tearing my eyes away. 'I'm sorry... what're you even talking about?'

He seems like a sweet enough old gent, but he must've forgotten what their conversation really went like and he's making all this up.

'You'd learned you couldn't have children and that cut you up. It was the only way she could figure out, you see, to keep you alive.'

*To keep me...?*

I swallow. 'No. That didn't happen,' I assert. This is... it's bullshit, but his words are leaving a strange bubbling feeling in my throat, nonetheless.

'That isn't what happened. Ava didn't make some sort of... pact with me, to keep my infertility quiet, that would be... It would be nuts!' I half stand to leave, but I can't bring myself to do it. The small, nagging doubt growing in my mind that I can't quite silence has reminded me of something. The fact that, for so long, I couldn't get anyone to answer why I'd refused the op.

Everyone had been so reluctant to say anything beyond that I hadn't wanted to have the operation because I was depressed, and sure, Ava's confession had solved that one for me, only...

I never did find out what persuaded me in the end to change my mind on that, did I?

If I was so depressed and refusing to have it, *what changed*?

I look back at Harry, frowning deeply and he's saying, 'Ava got herself into a real double-bind with you, over it. She was desperate for you to live – of course she was! She willingly agreed to keep that lie going so you'd let them operate but then, the minute you awoke, you needed her to be transparent, open and honest... the grand Keeper of the Truth for you.' He points out reasonably, 'There was no way she could keep *both* of those promises, as I'm sure you'll agree.'

I gulp, feeling my face colour.

'Ava *has* already told me something, though!' Then I add, because he clearly already knows it, 'She told me the child she was carrying isn't mine. If she was willing to come clean and tell me that much, why not go on and tell me all the rest? If we'd ever really had this... this pact you're making out, why wouldn't she have simply *said*?'

'That you, too, were in on it?'

'Precisely.'

He looks thoughtful, taking that on board for a bit. I fold my arms thinking: *there you go, it's all a lot of claptrap, isn't it? There was never any so-called pact.*

And then he says, 'Would you have believed her?'

'What?'

'Once the trust between you was broken, would you have believed the truth even if you heard it?'

'I...' I stand straight up as the unchallengeable truth hits me right between the eyes.

'No,' I admit, feeling sick to my stomach. 'I wouldn't have.' She had other things to say to me that day when she told me about the baby, didn't she? I recall how I blocked her out. When she tried to tell me everything else she wanted to share, I didn't want to know, did I? didn't let her speak.

Dear God...

I grasp his hand tightly for an instant, the implications of what he's told me hitting thick and fast.

'Are you absolutely *certain* about the things she said to you?'

He's got memory problems. It says so on the badge attached to his lanyard. Maybe I'm hoping he'll come up with some way out piece of nonsense that'll give the lie to everything else he's said, but he only nods.

'My memories of things long past and anything that's happened in the last two hours or so is impeccable, they tell me. It's only the stuff in between I have the trouble with.'

I blink, taking this on board. If his timing is accurate, then...

'You're telling me that... you saw Ava and had this conversation with her some time *in the last two hours*?'

'I did, young man, or else I never would've remembered any of it.'

I let out a long, disbelieving whistle. If she was on her way to the hospital so recently, the child might not even have been born yet! Perhaps, she might not be too far away, after all?

More importantly, if he's right, Ava never wronged me in the way I thought. With growing mortification, I'm seeing that I might have done something terrible. I let myself get so hurt I ran off and left her alone when all along it was *me* who'd asked her to keep the truth from me.

I'm the one who lied to myself!

# 64

## AVA

Someone just said, 'We've pumped her stomach, all we're waiting for is...'

The rest of the sentence got lost as they moved away but the two women on the other side of the blue curtain have started up their argument again in hushed, agitated voices.

'It should be me, I'm telling you!'

'Under the circumstances, I hardly think she'd want you in there with her. She'll be feeling...'

'She'll be feeling devastated!' *Robyn*. That's Robyn's voice. And she's talking to Mum. 'I know her better than anyone else and I know what she'd want.'

The staff gave me something for the pain and I've been groggy, in and out of consciousness a little. I try and move to sit up a little on the trolley and call out to them but, with my throat and mouth feeling so scratched and dry, there's no way.

This is all happening too fast... I manage to get my hand up to my face, wiping away the big, fat tears that are springing out of nowhere. I didn't expect to have this baby tonight. I thought I still had a couple of weeks to go, and that in that time... maybe a miracle would happen and I'd start to feel what I ought to be feeling, somehow, more... *ready* or this.

But I'm not. I'm not ready at all! And Robyn's wrong, I'm not feeling devastated, *I'm feeling terrified.*

The sister in charge of the ward has arrived; brisk and efficient, she's checking the cannula in my arm, but I don't miss the sense of urgency beneath her quiet enquiry.

'Everything still okay in here? We're fetching the paperwork we'll need you to sign.' She's patting my hand kindly. 'Ava, you understand what's going to happen, don't you?'

I blink. Give her the tiniest nod. Someone explained it before. How that gush of bright red bleeding I'd experienced soon after we got here wasn't normal or okay. How it meant that the baby's placenta must've been covering the cervix and it had got partially detached, *placenta previa*, they said.

How that could spell a lot of danger if things didn't go to plan, all the potential implications of that and how an emergency Caesarean was necessary and I wouldn't be going home before I'd had the op.

I manage a scribble on the piece of paper someone's put in front of me. Sister glances at her fob watch. 'Baby's dad here yet?'

'He's not in the picture.' The other nurse's voice dips. 'Both mum and sister are duking it out, outside, as to who gets to go in with her.'

The sister does a clucking sound with her tongue. I hear her say, 'Okay. We need to get her into Theatre for the spinal block, asap.' Then she mutters something inaudible just as this terrible, searing pain goes right across my abdomen.

*So sharp*, it makes everything in front of my eyes go white, nothing but pure white, and the pain level hits the roof.

'I... don't want to be alone,' I get out.

'You won't be, Ava. That's all right.' The nurse calmly lifts my left hand to my face – it seems I've been clutching the mask all this time. 'Take in a little more of the gas and air. Nice and easy does it.'

Am I shaking my head? I hear the ward sister saying, 'She doesn't want the nitrous oxide?'

I don't want it.

Not at first. Icky, cold, it feels as if I'm drawing a dry, chemical breath into my lungs. The pain is racking my body right in two but then, as soon as I settle down to properly *breathe*, everything else in my life starts floating comfortably away. All the bad, sad, stuff, it's all still there, I'm aware of that. Nothing's really gone away. My baby's life is in danger and this operation is still about to happen, but the edge of all that bad stuff is... it's somehow blunted by the gas. So, I breathe. Keep breathing. Because the more I breathe, the more I can leave all this behind. The curtains have been opened and someone's gone to the head of the trolley and I can feel rumbling as the bed's being moved across the ward floor. Someone must've held the doors open because now, my eyes half closed, I'm aware of the lights down the corridor speeding past like I'm running, *like I'm flying*, and then, for one split second...

I am back with William in beautiful Florence.

Is it the gas and air doing this? If it is, I don't care, I want it to last forever, never want it to stop because in my half dream, drifting elsewhere, Will and I are still together.

'*Run!*' He's grasped hold of my hand and – our pursuer still close – we're flying over the Ponte Vecchio once more.

'*Just keep going.*'

'*Stop making me laugh!*'

The dappled light hitting my eyes as we dash over the bridge and out under the arched walkway is shining like pure gold. For one small moment, engraved onto my soul for all eternity, my heart opens wide. It's filled with all the laughter we shared that day. In a moment of razor sharp clarity, it comes to me. I'm *glad* of the lie I told that kept Will alive, because without that we could never have had those moments.

I'm glad I also found the courage, in the end, to tell him the truth. That was the most loving thing I ever did even if – especially if – he hated to hear it so much that he left. I'm *proud* of me. I'm proud of all the hugely important, painful decisions I've been making ever since. Besides, if I can do something as brave as that, then whatever comes next, I will surely be just fine.

The nurse is saying, 'We're about to go into Theatre, ladies. Which ne of you is going in with her?' I don't even lift my head to look.

She's saying more sharply, *'Excuse me?'*

'You've got to let me in!'

'I'm sorry,' the nurse is insisting. 'Only one person is allowed in ere with her and I'm afraid you're not even—'

'If there's only one person allowed in there it has to be me,' a amiliar male voice is saying, 'because I am the baby's father.'

My eyes shoot wide open. Then close. Because I have no choice. he meds just kicked in and maybe...

Maybe, after all, I'm only dreaming?

*  *  *

'ou came back?'

Will's got dark rings under his eyes, looking full of remorse, but... e's here, and I can't begin to say how much that means to me.

'Hey,' he says, his fingers closing around mine. 'You did just great.'

I give a quiet laugh.

'I think the doctors did most of the work.' Now it's over, my baby aken up to the neonatal intensive care unit, we've got a few quiet ninutes to ourselves. The nurse will be back soon and I know the drenalin won't last, but... I search his face questioningly.

*'You came back*, Will?'

He nods. 'I wouldn't leave you without a proper goodbye, Ava.'

I swallow. 'Is that what you're here for?' I turn away, determined he von't see the gutted look on my face. Will's moved on. And I... I've noved heaven and earth in the past week to find a new place, make the eginnings of a home for myself and the baby. I need to remember hat: how far I've come.

'No.' His face twists in anguish as he squeezes my hand. 'I had a lot f time to mull things over in Leeds. I realised I've made so many nistakes with people I love, taken things the wrong way and left them nresolved for too long. I came back because I didn't want to leave

things like that between *us*. Ava, I was wrong! Sometimes, things aren
always the way they appear to be at first sight.'

I give a pained laugh. 'How true *that* is.'

'I'm sorry for the way I left you.' He gulps. 'I came back to let yo
know that. And then I met Harry.'

I start, making to sit up a little further but the searing pain acros
my belly soon puts paid to that. 'What did he...?'

His voice breaks. 'Ava. I *know* what we agreed, how you persuade
me to have that operation, in the end...'

*Harry told him?* In the storm swept ocean of his eyes I see so man
things: regret, sadness, and... maybe something else, too.

'Hey. It's okay...'

'Only... it isn't okay, is it?' Hurt climbing my throat, I'm aware fc
the first time at how angry I've also been with him for leaving me. H
went when I needed him the most! I've let Beach Cottage go and nov
there is no going back, Will must know this.

He's saying, 'If you want me, I still want to be in your life...'

I do want that. *More than anything*, but... 'I thought you didn't tru:
me, any more?'

'I trust you,' he breathes. 'I should've given you a proper chance t
explain.'

I hold his gaze.

'Instead of running,' he finishes, full of remorse. 'I shouldn't hav
done that.'

'No.' I wipe my eyes with my sleeve, feeling wrung out. 'I've been s
unhappy without you and I'm still cross at you for what you've put m
through, but...'

He's sorry and I can't stay angry with him.

'We always knew this is how it would be, Will.'

Our time is up. Nurse has popped her head around the curtai
'They're bringing baby down from the neonatal unit, now. Ready to sa
hello, Mum and Dad?' She's smiling reassuringly. 'Don't worry. He'll b
here any minute and he's doing okay.'

Thank God.

And... *us*? I look over at Will, asking silently, *Are we doing okay?*

But they've already wheeled the plastic cot over to my bedside. My heart fills to overflowing as she places the tiniest, yawning scrap of a person I ever did see in my arms and I gasp.

'Oh, my word. *You're so small!* How am I ever going to do this?'

Will reaches out to gently stroke baby's cheek with the back of his hand.

'We,' he says, smiling softly. 'How are *we* gonna do it?'

# EPILOGUE

When I opened my eyes this morning, the snow was falling, softly and steadily outside. It took me back. Getting up to open the window, holding out my hand to catch the snowflakes, I had trouble believing it could really be one year to the day since Will and I went our separate ways.

Could it really be a whole year, since the dream of the life we'd longed for began to shimmer and fade? I know we never wanted it to. We did everything we could think of, to keep it alive, but sometimes it seems you have no choice and life has other plans. Sometimes, there's even a new dream that you never saw, growing quietly in its place.

Outside, the 'For Sale' sign the owners of Beach Cottage installed after deciding not to renew the lease is swaying a little, all forlorn. Given the circumstances, they've allowed us to move back in but only till the end of the year. We'll be gone, soon.

'This time last year, it felt like the end of my world.' I turn to pluck little Harry out of his crib. 'And yet, look at me now... a mum! Best job in the world, if you ask me.'

He smiles back, softly. He's only eight weeks old. Does it matter if he can't grasp a word I'm saying? I talk. He listens. And, just like old Harry, there is wisdom in his eyes, all the same.

'For so long, I tried to squash my life to fit this ideal vision of how I thought things *should* be. But there was so much waiting out there for me that I couldn't begin to imagine.'

I have no plans to go back to work for either Ginny or the bank again, but in my mind, and half scribbled down here and there, I've already got a whole bunch of ideas for one-off children's party clothes for the high-end children's store owner Hayley introduced me to. There's an advance waiting for me as soon as I'm ready, an opportunity I'm excited to get my teeth into. As for my other plans...

Will is knocking, very quietly, on the door. He's brought up tea, but can tell he's not rested much, his voice a little hoarse. 'I wasn't sure if you'd both still be sleeping?'

'We're awake.' Even first thing in the morning, only half dressed and in his PJ bottoms, he brings a smile to my face. 'I missed you being in bed beside me last night.'

'Hey, I missed you, too.'

I do a half turn, so the little guy can see him, over my shoulder. The way these two smile each time they catch sight of each other would light up a room.

'Up late doing online work with Toby, again?' I've been preoccupied with looking after Harry, but I know Will and his mate have been working hammer and tongs, making up for lost time. He breaks into a grin, nodding, stretching his arms overhead, luxuriously. 'Very late, but tonight, I'll be back in your bed, hopefully.'

I lean in to touch his hand.

'You're *done*?'

Taking Harry from me ever so gently, he smiles. 'Not only are we done, but the producer's already heard it and he loves it.' His dream. What he's been struggling with, for so many months... I clap my hands together.

'Will, I am so happy for you!'

In response, he holds our baby up high, facing the window.

'See that? This is the view from your bedroom, young man. You can't see too much yet,' he's saying. 'But, one of these days, when you're

older and taller, you'll appreciate you have the one room here tha
looks out over a sea view.' Will glances over at me mischievously. '*If* yo
squint very hard and imagine that the trees aren't all there in the way..

I give a snort. The cottage is up for sale. We're leaving and he mus
have forgotten that we won't... And then the penny drops.

I grasp at Will's hand. 'You're putting in an offer for this place?' No
he's got his latest project off the ground – perhaps he knows we ca
afford it?

Ever so gently, he's placed the baby back in his crib.

'That depends, I guess, on whether *you're* ready to accept the offer
already made you, once before?'

And now Will's bringing something small and sparkly out of h
pocket. He's leaned in to place it on my finger where it belongs and fo
a moment, lost in a kiss, we are in the best place in the world.

Behind him, the sun just came out, shining like a beacon across th
flat white plain of snow.

# ACKNOWLEDGMENTS

or this book, which has taken me the longest of all to write, my grateful thanks go once again to my husband, Eliott. For the hard work f being my first beta reader; for sticking in there with me during the ong months when the story wasn't working, and always, always, elieving I would put it right when the time was right. You are so ppreciated!

Thanks so much to beta readers, Anne Williams and Michelle yles. both for your freely given time and for putting down your noughts: your comments helped me get the pulse of the story.

Thank you to my lovely editor, Sarah Ritherdon, it's been a delight working with you and I am so looking forward to what comes next! ikewise, to all the other supportive members of the Boldwood family, with a special shout-out to Caroline Ridding, because the day you eminded me to 'Keep the faith,' I really needed to hear it.

# BOOK CLUB QUESTIONS

- At the begin of novel, Ava makes a pact with Will to keep their secret: later, she promises him that she'll always be honest. On both occasions, she makes her decision based on what she believes will be best for HIM... can breaking a promise or lying to your partner ever be deemed acceptable, if it's intended to save them a lot of hurt and heartache?
- After Will wakes up, Ava makes the decision not to tell him straight away about the pregnancy because she wants him to fall for her, first... is this the right decision, or should she have been upfront about it straight away, given she could have run the risk of him rejecting her?
- Harry's comment to Ava that 'the heart always remembers' indicates he doesn't think all memories are stored in the brain. Studies have shown that older people with dementia who've had a joyful visit from a loved one can retain their elevated mood following the visit, for longer than they remember the actual visit. Do you think that people with compromised memory can retain 'feeling memories' and is this what Harry means?
- Soon after waking up, Will goes through a mini 'identity crisis' when he realises his life is no longer the way he left it,

seven years ago. Do you think our sense of self is formed
from a sum total of all our memories? Or is there an
underlying 'self' underneath that will always be retained,
no matter how many memories go?

- Will tells Ava that, according to his grandpa Geoff, 'So much
  in life depends on where you're standing.' Implying that the
  stories we tell ourselves, ie our narratives about our life, will
  shape a lot of how and what we end up experiencing.
  Do you think this is true? What does Will learn about the
  truth or falsehood of this?

- Soon after Ava elects to leave Beach Cottage (after she and
  Will part), she also decides against moving into her parent's
  house, despite her baby being nearly due. Why is this an
  important decision for her - when she had two chances to
  remain in a comfortable home, was she right to turn them
  both down?

- Ginny uses an underhand method to get her business
  underway, but she justifies it by implying that sometimes
  the truth has to be stretched, in order to reach your goal.
  Ava cuts her friendship ties with Ginny over just this issue...
  and yet she herself has done a similar thing. Is Ava showing
  double standards or does she have a good justification,
  here?

- We learn that Will's been hugely upset, before the story's
  start, on learning that Ava's baby isn't his. Still, he seems to
  come to terms with this and be willing to accept the child by
  the end. Is he right to change his mind, and what's the key
  factor that facilitates this?

# MORE FROM GISELLE GREEN

We hope you enjoyed reading *The Girl You Forgot*. If you did, please leave a review.

If you'd like to gift a copy, this book is also available as an ebook, digital audio download and audiobook CD.

Sign up to Giselle Green's mailing list for news, competitions and updates on future books.

https://bit.ly/GiselleGreenNewsletter

## ABOUT THE AUTHOR

Giselle Green is an award-winning, bestselling contemporary women's fiction author. Mum to six boys (half of whom have flown the nest) and owner of one bright orange-and-cinnamon canary who hopefully never will, Giselle enjoys creating emotionally-gripping storylines about family and relationships.

Visit Giselle's website: https://gisellegreen.com/

Follow Giselle on social media:

- facebook.com/gisellegreenauthor
- twitter.com/gisellegreenuk
- BB bookbub.com/authors/giselle-green

# ABOUT BOLDWOOD BOOKS

Boldwood Books is a fiction publishing company seeking out the best stories from around the world.

Find out more at www.boldwoodbooks.com

Sign up to the Book and Tonic newsletter for news, offers and competitions from Boldwood Books!

http://www.bit.ly/bookandtonic

We'd love to hear from you, follow us on social media:

facebook.com/BookandTonic
twitter.com/BoldwoodBooks
instagram.com/BookandTonic

Lightning Source UK Ltd.
Milton Keynes UK
UKHW022155070622
404067UK00008BC/2064